TOUR WARS

ROMANCING THE RUINS #3

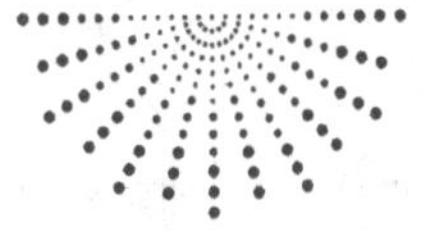

CARLA LUNA

MOON MANOR PRESS

First paperback edition: March 2024

Cover Design: *Bailey McGinn*
Editing: *Free Bird Editing*
Proofreading: *One Love Editing*

ISBN: 979-8-9894130-1-0 (paperback)
ISBN: 979-8-9894130-0-3 (ebook)

Published by Moon Manor Press
www.carlalunabooks.com

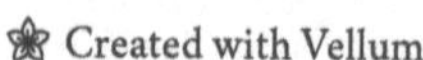 Created with Vellum

Dedicated to the memory of my father, Mario Salas Luna, who was taken from this world too soon.
Thanks, Dad, for sharing your passion for art history, anthropology, and cheesy B-movies.

AUTHOR'S NOTE

The ancient ruins of Pompeii, located in southern Italy, have been under continuous excavation since the mid-eighteenth century. Over the decades, archaeologists have exposed villas, temples, baths, and entire streets lined with shopfronts. To this day, investigation into the site continues, conducted by various international teams. However, the Via Stabiana Project and the House of Venus are fictional creations, as is the project's director, Dr. Maurizio Roberti.

Content warning: while *Tour Wars* is meant to provide an escape from the harsh realities of everyday life, the book contains backstory involving parental loss, as well as a scene of sexual harassment.

CHAPTER ONE

Emilia Flores had twenty minutes to pull herself together. Twenty—*no, nineteen*—minutes to cool down, fix her appearance, and get in the right headspace before her first set of job interviews. Three interviews back-to-back, all for teaching posts at prestigious colleges. No easy feat, especially when she was still reeling from a panel session that had gone wildly off the rails.

Why had she ever thought she liked academic conferences? Right now, this one felt like the seventh circle of hell.

As she entered the women's restroom, she recoiled at the reflection that greeted her in the mirror. Her long dark hair had come loose from her braid, leaving messy wisps straggling around her face. Little remained of her artfully applied makeup except a smudge of mascara under one eye. And the beads of sweat glistening on her forehead made her look like she'd just returned from a five-mile run.

All because she'd lost her temper during that disastrous panel session. When challenged by her rival, fellow archaeologist TJ Mayer, she hadn't responded with calm professionalism. Instead, she'd disputed his claims in a heated exchange that sent her blood pressure soaring.

Grabbing a paper towel from the dispenser, she moistened it, wiped off the smudge, and blotted the sweat from her face. She undid her braid and ran her fingers through her hair, only to remember she'd left her hairbrush in her hotel room.

"Dr. Flores?" A timid voice caught her attention.

She whipped around in frustration. With so little time to spare, she didn't have the bandwidth to deal with any distractions. Standing behind her was a petite young woman who looked college-aged, with curly black hair and light brown skin just a touch darker than hers. Around the woman's neck was a lanyard that read Viviana Orozco, Penn State University. No doubt an undergrad, possibly attending her first big conference.

Emilia replaced her frown with a welcoming smile. Even at age twenty-eight, she could still remember how it felt to be so young and inexperienced. And she was always happy to see more Latinas pursuing archaeology.

"As much as I appreciate the title, I'm not *officially* Dr. Flores yet," she said. "I still have to defend my dissertation." If all went well, she'd finally be done with grad school in a few months. "Was there something you wanted to ask me?"

"I wanted to tell you how much I enjoyed your presentation on the collapse of the Late Bronze Age in the Mediterranean. Your paper was the best one there."

"Thank you. It's nice to hear that." Up until the last twenty minutes of the panel, Emilia had felt the same way. Like she was crushing it. Until TJ had derailed her.

"Once I'm done with college, I was thinking of pursuing a PhD in archaeology like you. My parents said I'd be wasting my time because it's so hard to get a teaching job. Is that true?"

If Viviana hadn't seemed so earnest, Emilia might have laughed at the question. It wasn't just hard. It was nearly impossible. But it wasn't something she had time to explain.

She reached into the front pocket of her briefcase and pulled out a business card. "I've got to rush, but my email address is right here. Send me your questions, and I'll answer them once I'm back at Yale."

Viviana smoothed her hand over the embossed card. "Thanks, and…um…this is just my opinion, but I think the last guy on the panel was totally disrespectful. He acted like he was trying to show you up. I don't blame you for getting mad at him."

Emilia took a deep breath, not wanting to succumb to the anger she'd shown earlier. During her talk, she'd presented archaeobotanical evidence—ancient seeds and pollen grains—to prove that the fall of the Bronze Age in the Mediterranean had been brought about by drought and famine, mainly due to climate change. Given that she'd written her dissertation on this exact topic, she knew the material inside and out. She always felt confident presenting it.

But when it was TJ's turn at the mic, he didn't just counter with his own theory; he claimed it was superior to hers. Rather than blame the collapse on natural disasters, he insisted a marauding group of invaders, known as the Sea Peoples, had triggered the devastation.

Wasn't that just like a man to blame everything on warfare?

If the panelist had been anyone but TJ, she might not have responded as forcefully. But whenever he provoked her, all her self-control went out the window. As a result of their argument, the session had run overtime, she'd gotten overheated, and now she was woefully behind schedule.

"It's all right," she said. "That sort of thing happens in academia all the time. I've got to run, but it was nice to meet you. Good luck with the rest of the conference."

With a quick wave, she dashed out of the restroom and headed down the hall, but speed walking in heels wasn't in her skill set. As the heel of her right pump twisted under her, she stumbled and smacked into a wall, bruising her elbow. Wincing in pain, she took a minute to get her bearings, only to be accosted by a sarcastic male voice.

"Em. I didn't realize I'd thrown you that much off-kilter."

She grimaced. TJ Mayer. The same jerk who'd attempted to upstage her on the panel session. Who'd aggravated her all last summer when they'd worked together excavating the site of Troy in Turkey.

"I'm fine," she snapped. "Just in a rush, that's all."

"Headed for your first interview of the day? Georgetown, right? Mine's with Cornell University. I figure I've got a decent chance since I spent a summer digging at Sardis as part of a joint excavation between Harvard and Cornell. Never hurts to use my Harvard connections."

Of course he would mention Harvard. If she had a dollar for every time he brought it up—*and* dismissed Yale as second-rate— she'd be halfway to paying off her student loans. Equally vexing was his insistence that his hometown of Chicago was culturally superior to hers in Milwaukee. Sure, his city had more museums, but she'd pick Wisconsin over Illinois any day, especially when it came to sports.

As if it wasn't bad enough that he was her academic rival, what irked her even more was that she found him attractive. Though he wasn't as jacked as a lot of her dig buddies, he had a lean, muscular frame—a runner's build—and his height matched hers almost exactly. Last summer, his light brown hair had been a shaggy mess, but he'd had it trimmed since then, and it curled, ever so slightly, at the back of his neck. Sealing the deal were his vintage glasses, which drew attention to his warm brown eyes. Why did guys with old-school glasses always get her hot and bothered?

But even if he was hot, he was a giant pain in the ass.

"I'll go with you since I'm headed that way," he said. "If you want, I could toss you a few practice questions. Or vice versa. Couldn't hurt, am I right?"

"Keep your distance," she muttered. "You've already done enough damage."

"All I did was present my own research. My evidence is solid, and you know it. From the analysis of the bronze artifacts and other lithic material found in Cyprus and Greece, I—"

"Just stop. Like I haven't heard about your damn Sea Peoples a dozen times already? Today was even more painful than usual. Not only was I forced to listen to your outdated theories, but then you had the balls to single me out for criticism to make yourself look good."

He crossed his arms. "If you can't handle a little competition, then you'll never survive in academia."

Jerk. He was baiting her, like he always did, no doubt hoping to push her over the edge again. "I can handle anything, but your attitude sucks. You just wanted to mess with my head so that I'd screw up my interviews."

"That's not why I did it. Actually, I—"

"Save it. I'm going to be late." She was about to make a hasty exit, but he placed his hand on her arm.

"Hang on. You have something on your face." He leaned in closer and brushed his finger across her cheek. Just the slightest touch, but it made her nerve endings tingle.

She wanted to push him away but couldn't make herself move. Only after he withdrew his hand did she regain the power of speech. "What the hell?"

"Sorry. Shouldn't have touched you without your permission, but you had a smudge on your cheek. Maybe pen? Or...mascara? I didn't want you to go into your interview that way."

How had she missed it? She'd probably made matters worse when she cleaned up in the restroom. But her unexpected reaction to his touch only added to her discomfort. "Thanks. I have to go."

She didn't spare him a backward glance as she strode down

the corridor. All she cared about was getting to her first job interview on time.

I just want this to be over.

In all her years of grad school, she'd never missed the annual conference put on by the American Institute of Classical Archaeology. This year, it was being held in Philadelphia, which meant she'd been able to save money by taking the train from Yale University, less than four hours away. Since the conference always took place in January, it was the ideal time to catch up with her colleagues between summer dig seasons. In addition to the social aspect of the meetings, she enjoyed attending panels on groundbreaking research and debating topics like the impact of racism and colonialism on the field of archaeology.

But with her doctorate so close at hand, this year's conference took on a whole new urgency. Namely, the painful prospect of finding a full-time job in her field. Even if a lot of colleges now conducted their first-round interviews via Zoom, some still hosted them in person at conferences like this one. After applying to dozens of places, she'd lined up six interviews for the upcoming academic year. Though the teaching jobs wouldn't start until August or September, the sooner she secured one, the sooner she could relax.

Maybe she'd get lucky, like her friends Stuart and Olivia. They'd gone through this hellscape last year and emerged with tenure-track teaching positions. But she suspected the odds weren't in her favor.

As she approached the wing of the hotel where the interviews were taking place, she paused and gave herself a quick pep talk.

You've got this. You're a kick-ass archaeologist with tons of field experience, you speak four languages, and you've published three papers. Go in there and give them hell.

Even if TJ had thrown her off her game, she wouldn't let him get to her.

~

EMILIA SAT AT THE HOTEL BAR, DRINKING HER SECOND MOJITO OF the night. To say her interviews hadn't gone well was putting it mildly. When the first hiring committee had asked about her long-term research goals, she'd floundered. She'd been awkward and anxious, nothing like the image she usually projected in the field or the classroom. By the time her second interview rolled around, she was a hot mess.

As would be expected with a gathering of archaeologists, the bar was packed. On her left, raucous laughter from a noisy group made her bristle with irritation. The four guys clustered together didn't appear to have a care in the world. All male, all white, all smug as hell. If she had to guess, she'd say they were full professors secure in their jobs.

At least she wasn't drinking alone. Her friend Dusty Danforth perched on a stool beside her, sipping a glass of white wine.

Though Emilia had met dozens of archaeologists during her seasons in the field, she regarded most of them as colleagues. She'd always struggled with letting people in, which was why she only had a handful of close friends. Dusty was one of them. Like Emilia, she was an archaeologist by training, but she'd left academia last year and had no regrets about it. She'd come to the conference to support her boyfriend, Stuart Carlson, who was giving a presentation on recent archaeological discoveries at the site of Troy.

Dusty nudged her. "Stop moping. I'm sure your interviews weren't that bad."

"They were abysmal. I kept choking up. Like I couldn't remember a damn thing I've ever written. All because TJ pissed me off when we were on that panel."

"What happened between you two? When we left Troy last summer, you were getting along. When did you turn into enemies again?"

At Troy, Emilia and TJ had spent most of the summer squabbling, but they'd bonded while playing matchmaker between Dusty and Stuart. Then, after they teamed up to take down their scheming boss, they'd become allies.

Their truce had lasted less than a month.

"Once the academic year started up again, we were back at each other's throats," Emilia said. "It doesn't help that we're always competing for the same opportunities, and he's usually the one that gets them. It's so unfair. Do you remember when he got accepted to be a panelist at that big archaeology symposium in DC?"

Dusty nodded. "You applied, too, didn't you?"

"Yeah, but I got rejected. Then I found out TJ was super tight with the professor who organized the panel. When I accused him of having an unfair advantage, he insisted he'd gotten accepted on his own merits. Which is total bullshit. What made it worse was that he kept bragging about all the amazing connections he made at that symposium."

To be fair, a lot of academics were just as boastful as TJ, but none of them grated on Emilia's nerves like he did.

She continued. "Then, in December, we got into a month-long debate on ArchForum."

Dusty groaned. "*No.* That online forum is full of toxic archaeology bros."

"No kidding. I made the mistake of starting a discussion about Bronze Age climate change. Naturally, TJ came at me with his own theories and got his buddies to take his side. He's always looking for ways to undermine me, like at today's panel."

What made it infinitely worse was that TJ never got riled up the way she did. He was so sure of himself that he sailed through life with a smug confidence she secretly envied.

When Dusty didn't reply right away, Emilia's hand tightened around her cocktail glass. "I sound paranoid, don't I? Do you think I'm blowing things out of proportion?"

Her friend gave her an impish smile. "What I think is that you mention his name *a lot*. I get that you've decided he's your personal nemesis, but…"

A rush of heat flooded Emilia's cheeks. "But what? Are you suggesting I'm secretly pining for him and trying to cover it up by acting like he's my sworn enemy?" The words tumbled out with more fury than she'd intended, but Dusty's grin only widened. Like she knew she'd hit her mark.

Dusty raised her wineglass in a salute. "You said it, not me. For what it's worth, I don't think TJ was trying to sabotage you today. Sounds like he was just presenting his own research. I mean, the topic of the session was *contrasting* theories on the collapse of the Bronze Age."

While her friend's logic made sense, Emilia couldn't bring herself to agree. "Sure, but he didn't have to be a dick about it. Now I'm worried I botched everything."

"You have more interviews tomorrow. Maybe then you'll be in a better frame of mind."

"Maybe." Pushing aside her anger, Emilia tossed back the rest of her drink and crunched the last bits of ice between her teeth.

Dusty drained her wine and set down the glass. "If it helps, last year when Stuart did his interviews, he was sure he'd tanked. Then he landed an awesome teaching job at the University of Boston." She scanned the room. "This whole scene makes me so grateful I dropped out of grad school last fall. I'm just happy to be here as Stuart's plus-one. Speaking of which…" She waved him over. "He must be done schmoozing."

In Emilia's opinion, Stuart was a little too tightly wound, but Dusty adored him, and he treated her like a queen. The two of them had known each other since childhood, but they'd only started dating last August, after they worked together at Troy.

Stuart came to stand beside them at the bar. He placed his hands on Dusty's shoulders and kissed the top of her head. "Having fun? Or plotting future shenanigans?"

Dusty grinned up at him. "What makes you think I would ever get up to any trouble? I've only had two glasses of wine."

"Do you want another round?" he asked. "Or are you ready to call it a night?"

Emilia couldn't miss the way he caught Dusty's eyes and the smile she gave him in return. That secret, knowing smile of a couple that can't wait to get into bed and start screwing like rabbits. She waved them away. "Get going. I'll be fine."

"You sure?" Dusty asked.

"Yeah. I'm just about done for the night. I'll see you tomorrow, right?"

"Definitely. Let's meet up for lunch. I'll text you." Dusty pulled a few bills out of her wallet and left them on the bar. "Have a good night. I'm sure you'll crush those interviews."

Emilia fought off a pang of wistfulness as she watched them walk away. Her romantic life was nothing like Dusty's. For the past year and a half, she'd been on a self-imposed dating hiatus. All because her last partner had broken her trust and left her emotionally gutted.

Rather than go up to her room, she ordered another mojito. She sipped it slowly, savoring the taste of mint and lime. If she was lucky, the buzz would ease the negative voices in her head.

Until another, more annoying voice broke into her thoughts. "Anyone sitting here?"

And because fate was such a fickle goddess, of course it was TJ.

CHAPTER TWO

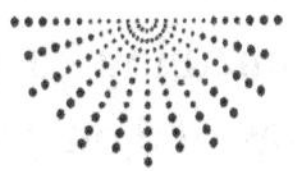

Emilia scowled at TJ, who stood beside her, holding a bottle of beer. He'd changed out of his business attire but still looked maddeningly attractive in jeans and a dark green Henley.

He gestured to the empty seat. "Okay if I join you?"

"Go away."

"Come on, Em. Don't you know you shouldn't drink alone?"

"I wasn't drinking alone." Did he think she was that pathetic? When he raised his eyebrows, her scowl deepened. "Dusty was with me. She and Stuart left a few minutes ago."

"Right. So?" He pointed to the barstool.

"Whatever. But I'm not going to talk to you." She downed the rest of her mojito in a hasty gulp, shivering as the rum coursed through her system. She was tempted to get up and leave but didn't want TJ to assume he'd driven her away. Instead, she foolishly ordered another cocktail.

She was hoping he'd let her drink in silence, but he couldn't keep his mouth shut. "How'd your interviews go?"

"Terrible. Is that why you're here? To rub it in? I'm sure you aced yours." She waited for him to tell her how well they'd gone.

How he'd wowed the hiring committees with his knowledge and experience. Because he was nothing if not boastful.

He scraped a hand through his tawny brown hair. "I'm not usually lacking in self-confidence, but..."

Truly, that was the understatement of the century.

"I didn't feel great about them," he said. "Too much is at stake. You know?"

For once, this was something they could agree on. "Yeah. There are hardly any listings, and only four are tenure-track."

She'd gotten a sick feeling in the pit of her stomach when she reviewed the available postings. Landing a job as a tenure-track professor—a position with guaranteed job security in the cutthroat world of academia—seemed as elusive as discovering a lost tomb laden with golden artifacts.

TJ drove out a harsh sigh. "There aren't a lot of museum posts, either. If I can't line up something, then I'm screwed."

"There's always contract archaeology." Before starting grad school, she'd spent a year working in cultural resource management, or CRM, doing salvage archaeology in Arizona. Even if the pay hadn't been ideal, she'd gotten hands-on experience conducting records searches, ground surveys, and excavations on sites designated for construction.

"You did that before, right?" he asked. "Would you consider it again?"

"Maybe. Now that I have a graduate degree, I could be a project manager, but..."

"But it's not the dream, is it?"

She shrugged. "You've seen the stats. Most archaeologists end up in CRM."

Some people—like her friend Rick Langston—preferred it to the academic grind. But if she went that route, her dad would be so disappointed. Though she'd warned him an academic gig wasn't a sure thing, he'd already started referring to her as "Professor Flores" in the family group chat.

By pursuing a teaching career, she was carrying on the legacy left by her mom, who'd been a devoted third-grade teacher until her untimely death from a car accident sixteen years ago. A loss that had left a painful void in Emilia's heart. Even though her extended Mexican American family provided her with plenty of love and support, no one could ever take her mom's place.

"There's always the post-doc option," TJ said. "That's my fallback. Get a sweet post-doc for a year or two, then look for something more permanent. If that fails, there are fellowships to travel and do research overseas."

While she didn't want to boost TJ's ego any more than necessary, she couldn't deny his idea had merit. "That's not a bad plan. A paid stint in the Mediterranean would be awesome."

"Wouldn't it, though? Any preference on where you'd want to work?"

As hesitant as she was to reveal too much of herself to him, she couldn't stop the response that slipped out. "Italy. Nowhere else comes close."

In addition to working on three excavations there, she'd spent five months on a conservation fellowship in Florence. She'd never been happier than when surrounded by all that history and culture, not to mention the delicious food.

"I'm gonna look into those travel fellowships," she said. "You okay with a little competition?"

"I've never been afraid of competition. You know that."

"You don't have to sound so smug about it." She downed the rest of her cocktail in a quick swallow. Time to put an end to this miserable day. But when she eased off the barstool, her legs wobbled, and her head spun. She clutched her stomach, fighting off a sudden wave of nausea.

What the hell? She'd only had three drinks. Or was it four?

Four. Or five, if you counted the tequila shots she and Dusty had done earlier. Just enough to push her over the edge.

Clutching onto the stool for balance, she tried to right herself. At least she'd had the sense to change out of her heels.

"I'd better get up to bed," she said. "Big day tomorrow."

He narrowed his eyes at her. "Are you okay?"

"I'm fine." A total lie. She was woozy as hell. If she let go of the stool, she'd go crashing to the ground.

"Let me help you." He came over to her and put his arm around her waist.

Her first instinct was to pull away, but he felt so warm and solid. She leaned into him, masking her vulnerability with a growl. "I don't need your help."

"You really want to faceplant here?" He nodded toward the noisy bros seated beside her. "Those guys? Two of them are on the hiring committee for ASU. Don't you have an interview with them tomorrow?"

She did. Acting like a drunken fool wouldn't be a good look. "Fine. You can help me to the elevator."

"I'll do more than that. I'll make sure you get to your room okay."

"That's not necessary." She'd been traveling alone since she was eighteen. Ten years of working at archaeological sites in Mexico, the Middle East, and the Mediterranean meant she'd dealt with all kinds of shit. But she also didn't want to make an ass of herself.

Rather than push TJ away, she leaned on him as they left the bar. They walked toward the bank of elevators located off the hotel lobby. When their elevator arrived, she pushed the button for the eleventh floor.

"Perfect," TJ said. "That's my floor, too."

As the elevator made its ascent, her stomach pitched again. She wasn't going to be sick now, was she? When had she turned into such a lightweight? During her summers in the field, she'd won more than a few drinking competitions with men twice her size. Then again, she'd been so anxious about today's panel that she hadn't eaten anything since breakfast.

Once they reached her room, she broke away from TJ. With painful slowness, she inserted her key card and opened the door. "I'm good for now."

He wasn't listening. Instead, he followed her inside like he had every right to be there. She made her way over to the bed and sat on the edge. Taking a deep breath, she rubbed her hands over her face. "I don't get it. I usually handle my booze a lot better than this."

"Maybe so, but you're under a ton of stress right now. I'm going to grab you some water. You should take some ibuprofen, too."

Why was he being so helpful? Did he have an agenda? "You'd better not try anything."

He held up his hands and backed away. "As if I would? Even drunk, you could kick my ass."

A hint of a smile crossed her lips. "True enough. My toiletries bag in the bathroom has a bottle of Advil."

When he came back, she didn't flinch as he sat on the bed next to her. For as much as he annoyed her, he didn't seem like the type to take advantage. She shook out a couple of ibuprofen capsules and chased them down with a swig of water.

Even if he'd done nothing to deserve her anger, she couldn't stop herself from lashing out. "Aren't you going to mock me for almost humiliating myself in the bar? As a matter of fact, why didn't you let me humiliate myself? You want that ASU job as much as I do."

"Give me some credit. I'm not that underhanded." He flashed her the cocky grin she was used to. "If I get that job—no, *when* I get that job—it'll be on my own merits, not because my rival passed out at the hotel bar."

"Ugh." She drained the rest of the water and set the empty

glass on the nightstand. "Do you have any idea how infuriating you are?"

"Yeah, but you kind of like it, don't you?"

No. Of course she didn't.

Dusty's earlier words echoed in her brain. *Did* she like it? If she was being completely honest, she'd had a lot of fun sparring with him when they'd worked together at Troy. Every time she beat him at cards, shut him down with her exceptional language skills, or drank him under the table, she reveled in the thrill of victory.

But she'd never admit it.

"No," she muttered.

"Really?"

He was sitting so close. Too close, but she couldn't bring herself to push him away.

She caught a whiff of something delicious. His aftershave. Not too cloying but nice and citrusy. Behind his glasses, his inquisitive brown eyes were fixed on hers, like they could see right into the depths of her soul. Under normal circumstances, she would have denied her feelings and called him out on his arrogance. But she couldn't do it tonight.

Instead, she asked the question that had needled her for hours. "Why did you undermine me today? Why didn't you target anyone else on that panel?"

He gave a small chuckle. "Because you were the only one worth challenging."

Damn. How was she supposed to respond to that?

"I tried to tell you earlier, but you wouldn't let me," he said. "I knew you could hold your own. You're just like me—nothing excites you more than a good battle of wits."

"I'm nothing like you."

"So you say, but I've never seen you concede defeat in an argument. We're more alike than you want to admit."

Instead of firing back an angry retort, she stared at him in silence, unable to break free of his spell. She hated that she was even the slightest bit attracted to him. That she was suddenly gripped with the desire to break down their barriers and feel his mouth on hers.

Without thinking, she grabbed his shirt and pulled him closer until their lips met. Soft at first. Tentative. But then deeper, tasting beer on his tongue. And when his hands threaded through her hair and he plundered her mouth with a passionate kiss of his own, desire shot through her, igniting her entire body. An ache built up between her legs, reminding her it had been far too long since anyone had kissed her like this. With lust and longing. Like she was the only thing that mattered.

Until he pulled away and sprang up from the bed. Raking his hand through his hair, he stepped back. "Em...I...this is a bad idea."

Fuck. He didn't want her. Even if he'd kissed her back, he hadn't meant it. Mustering up a tiny shred of dignity, she wiped her hand across her mouth, as though she was a prickly five-year-old trying to erase a kiss from her abuela. "You should go."

"Right. Yeah. Sorry." He inched away. "I'll see you tomorrow. And...um...good luck with your interviews."

Then he was gone, slamming the door behind him.

How could she have thrown herself at him? Even if he enjoyed their rivalry, he didn't want any more than that. Neither did she.

She lay down on the bed and let out a groan.

Worst. Conference. Ever.

CHAPTER THREE

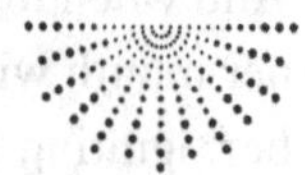

TJ leaned against the hallway, trying to catch his breath. Had he been hallucinating? Or had Em just kissed him?

Emilia Flores, who had once claimed she'd rather eat dirt than spend a minute alone with him. All because they'd gotten off to such a disastrous start last summer.

Even before he learned they'd be digging together at Troy, she'd been on his radar. Hard to ignore her when she'd already made a name for herself in Bronze Age archaeology. Three published articles, four presentations, and two panel sessions. He'd been keeping track. Since her theories conflicted with his, he'd quarreled with her in a few online forums. It didn't help that they were academic rivals, what with him being a Harvard grad student and her being at Yale.

But last June, before leaving for Turkey, he'd offered her an olive branch. Upon discovering they were arriving in Istanbul on the same flight, he'd reached out to her. Thanks to a hot tip from a friend, he'd gotten a lead on a bargain-priced hotel in the popular Sultanahmet district. When he'd asked Emilia if he should book it for them, she'd agreed. But he'd screwed up.

His first mistake had been reserving only one room for the

two of them as a way to cut costs. His second? Not taking the time to check the hotel's reviews on Tripadvisor or Yelp. The place had been a filthy, one-star dump that smelled like a sewer. Naturally, Emilia hadn't been impressed. Instead of apologizing, he'd gone on the defensive and accused her of being a diva.

He'd definitely been the asshole in that situation.

They'd spent the whole summer trying to one-up each other, until they'd bonded to save the project from their glory-hog of a dig director. By the last week at Troy, they'd started acting like friends. They'd even shared one memorable night where they'd spent hours talking about their shared Midwestern roots and the crushing weight of family expectations. But their animosity had returned after they'd flown back to the States and revived their academic feud. Now, they were competing for the exact same jobs.

The truth was, even if Emilia was a little strong-willed for his liking, he admired her. And he *loved* challenging her. Not just because he enjoyed watching her dark eyes flash with anger whenever he bested her but because he considered her a worthy opponent. She was smart, driven, and just as competitive as he was. And a total knockout, with a sexy, toned figure and long black hair that fell past her shoulders in silken waves.

It pained him to admit he'd had more than a few fantasies about her. Not that he'd ever tell her. She'd either laugh at him or threaten to punch his lights out.

But damn, that kiss.

He'd wanted to keep going. To forget about everything except the taste and feel of her.

Get your shit together. You have three interviews tomorrow.

He pulled his key card out of his wallet, ambled down the hall, and let himself into his room. After changing for bed, he opened his laptop and reviewed his notes. Tomorrow morning, he had first-round interviews with Arizona State University, Northwestern, and UNC-Chapel Hill. Though he'd gladly take any of them, the Northwestern job would bring him closer to his family, who lived in the Chicago suburbs. Knowing Emilia, that was her top pick as well since it would put her less than two hours away from her family in Milwaukee.

Stop thinking about Emilia.

He tried to focus, but it was impossible. He imagined running his fingers through her hair and kissing her everywhere until she moaned in ecstasy. As his body reacted, he let out a groan.

Time for a long, hot shower. Otherwise, he'd be distracted all night.

THE BREAKFAST BUFFET AT THE CONFERENCE WAS SET UP IN ONE OF the hotel's ballrooms, spread out over dozens of tables. TJ searched for a familiar face until he spotted his colleague Olivia Sanchez. He'd met her on a dig in Cyprus a year and a half ago, and they'd stayed friends ever since. Upon getting her doctorate last spring, she'd snagged a primo teaching gig at UC Santa Barbara, which was basically the dream. When he'd first learned about it, he'd had a hard time controlling his jealousy, but if anyone deserved a great job, it was Olivia.

After setting down his plate and coffee mug, he plopped into the seat across from her. "Good morning, Olivia."

Clad in a t-shirt and sweats, her curly hair pulled into a messy ponytail, she looked like she'd rolled out of bed. "Morning, TJ. Nice tie. Glad to see you're more polished than I am."

He smoothed a hand over his tie. The maroon shade was a nod to the school colors of the University of Chicago, where his father had taught for years before succumbing to pancreatic cancer when TJ was eleven. "Thanks. Did you just get up?"

She grinned. "Busted. Since I'm not presenting until eleven thirty, I figured I might as well sleep in. I have plenty of time to go back to my room and change."

"It must be nice to be so relaxed." He added cream to his coffee, then took a sip. *Blech.* Hotel coffee was the worst, matched only by the weak-ass Nescafé he'd had on some of his digs.

"Don't forget, I went through this circus at last year's conference," she said. "Nine interviews in two days. It really sucked. I'm just glad it ended well."

"For you, maybe, but the listings are pathetic this year. I'm not holding my breath."

"Where's the self-confident TJ I know so well? The guy who said, 'Seriously bro, I'm connected,' back when we were in Cyprus?"

He cringed. Younger TJ had been such an ass. "I was an idiot. I don't know how you put up with me. Even if I've got Harvard connections, they only go so far."

"Did someone mention Harvard? That must mean TJ has joined the chat." Olivia's boyfriend, Rick Langston, sat next to them, carrying a plate laden with eggs, bacon, sausages, hash browns, and a stack of pancakes.

"That's quite a breakfast," TJ said.

"Hey, it's free food. You take it where you can get it." Rick popped a piece of bacon into his mouth. "You ready to rock those interviews?"

"No," TJ muttered. "I'm having a crisis of confidence."

"If nothing comes through in academia, you can hit me up," Rick said. "There's so much construction going on in Ventura County that the CRM firm I work with is stretched thin. We don't have enough archaeologists on staff to manage all our projects. Salvage archaeology might not be glamorous, but it pays the bills, and you still get your hands dirty."

TJ managed a half-hearted smile. "I appreciate the offer, but I'm still holding out for a teaching job or something at a museum. I just wish the field wasn't so competitive. It doesn't help that Emilia…" He trailed off as he caught a knowing smirk between Rick and Olivia.

"So…you and Emilia, huh?" Olivia asked. "I thought you couldn't stand each other. But last night, I could have sworn I saw you leave the hotel bar together."

Rick grinned. "You two looked pretty tight."

Fuck. "You…you were there?" TJ swallowed quickly, then coughed as a chunk of waffle lodged in his throat.

"We were in the back, with a group from UCLA," Olivia said. "But no judgment. A conference like this is the perfect place to let off a little steam."

"Nothing happened. Really." TJ's forehead prickled with sweat. "She had too much to drink, so I was helping her get to her room. I wasn't taking advantage of her."

Until she kissed me passionately, and I kissed her right back.

He wiped his brow with his napkin only to realize it was sticky with syrup. "Please don't mention this to Em. She didn't even want my help, but I…um…I…" How could he explain his actions? He wasn't even sure why he'd helped her in the first place.

"We were just teasing," Rick said. "If you and Emilia want to keep things quiet, it's totally cool. What happens at conference stays at conference."

"Damn right," Olivia said, giving Rick a fist bump. "We won't breathe a word."

"Thanks." TJ could only imagine how furious Emilia would be if she learned she'd been the subject of gossip. Pushing aside his plate, he stood up. Right now, the thought of food—even waffles doused in syrup—made his stomach churn. "I'm going outside. I need a dose of fresh air before my first interview."

"Knock 'em dead," Rick said. "Don't forget we're doing a bar crawl at eight with a group from the old Cyprus crew."

"I'll try to make it." Setting his napkin on his plate, he left the two of them.

Why couldn't he be at that stage of his life? With a job he liked, a partner he cared about, and a sense his career was on track. Instead, he was floundering, unsure of where the road would take him. He'd always been so driven, willing to do whatever it took to get ahead in academia so that he could follow in his late father's footsteps. But the ball wasn't in his court anymore.

Once he was outside, he regretted his decision immediately. Philadelphia in January was bitterly cold, with an icy wind that cut through his suit jacket. The streets were covered with a mix of slush and ice that could easily destroy his only pair of decent loafers. Within minutes, he turned around and headed back to the hotel.

After checking his appearance in the men's restroom, he made his way to the wing of the hotel reserved for interviews. Outside the row of suites was a small waiting area filled with sharply dressed grad students. None of them looked happy to be there.

As he was about to join them, someone cursed behind him. "Fuck me. Not you again."

At the sight of Emilia, regret and shame washed over him. Even if she'd been the one to initiate last night's kiss, he shouldn't have kept going. "Hey, Em. Can we talk?"

She let out an exasperated breath. "Can we not?"

He still found it hard to reconcile this polished version of Emilia with the woman he'd known last summer. On the rare occasions when she'd changed out of her grubby dig clothes, she'd rarely worn anything fancier than a sundress. But today, her hair was pulled into a bun, her makeup was flawless, and she was clad in the same navy blazer and pencil skirt she'd worn for yesterday's panel. And the same heels. They accentuated her calves, which were toned from years of running.

She growled. "You're staring."

"Sorry. You look nice. Um...professional."

"I can be professional when the occasion calls for it. What do you want?"

"To apologize for last night. I was just trying to make sure you got to your room safely. It wasn't my plan to hit on you. And then I left abruptly and—"

"By the goddess, stop talking. Please." She rubbed her temples. "There's nothing to apologize for. I was drunk and horny and made a mistake. Don't give it another thought."

But he *had* given it another thought. All through his steaming-hot shower and in bed afterward, he'd fantasized about her. About what he'd do if they could ever move past their animosity and give in to the physical attraction simmering beneath the surface. But he wasn't about to share that with her.

"I won't mention it again, but can we call a truce while we're at this conference?" He put out his hand. "Friends?"

A pained expression crossed her face. Did she regret the way he'd ended things last night? Had she wanted him to stay? Was she secretly wishing they'd done more than kiss?

But she quickly dispelled his delusions with a firm shake of her head. "I don't think that's a good idea. We both need to focus, and we're competing for the same teaching positions."

She joined the others in the waiting area, choosing to lean against the wall rather than take the last available chair. Meanwhile, he stood there like an idiot, wishing he hadn't said anything. Even if he'd spent far too long dreaming of her last night, she'd clearly dismissed the entire incident.

Besides, she was right. He needed to focus on his interviews.

He couldn't waste another minute obsessing over her.

Even if she did look really hot in those heels.

CHAPTER FOUR

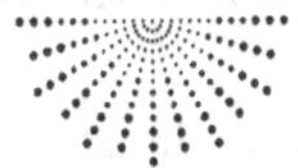

Seven Months Later

Emilia maneuvered her way around the crush of people clogging the Via dell 'Abbondanza—one of the wide stone streets that traversed the archaeological ruins of Pompeii. Even at six in the evening, the place was crawling with tourists. Given that August was almost over, the summer travel season should have been winding down. Instead, the site was packed from the moment it opened until the gates closed at eight. All the more reason Emilia was grateful to be working in an area that was off-limits to visitors.

A familiar voice called out her name. "Emilia. Wait up."

Smiling, she halted until Paulo caught up to her. Over the past three months, they'd grown close while working together at Pompeii. Though she'd done little more than flirt with him, she could easily see herself succumbing to his charms. What did it matter if he had a reputation as a player? He was smart, fun, and easy on the eyes, with a sexy Italian accent tailor-made for seduction.

It was high time she ended her dating hiatus. Or at least

indulged in a casual hookup. As long as she didn't fall in love again, she wouldn't get her heart broken.

"Hey, Paulo. Ready to head back?" She took off her baseball cap and wiped the sweat from her forehead. The sun had been brutal today, with the midday temperature spiking to ninety degrees. "I'm so glad it's Friday. I'm dying for a cold beer."

"Enjoy it while you can since you're on duty here this weekend."

"I am?" A sinking sense of dread overtook her as she recalled penciling her name on the master calendar earlier in the week. "Shit. I totally forgot."

He flashed her a sly grin. "Lucky you. I know how much you *love* leading tourists around Pompeii."

"Don't remind me."

"I don't understand why you always say you're available to give tours. You know it's optional, right?"

For you, maybe. Unlike the Europeans working at Pompeii, who weren't burdened by crushing student loans, Emilia never turned down a chance to boost her income. Even if she'd been hired as an archaeologist, moonlighting as a weekend tour guide was a convenient side hustle. She didn't even need a license since the company she worked for—Buon Viaggio Tours—was owned by the dig director's brother. Weekends at Pompeii were so busy that his company was always in need of extra help. While she didn't enjoy coddling needy tourists, the pay was decent, and the tips were great.

"I wouldn't mind giving tours if I didn't get stuck with Americans," she said. "They're the worst, and I'm saying this *as* an American." Case in point, they were now stuck behind an English-speaking group that was blocking the street in an unwieldy clump, oblivious to those trying to get around them.

Paulo grimaced. "I had a group from Texas two weeks ago. Three of them kept asking me when we were going to visit the 'infamous brothel.' They were so disappointed when they realized the lupanar was just a few empty rooms and some faded paintings."

"It doesn't live up to the hype. In most of the murals, you can barely see what the people are doing." Even if the wall paintings adorning the ancient brothel depicted couples in various sexual positions, the colors were dull and faded from decades of exposure.

Paulo lowered his voice to a sexy whisper. "Does that mean you've studied the pictures closely? For ideas?"

"I don't need them for inspiration. I can come up with plenty of ideas on my own." When he chuckled, a flush of excitement raced through her. It was time she took things further than flirtation.

Once the group of Americans moved on, she and Paulo made their way through the ancient Forum, an open area of the site lined with tall stone columns. Around them, tourists posed for group shots, pored over guidebooks, and took selfies next to the statue of the Greek god Apollo. Emilia had lost track of how many photos she'd been asked to take as a guide—the same poses, over and over, with a multitude of different phones.

After passing through the western exit of the ruins, known as the Porta Marina, she and Paulo strolled past idling minibuses, souvenir stands, and clusters of tourists gathered around the outdoor snack bar across from the site. They bypassed the crowds and headed for the train station, which was less than five minutes' walk.

Though living in modern Pompeii would have been more convenient, all the archaeologists in her cohort were staying at a hostel in the nearby town of Ercolano. Not that Emilia had any complaints. The hostel was cheap and comfortable, with a funky rooftop patio that overlooked the city.

In all honesty, she would have been equally happy living in a tent or crashing on someone's couch. All that mattered was that she'd landed a job at one of the best-known sites in the ancient world.

Back in the spring, as each teaching post slipped through her fingers, she'd had to recalibrate her goals. Rather than wallow in self-pity, she'd sent out a flurry of applications: post-docs, research grants, fellowships, and lab tech positions.

She'd almost resigned herself to going back into cultural resource management when she received a traveling fellowship to work in the Mediterranean. As luck would have it, that same week, Stuart told her about a six-month dig in Pompeii called the Via Stabiana Project. Led by Italian archaeologist Dr. Maurizio Roberti, the project was accepting applications from archaeologists all over the world, provided they spoke Italian.

When she found out she'd been accepted, her relief was so intense she almost burst into tears. With her fellowship covering her travel and lodging expenses, she could save every euro she earned from the Pompeii job to set aside for the future.

At the arrival of the local train, known as the Circumvesuviana, she stepped back to avoid the throngs of tourists disembarking. As she was following Paulo on board, a familiar voice made her wince. "Just made it. Talk about good timing."

If there was one thing that she didn't love about the Via Stabiana Project, it was having to work with TJ. *Again.*

Like her, he hadn't been able to find a permanent post at a college or a museum. In all fairness, he'd been the one to tell her about the traveling fellowships offered by the Carter Institute of Classical Studies. And they'd both learned about the Pompeii gig from Stuart. But Emilia hadn't expected she and TJ would be the *only* two Americans accepted on the dig.

Standing beside him was Marie, a petite Swiss woman with a blond bob and an irritating giggle. Emilia couldn't tell if TJ was interested in her, but she'd clearly set her sights on him. Every time she laughed at one of his jokes or gushed in excitement over his dig stories, Emilia wanted to roll her eyes.

Not that she was jealous. So what if she and TJ had shared a passionate kiss seven months ago? It had merely been a lapse of judgment on her part. True, she'd had a few dreams where they'd done more than kiss, but only because she'd gone without sex for so long. Once she got together with Paulo, her dry spell would be over.

As the train left the station, she squeezed in next to Paulo, grateful their car wasn't packed with hot, sweaty tourists. Even so, the AC barely seemed to be functioning. She took off her hat and tightened her ponytail to ensure her hair wasn't sticking to the back of her neck.

Paulo leaned across the aisle to address Marie. "Ready for the weekend? Is the Swiss contingent headed for Positano again?"

"Of course," Marie said. "Swimming, sunbathing, and limoncello. We've got the perfect weather for it. How about you?"

"Taking the train up to Roma to meet with a few friends," he said.

During their weekends off, the archaeologists on the Via Stabiana Project could spend their time however they chose. Since Emilia was on a tight budget, she rarely ever traveled. Over the past three months, she'd only spent two weekends in Naples and one on the Amalfi Coast.

"No time off for me," TJ said. "I'm leading tours of Pompeii on Saturday and Sunday. With Emilia."

Marie placed her hand on his shoulder. "You poor thing. You'll be so tired on Monday."

Emilia groaned. If giving up her weekend wasn't bad enough, now she had to spend it with TJ. "Why do they insist on pairing us up? They should know we don't work well together."

"Don't blame me," he said. "You always rush through your spiel, and then my group can't catch up. It's like you just want to get it over with."

She fought back a surge of irritation. If she let him set the pace, they'd spend all day running behind schedule. "I *do* want to get it over with. Being a guide sucks. Having to wait for your slow ass sucks even worse."

He glared at her. "I'm trying to do my job. If people in my group have questions, I don't want to ignore them, like you do."

Did he have to sound so self-righteous about it? True, she didn't take the time to answer every question, but she needed to keep things moving. They only had so many hours to get through all the stops on their itinerary. On days when they had to do two tours, back-to-back, they couldn't afford any delays.

She jabbed a finger in his direction. "It wouldn't be a problem if you could give short answers, but you bombard them with more information than they need. You're just showing off."

Paulo chuckled. "You two are always fighting. What's that saying in America—why don't you bang it out of your system?"

Marie wrinkled her nose in disgust. "Really, Paulo? Eww. They're not together."

"You've been reading too many of Marie's romance novels," Emilia said to him. "There's nothing between us."

TJ placed his hand on Marie's arm. "Just because Em and I are the only two Americans here doesn't mean we like each other. Back in the States, we're not even friends."

Paulo waggled his eyebrows. "I don't believe it. You worked together at Troy last summer, no? Did something happen then?"

Why did he sound so amused about it? If anything, he should be jealous. Maybe he was excited at the prospect of stealing her away from TJ.

Spurred on by the thought, Emilia answered his question with a sly laugh. "Well, since you asked...I can't deny it any longer. During the day, TJ and I fought constantly. But at night, we gave in to our deepest urges. Sneaking off to the site after hours. Having wild, passionate sex inside the giant wooden model of the Trojan horse. Keeping it hidden from the rest of the crew all season long. The fear of getting caught made it a total adrenaline rush."

In theory, it could have happened since tourists were allowed to climb up the ladder of the forty-foot wooden horse and clamber into its belly. Once inside, they could pretend they were Greek soldiers, waiting on the signal to attack Troy. But Emilia didn't think anyone had ever entertained the possibility of using it for after-hours sex.

Marie, however, appeared to be taking her seriously. She flashed sad puppy-dog eyes at TJ. "Is that true, Theo?"

Theo? As far as Emilia knew, the only time TJ went by his real name was when he was giving an academic presentation. How had Marie earned the privilege of using it?

TJ's mouth set in a grim line. "No. Em's just being obnoxious. Nothing happened."

As the train continued its journey, the rocking motion made Emilia drowsy. She gazed out the window at the rows of apartment blocks rushing past and tried not to think about TJ.

Focus on Paulo. He's hot, he's into you, and you know he'd be up for a fling.

Next week, she wouldn't sign up to do any tours. Instead, she'd ask Paulo if he wanted to get away for the weekend. All she needed was a night alone with him. Then, she could banish the memory of TJ's kiss forever.

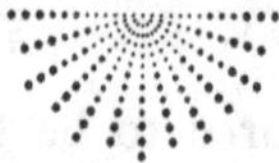

CHAPTER FIVE

During the train ride to Ercolano, TJ couldn't stop himself from imagining the scene Emilia had planted in his brain. Sneaking away with her at Troy, getting naked inside the Trojan horse, and indulging in hot, furtive sex, like some kinky *Iliad*-inspired fantasy. They'd have to bring blankets to prevent splinters. Maybe some booze to loosen up. And they'd have to keep quiet so they wouldn't be discovered by a roaming security guard.

Though he'd never attempted anything that bold before, the idea was titillating.

Get serious. Like Em would ever have sex with you?

Besides, she'd clearly concocted that Trojan horse fantasy to mess with him. Had she said it out of jealousy? Did she think he and Marie were hooking up? The thought had crossed his mind, particularly when Marie had asked him to join her in Positano last weekend, but he hadn't acted on it.

Not because of Emilia. If anything, she was more combative than ever. When they'd first arrived in Pompeii, they'd gotten along, albeit grudgingly. Since they were no longer competing for the same jobs, their rivalry had eased up a little. On the site, they each had their own specialties. She worked with Paulo and three other members of the archaeobotanical team, who were tasked with studying the ancient plant remains, while TJ and his group focused on the bronze and iron artifacts found on the site. Occasionally, they conferred together, but they kept their interactions professional.

But once he and Emilia had been assigned to work together as guides, they'd started squabbling again. She claimed he spent too much time showing off, while he resented the way she rushed her groups through each spot on the tour.

When the train reached Ercolano, the four of them got off and headed toward the hostel. In addition to the sixteen archaeologists living there, the place housed a motley mix of digital nomads and scruffy Europeans traveling on the cheap. It offered a breakfast buffet, a decent bar, and a rooftop patio where people gathered at night to hang out and drink beer.

While TJ enjoyed the lively atmosphere, he was getting a little old for this shit. He wasn't a twenty-year-old backpacker bumming his way through Europe. He was a professional archaeologist with a PhD from Harvard. As fun as the hostel was, it was a far cry from where he could have been living if he'd gotten a job as a college professor in the US.

No whining, remember?

At least he'd found work in his field, which was more than he could say for some of his colleagues. Instead of toiling away at a minimum-wage job, he'd scored a gig that made use of his archaeological training and looked good on his resume.

The walk from the train station to the hostel took twenty minutes along paved sidewalks lined with small shops and apartment buildings in muted tones of yellow, peach, and orange. Compared to a bustling city like Naples, Ercolano was far more low-key. Located on the Tyrrhenian Sea, it was a popular spot for people visiting the ruins at Pompeii and Herculaneum, but it wasn't as packed with tourists as the towns along the Amalfi Coast.

When TJ's phone buzzed, he glanced at it. His younger sister, Romily, had sent him a text.

> Romily: Mom and Al are already planning the big Labor Day BBQ and it's gonna be painful. Way too many people and too much meat. You're lucky you get to skip it.

> TJ: Not sorry I'm missing it. The Memorial Day BBQ was bad enough. Any chance you can get Al to make you a veggie burger?

> Romily: As if. I'll be stuck eating nothing but potato salad and three-bean casserole.

> TJ: Don't forget pie. If there's one thing I miss here, it's Mom's pies.

As he walked with the others, TJ cast his mind back to the last family cookout he'd attended. Before leaving for Italy, he'd flown home to see his family over the Memorial Day weekend. Though he always enjoyed spending time with his mom and Romily, he hated coming under the scrutiny of his two stepbrothers and his stepdad, Al. When he'd explained what he'd be doing in Pompeii, he'd gotten the usual backlash.

"So, this isn't a permanent job?" Al asked. "What are you going to do when you get back in December? It'll be the dead of winter."

"I can apply for jobs while I'm in Italy," TJ said. "Either that, or I'll see if I can find another dig in the Mediterranean."

"That's your whole plan?" Al said. "Sounds like a recipe for failure."

TJ's mother gave him a sympathetic smile. "I still think you should consider teaching high school. Do you remember Mr. Carruthers? You had him for AP European History. He's retiring next year. Maybe you could take his place when you get back."

Like it was that easy? No doubt Mr. Carruthers' spot would attract dozens of applicants, all of whom had actual teaching degrees. "Thanks, Mom, but we talked about this before. I don't want to teach high school."

His stepbrother, Randy, slopped a giant spoonful of potato salad onto his plate. "You should sign up for one of those coding boot camps. The kind where they teach you the basics in a couple of months. Lots of jobs in CS."

Randy should know. He'd gotten a bachelor's degree in computer science eight years ago and was now making six figures. Something he mentioned at every family gathering.

"You should come work for me," Al said. "With your people skills and your knack for networking, I'm sure I can find a place for you. Sports management's a great field."

TJ's other stepbrother, Jake, snickered. "Yeah, but that would mean TJ needs to give a shit about sports."

"Stop it," Romily said. She'd always been his staunchest supporter. "He's going to be working at Pompeii, for fuck's sake."

Their mom frowned. "Language, sweetie."

"Sorry, Mom, but we're talking about one of the most incredible archaeological sites in the world. After Mt. Vesuvius erupted, Pompeii was covered in ash and pumice stone and frozen in time for centuries."

TJ flashed his sister an appreciative grin. "Romily's right. It's like the entire city was sealed in a time capsule. Only two-thirds of it has been excavated, so there's lots left to explore."

Al doused more ketchup on his burger. "I still think it's a dead end. You finish this, then you're stuck back where you were last winter. No job, no prospects, no practical skills. You're twenty-eight, which means you need to stop dicking around. I know you put a lot of effort into getting a PhD, but—let's face it—you might have been wasting your time."

Rather than defend himself, TJ smiled and nodded. Better to play along with his stepdad than get into a heated argument. Been there, done that. But TJ knew if his *real* father had been alive, if Dr. Theodore Mayer, Sr. had been seated at the table, he wouldn't have discouraged his son. As a Roman history professor at the University of Chicago, he'd imbued his two children—TJ and Romily—with a passion for the ancient world.

During his years of grad school, TJ had often wished he could ask his dad for career advice. Had his dad ever doubted his decision to go into academia? Would he advise TJ to keep trying or to give in and take a job with his stepfather?

A soft voice shocked TJ out of his reverie. "TJ? You okay there?"

"Wha…?" He startled as he realized they'd reached the entrance of the hostel. Emilia, Paulo, and Marie were staring at him.

Marie placed her hand on his shoulder. "We lost you for a few minutes."

"Sorry. Just daydreaming."

Paulo smirked. "About having sex in the Trojan horse? I can only imagine."

Emilia rolled her eyes. "I was kidding about the damn horse. Let's grab a beer. I need one before I have to deal with the hordes tomorrow."

Now wasn't the time to dwell on the past. Or worry about the future. TJ needed to live in the moment and celebrate Friday night with his colleagues. A few beers on the rooftop sounded like the perfect way to decompress.

And not once would he allow himself to envision the Trojan horse scenario.

Nope. Not even a little bit.

~

THE NEXT MORNING, AS TJ WAS FINISHING HIS BREAKFAST IN THE hostel's common room, Marie came up to him and leaned on his chair. Over her shoulder was a red-and-white striped weekend bag. "I wish you could come with us. Wouldn't you rather spend the weekend in Positano than work at Pompeii?"

He inhaled the faint scent of her honeysuckle perfume. "Definitely, but whenever Dr. Roberti's brother needs guides, I don't want to turn him down."

"You should stand up for yourself, like I do. Last weekend, he asked me if I wanted to work, but I told him I had plans. You could do the same thing."

"It's not that easy." First of all, he needed to stay on Dr. Roberti's good side so he could get a killer recommendation once the project ended. Second, he was trying to squirrel away money for the winter. Once he was done working in Italy, he didn't want to return home flat broke.

"Try to get next weekend free, okay?" She ruffled his hair. "Then we could go to the Amalfi Coast together."

A tempting thought. Even if she didn't make his pulse race with excitement, she was sweet, cute, and obviously into him. And he hadn't been with anyone for over a year, which made him feel like a damn monk. "I'll try. Okay? Right now, I have to take off. I'm sure Em is waiting outside, thinking up new reasons to snipe at me."

Marie squeezed his shoulder. "Do you promise nothing happened between the two of you?"

"Nothing happened, and it never will." He wasn't about to mention the kiss he and Em had shared in Philly seven months ago. Or last night's fantasies, which had involved Emilia, the Trojan horse, and a couple of *actual* Trojans.

After Marie left, he dashed up to his room to grab his backpack. Even though he was running late, he checked it over to make sure he had everything he needed for the day: sunscreen, a water bottle, a sun hat, a site map, a clipboard, and a red flag bearing the company's logo. The one time he'd forgotten his hat, he'd gotten a blistering headache from the sun.

Outside the hostel, Emilia leaned against the bright blue gate that marked the entrance to the building. She looked up from her phone and scowled. "You're late."

Was she going to be this surly all day? "Only by a few minutes."

She stuck her phone in her back pocket and started walking. "We need to hurry if we're going to catch the eight o'clock train. We're supposed to be at Pompeii at least twenty minutes before it opens."

"We'll be fine."

Giving a resentful grunt, she strode on ahead. Rather than engage her further, he let her stew in grouchy silence.

When they reached the platform for the train station, they were ten minutes early. No one else was waiting, save for an elderly woman peering at a map. TJ wanted to point out that they'd rushed for nothing, but he didn't need to rile up Emilia. Still, he couldn't let things stand the way they were. If he didn't find out what was wrong, he'd have to be extra cheerful to compensate for her grumpiness.

"You doing okay?" he asked.

She plopped down on a metal bench facing the track. "I'm fine. Why?"

He sat beside her, putting a generous amount of space between them. "Because you're giving off a hostile vibe." *And you're going to be a crappy tour guide if you keep it up.*

"It's nothing."

"No, it's not. If I did something to piss you off, can you please yell at me and get it over with?"

He honestly couldn't think of anything he'd done to her. Last night, they'd hung out on the rooftop with the other archaeologists, drinking beer and swapping dig stories. She'd joked with him more than usual, especially after Paulo brought up the Trojan horse *again*.

"It's just…" She looked away. "Marie and her friends left the hostel as I was waiting for you. Naturally, she had to brag about her fabulous weekend plans and offer her deepest sympathies that I was stuck working. Oh, and she made sure to tell me you're going to the Amalfi Coast with her next weekend."

Was that why Emilia was so sullen? Because she was jealous? He could have strung her along, but he didn't have the energy to bicker. "I didn't say I was going for sure. I might consider it, but only if I'm not needed here. If they ask for guides, I won't say no. The money's too good to turn down."

"Agreed. Every little bit helps." She let out a ragged sigh. "Being broke really sucks."

Though he knew she was as desperate for money as he was, she usually blew it off like it was no big deal. Her rare display of vulnerability surprised him. "Do you have a lot of debt?"

When she didn't answer right away, he wanted to kick himself for prying. But she turned to face him with a wry smile. "It's not as bad as it could be. I've been hustling nonstop since I was seventeen. If there was a fellowship, a research grant, or a source of financial aid I could apply for, I went after it. Most of the time, I got it."

He regarded her with admiration. "I'm impressed. That sounds like a ton of work."

She shrugged. "You do what you have to. You're the same way."

"Yeah. I've gotten enough scholarships that my student debt isn't too overwhelming. But even without a massive loan looming over my head, I'm in crappy financial shape. I barely have any savings."

"Same here, and once this job ends, I've got nothing lined up. If I can't find a contract archaeology gig, I could always move back home and work at my dad's landscaping company or my aunt's garden shop. The Flores family takes care of their own. But I'm twenty-eight, damn it."

He envied her, coming from a large Mexican American family that genuinely seemed to care about each other. They were probably a lot less focused on making six figures than his stepdad was.

"I'll be twenty-nine next month," he said. "A little old to end up in my childhood bedroom. And honestly? I'd rather live in a shack than move back home. My stepbrothers would *never* let me hear the end of it."

When the train arrived at the platform, they got on board. He followed Emilia to the back of the car, where they found two aisle seats across from each other.

Rather than lapse into silence, she kept the conversation going. "Do you ever worry about what comes next? I get so tired of scrambling for work."

"Me too. But then I remind myself that, right now, I love what I'm doing. I mean, other than guiding hormonal teenage boys through the brothel."

She snorted with laughter. "Paulo and I were talking about that yesterday. Maybe if they installed some neon signs and brightened up the sex paintings, it would be less disappointing."

A flicker of annoyance flared up inside of him. "You and Paulo, huh? When are the two of you planning *your* getaway?"

Her familiar scowl returned. "Jealous?"

"Hardly. But…fair warning, he gets around. At least that's what Marie told me. She worked with him at Pompeii two years ago."

"I'm sure she loved sharing that tidbit of information now that you two have been getting cozy, *Theo*. I didn't realize you'd started going by your real name."

Her irritation filled him with a swell of glee. "I haven't. It's a special privilege, reserved only for a select few." He was tempted to push the joke further, but he couldn't risk antagonizing Emilia, not when they had to spend the next eight hours giving tours together. "I'm kidding. Marie took it on herself to call me Theo, but I prefer TJ."

"Really? Why?" This time, there was no snark in her tone, just curiosity.

"Because Theodore was my dad's name. Even though he's been gone for seventeen years, I still feel like it belongs to him. My younger sister, Romily, started calling me TJ when she was two, and the name stuck."

"She's the one who's into rom-coms, right? I remember you mentioning her last summer."

"Yep. She loves them. She had a rough time in middle school, but watching those movies always cheered her up. You can judge me if you want, but I can't resist a good rom-com."

"Is that what you're hoping for with Marie?" Emilia asked in a mocking voice. "A jaunt along the Amalfi Coast, worthy of a Netflix rom-com?"

Why was Em being so petty? "What have you got against Marie, anyway? She's always nice to you."

Emilia's jaw tightened. "On one of our first weekends here, she invited me to join her friends in Positano. I went with them but regretted it right away. Here they were, blowing a small fortune on overpriced cocktails, and I could barely afford a beer. Dinner that night ate up most of my food budget for the week. I could tell she felt sorry for me, and I don't need that shit."

From what he knew of Emilia, she hated being the object of anyone's pity. "I'm sure she was just being nice."

"I don't think so. Whenever she's around me, she gives off this weird passive-aggressive vibe. Her friends don't treat me that way, but I can tell she doesn't like me."

"Maybe she's jealous of us. Because of our relationship."

"Our *relationship*? What are you talking about?" Emilia's voice was so loud that the woman next to her—a Sicilian grandma type dressed in black—gave them both the stink-eye.

He struggled to come up with a response that wouldn't aggravate Emilia further. What they had wasn't exactly a friendship, but they weren't strangers, either. "The fact that we dug together as colleagues when we were at Troy last summer." He frowned. "It didn't help that you fed her that bullshit about us having sex in the Trojan horse."

For this, the Sicilian grandma hissed at them.

"Lower your voice," Emilia said. "I was just teasing. I didn't mean it."

"Didn't you? The fact that you brought it up suggests you wanted it at some point."

"Hell, no. It's not like we *ever* would have considered it."

"That's what you think." He gave her a wolfish smile. "If you'd asked, I would have taken you up on it in a heartbeat."

She stared at him in shock, flushed bright red, then clammed up for the rest of the ride.

At least now he wouldn't be the only one fantasizing about it.

CHAPTER SIX

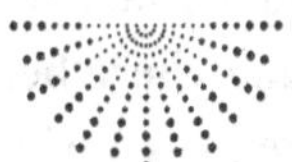

When Emilia had teased TJ about the Trojan horse during yesterday's train ride, she'd scored a point in their ongoing feud. But now? He'd trounced her. By admitting he would have been into it, he'd turned it from a joke into a challenge. All of a sudden, she couldn't stop envisioning how the scene would have played out. Hot, sneaky sex in a forbidden location, which was the *best* kind of sex.

She tried to dislodge the steamy images from her brain. Other than having to defend her attitude toward Marie, she'd enjoyed talking to TJ this morning. With most people, she put up a good front, using sarcasm and self-deprecating humor to mask her uncertainty about the future. Like the fear that she'd never land a decent job in her field. Or pay back her student loans.

For once, it had been a relief to let down her guard and speak honestly about her financial situation with someone who could relate. Unlike the rest of the group, TJ was under just as much financial pressure as she was. Neither of them could afford to spend every weekend on the Amalfi Coast or drop a bundle on an expensive dinner with friends.

That was why they signed up for tours almost every weekend.

Even if their side hustle left them exhausted by Monday, they couldn't pass up the chance to make extra money.

When they got to the Porta Marina entrance of the site, the representative from Buon Viaggio Tours stood waiting for them. Giada, the local tour wrangler, might have been barely five feet tall, but she was a force to be reckoned with. Her short, dark hair was streaked with gray, and her face was weathered from the sun, but she could have been anywhere between forty and sixty. She spoke six languages, worked tirelessly at her job, and had a low tolerance for bullshit.

"Good. You're early." Giada handed each of them a printout. "Here are your lists for this morning's tour. It's a big group—fifty people—so you each get twenty-five."

Emilia bit back a groan. "Twenty-five?" Anything over twenty was hard to control.

"It's Saturday, so we're fully booked. Your first tour is four hours long. You'll be starting right at nine, and you need to wrap it up no later than one o'clock." Giada nailed TJ with a fierce glare. "Understand?"

"Why are you looking at *me* like that?" he said.

"Because you're a big talker. I get it—you like to show off, but this group needs time for lunch before they board their bus for Positano. Then, make sure you're both back here by one forty for your second group. Their tour starts at two o'clock sharp."

TJ nodded. "We won't be late."

On the street facing the entrance to the site, two coach buses idled as their groups disembarked, three smaller minibuses jockeyed for space, and a snaking line of tourists waited for the gates to open. Just another busy morning at Pompeii.

Giada turned her focus to Emilia. "And you—smile more. Even if some of the men can be a little hands-on, we need those five-star reviews."

Emilia plastered a bright smile on her face. "Will do, G. Anything else? Any VIPs?"

"Yes, indeed. We have a big-deal VIP today. He's not part of the tour group, so he'll be arriving separately. His name is Luca Roberti. Emilia, he's with you, so you'll need to be extra nice to him."

Emilia was starting to wish she'd taken the day off. Just what did "extra nice" entail? Did that mean she had to keep her mouth shut if he grabbed her ass? "What kind of VIP? Is he a business exec? A celebrity?"

"Wait—Luca *Roberti?*" TJ said. "Is he related to our boss?"

Giada let out a huffy breath. "Both of you—listen. I don't know why I have to explain everything to you clueless Americans. There are three Roberti brothers." She ticked them off on her fingers. "The youngest is Angelo Roberti, the owner of Buon Viaggio Tours. He's *my* boss. The middle brother is Dr. Maurizio Roberti, who runs the archaeological project in Pompeii. He's *your* boss. And the oldest is Lorenzo. You've never met him. He lives in Milan and is the most successful of the three. Luca is his son. Got it?"

"Got it," Emilia said. "So...Luca's here for a visit?"

"More than that," Giada snapped. "You know Angelo wants to expand Buon Viaggio, right?"

"Sure. It's not exactly a secret." Emilia had heard the gossip from one of the other guides. Right now, the company was focused on Tuscany and southern Italy, but for Angelo to stay competitive, he needed to add tours that covered the entire country, and he was hoping to add an office in Milan.

"Angelo wants his older brother to invest in the company," Giada said. "But Lorenzo—well, he's skeptical. He's always looked down his nose at Angelo and isn't sure if the company is a worthwhile investment. So he's sending his son, Luca, who has a degree in business, to spend a few months working with Buon Viaggio. He'll be joining some of our tours and observing how we operate."

"Like a spy?" TJ said.

"This isn't a James Bond movie, but yes, he'll be reporting his findings back to his father. Which means we need to impress Luca. His father isn't just wealthy; he's got significant ties to the Italian Ministry of Tourism."

"Isn't that a conflict of interest?" TJ asked. "I mean, if he's planning on investing in a private tour company?"

Giada waved her hand in dismissal. "Enough questions. Just do a good job, okay? With that in mind—here." She tossed Emilia a plastic bag. "Freshen up a little."

Emilia's heart sunk as she peeked inside the bag. "Can't I just wear my polo?" She hated the company's ugly red polyester polo, but it was better than the shirt in the bag—a tight, scoop-necked tee that would put her cleavage on full display.

"Go change!" Giada barked. "While you're at it, put on some lipstick."

When TJ started laughing, Emilia shot him a withering glare, then tromped off to the restroom to change. The clingy shirt made her feel far too exposed, but she wasn't about to ignore Giada's orders. Not when the woman would report any infraction to her boss.

As Emilia came out, Giada was waving a large group over. With practiced efficiency, she greeted them enthusiastically, divided them up, and distributed their headsets. On tours like these, TJ and Emilia were meant to keep the entire group together, even though they often had to split up to herd their sections into the smaller spaces on the site.

Emilia put on her headset and adjusted her mini microphone. Remembering to smile, she gestured for her group to move in closer. Most of them looked to be at least sixty, if not older, but none were using a cane or a walker, which was a relief. More than one person had gotten injured on the uneven stones lining the ancient Roman roads at Pompeii.

"Buongiorno!" she called out. "I'm Dr. Emilia Flores, an archaeologist from the United States, and I'm working here at

Pompeii on a six-month excavation project. Getting to dig in a place with this much history has been amazing, and I can't wait to tell you everything about it. During our tour, we'll make a series of stops, clearly marked on the maps you've been given. I'll try to explain everything in detail, but if you have questions, don't hesitate to ask. Please try to keep together. The site is so big that it's easy to get lost. Since it's hot out, make sure to drink plenty of water, and let me know if you feel dizzy or need to rest in the shade."

As she scanned the group to make sure everyone understood her, a tall man with slick dark hair and aviator shades approached them. If she had to guess, she'd say he was in his early thirties. He moved through the group effortlessly until he reached the front and took her hand. "Dr. Flores? I am Luca Roberti, and I'm here to observe your tour. I hope you won't find my presence too intimidating."

His voice was low and warm, so smooth and confident that it took her a moment to respond. He wasn't just attractive; he was movie-star gorgeous, with a sense of presence. She swallowed, suddenly unnerved at the thought of keeping him entertained for the entire tour. He'd probably been to Pompeii before. If she didn't want him to get bored, she'd need to channel as much positive energy as possible. No wonder Giada had asked her to smile.

"It's nice to meet you," she said. "Thank you for joining my tour."

"The pleasure is all mine, bellissima. What good luck to have such an alluring guide for my visit to Pompeii."

Bellissima. It was a bold move on his part, calling her "very beautiful" from the second he met her. Then again, he was Italian. "Uh...thanks." She turned her attention back to the group. "Let's start the tour, shall we?"

~

THE HALF-DAY TOUR ALWAYS ENDED AT THE OUTDOOR THEATER near the southern edge of Pompeii. Since everyone could spread out and sit on the ancient stone benches, she and TJ did this last part together. When they were in a rush, she liked being the one to wrap things up so that they wouldn't run late. But since they were ten minutes ahead of schedule, she let him take the lead.

She drained the rest of her water bottle as he described the features of the outdoor theater and the type of performances it would have hosted, like musical comedies and Greek dramas. Even if he tended to be a little long-winded, his enthusiasm was admirable. He always sounded like there was nothing else he'd rather do than spend hours talking to tourists.

"Any last questions?" he asked.

An older dude with a shaggy white beard and a tie-dyed shirt raised his hand. "What about Pink Floyd? Didn't they have a concert here in 1972?"

TJ grinned. "Good one. They did, but not at this theater. It's too small. They held their concert at the big outdoor amphitheater at the eastern end of the site. We don't include it on the tour because it takes about twenty minutes to get there."

When the guy's face fell, Emilia spoke up. She never wanted anyone to leave feeling unsatisfied. "You can walk over there if you want since you don't have to be back on the bus until two. But then you might miss a chance to grab lunch."

As if to cheer him up, TJ asked, "What's your favorite Pink Floyd album? I'll bet you've listened to all of them."

"*Echoes,*" Tie-Dye said. "The old stuff's the best. You?"

"*Wish You Were Here.* It's a classic." TJ gestured to Emilia. "Em is partial to *Dark Side of the Moon.*"

How just like TJ to make her sound so basic. She'd barely given Pink Floyd a thought before coming to Pompeii. It just seemed like another example of "dad rock" enjoyed by white guys in their fifties and sixties. But since the Pink Floyd question came up a lot, TJ had made a playlist of their best albums and insisted she listen to it. She'd liked it more than she expected—something she had yet to divulge to him.

"Anyone else a Pink Floyd fan?" TJ asked.

While he entertained the crowd, Emilia inched away and found a quiet spot in the shade. She pulled out her phone and texted Giada.

> All done. TJ's finishing up at the theater. We'll start heading back in 5 minutes.

Giada always wanted to be kept in the loop. Otherwise, she sent all-caps texts demanding to know their status.

Emilia recoiled as someone placed a hand on her shoulder. She dropped her phone, sending it clattering onto the stone steps. Before she could grab it, Luca bent down and picked it up. He handed it back to her, letting his fingers graze her palm. "So sorry, bellissima, I didn't mean to frighten you."

"It's…ah…it's okay."

It wasn't. Not really. She didn't like anyone on the tours touching her. Given that their groups often squeezed into tight spaces, she needed people to respect her physical boundaries. Normally, she shut down the handsy types with a glare, but when Luca had brushed up against her—more than once—she'd put up with it because he was her boss's nephew. She hadn't snapped at him when his hand had rested on her back or even when it had grazed her ass. But after the way he'd behaved on her tour, she didn't want to spend any more time around him than necessary.

He pinned her in his gaze, making it impossible for her to look away. "I wanted to tell you what a marvelous job you did. Your passion for ancient history made the site come alive."

He was standing so close that she caught a powerful whiff of his aftershave. Something with sandalwood. A bit too potent for her liking. She tried to shake off her uneasiness. In fifteen minutes, the tour would be over, and she wouldn't have to deal with him any longer.

"Thank you. I love working at Pompeii. Sharing my knowledge with all these visitors is always a pleasure." Did she sound convincing? She hoped so since she was sure Luca would report his observations to his uncle Angelo.

"It was a delight to spend the morning in your presence. Would you like to join me for lunch? I'd love to hear more about your experiences here."

Even if he was stunningly handsome, he made her uncomfortable, and not just from the way he'd touched her on the tour. It was the power imbalance, the sense that he'd be calling the shots. Thankfully, she had a legitimate excuse. "I'd love to, but I don't have much time. I'm giving another tour at two. If I'm late, Giada will have my head."

"Of course. Wouldn't want to upset Giada. Angelo told me she has quite a temper. Another time, perhaps?"

"Um…sure. Thanks." When her phone buzzed, she checked it. Sure enough, Giada had responded in her usual demanding manner.

DO NOT let TJ go off on a long tangent!! Bring them back here NOW.

"We'd better get going," Emilia said.

She tucked her phone in her back pocket and went to stand next to TJ. After waiting for a break in the conversation, she addressed the group. "I'm sorry, but we need to bring the tour to an end. Your bus is leaving at two, and we don't want any of you to miss lunch before that."

As everyone got to their feet, she sidled closer to TJ. Usually when lunchtime rolled around, she ate by herself to get a break from peopling. Today, she didn't want to be alone. "Want to grab lunch together?"

"Sure. Everything okay?"

She nodded, not wanting to reveal anything until after the tour was over. With her leading the way and TJ bringing up the rear, they escorted their group to the entrance, where they bid them farewell and collected their tips.

At the outdoor snack bar across from the site, TJ ordered sandwiches, and she grabbed them a couple of icy lemonades. They found a spot in the shade where they could eat quickly.

She hadn't even thought to give TJ her order, but he'd gotten her favorite sandwich—a hero on a crusty white roll with mozzarella, tomato, basil, and prosciutto drizzled with olive oil. "Mmm. This is great. Thanks."

He handed her a couple of napkins. "You sure everything's okay? That Luca guy seemed kind of intense. I hate to say it, but he was checking you out. I caught him staring at your butt, and he didn't even attempt to be discreet about it."

Rather than snap at TJ for acting protective, she sighed in resignation. "Yeah, he was giving off creepy vibes. A few times on the tour, he deliberately brushed up against me, and I let it go because he's Angelo's nephew. Then he asked me to have lunch with him, which shouldn't be a big deal. Maybe he just wanted to learn more about the tour company, but..."

"But then he could have asked both of us. Let's face it, I'm a better guide than you are."

She couldn't help but laugh. "You're the worst, you know that?"

"At least I'm not a lecherous dude trying to hit on you." TJ sipped his lemonade. "If Luca comes on another of these tours, I can take him in my group. Okay?"

"Okay. But now that he's done the Pompeii tour, I'm sure Angelo will want him to go on all the other jaunts Buon Viaggio offers. Maybe he'll send him on one of those long-ass bus tours through southern Italy. By then, he'll have forgotten all about me."

In all likelihood, she was blowing things out of proportion. Luca was just being friendly in the same way Paulo was. An Italian male who enjoyed complimenting women and occasionally got handsy. And yet, his behavior had set off alarm bells in her head.

Because there's a power imbalance. You know what a slippery slope that is.

She'd made that mistake before, only to get burned. But for now, she wasn't going to worry about it.

CHAPTER SEVEN

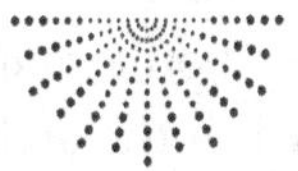

Emilia dabbed at her forehead with a damp bandanna. She wasn't the type to whine about the weather, but the extended heat wave had made her cranky. Ever since last weekend, the temperature had been in the nineties, with poor air quality due to the residual smoke from a series of wildfires in Sicily.

It didn't help that she spent her mornings working outside. She and the other archaeologists had spent the past few months excavating the ruins of a recently discovered Roman house known as the House of Venus. Most days, they dug until one, took a lunch break, then spent the rest of the afternoon analyzing their finds in three makeshift labs near the excavation area. The lab work was meant to give them a break from the sun, but the stifling buildings lacked air-conditioning.

For the past few days, Emilia had been working up the nerve to ask Paulo about his plans for the weekend. Her hesitancy wasn't because she was afraid he'd turn her down. He'd given off enough signals that she was certain he'd say yes to a steamy, no-strings hookup. But TJ had gotten into her head. Whether it was because of that stupid Trojan horse joke or because she'd opened up to him last weekend, he'd been on her mind a lot. Which was ridiculous. They weren't even friends.

Still, that hadn't stopped her from indulging in a few steamy fantasies about him that had left her overheated and frustrated. She needed to take care of these urges before she did something regrettable—like proposition him.

She drained her water bottle and set it on the lab table. Everyone else who worked in the archaeobotanical lab had left for the day, but she'd lingered behind with Paulo. He stood beside her, his brow furrowed in concentration as he peered into a microscope. At the moment, he was studying a cache of carbonized seeds they'd found while excavating the kitchen area of the house.

When he looked up, she cleared her throat. "So…Paulo? Any plans for the weekend? I followed your advice and decided to take a break from giving tours."

"About time you cut loose. I wish I was free, but my cousin's visiting from Pisa. I said I'd show him around the site on Saturday. We might hit up the Lumos Bar that night if you want to join us."

While Paulo's answer was disappointing, it wasn't an outright no. "Saturday night would be great. But…um…I was kind of hoping we could get away sometime. Just the two of us? How about next weekend?" The neediness in her voice made her cringe.

"That's the start of our break, remember? Aren't you coming on the Greece trip?"

Damn. She'd totally forgotten. The Via Stabiana Project was taking a weeklong hiatus in mid-September because their boss, Dr. Roberti, had to attend an international conference in Zurich. Most of the Pompeii archaeologists were traveling to Greece on a trip organized by Marie and her friends.

"I'm not going to Greece," Emilia said. "I've been on a couple of digs there, so I've already seen most of the sites." She paused, hesitant to admit she couldn't afford the cost.

"Who said anything about visiting archaeological sites?" He chuckled. "This is a vacation. We're going to Mykonos and Paros, which means lots of beach time and clubbing."

That's what I'm afraid of. A trip like that would eat into her savings, especially since Marie didn't understand the concept of low-budget travel.

"Come on," Paulo said. "Everyone's going. Even TJ."

"He is? The last time I talked to TJ, he said he was staying behind."

"I'm what now?" TJ approached their table, followed by two other archaeologists from his lab. He ambled over to Paulo and Emilia, flashing his usual cocky grin. "Admit it, Em—you were talking about me. Can't stop thinking of me, can you?"

Even if his comment was eerily accurate, she wasn't going to admit it. "It wasn't like that. Paulo said you were going on the Greece trip. I thought you planned to stay here."

"I thought so, too, but Marie talked me into it." He winked at them. "She can be very persuasive."

Emilia bristled with irritation. The news annoyed her more than it should have.

"You see?" Paulo said. "Think of all the fun we'll have. If you need to save money, you can share a room with me."

When he caught her eye, there was no mistaking his implications.

Sex on a Greek island? With a hot Italian guy? Maybe it was time to stop obsessing over her budget and have a little fun.

Before she could reply, her phone buzzed with a text.

> Giada: You're needed for a meeting with the
> brothers in Dr. Roberti's office. NOW.

Shit. Was she in trouble? She couldn't think of anything she'd done wrong.

Emilia: Be right there.

Giada: BRING TJ. That idiot isn't answering his texts.

If TJ was being summoned, then they must have screwed up on one of their tours last weekend. She stuck her phone in her back pocket and turned to TJ. "We're needed in a meeting with Dr. Roberti and his brother Angelo. I think it's about our last set of tours."

TJ gawked at her. "Why? What did you do?"

"What did *I* do? Nothing. It's probably because you made us run late on Sunday. Come on." Before leaving, she turned to Paulo. "Can you clean up my station? In case I don't get back in time or end up getting fired?"

He placed a hand on her shoulder. "You won't get fired. He probably wants to praise you for doing a good job."

"That's not what Giada's text sounded like." Then again, the woman's tone never changed, regardless of whether she was delivering good news or bad. Emilia gestured to TJ. "Let's get it over with."

Dr. Roberti's office was located on the other side of the House of Venus. Like the labs, it was a temporary structure, containing storage shelves crammed full of artifacts—pots, vases, ceramic lamps, coins, iron tools—and buckets of mosaic tiles. Along another wall was a bookshelf lined with historical tomes and excavation reports. A noisy box fan stood in one corner, offering a semblance of a breeze. Dr. Maurizio Roberti—their boss—sat behind his desk. Standing beside him was his brother Angelo, the owner of Buon Viaggio Tours, and Giada.

Emilia had never warmed up to either of the Roberti brothers. Both were tall and thin, with bristling mustaches and a sleazy air about them. So far, they'd treated her respectfully, but they had a reputation for being petty and vindictive. At least that's what she'd heard from Paulo, who'd worked with them in Pompeii two summers ago.

"Have a seat, please." Dr. Roberti pointed to two folding chairs facing the desk.

Yep, they were in trouble.

She felt like a kid being called into the principal's office. Not that she'd been much of a troublemaker. She was the type who got straight As and followed the rules. The one time she'd been suspended was because she'd given a beatdown to a sixth-grade bully that had been harassing her friends. It had happened shortly after her mom died, when her rage had been so intense she'd had a hard time channeling it.

As she sat next to TJ, she had a sudden urge to grab his hand in solidarity. Instead, she faced her boss with an earnest smile. "Dr. Roberti, is everything all right?"

TJ wasn't as diplomatic. "Did we mess up?"

"No need to worry," Dr. Roberti said. "If anything, you two should be commended. Giada told us you've signed up for more weekend tours than all the other archaeologists combined."

"They're hard workers," Giada said. "You know how Americans are. Always hustling. Always competing to be number one."

A backhanded compliment, to be sure, but coming from Giada, it was high praise.

Emilia spoke up quickly. "I love giving tours. I've learned so much about Pompeii this way." That last part wasn't a lie. Thanks to all the extra hours she'd logged leading visitors around the site, she had the layout memorized.

"Same here," TJ chimed in. "It's an honor to work for Buon Viaggio."

"You see?" Giada said. "One of them will be fine for the job. Can I go now? There's a group finishing up at six, and I need to meet with them."

"Go ahead," Angelo said.

"Grazie. I'll talk to you later." She left, closing the door behind her.

Angelo addressed Emilia and TJ. "According to Giada, your reviews have been consistently high. Lots of five stars, which is what we aim for. We may be a small company, but our customers' opinions are vital to our survival. With that in mind, I have a proposal for one of you. Maurizio tells me the Via Stabiana Project will be taking a break in the middle of September. As chance would have it, we have an English-speaking tour scheduled during that time. A ten-day jaunt through southern Italy, starting and ending in Rome. Normally, Mateo—who's our most experienced tour leader—would handle the trip, but he's laid up in the hospital."

"The hospital?" TJ asked. "Is he okay?"

"A few broken bones, but he'll recover. He fell while leading a group on a trek up Mt. Etna. If we weren't so busy right now, I'd ask one of our other guides to take his place. But with the end of summer approaching, we're stretched thin. So, we're asking if one of you would be willing to lead the tour. The group consists of about thirty-five American tourists, which means you'll feel right at home. In addition to covering your hotel stays, the company will pay you for your efforts, and you'll be allowed to keep any tips you earn."

A ten-day tour? Emilia shuddered. That was a lot of time to spend herding people around Italy. People who'd push her to the breaking point with their questions and demands. But ten days of extra pay? Lodging in hotels along the way? How could she turn down the opportunity? Not to mention, she'd earn the gratitude of the Roberti brothers, which might result in a stellar recommendation after her time in Pompeii ended.

"If neither of you are available, I'll offer it to the other archaeologists," Angelo added. "But given your dedication to our company, I wanted to let you two have the first crack at it."

Before Emilia could second-guess herself, she raised her hand. "I'll do it."

TJ glared at her. "Wait a second. I'd like to be considered, too. This is a huge honor."

An honor? Bullshit. You just want the money. Maybe TJ would be better at handling a lengthy tour than she would, but she wasn't going to give him the chance. "Aren't you spending the break in Greece? With Marie and the others?"

She could imagine the wheels turning in his head as he considered his options: frolicking with Marie on a Greek island versus a shit-load of extra cash. She was hoping he'd concede, but he didn't back down.

"Are you sure Emilia can handle this?" he asked. "It's a huge amount of responsibility compared to leading half-day tours at Pompeii."

Shut up, TJ. "I can handle it," she said. "I assume we'll be using local guides for some of our excursions, but if you need me to research any stops along the way, I can do it between now and when we leave."

Angelo lifted an enormous binder off his brother's desk and walked it over to her. "I'll need you to read through this from cover to cover. Even if you won't be leading all the tours, you should be well versed on every place your guests will be visiting. You'll also need a working knowledge of the best bars and restaurants in each city."

The binder weighed at least ten pounds, but she had over a week to review it before the tour started. "No problem. By the time I'm done, I'll be a total expert."

The door opened suddenly, and Luca Roberti strode in, dressed in a cream linen suit. As he caught Emilia's eye, a chill iced her spine.

He flashed his uncles an oily grin. "Maurizio. Angelo. I hope I didn't miss much."

"Not at all," Angelo said. "You'll be pleased to hear that Dr. Flores has signed up to lead our ten-day tour of southern Italy."

He beamed at her. "Excellent. Bellissima, it will be a pleasure to spend ten days exploring Italy with you."

She swallowed, her mouth dry, her heart pounding. "You… you're going, too?"

"But of course. How better to judge Buon Viaggio than to come along on one of their most popular tours? You needn't worry. Feel free to treat me like any other guest."

Shit.

What had she gotten herself into?

CHAPTER EIGHT

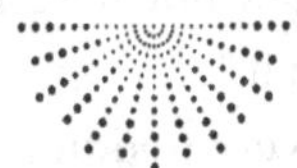

If there was one thing TJ had learned from years of playing cards with his family, it was how to read people's tells. Right now, he could read Emilia like a book. Even if she was smiling at Luca, her spine was rigid, her hands clenched.

He knew damn well she didn't want to spend ten days leading a bunch of tourists across Italy. She'd only volunteered because she was desperate for money. But she hadn't known Luca would be joining the tour.

TJ couldn't sit back and let her suffer. Even if she could barely tolerate him, he didn't want her thrown to the wolves. Or one wolf in particular. She might have been able to handle Luca during a four-hour tour of Pompeii. But for ten days? On a trip involving overnight hotel stays? The risk was too great.

"Actually," TJ said. "I'd like a chance to lead the tour as well."

Emilia nailed him with an icy glare. "What about Greece?"

"I'd rather lead the tour."

"Than go to Greece?"

He was going to have to sell it. Hard. He flashed his smarmiest, most kiss-ass smile at the Roberti brothers. "As you can probably tell from the reviews I've gotten, I excel at giving tours. It's one of the things I've enjoyed most about this Pompeii job. If academia doesn't pan out for me, I was thinking of getting into the tourism industry. It doesn't hurt that I speak three languages and have an undeniable knack for engaging people."

"What the fuck?" Emilia hissed under her breath.

He refused to back down. "In fact, my reviews have been better than Emilia's. Giada's not here right now, but if you ask her, I'm sure she'd confirm it."

The Roberti brothers were nodding, as though taking it all in, but Luca frowned. "That may be the case, but I observed Emilia closely last weekend. She has a 'way' with tourists, especially those of the male persuasion. Don't you, bellissima?"

Even if she was cringing inside, Emilia's smile never faltered. "I do indeed, Luca. I've been called, 'charming,' 'winsome,' and 'lovely' in my reviews."

"As is only right," he said. "Naturally, I was looking forward to spending time with you on this tour."

"Then it's settled," Angelo said. "My nephew is an excellent judge of people. If he feels Emilia is the best candidate for the job, then I'll—"

"Wait." TJ spoke quickly, his pulse racing. "This tour is a huge responsibility. Ten days, multiple cities, and a large group of Americans. It's a lot. What if Emilia and I took it on as a team? We could split the pay and share the experience."

"We've never had two tour leaders," Angelo said. "Though Mateo did admit he was run ragged last month with some very demanding groups."

"Exactly," TJ said. "Given your company's tremendous reputation, their expectations are sky-high. Neither I nor Emilia have ever handled three dozen tourists on our own. At Pompeii, our groups are limited to twenty-five people each. If we co-lead the tour, we can easily accommodate the guests if they choose to split up or if some of them opt for an alternate excursion. It'll make the trip that much more enjoyable."

As Emilia huffed out an angry breath, TJ wondered if he was making a huge mistake. Maybe she'd be fine dealing with Luca on her own. But she hadn't acted that way last Saturday when she'd mentioned feeling uneasy around him.

"All right," Angelo said. "We'll give it a go."

Luca's frown deepened, but he merely nodded.

"Stop by my office tomorrow morning to sign the paperwork," Dr. Roberti said. "You can also pick up the pouch you'll need for travel expenses. It contains a company credit card, along with extra euros for tips, incidentals, and any meals taken on your own." He gave them a stern look. "Don't abuse the privilege. No ordering room service."

"I wouldn't dream of it," Emilia said.

TJ nodded. "Same here. I'm a frugal traveler."

"That's the attitude I like to see," Dr. Roberti said. "But I must warn you—if you mess up this tour, you'll be off the guide circuit permanently. If you succeed—and get us the five-star reviews that Buon Viaggio needs—then you might earn a spot on next year's team at Pompeii."

Next year's team? In all the talks Dr. Roberti had given about the Via Stabiana Project, he'd never hinted it might extend beyond the six-month time frame.

"I thought the project was only funded through the middle of December," TJ said.

Dr. Roberti placed a finger against his lips. "Shh. For now, it'll be our secret. Don't tell the other archaeologists, but it looks as though we might receive another round of funding. If all goes well, we should be able to start up again in January and continue until next June. Rather than keep everyone in place, we only want team members who've pulled their weight. Anyone who goes the extra mile will rank more highly."

TJ was tempted to pump his fist in enthusiasm but didn't want to appear too eager, especially with Emilia glowering beside him. She probably resented him even more now, knowing they'd both be competing for a chance to extend their stay. He gave the Robertis a dazzling smile. "I promise I'll keep it quiet, but I'd love to stay at Pompeii for another six months. In the meantime, I'm grateful for the opportunity to co-lead this tour with Emilia."

"The same goes for me," Emilia said. "We won't let you down."

"I sincerely hope not," Angelo said. "Before you go, let me give you a quick overview of the trip."

The overview was hardly quick. For the next twenty minutes, he outlined the entire tour, describing each stop they'd take along the way, as well as all the sites they'd be visiting. If TJ was being honest, the trip sounded exhausting, with far too much crammed into ten days. At least he and Emilia would have the binder for guidance. Right now, she was clutching it like a life preserver.

Once Angelo was done, Dr. Roberti dismissed them. TJ left the office with Emilia, making sure to shut the door behind them. They walked through the dig site, passing one of the rooms they were excavating—the triclinium, or dining area of the house— whose walls displayed a series of well-preserved paintings dedicated to the goddess Venus. The site was quiet, the buckets and tools arranged in a neat pile.

Just before they entered the lab, Emilia whirled around and pinned TJ up against the hard stone wall. Her grip was surprisingly strong.

Her dark eyes flashed with fury. "That tour was mine. You had no business poaching it."

His heart hammered against his rib cage. "Em, listen, I—"

"No, you listen. You already had plans. A week in Greece. A little fling with Marie. Now you act like it's your life's ambition to be a tour guide?"

Her voice had risen so loudly he was afraid someone might hear them. Still squished against the wall, he tried to break free. "Lower your voice, okay?"

"Did you know something I didn't? About the Pompeii project being extended?"

He swallowed. "No. That was the first I'd heard about it."

"Then what made you change your mind?"

He could have lied to her. If he told her he'd done it because of the money, she'd believe him. But he didn't want her to hate him more than she already did. "I saw the way you reacted when Luca walked in. You looked unsettled."

"Bullshit."

"I know what I saw. You went rigid. Last Saturday, you said he creeped you out when he was on your tour. Do you really want to spend ten days alone with him?"

She released her grip on his shirt and stepped back. "I wouldn't be alone with him. There'll be at least thirty other people on that tour." But already, her rage had diminished. "Besides, I can take care of myself."

He brushed off his shirt. "I know that. But if something happened with Luca—something you didn't want—then I'd feel terrible."

"Why? You don't even like me."

Actually, I do. Even if they argued constantly, he always got a rush out of it. He hadn't even wanted to spend a week with Marie in Greece. He'd just agreed to it in the hopes of getting Emilia off his mind.

He scraped a hand through his hair, trying to think of an answer that wouldn't piss her off. "It's not just about you. I don't like it when women are forced into uncomfortable situations. When Romily was a freshman in college, one of her classmates started stalking her. A guy she'd dated but hadn't clicked with. At first, I didn't take her complaints seriously. She tended to be a bit of a drama queen. But then..."

Emilia blanched. "What happened?"

"She was walking back to her dorm one night, and the guy cornered her. When he grabbed her, she yelled at him to back off, and someone from campus security heard her. She was unhurt but really freaked-out. That was it, but I wish we'd listened to her from the start."

The memory still pained him. How Romily had called him that night, her voice shaking with sobs. He'd spent hours on the phone with her, reassuring her that she'd done nothing wrong. Any guy who couldn't take no for an answer was a dick who deserved to get his ass kicked.

"I'm sorry," Emilia said softly. "That must have been awful. But I'm not an inexperienced freshman living away from home for the first time. I've got this. If you come along, you'll be cutting into my pay."

"Then I'll give you my half." The words tumbled out before he could stop them.

"Why? You need the money as much as I do."

Stop being so stubborn. But this was Emilia, who was proud as hell. If she suspected he was offering her the money out of sympathy, she'd boot him into the nearest trench.

"Honestly? I'll be saving a lot by not going to Greece. Marie and her friends will probably spend a fortune on drinks and clubbing. Even if the tour won't be a real vacation, I'll get to spend every night in a cushy hotel room."

That alone was worth the hassle of leading a bunch of Americans through Italy.

"What about Marie?" Emilia demanded.

"There'll be another time." *If she even wants me.* Marie was bound to be annoyed once she learned about the tour. "Here's something else to consider. Ten days is a long time to be on the road with a group of high-maintenance tourists. If you ever need a rest from all that peopling, then you can tap out, and I'll wow them with my jokes and good humor. It might be fun."

Did he believe it? Not quite. But he wanted her to.

She smacked him in the chest with the binder. "You're going to spend every spare minute memorizing this tome with me until we leave for Rome. Got it?"

He winced. "I can't think of anything I'd rather do more."

～

THAT NIGHT, TJ JOINED EMILIA ON THE ROOFTOP PATIO OF THE hostel. Seated on a wooden bench with the binder between them, they'd already started on their homework. At the moment, they were alone since the rest of the archaeologists had walked to a nearby pizzeria for dinner.

TJ leafed through the binder, which was crammed with information. "This is more overwhelming than I thought."

"You can still back out," Emilia said. "I'll be fine on my own."

"Nope. I just wish I didn't need to know so much about places I've never visited." He'd be out of his depth, something he hated. Whenever he traveled, he liked to command a certain level of expertise.

She pointed to the map that outlined all the stops on the tour. "I've been to most of these places. It's too bad we're not going to Florence because I spent five months there. I have that city down cold."

"Were you on a dig? Or was it a semester abroad thing?" If she'd mentioned it before, he couldn't remember it.

"No, I had a conservation fellowship. I figured the training would give me another set of skills. My focus was on the study and treatment of frescoes, like the wall paintings found in Pompeii and Herculaneum. I thought we'd spend most of our time studying art history, but I also learned a ton about chemistry."

He regarded her with a mixture of admiration and jealousy. "That's awesome. I took a chem class in grad school to learn more about metallurgy. It was tougher than I thought."

"Couldn't handle all the formulas, huh?" She grinned. "But seriously, I'd love to use my knowledge. I mentioned it to Dr. Roberti back in June, but nothing came of it. I'm hoping he'll consider me once we start restoring the wall paintings in the House of Venus."

Now TJ was even more jealous. Doing conservation work at Pompeii would be an incredible opportunity. And it might mean Emilia would have a better chance at getting to stay an extra six months. Then again, if they pulled off this tour successfully, they'd both be among the top contenders for the next phase of the project.

Rather than dwell on the future, he switched his focus back to the tour. "Since there's so much to cover, why don't we split up some of the places on the map?"

"Good idea. We can take turns memorizing stuff."

"Then we can quiz each other until we get it right. We're going to be a kick-ass team." He was starting to get excited. As long as they were fully prepared, it could be a fun challenge.

Emilia gave him another of her trademark eye rolls, but not without smiling first. Like she was more on board with the "team" concept than she wanted to admit.

As they were removing pages from the binder, Paulo emerged onto the rooftop. With him were Marie, her friend Chloe, and two other Italian archaeologists.

"Well, well, if it isn't our naughty Americans," Paulo said. "Did you get fired?"

Marie glared at him. "Don't even joke about that. You know how vindictive those Robertis can be."

Vindictive? TJ hadn't seen any evidence of that, though both Paulo and Marie had worked with Dr. Roberti before, so maybe they'd experienced another side of him.

"We're not fired," TJ said. "But I do have bad news. About the trip to Greece, I—"

"TJ and I were asked to lead a group through southern Italy," Emilia said. "For Buon Viaggio. The regular tour manager can't do it, so Angelo wanted us to fill in because we've spent so much time guiding tourists around Pompeii."

He stared at her in shock. Rather than tell the others the truth—that he'd insisted on doing the tour with her—she'd made it sound like he didn't have a choice. Was she trying to placate Marie? If so, he appreciated the effort.

"Yeah, this tour's kind of a big deal, so we couldn't turn it down," he said. "Plus, the group is from the US, so we're the ideal candidates for the job. The money's great, and we'll get to stay in decent hotels during the trip."

"What the hell?" Marie stared Emilia down. "What's going on with you two, anyway?"

"Not a damn thing," Emilia muttered. "I'd rather be paired up with anyone else on Earth, but they wanted both of us. It's just work."

Paulo chuckled and draped his arm around Marie's shoulders. "Relax. They're not going to have time for sex, what with catering to all those needy Americans. But if you want to share a room while we're in Greece, you might be able to convince me."

She shrugged off his arm. "No, thanks."

Her friend Chloe snickered. "Been there, done that, right, Marie?"

Had Paulo and Marie hooked up before? Maybe that was why they were constantly bickering. To his surprise, TJ barely felt a flicker of jealousy. If they wanted to reconnect in Greece, so be it. After all, he'd be spending the entire break with Emilia. Not that *anything* would happen between them.

Emilia took a page out of the binder and handed it to Marie. "Check out this list of instructions. Even if TJ and I wanted to have sex—which we definitely don't—it's expressly forbidden."

As Marie scanned it, her sour expression vanished. "You're right. Those are some intense rules." She passed it to TJ. "You'd better behave yourself."

TJ reviewed the list. The last rule was in all-caps, which made him wonder if Giada had written it:

RULE 10: UNDER NO CIRCUMSTANCES ARE GUIDES TO ENGAGE IN ROMANTIC OR SEXUAL ACTIVITY WITH ANYONE ON THE TOUR, INCLUDING THE GUESTS, THE DRIVER, OR ANY OTHER GUIDES. SUCH ACTIONS ARE GROUNDS FOR IMMEDIATE DISMISSAL.

Not a problem. Given how much Emilia disliked him, this was one rule TJ wouldn't have trouble following.

After three months of bunking in a dorm-style room with five other archaeologists, Emilia was blissfully alone. She had her own room at the Hotel San Pietro, outfitted with a comfortable double bed, a large flat-screen TV, and a private bathroom. So what if the view outside her window displayed a boring brick wall? She was in Rome, on someone else's dime.

As with all good things, this delightful solitude wouldn't last. Starting tomorrow, she and TJ would be responsible for leading a ten-day tour across southern Italy. A tour consisting of thirty-three people, all from the US. Fortunately, Mateo—the former tour leader—had already arranged the airport transfers. All Emilia had to do was greet the guests when they arrived at the hotel and ensure check-in went smoothly. To ease everyone into the first day, the only activity on the agenda was an evening reception at the hotel bar, followed by dinner in a nearby restaurant.

After that, the job would entail a lot more work.

Don't think about it now. One day at a time.

While Emilia prided herself on being self-sufficient, this was one of those occasions when she wished she could call her mom for advice. As a third-grade teacher, her mom had always relished the chance to take her class on field trips. She'd embarked on each excursion with the same level of energy as Ms. Frizzle, the excitable science teacher from the TV cartoon *The Magic School Bus*—one of Emilia's favorite shows when she was in kindergarten.

When Emilia had asked her mom how she kept up her enthusiasm while visiting the Milwaukee Zoo for the fifteenth time, her mom had said, "It might be my fifteenth time, but some of these kids have never been to a zoo. I want to make it fun and memorable."

But was Emilia capable of making *anything* fun and memorable? Unlike her mom, she wasn't known for her cheerful disposition.

At times like this, the grief over missing her mother hit her like a physical blow. Swallowing back her tears, she reached for the shopping bag she'd set on the bed. She opened a container of cookies, took one out, and bit into it, savoring the taste of the rich, buttery shortbread. Earlier that day, when she and TJ had first arrived in Rome, she'd stocked up on cookies, chocolate bars, and toffee, in case they needed a boost of energy while leading the tour. She still wasn't sure how she was going to handle so much socializing, but at least he'd be with her to share the burden.

When a loud knock broke the silence, she suspected it was TJ. Who else would be pestering her? She got up and opened the door to her room.

TJ stood in the hallway. "I thought I'd check in and see how you're doing. What'cha up to?"

In the past, she would have chafed at the intrusion, but she wanted to share what she'd accomplished. "Come on in. I'll show you."

After he shut the door behind him, she led him over to the

bed, then scooted back onto it and picked up her laptop. "I've been doing background research on our guests. Most of them are on LinkedIn, Facebook, or Instagram—or all three." She rarely dipped her toes into the world of social media, but people's posts revealed a lot about them. Or, rather, what they wanted others to think of them.

TJ plopped down beside her on the bed. Like her, he was wearing a t-shirt and shorts. His hair was damp, as though he'd come from the shower. She caught a whiff of his citrusy aftershave, which triggered a vivid memory. The last time they'd sat together on a bed had been that mortifying night in Philly when she'd kissed him. And hadn't wanted to stop.

Maybe he'd forgotten it. She sure as hell wasn't going to bring it up.

"Did your research turn up any red flags?" he asked. "Anyone who might be a problem?"

You're the problem. You're sitting too close. She wanted to inch away or put a pillow between them as a barrier, but she'd look ridiculous. Instead, she passed him a composition book. "See for yourself. I'm keeping track of all the details here."

He scanned the page where she'd jotted down notes about everyone, including their ages and where they were from. "Let's see—we've got a lot of folks in their sixties and seventies. A few younger couples. Pretty much what I suspected. But this Davis McGowan guy is traveling solo, and he's the same age as us. Weird, huh?"

Emilia turned her laptop so it was facing him. "Here's his profile. He lists himself as a digital nomad. From what I can tell, he's trying to get a foothold as a travel influencer, but he doesn't have a lot of followers yet. Two months ago, he did a scathing takedown of Global Adventures, which got the most views of any of his videos. He took their six-day tour of Portugal and hated it. Apparently, the tour leader was a prick, the schedule was brutal, and the hotels were second-rate."

"Yikes. We need to get on his good side. Make sure to be extra nice to him."

She scowled. "Now you sound like Giada. I'm going to be extra nice to all our guests. Especially with creepy Luca watching my every move." She pointed to another set of names on her list. "These two could be a problem. The Mangolds—Giles and Irene. They've traveled a lot, and they always post very honest, super-detailed reviews."

He passed back the notebook. "This is great. I've been memorizing facts about Rome for two hours, but I didn't think of stalking anyone on social media."

"I'm not stalking. Just getting prepared. It's easier for me to deal with people when I know what to expect."

"Makes sense. I don't know about you, but I'm ready for a study break. Want to watch *Gladiator*? It'll get us in the mood for Wednesday's tour of the Colosseum and the Forum."

"We're not leading that tour." For that one, Buon Viaggio was using a local guide with ten years of experience in Rome.

"So? I'm sure we'll get at least one question about the Colosseum. Watching the movie will get us in the right frame of mind." He stretched out his arms and proclaimed, Russell Crowe–style, "Are you not entertained?"

As pathetic as his *Gladiator* impression was, it made her smile. If she was being honest, she'd rather relax with a movie than spend the next two hours doing research. But she wasn't sure if she should be alone with TJ in her room. Not because he annoyed her but because she didn't trust herself. No matter how much they bickered, she couldn't deny the flicker of attraction growing between them.

All last week, they'd spent their nights on the hostel rooftop in Ercolano, sharing beers and studying the binder. Amid all the challenges and teasing, there had been those moments when their eyes had met and she'd had to look away, afraid of what she might do. When she'd felt a gravitational pull toward him, like she wanted to kiss him without stopping.

Which couldn't happen. Especially now, when the rules of the tour expressly forbade sexual relationships.

"Come on, Em, it's on Netflix Italy," he said. "And you already have snacks." When she didn't answer, he clasped his hands together and flashed her a plaintive look. "Please. It's our last free night before the horde arrives."

Why was he being so insistent?

Then again, what did she gain by shutting him out? For the next ten days, they'd need to operate like a team. Just because she'd kissed him once didn't mean it would happen again. She scooted over and set her laptop on the nightstand. "You win. Just don't leave cookie crumbs everywhere."

He sprang off the bed, turned off the overhead lights, and grabbed the remote. When he sat back down, he put a little space between them, but his presence was still palpable.

Relax. Nothing's going to happen. Not unless you want it to.

She didn't. Even if he smelled good, even if she was suddenly possessed with the urge to run her fingers through his damp hair and pull him closer until their lips met, she'd never do it. Instead, she passed him the container of butter cookies. "Help yourself."

He took two. "Thanks. You know what would make this even better? A big tub of popcorn."

"Are you insinuating my snacks aren't adequate? Just start the movie already."

By the time the credits rolled, TJ was struggling to keep his eyes open. The stress of the past two weeks, spending every spare minute preparing for the tour, had wiped him out. Beside him, Emilia was unusually quiet. Odd, since she'd been making snarky comments for most of the movie.

"Em?"

She didn't answer. Though he couldn't make out much in the dim light of the flickering TV screen, she was slumped against the headboard with her eyes closed. He stared at her, torn over what to do. Should he rouse her? Or was it better to leave her this way? Like him, she probably needed her sleep.

For the briefest of moments, he was tempted to brush his hand across her cheek. To place a soft kiss on her lips and wake her up, Sleeping Beauty–style. He wouldn't do it, of course. He'd never violate her boundaries while she was asleep. But his mind traveled back to that night in Philly when they'd been alone in her room. Even if she'd been drunk, that kiss hadn't been an accident. She'd *wanted* him. If he hadn't pulled away, she might have kept going.

Was there a version of Emilia that actually liked him?

Idiot. She's into Paulo.

Was she? In the three months they'd been at Pompeii, she'd flirted with Paulo constantly but never spent a weekend alone with him. They hadn't even gone out on a date. Living in a hostel made hooking up a challenge, but other archaeologists had managed it. If Emilia had really wanted Paulo, nothing would have stopped her.

You're no better. Marie is into you, but you haven't made a move, either.

Because of Emilia. If he could only get his prickly rival to let down her guard, maybe she'd reveal how she truly felt about him.

With a sigh, he eased off the bed, turned off the TV, and let himself out, closing the door softly behind him.

Once he was back in his own room, he got ready for bed. In addition to his phone alarm, he set one on the digital clock on his nightstand. He lay on his bed, relishing the silence, but couldn't tame his restless mind. When his phone buzzed, he half hoped it was Emilia.

Instead, his sister had sent him a text.

Romily: How's Rome? Any good stories? Call me
if you're around.

Perfect. By now, it was the middle of the afternoon in Chicago. Since Romily worked from home, she was probably itching for a distraction. He called her immediately.

"TJ!" she said. "I wasn't sure if you'd be asleep yet. When do the tour wars start?"

He snorted. "The tour wars?"

"Yeah, that's what I'm calling your little adventure. It's the perfect setup, right? You and Em, two rivals forced to work together despite your bitter animosity. Who knows what might happen once you're on the road?"

Now he was outright laughing. Only his kid sister, with her passion for cheesy rom-coms, would assume this tour had the makings of a love story. "Trust me, nothing's going to happen. First of all, it's against the rules. Second—well, you know how she feels about me."

Romily was the only one who knew about the drunken kiss. In hindsight, confiding in her might have been a mistake because she'd spent the past seven months rooting for them to get together.

"If she really hated you, she'd ignore you," his sister said. "But she argues with you all the time. That's gotta mean something."

Her persistence was maddening. "Why are you so invested in this?"

"Because I'm bored. Right now, my job is dull, I'm still getting over my ex, Derek-the-dickweed, and Mom is driving me up the wall. She keeps calling to check on me because she's worried I'll never find 'the one.' News flash, Mom—I'm twenty-six. I've got plenty of time to find the guy of my dreams. She doesn't nag *you* about it."

He tossed off the comforter. Even with the air-conditioning kicking up a decent breeze, he didn't need it. "She's given up on me. I'm going to die alone as a poor, pitiful academic, surrounded by piles of books and ancient manuscripts. My luck with women has been epically bad."

"You know why, right?"

"I suspect you're going to tell me." Romily never sugarcoated anything.

"It's because you try too hard to impress them. Bragging about your digs and constantly bringing up your Harvard connections. That routine gets old fast."

Ouch. Had he really been that bad? "Don't go easy on me or anything."

"I wouldn't dream of it. That's why Emilia is perfect. She already knows all that shit, and she's totally unimpressed. But deep down inside, I think she likes you. Not for the stuff you've bragged about but for the guy underneath."

"Even if she secretly likes me, we won't be getting together on this tour, no matter how much your rom-com-obsessed heart insists on it. If we break the rules, we could get fired."

That couldn't happen. Far too much was at stake. Now that he knew the Via Stabiana Project might extend into next year, he desperately wanted a spot on the team. The best way to secure his place was by bringing his A game to this tour. That meant no mistakes and no hooking up. *With anyone.*

"What about after the tour?" Romily said. "Once you're back in Pompeii and working as archaeologists again, what's stopping you from taking things further?"

What *was* stopping him? Fear of rejection? Fear of humiliation? It wasn't as though Emilia would be any meaner to him than she was now.

"Well?" Romily demanded. "I want answers, bro."

He paused to imagine Emilia's reaction if he approached her honestly. For once, he'd be open and vulnerable and tell her how much he respected her. That he wanted more from her than just rivalry and one-upmanship. She'd probably think it was a joke.

"You know what Al always tells us, right?" Romily said. "You miss one hundred percent of the shots you don't take."

TJ groaned. Having a stepdad in sports management meant enduring a *lot* of motivational quotes. "The last thing I need is one of Al's clichés, but you've got a point. After the tour ends, I'll see where we're at. If we get through it without wanting to kill each other, then..."

"Then what?"

"Then I'll consider it."

In all possibility, spending ten days leading a tour with Emilia would push them both to the breaking point. They'd get so fed up with each other that they'd never want to work together again.

But if they didn't?

Then maybe he had a chance.

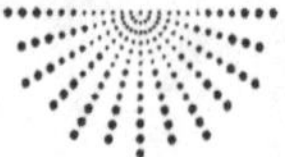

CHAPTER TEN

Emilia scanned the hotel bar. A quick head count confirmed that all thirty-three members of the Buon Viaggio tour group had shown up for the welcome reception. Most of them were white, well-off, and in the sixty-plus age range. Sprinkled among the gray-haired set were a few younger travelers, including Davis McGowan, the aspiring influencer. But no sign of Luca Roberti yet.

Did that mean he'd decided to bail on the tour? Or did he think it unnecessary to attend the meet and greet? Either way, Emilia was grateful not to deal with him. The last time she'd seen him, during their meeting in Dr. Roberti's office, his presence had sent cold shivers down her spine.

By now, everyone had ordered an aperitivo—a refreshing pre-dinner cocktail meant to whet their appetites. They clustered in small groups, taking up most of the dark leather booths and armchairs in the dimly lit bar. At this stage, they were still strangers, but that would change after they spent the next ten days together touring Italy.

Emilia sipped her Pellegrino. Though she'd been tempted to order an Aperol spritz—tonight's drink of choice—she wanted to pace herself since they'd be having wine with dinner. Under no circumstances could she drink too much and lose her inhibitions. TJ stood beside her, drinking a Coke. Like her, he'd changed out of the hideous red Buon Viaggio polo shirt into attire more suitable for an evening out. Just khakis and a dark green button-down, but they looked good on him. She was wearing one of her few decent outfits—an embroidered blue sundress topped with a cream-colored cardigan.

TJ set his drink on a nearby table and caught her eye. "Ready?"

A wave of nerves rolled over her. She'd met most of the group when they'd checked in earlier, but they'd all been so tired and travel-worn that she'd barely interacted with them. All she'd done was secure their room keys, hand out their welcome packets, and order their luggage sent up to their rooms. Now it was time for her to be a tour *leader*.

"You're speaking first, right?" she asked.

"Naturally. I've got this."

While she could have done without his smug attitude, she envied his self-confidence.

"Before I start, are you sure you don't want to do an icebreaker with the group?" he said. "Something to kick-start the bonding process?"

"Absolutely not. No trust falls, no games, no improv." The thought of engaging in a team-building exercise made her cringe. She hated forcing anyone out of their comfort zone.

To his credit, TJ didn't argue. "Okay, then. I'll just warm them up myself."

"Thanks. Go for it."

Without a hint of shame, he clambered onto a chair and called the group to attention with a whistle. "Buonasera, everyone! I'm so glad you arrived in one piece. I'm Dr. Theodore Joseph Mayer, Jr, but I go by TJ." He gestured to Emilia. "This is my lovely co-leader, Dr. Flores, but you may call her Emilia. We're archaeologists from the United States who've been working at Pompeii for the past three months. When we're not digging up artifacts or studying ancient history, we love giving tours of the site. Lucky for you, Pompeii's one of the stops on your itinerary, so we'll get to tell you all about it."

His cheerfulness appeared honest and unforced. All day, he'd maintained that level of enthusiasm, whereas Emilia had already gotten testy when one of the guests had complained about the size of his room. She'd been tempted to say, "Get over it, buddy. European hotel rooms are just smaller than American ones." Instead, she'd apologized and begged the clerk to put the guy in a bigger room.

TJ continued. "Now that I have your attention, I need to share a little secret. This is the first time Emilia and I have ever managed a tour like this. Sure, we've done plenty of full-day tours at Pompeii, but we've never led a group for ten whole days. I know what you're thinking. A couple of newbs, right?"

Emilia hadn't asked him to address this issue, but she appreciated his decision to tackle it right away. At check-in, a few of the Buon Viaggio regulars had expressed their disappointment at Mateo's absence.

"Here's the thing," TJ said. "Em and I might be new to this game, but it means we'll be trying extra hard to create an exceptional experience for all of you."

An older man spoke up. Giles Mangold, age seventy. A retired financier from New York. He and his wife, Irene, had traveled with Buon Viaggio twice before and were known for leaving detailed reviews. He was the type who docked hotels a whole star for the slightest misstep, like an elevator outage or a forgotten wake-up call.

"What happened to Mateo?" he asked. "I thought he was in charge. He did such a good job with our tour of Tuscany."

Mrs. Mangold nodded. "Such a charming man. He told the most fascinating stories."

"Sadly, Mateo suffered a hiking injury while leading a group up Mt. Etna," TJ said. "He's still not able to navigate stairs very well, so he's out for another few weeks. Emilia and I will do our best to stand in for him. Not only will you learn a lot, but there will also be fabulous food and wine at every city we visit. I can't wait to get started." He gave a little bow, then focused his attention on Emilia. "Now, my partner is going to fill you in on a few of the details."

When he reached down to offer his hand, she repressed a groan. Standing on a chair made her feel like a kid trying to get the attention of the grown-ups. But she couldn't leave him hanging. She climbed onto the chair next to his.

Remember to smile. Act like you want to be here.

"Buonasera," she said. "I just wanted to remind you that all the information you need, including the itinerary for our entire tour, is in the welcome packets we gave you at check-in. You also received your lanyards, which you should bring along for every excursion. Each day's activities are listed in the itinerary, and they're also on the Buon Viaggio app, if you chose to download it."

"What if we don't want to be glued to our phones?" demanded an older woman. Sylvie Galloway, age seventy-six. A wealthy owner of a gallery in New Mexico, clad in attire that screamed "upscale artsy." Today's ensemble included a dark green caftan and an exquisite, seven-strand turquoise necklace. "I hate how you need an app for everything these days."

Her clique—three other women, all her age—nodded in solidarity. Emilia itched to remind them that apps weren't a brand-new invention. Instead, she gave the four older women a knowing smile. "You're in luck because all the information on the app is also in the welcome packet, which is printed on good old-fashioned paper."

"If we need to get hold of you, what should we do?" Mrs. Mangold asked.

"We've listed our cell numbers at the top of the itinerary," Emilia said. "You might want to enter them into your contacts now so that if one of us calls, you won't think we're a telemarketer asking if you'd like to refinance your mortgage." For that, she got a few chuckles, which went a long way in boosting her confidence. "If you have any questions or wish to sit out an excursion, just let us know. You can call or text us at any time—day or night. I mean it."

She didn't. Not really. If she was asleep, she didn't want to be woken by needy questions, but she was hoping it wouldn't come to that.

TJ took over, giving a brief rundown of the evening's dinner and the following day's activities. "We'll leave for the restaurant in fifteen minutes," he said. "It's a short walk from here—about three blocks. Any more questions?"

Davis McGowan raised his hand. Of all the guests on the tour, he was the easiest to recognize because of his travel videos. Tall and rangy with a deep tan and floppy blond hair, he looked like he belonged on a Malibu beach, though his profile listed him as being from New Jersey. "Are you two a couple?" he asked.

The question caught Emilia off guard. Were they behaving like a couple? Maybe she'd gone overboard in trying to act like a team player.

TJ answered with a quick grin. "Nope. We're just colleagues. Back home in the States, we're rivals. Even though we both wrote dissertations about the collapse of the Bronze Age, we have opposing theories. Don't get us started on that one unless you're ready for major fireworks. But I promise we'll be civil while leading your tour."

A few people laughed, but no one followed up on Davis' question. Emilia stepped down from her chair, and TJ joined her.

"That okay?" he whispered. "Did I sound enthusiastic enough? I wanted to convince them we'd be just as good as Mateo."

While she wasn't sure if that was possible, given that Mateo had ten years of experience, she didn't want to add to TJ's stress. The more time she spent with him, the more she realized he used his boastful persona to mask the anxiety simmering under the surface. "You did great. I think they were totally on board. Or they will be after tonight's dinner, which sounds incredible."

Davis walked over to them and addressed Emilia. "Dr. Flores? Did you get the text I sent earlier?"

Out of the corner of her eye, she noticed the Mangolds approaching, but TJ went over to intercept them. She faced Davis with her friendly tour-guide smile firmly in place. "Please call me Emilia. You wanted to talk to me about the videos you're making?"

"I don't know if you've checked out my YouTube channel—Davis Destinations—but I do travel reviews. For tours, I usually post a brief video with my overall thoughts, including my rating of each aspect of the experience. I follow this up with a series of vlogs and shorter videos about the sites I enjoyed visiting. In general, I aim for an upbeat vibe, but I'm not afraid to be honest. I owe it to my subscribers."

She'd now watched enough of his content to get a good sense of his online persona. Most of the time, he came across as low-key, friendly, and open to adventure. But when leaving a bad review, he had no qualms about speaking his mind. "It's fine as long as you check with the guests to make sure they're okay being filmed. If you have a problem with the tour, I only ask that you come to me or TJ first. That way, we can try to fix things before you post a negative review."

He smirked. "Obviously, you're referring to my scathing takedown of the Global Adventures tour I took in July?"

"Yeah. It was…rough, but I get it. When you sign up for a tour, you're putting down serious money, so you expect a certain level of service."

"Honestly? You and TJ showed more enthusiasm in that short

welcome speech than our guide did during our entire six days in Portugal."

With that in mind, she was determined to maintain her cheerful disposition, even if it killed her. "We'll do our best, but we're new to this. Do you have any suggestions?"

"Sure. Answer everyone's questions, even if the information they need is literally right in front of them. Most people are shit at reading instructions. If they're tired, don't give them a guilt trip if they choose to skip an excursion and rest at the hotel."

"Your guide did that?" Even at her grumpiest, she'd never treat anyone so rudely.

"Oh, yeah. He hated it when anyone tried to deviate from the schedule."

Though Emilia couldn't let down her guard too much around any of the guests, she sensed Davis could be a potential ally. "Thanks. We'll try to be as flexible as we can."

"Emilia. *Bellissima.* There you are." At the sound of Luca's lightly accented voice, her jaw tightened. He moved in closer and placed his hand on her shoulder, as though marking his territory. "I am so sorry I missed your welcome introduction, but I am delighted to be joining you on this tour. With you at the helm, I am certain it will be a memorable experience."

"Thank you. Luca, this is Davis McGowan, one of our guests."

Davis extended his hand. "Pleased to meet you."

Luca didn't take it. Instead, he regarded the other man with disdain. "Yes, I've heard your name. One of those *influencers*? I hope you'll be judging us fairly."

The light vanished from Davis' eyes. "Of course. I wouldn't post anything negative without a good reason."

Luca gave a cool nod. "So you say, but I remain skeptical. Emilia, we should leave for dinner soon. I have a few questions about the tour, so I insist you join me at my table."

His table? What made him think he was in charge of an entire table? But Emilia didn't allow her smile to falter. "Whatever you wish. We'll gather up the group in ten minutes."

"Excellent. I will go remind TJ as well." Giving her shoulder a gentle squeeze, he strode over to TJ, who was deep in conversation with the Mangolds.

Emilia shuddered. Just what was Luca's role exactly? Had he been assigned to act like her boss? Or was he the type who insisted on asserting his authority in every situation?

As if sensing her discomfort, Davis addressed her in a low voice. "Are you okay? You looked like you did *not* want him to be touching you."

"Not really, but he's my boss's nephew, so I couldn't tell him to back off. Given his connections, I have to do what he says. Not…um…sexually, or anything, but you know what I mean?" Now, she felt even more awkward.

"I do, but if you ever need backup, let me know. I've cock-blocked more than a few lecherous male travelers in my time."

"Thanks. Right now, my goal is to keep him happy without compromising myself. I can't risk antagonizing him."

It was a fine line to walk, but she'd make it work.

CHAPTER ELEVEN

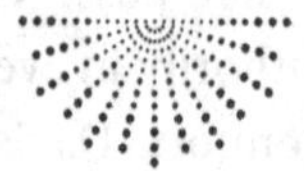

A sense of lazy contentment overtook Emilia as she set her plate to the side. After a delicious meal and multiple glasses of wine, she was more relaxed than she'd been all day. Dinner had far exceeded her expectations. They'd started with antipasti—a selection of olives, marinated red peppers, artichoke hearts, cured meats, and cheeses, along with delicious slices of bruschetta topped with tomatoes, zucchini, and pancetta. Their first course, or primo, had been a savory bowl of spaghetti alla carbonara. For the secondo, they'd enjoyed a sublime dish of beef braised in red wine with caramelized pear. Upon taking her first bite, Emilia had groaned out of sheer, hedonistic pleasure.

Even if she'd been living in Italy for almost four months, she rarely got to indulge in food of this quality. Due to her limited budget, her typical dinner usually consisted of a salad or a bowl of cheap pasta.

After the waitstaff had cleared their plates, their server reappeared to announce the dessert course, or dolce. "Our final dish will be a creamy panna cotta, a traditional Italian custard, topped with fresh raspberries and blackberries. Would everyone like to partake?"

All the hands went up at their table except those of Sylvie and her three elderly friends, whom Emilia had secretly nicknamed "the Golden Girls."

Luca favored them with an indulgent smile. "Come now, ladies. How can you pass up this classic Italian dessert?"

"I've already eaten far too much," Sylvie said. "Not to mention all the wine I've had. That's a lot of calories."

"Are you worried about your girlish figures?" Luca asked. "Trust me, you all look so lovely that one little dessert won't make a difference."

One of Sylvie's friends giggled. "You're such a flatterer."

"I'm only stating the truth." He placed a hand over his chest. "Do I look like the type to feed you a line?"

"I suppose it wouldn't hurt." The woman addressed their server. "I'd like to try the panna cotta as well." Her friends followed suit.

Luca raised his wineglass. "That's the spirit. What is life without a few indulgences, eh?"

Emilia resisted the urge to roll her eyes. He'd been like this all night, working his charms on everyone at their table. He'd joked with their server in Italian, ordered a few extra bottles of wine, and amused the group with his travel anecdotes. All of which suited Emilia just fine since she was grateful not to be the sole focus of his attention. At the start of dinner, he'd asked her a few questions about the tour but had changed course after Sylvie inquired about his recent trip to Switzerland.

The dessert was heavenly—the creamy, sweet panna cotta contrasting with the slight tartness of the blackberries. Emilia licked the excess off her spoon. "Mmm. This is so good."

"Have you been enjoying the meal?" Luca asked. "You've been so quiet."

Whose fault is that? He'd pretty much dominated the

conversation at her end of the table. "I've been focusing on the food. It's not often I get to enjoy an elaborate meal like this."

"Such a shame. A woman like you deserves to be wined and dined in the finest restaurants in Italy."

Just stop. Fortunately, one of the guests diverted him with a question about skiing in the Alps.

After dessert, espresso, and another half hour of small talk, Emilia was reaching the limits of her sociability. When TJ stood to address the group, she shot him a look of gratitude.

"Wasn't that a marvelous dinner?" he said. "I don't know about all of you, but if I ate another morsel, I wouldn't be able to keep my pants buttoned. By now, you're probably ready to call it a night. If you'd like to follow me, we'll head back to the hotel."

Perfect. Emilia set her cloth napkin on the table beside her, but before she could stand up, Luca placed his hand on her arm. "Wait. Please."

"Is everything all right?" she asked.

"I owe you an apology. I was hoping we'd have more time to talk, but I was in constant demand. I had no idea those women would find my travel stories so amusing."

Sure you did. That was exactly what you wanted. "It's fine. You were a delightful host."

"Even so, I'd like to make it up to you. Stay and share a drink with me."

Hell, no. She wanted to retreat to her room, change into her pajamas, and zone out with an hour of mindless TV. Not spend another hour entertaining a man whose compliments made her squirm with discomfort.

She gave him an apologetic smile, hoping to convey the proper amount of regret. "Thank you for the offer, but TJ and I need to escort the guests back to the hotel. Even if it's only a few blocks away, I wouldn't feel right letting them wander on their own."

"I'm certain TJ can take care of them. As you said, it's a short walk."

As if summoned by the sound of his name, TJ appeared at Emilia's side. "Ready to go, Em? Some of our guests are looking mighty sleepy."

Luca's grip tightened on her arm. "I'd like it if you stayed." He directed his gaze at TJ. "Would that be a problem for you?"

"No, of course not, but…" TJ caught Emilia's eye. "It's late, and…um…Em might not want to walk back to the hotel by herself."

Before she could respond, Luca spoke up. "She'll be fine. I'll make sure she gets back safely."

The challenge in his voice sent her pulse racing. This wasn't a man who liked being denied anything. She'd already turned down his offer for lunch when they were at Pompeii. If she didn't concede this time, he might suspect she was trying to avoid him. As long as they stayed at the restaurant, she'd be safe.

"Do you want me to stay?" TJ asked her.

Yes. But she couldn't say it, not when his first responsibility was to look after the guests. "I'll be okay. It's just one drink."

He gave a quick nod. "All right, then. I'll see you tomorrow at the breakfast buffet. We should get there just before it opens."

She was gripped with the urge to grab his hand and squeeze it for reassurance, but such a bold act would surely upset Luca. "Sounds like a plan. Thanks."

As he gathered up the guests, she longed to join them but turned back to Luca, her polite smile firmly in place. "Just one drink. I shouldn't stay too late."

"I understand. We'll have a digestivo—a little drink to aid in the digestion. Perhaps some amaretto or sambuca?"

"Amaretto sounds lovely. Thank you." To be honest, she didn't want any more alcohol. During dinner, their server had constantly refilled everyone's wineglasses, making it difficult for her to keep track of exactly how much she'd imbibed.

Once their drinks came, Luca leaned in closer, his voice a soft purr. "Now that we're alone, I must speak honestly. You look positively radiant tonight. A true goddess. That dress suits you far better than the Buon Viaggio polo shirt."

Though his praise sent uneasy prickles along her spine, she kept her tone light. "You think so? Don't tell Angelo because he might be hurt. He loves red so much that it's the signature color for Buon Viaggio—our tour flags, our polo shirts, the company logo, everything."

He chuckled. "I suppose it makes for good branding, but I prefer you dressed like this."

"Um…thanks."

"I imagine you're used to receiving compliments from the men on your tour. I'll bet they can't keep their eyes off you."

Stop it. Please. Not only was his behavior inappropriate, but it also reminded her too much of her ex. Right from the start, he'd praised her beauty and acted like she was the most important person in his life. In reality, she'd been anything but. She suspected Luca operated the same way. A manipulative narcissist who knew how to present the best version of himself while hiding a darker underbelly.

She sipped her amaretto slowly, savoring the sweet taste of the almond liqueur. "Will you be joining us for the entire tour?"

"I hope so, but I won't be able to participate in all our activities in Rome. I need to take care of some business in the city." He reached over and took her hand. "Am I correct in assuming you won't be leading tomorrow's tour?"

"For the next two days, we'll have local guides who are area experts. TJ and I will be accompanying the group but not leading it. Once we leave Rome, that will change, and we'll take turns switching off or split everyone into two groups so that we can give them our full attention."

"Please ensure that I'm in *your* group, not TJ's. When we were at Pompeii, your lively presentation was a joy to watch."

"I'll do my best." She cringed inwardly, remembering how he'd behaved. How his eyes had rarely strayed from her figure. How he'd let his hand linger on the small of her back or brush up against her ass. Even TJ had noticed it.

"Wonderful," Luca said. "I look forward to our days ahead."

Just where was he going with all this flattery? Was he trying to woo her into bed? Or was she reading too much into tonight's conversation? Thanks to her ex, she found it hard to trust any man who lavished her with compliments. Maybe Luca was the type who took pleasure in charming women of all ages.

It's more than that. You need to trust your gut.

When her phone buzzed with a text notification, she flipped it over and glanced at it.

> TJ: The guests are secured. Are you okay? Do you need me for backup?

"Everything all right?" Luca asked.

She swallowed, trying to clear the knot from her throat. "Um...yeah. I just had to check in case one of the guests needed me."

"Do they?"

"No. It was TJ. He said everyone got back okay." She was tempted to respond to his message but sensed Luca wanted her full attention. She flipped her phone back over and asked him about his recent trip to Sardinia. Having spent two seasons digging there, she knew the island well. If they shared travel stories, maybe he'd ease up on the personal comments.

As their conversation continued, his touches were so frequent that she was tempted to call him out. If they'd been in the States, she would have. But she didn't know if his behavior was a by-product of his upbringing or if he was just plain creepy. While she didn't appreciate it, she hesitated to confront him outright. Not only was he Angelo's nephew, but he was also on this tour to observe and report back to the Robertis. If she crossed him,

Angelo might retaliate by bumping her off the tour guide circuit at Pompeii, and she needed the extra money.

When she let out an involuntary yawn, Luca ran his hand along her forearm. "I'm sorry to have tired you out, bellissima. I have one more thing to discuss with you before we head back."

Here it comes. She girded herself, waiting for him to proposition her. No matter how much power he wielded, the answer would be no.

"I hate for our conversation to take a less pleasant turn, but I need to speak honestly," he said. "I'm not pleased Davis McGowan is on this tour."

"Huh?" His statement was so unexpected that she couldn't form a response.

Luca's hand tightened around his glass. "People like him are despicable. Influencers. Social media hacks. They're not real travelers, just parasites obsessed with building up a following. And how do they do it? By filling the internet with negativity. Spewing hatred so they can get more likes. It's loathsome."

Emilia drew back, unnerved by the hostility in his voice. "I don't think he's that bad."

"Have you seen the video he did about his tour with Global Adventures? Complete trash."

"I'll admit he could have been more diplomatic, but he was being honest. From what he told me, their guide did a poor job. Negative reviews can be malicious, but they also help other travelers make decisions, and the positive ones can have a huge impact on small businesses."

"I have yet to see that happen."

While she didn't want to offend him, she couldn't bring herself to agree with him, either. "My friend, Olivia, has a younger sister—Sofia—who's a foodie influencer. She's traveled all over the world, but she got her start by spotlighting small restaurants in San Diego, where she's from. Her videos were so popular they put a few of those places on the map. Before starting this tour, TJ and I asked her advice for places to eat in Matera and Bari since we'd never been there before."

Luca frowned. "Perhaps this Sofia is the exception to the rule, but I doubt Davis is as ethical. I want you to be careful around him. No doubt he's hoping to earn your trust, only to destroy it if he decides to post a negative review. Do *not* let him get to you. Do you understand?"

His eyes drilled into hers, his anger simmering beneath the surface. More than anything, she wanted to put an end to this conversation. "Yes, I'll be careful. Thanks for the warning."

"Good. Let's get you back to your hotel room, shall we? Thank you for allowing me this brief time alone with you. I hope we can do it again soon."

Not if I can help it. For now, she'd placated him. Maybe that would be enough for the next few days. She couldn't handle much more than that.

By the time she returned to her room, she could barely keep her eyes open. Not only had the food and wine made her drowsy, but the sheer effort of conversing with Luca had exhausted her. She kicked off her sandals and lay on her bed. When her phone buzzed, she remembered TJ's earlier text. As she picked it up, a wave of fatigue crashed over her, making the words blur on the screen. She set the phone beside her and closed her eyes. She just needed a minute to recover, and then she'd text him back.

But two minutes later, she was out cold for the night.

CHAPTER TWELVE

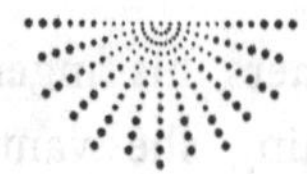

When TJ's alarm went off at 6:15 a.m., he could barely open his eyes. He'd stayed up long after midnight, desperate to know how Emilia's evening had gone. If she'd given him a sign that she was all right, he might have been able to tame his anxious thoughts. But she hadn't responded to his messages. The first time he'd texted her, her silence hadn't worried him. He'd assumed she wasn't checking her phone in the restaurant. Or that she'd been hesitant to text him in Luca's presence.

After an hour, he'd tried again with no response. The same with his third message, sent an hour later. That was when he'd grown worried. Emilia might be a strong, independent woman who could fend for herself, but she wasn't on an even playing field. Telling Luca to fuck off wasn't an option, not without risking her job.

There could be another reason why Emilia hadn't answered. A reason TJ didn't want to consider, even as the negative voices in his head harped at him. What if she hadn't replied because she was having fun with Luca? In theory, that wouldn't be a bad thing, since she needed to stay on his good side. But the thought of her kissing that slick bastard made TJ heat up with a slow-burning anger.

This isn't about protecting her. You're jealous.

No, he wasn't. He'd offered to co-lead the tour with her so that she wouldn't have to deal with Luca on her own. So what if he had a bit of a "knight in shining armor" complex around women? Someone had to protect them from the wolves.

With a groan, he forced himself to sit up. At the sight of a text notification on his phone, he scrambled for his glasses, only to drop them on the floor. He groped around for them and put them on hastily. To his immense frustration, the message wasn't from Emilia. Their bus driver had sent them both a text, reminding them that he'd be at the hotel by eight thirty.

TJ jumped into the shower, got dressed, and headed down to breakfast. To reach the buffet, he went out the back entrance and crossed the hotel's inner courtyard. In the midst of a city filled with noise, traffic, and tourists, it served as a peaceful oasis, replete with shade trees, flowering bushes, and wrought iron patio tables. Birds trilled in the trees, and the faint scent of jasmine lingered in the air. Off to one side, a marble fountain burbled softly. If he could squeeze in an hour of downtime today, he'd sit out here and read.

The buffet was set up in a separate building on the other side of the courtyard, inside a large, open room surrounded by full-length windows. To TJ's delight, the breakfast spread was lavish. One whole table was devoted to sweet offerings like cornetti, jam tarts, four different kinds of cake, and fresh bread with pots of honey, jam, and marmalade. Another held cold cuts, cheeses, hard-boiled eggs, yogurt, and bowls of fresh fruit. But the best feature of all was the pair of high-end coffee makers that occupied a third table.

A couple of servers bustled around the buffet, setting up the food, but no one was in the dining area other than Emilia. She sat at a table in the corner, flipping through the binder as she sipped her coffee.

He loaded up his plate and sat down across from her. Like him, she was wearing the ugly red company polo shirt. Her hair was back in a braid, but a few stray wisps had escaped, softening her appearance.

She glanced up with a faint smile. "Morning, TJ. Isn't this a great spread? I was tempted to steal some cake for later."

Wasn't she going to mention last night? Or explain why she'd ignored his texts?

He made no attempt to hide his irritation. "What happened with Luca after I left the restaurant?"

"Not much. We talked for about an hour, but that was it."

"Nothing else happened?"

For that, he got an eyebrow raise. "Were you expecting more?"

He knew that tone. She was skirting the edge of grumpiness—probably because she didn't want to discuss it any further. If he pushed too hard, she'd go into prickly hedgehog mode. But he wanted answers. "Why didn't you respond to my messages? I was worried about you."

She frowned. "I don't think Luca would have appreciated it if I'd texted you while he was talking to me. I didn't want to piss him off."

TJ downed half his cappuccino and ate a few bites of apple cake, hoping the caffeine and carbs would put him in a better frame of mind. But he was too peevish to behave rationally. "What about the text I sent after that? You should have let me know you were okay." Even to his own ears, he sounded needy and possessive, but he wanted her to understand how concerned he'd been.

"I was exhausted, and there was nothing for you to be worried about. I can take care of myself."

"I know, but these aren't normal circumstances. Didn't you

say you got a creepy vibe from Luca when he went on your tour in Pompeii?"

She closed the binder. "Can we drop it? Please? Yes, he's a little intense, and I could do without being called 'bellissima,' but he's also Angelo's nephew, and he's got a lot of power. Sharing a drink with him wasn't a huge hardship. I figure if I stroke his ego once in a while, that should be enough to keep him happy."

"Is that *all* you plan on stroking? If you want to hook up with him, then don't let me stop you." He was acting like a dick, but he couldn't help himself.

She stared at him, wide-eyed, the hurt evident on her face. "Seriously? What the fuck?" Grabbing her plate and coffee cup, she stood abruptly. "I'm not hooking up with *anyone*. Just let me do my job."

He held up the binder. "Do you want—"

"No. You hang on to it." She moved to a table across the room and slammed down her plate for emphasis.

Now you've screwed up everything. He hadn't meant to lash out, but he was worried she wasn't taking Luca seriously enough. Maybe the bastard hadn't made a move on her yet, but that didn't mean he wouldn't try it later. First, he'd earn her trust, and then he'd lure her into his trap.

TJ ate his breakfast in silence, trying to banish his toxic thoughts by studying the binder. Though he'd reviewed the section on the Colosseum last week, he could use a quick refresh. At seven thirty, when the guests were set to arrive, he stood and took a deep breath. If he and Emilia were going to work together, he needed to make things right.

He walked over to her table. "Em?"

She didn't spare him a glance. "What?"

"I'm sorry I was a jerk. I didn't sleep well last night." When she refused to meet his eyes, he kept going. "I can greet everyone this morning and answer their questions. Then I'll remind them we'll be gathering in the lobby at eight thirty." He set down the binder. "Why don't you take this for now?"

She nodded, then pointed to the buffet area. "The Mangolds are here. Better make sure there's nothing they need."

"Right." He wanted to stay and talk with her, to smooth over the rough edges, but now wasn't the time. He'd have to catch her alone later. "Enjoy your breakfast."

He went to the buffet table and greeted the couple. They had a slew of questions, mostly about things he'd already told them at last night's reception. The rest of the group trickled in slowly. Most seemed pleased at the breakfast offerings, but Sylvie Galloway pulled him aside with a sour look on her face. Today, she was decked out in a flowy purple caftan and a chunky necklace made of silver and turquoise. Beside her were her three friends, similarly dressed.

"There are far too many sweets here," she said. "If we eat these, we'll have a sugar crash by noon."

"Italian breakfasts tend to be heavy on the sweet options," he said. "But that table over there has cured meats, cheeses, and hard-boiled eggs. Plenty of protein."

"Plenty of fattening, unhealthy protein, you mean." She sniffed. "I'd like an egg-white omelet with fresh herbs. Please tell the cook to make one up immediately." She turned to one of her friends. "Doesn't that sound good?"

"It does," the woman said. "I'll have one, too. With fresh tomatoes."

As far as TJ knew, the hotel didn't have an actual restaurant, just a buffet and a bar. "Um…I'm not sure that's an option."

"Of course it is," Sylvie said. "There are eggs here, aren't there? How hard can it be to prepare an omelet? If need be, I'll do it myself. I'm an excellent cook."

He could only imagine how well *that* would go over with the hotel staff. "No need. I can go ask."

First Emilia, and now this. His morning was not off to an auspicious start.

~

THROUGHOUT BREAKFAST, TJ KEPT AN EYE ON THE GUESTS. He dropped by each table to chat with them and ensure they were coming on the day's excursion. With a little begging, he convinced the kitchen staff to make egg-white omelets for Sylvie and her friends. The only bright spot in the morning was the text he and Emilia had received from Luca informing them he'd be missing today's tour due to business meetings in Rome. A minor victory at best, but TJ would take it.

At 8:20 a.m., he called everyone to attention and announced they'd meet in the lobby in ten minutes. He also reminded them to bring anything they'd need for the day, like water bottles and sunscreen, since they wouldn't be returning to the hotel until five. Once the group had assembled in the lobby, he and Emilia herded them outside where their ride was waiting.

The bus did not disappoint—it was a luxury coach with comfy seats, Wi-Fi, and air-conditioning. TJ was grateful his duties didn't include driving the bus. He couldn't conceive of steering a behemoth like this through Rome's frenetic traffic. Thankfully, their driver, Nico, had twenty years of experience.

Though TJ had exchanged texts with Nico before, this was his first time meeting the driver in person. Nico was a bear of a man— large, swarthy, and bearded—who looked like he could destroy you in a fight or engulf you in an enormous hug, depending on his mood.

He greeted TJ and Emilia warmly. "It's good to meet you in person. Are we ready to embark?"

"We are," Emilia said. "I'm so glad you're driving. I can't imagine piloting this beast through Rome."

"Eh, you get used to it," Nico said. "Besides, my bus is so big that everyone needs to get out of my way. Scooters and motorcycles are no match for me."

"You have our itinerary?" TJ asked.

"On my phone. We shouldn't have any problems. Of course, I can't predict the traffic, the weather, or acts of God, but I can drive us anywhere buses are allowed."

"Thank you so much," Emilia said.

After all the passengers had boarded the bus, she placed the binder next to TJ and sat in the aisle seat across from him. From the way her head was drooping, he suspected she was still tired from last night. Rather than ask her to pitch in, he decided he'd take charge.

"I'm going to lead us off. That okay with you?"

When she nodded, he turned on the mic and began his spiel. "Buongiorno! Welcome to day two of the Buon Viaggio tour of southern Italy. If you're thinking, 'Wait, I'm meant to be with a different group,' speak now or forever hold your peace. Anyone? Okay, so today is going to be all about ancient Rome. We'll be taking you to the Colosseum, where a local expert will lead you on a four-hour tour, which includes the Forum and Palatine Hill. You'll be in the shade a fair amount, but make sure to apply sunscreen and drink plenty of water. Any questions?"

"What about lunch?" Sylvie asked.

"At one, we'll meet you at the end of the tour and walk to a nearby restaurant. After that, we'll visit the Capitoline Museums, three buildings located in the Piazza del Campidoglio, housing an incredible collection of statues, paintings, and sculptures. We'll return to the hotel by five for a bit of a rest before dinner at seven thirty."

In all, it was an exhausting first day, especially since the temperature was expected to reach eighty degrees by noon. At least the bus and the museums would be air-conditioned.

"During our drive to the Colosseum, I'm going to give you a few fun facts about it," TJ said. "In case you didn't know, it's one of the seven wonders of the world. By my count, I've only been to two of them, but I'm hoping to visit more. How about the rest of you? Have any of you visited the Colosseum before? Or any of the other six wonders, like the Taj Mahal, the Great Wall of China, or Machu Picchu?"

One thing he'd learned in giving tours of Pompeii was that people loved to recount their travel experiences—both good and bad. He was the same way. If anything, he'd been far more obnoxious in the past, constantly bragging about where he'd worked, acting like he was the most hard-core archaeologist on the planet.

As he tossed in a few jokes, he occasionally glanced at Emilia, hoping she'd respond with a smile. Instead, she was leaning back in her seat with her eyes closed. Was she tired? Fighting off a headache?

Or did she just want to be anywhere else but on this bus with him?

CHAPTER THIRTEEN

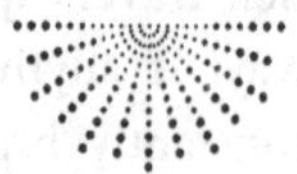

When the Buon Viaggio bus pulled up at their designated stop, TJ helped everyone disembark. The guests had been able to glimpse the massive Colosseum from the bus windows, but up close, it was more impressive than any postcard or photo could convey. Hard to believe an ancient monument of such significance could exist in the middle of a congested, modern city.

Though TJ had seen it numerous times before, the sight of it always filled him with awe. The largest amphitheater ever built, able to hold over fifty thousand people, a testament to the might of the Roman Empire. He could only imagine all the historic figures that had stepped through its gates—the powerful emperors, the fierce gladiators, the wily senators. At times like these, he had no regrets that he'd devoted so many years to studying ancient history.

With Emilia's assistance, he handed out the wireless receivers that would allow each person in the group to listen to their guide via headphones. As he was finishing up, a tall, blond woman approached them. She looked to be in her thirties and was carrying a messenger bag with a bright red flag sticking out of it.

TJ assumed she was the local expert who'd be giving this morning's tour.

"Is this the Buon Viaggio group?" she asked.

"It is indeed," he said. "Are you our guide? It's nice to meet you. I'm TJ, and this is—"

"I need to get your group moving. We've got a lot of ground to cover. Is everyone ready?"

"They are, but—"

"I'll be done at one o'clock. *Sharp.* You can collect your group at Palatine Hill by the Museo Palatino. Angelo sent me your contact information in case of emergency. If I text you, I expect you to answer immediately. Is this understood?"

Like he was going to argue? This stern woman wasn't someone he wanted to mess with. "Yes, ma'am. Thank you. Would you prefer it if one of us joined you on the tour? To help out?"

"Definitely not. I don't need an amateur tour guide mucking things up. Just keep your phones on." She addressed the group. "Everyone! Tune your receiver to channel 14. We are marching. If you lose sight of me, follow the red flag. Andiamo!"

Around them, similar groups were assembling. Some guides held up flags, while others carried umbrellas or signs, every one of them hoping to get their charges through the gates of the Colosseum when it opened at nine. Groups upon groups, speaking English, German, French, Italian, Spanish, and Japanese. A hop-on/hop-off bus pulled up, and a glut of people emerged, all hastening to reach the entrance. Even if TJ could appreciate the majesty of the Colosseum, he was grateful the cranky tour guide hadn't wanted his assistance. With the site this crowded, he preferred to observe it from a distance.

As the group marched away, Emilia let out an audible shudder. "Holy crap. I thought I was grumpy, but that guide is next-level. She's positively terrifying."

Nico stepped off the bus and lit a cigarette. "You mean

Sandra? She's only like that at first because it's so chaotic out here. Once she has the group together, she does a masterful job of leading them. She has a PhD in classical history and knows everything about the Colosseum."

"She has a PhD?" TJ asked. "Why isn't she teaching somewhere? Or working in a museum?"

"Eh." Nico shrugged. "There are a lot of archaeologists and historians in Rome and only so many university jobs available."

Ouch. Was that what TJ had to look forward to? Leading tours for the next two decades? "Does she do the same tour every day? It must get old."

"I think she mixes it up," Nico said. "But the Colosseum is so popular that she's always in demand."

A petite woman with olive-toned skin and a pink pixie cut approached them and addressed Nico in Italian. "Ciao, Nico. Do you have the scoop on Mateo? Did he get fired for misconduct? I'm pretty sure he was banging two women on his last tour."

Nico waved his hand in dismissal. "Eh, he wouldn't get fired for that. He was in a hiking accident, but he's coming back next month. We've got two Americans leading the tour right now—TJ and Emilia."

"Nice to meet you," the woman said, switching to English. She eyeballed TJ. "You're a cutie, though a little young for the women here. That Mateo, he was a silver fox. The ladies loved him."

Emilia burst out laughing, but TJ was thrown off-kilter. Was this woman the Roman equivalent of Giada? "I'm sorry, but who *are* you? Do you work for Buon Viaggio?"

"Nope. I'm Francesca Scioretti, but everyone calls me Cesca." She pointed to a coach bus parked behind theirs. "I'm with Roman Pathways Tours. Same shit, different bus. We're one of your direct competitors, so we follow the same route as you. Get used to seeing a lot of us."

"Wait," TJ said. "I thought this was a 'uniquely curated, one-of-a-kind experience.' You mean to tell me there are other tours following the same itinerary?"

Cesca snorted. "Believe it. First of all, there are only so many places you can visit on a so-called 'archaeological treasures of southern Italy' tour, so we hit up the same sites. And second, it's not always easy finding restaurants and hotels that want to accommodate large groups." She cocked her head to the side. "How'd you two get roped into this gig? You're obviously not Italian."

TJ answered. "We were hired because we're archaeologists, and—"

"Ha. That's what they tell all the guests," Cesca said. "A tour led by a 'real archaeologist,' when it's usually someone who's taken a few ancient history classes. Like me—one semester of Latin and two of Roman history, and that's it."

"No, we *are* archaeologists," Emilia said. "With PhDs and everything. We came to Italy to work at Pompeii. Giving tours is our side hustle. We're only doing this excursion as a onetime thing."

"So you say, but don't be surprised if you get sucked into the dark side. That's what happened to me." Cesca pulled out her phone and peeked at it. "We've got a few hours to kill, so let's grab a caffè. I know a place nearby where we can sit for a while. You up for it?"

Maybe Cesca was used to taking off, but TJ didn't want to risk leaving his post. On the chance Sandra contacted them with an emergency, she'd be mad if they were off having coffee. He'd hoped to use the break to talk with Emilia, but volunteering to stay with the bus might earn her forgiveness. "Em, you can go if you want. I'll hang out by the bus in case there's a crisis."

"Sorry to disappoint you, but the bus isn't staying," Cesca said. "None of them are."

Nico finished his cigarette and ground out the butt with his boot. "She's right. We can't linger after drop-off. Too much air pollution. As a matter of fact, there were a few years when we weren't allowed to drive around the historic district of Rome at all. I'll be back after lunch to take all of you to the museum. Grab anything you need before I leave."

"I'll get the binder," TJ said. "That way, I can brush up on my Roman facts while I'm waiting. If something comes up, I'll handle it."

Emilia brightened. "You sure?" When he nodded, she grinned at Cesca. "Lead on. I can always use more coffee."

As she walked away, TJ fought off a pang of longing. He wanted to be the one sharing coffee with her. Maybe this afternoon, once they were done with the day's excursion, he could seek her out alone and apologize again.

EMILIA WAS TEMPTED TO STAY BEHIND WITH TJ. AFTER THEIR argument this morning, she wanted to smooth things over. True, he'd grossly overstepped when he made that comment about her hooking up with Luca, but he'd only said it out of frustration. Last night, he'd reached out to her three times, and she'd left him hanging. To be fair, she'd been exhausted, but a simple message like "I'm okay, thanks" would have gone a long way in reassuring him.

As it was, she wasn't operating at full capacity. Falling asleep fully clothed had been a terrible idea. She'd woken at two, feeling out of sorts. After changing into her pajamas and brushing her teeth, she'd gone back to bed, only to toss and turn for hours. All because Luca had left her so unsettled. Even if he hadn't made a move on her, he hadn't kept things professional, either. He'd made too many comments about her appearance. And before bidding her good night, he'd kissed her on the cheek. She let it go without a word of protest, but she didn't want him getting into the habit of it.

Thank the goddess he'd gone off on his own today to deal with business in Rome.

"Come on," Cesca said. "My cousin works at a place nearby. We can sit there and gossip for hours, no problem."

"Sounds great." She followed Cesca away from the crowds gathered around the Colosseum and crossed onto a stretch of sidewalk lined with souvenir shops. Tourists pawed through spinner racks filled with postcards, key chains, and magnets. Every store displayed the same items, most selling for a couple of euros or less. Cesca skirted around them and led Emilia down a narrow side street toward a small café with a few tables set in the shade. Two of them were occupied, but Cesca placed her backpack on the remaining one.

"I'll grab us some drinks," she said. "What do you want? Caffè? Cappuccino?"

Emilia fished her wallet out of her pocket. "I'll take a cappuccino."

"Don't worry about the money. My cousin never lets me pay. I'll be right back." Cesca ducked into the café.

A stray cat brushed against Emilia's ankles. When she scratched it on the head, it gave a sweet meow. Rome had a lot of stray cats—so many, in fact, that they appeared in postcards and calendars. She wished she had something to feed this one. Next time she went to the grocery store, she'd buy a few pouches of kitty treats.

Cesca returned with two ceramic cups and set one in front of Emilia. "Your drink, signora."

"Thanks," Emilia said. "I have to ask—is this what you usually do when your group is on a tour? Relax and have coffee?"

"Most of the time, I'm the one giving the tours. I assume Buon Viaggio operates the same way. Rome's different from a lot of our other stops because there are scads of local guides, and they don't appreciate outsiders. Not many other sites in the south are like that except Pompeii, but it sounds like you're an expert there."

"I could do that tour in my sleep." Emilia took a tentative sip of her cappuccino. Still piping hot, so she forced herself to set it to the side. "Are you from Rome?"

"Napoli. Grew up there but came here for university. I started working as a guide during the summers and ended up doing it full-time once I graduated. I've been with Roman Pathways for five years."

"And you're not tired of it?" Emilia couldn't imagine being a guide for that long, leading tourists through the same sites over and over.

"I usually do the weeklong excursions, so there's a lot of variety. I've been all over the country—the Lake District, Tuscany, Sicily, Sardinia, you name it. Not like these Colosseum guides—the same thing, day after day. On the longer tours, you always get a fair amount of drama, and if you're lucky, a little romance. I live for that."

"I can see the appeal, but I'm not big on socializing. TJ and I are doing this as a side job, so we didn't have a lot of training. And that binder he was talking about? It's five hundred pages, and we're supposed to memorize all of it. We're lucky we can split up the responsibilities."

Cesca brought a bag of shortbread biscuits out of her backpack. She opened the bag and passed it to Emilia. "Want some?"

"Thanks." Emilia took two. She dunked a biscuit in her cappuccino, then popped it in her mouth. The crispy, buttery shortbread went perfectly with coffee.

"You said you came out here to work at Pompeii, right?" Cesca asked. "Was that what you wanted? Wouldn't a post at a university pay better? Or do you prefer doing fieldwork?"

Emilia sighed. "I've always loved being in the field, but that wasn't my goal when I got my PhD. I wanted a teaching job." She went on to explain the hoops she'd jumped through, only to end up without a single offer. "I lucked out when I got a traveling fellowship, though I didn't expect TJ to get one as well. If it wasn't bad enough that we spent the entire academic year competing for the same jobs, now we're stuck working at Pompeii together."

Cesca took another biscuit out of the bag. "Wait. So you and TJ *aren't* a couple? I assumed you were together since most tours only have one leader."

"We're not together. If anything, we're..." She was about to say "rivals" but stopped herself. She was getting tired of keeping up this ruse. Of acting like TJ was her sworn enemy when he'd been nothing but supportive.

"You're what?" Cesca asked with a smirk. "Friends with benefits? Rivals who occasionally succumb to a little hate-fucking? I won't judge."

A plaintive meow caught Emilia's attention. This time, it was a tabby cat with a white star on its forehead. She took a moment to pet it while trying to come up with a response. "Neither of those things. Even if we wanted to have sex, it's forbidden while leading this tour."

"Oh, please. It's not as if Mateo wasn't grabbing every piece of ass available. How else do you think he got all those rave reviews?"

Emilia laughed so hard she almost spit out her coffee. She wiped her mouth with a paper napkin. "But the rules seemed ironclad."

"Maybe so, but I'm sure your boss knew what Mateo was up to. He probably turned a blind eye because Mateo's a man. Typical." Cesca's eyes gleamed with excitement. "What if you *could* have sex with TJ? Would you?"

"Of course not." Emilia crumpled her napkin into a little ball. "We fight constantly."

"But do you enjoy it? Does challenging him rev up your motor, so to speak?"

Emilia let out a groan. Why was she denying it? Ever since

she'd met TJ in Turkey last year, she'd gotten a rush out of arguing with him. Trying to beat him at everything and rejoicing in those rare moments of victory. There were times when he'd genuinely infuriated her, like with the hotel in Istanbul or the panel session in Philadelphia. But the rest of the time? Being around him made her feel alive.

"Honestly? We both get a charge out of fighting with each other," she said. "Is that twisted or what?"

"Nah, it's hot as fuck." Cesca laughed. "Sorry for all the cursing. I learned English watching HBO, and I can't shake it."

"It's fine." The salty language reminded Emilia of her friend Dusty.

"Now that you've admitted it, are you going to make things happen with TJ?"

"Why are you so invested in this? You literally met me two hours ago."

"Like I said, I love drama. Forbidden-romance drama is even better. Do you want him or not?"

The more Emilia thought about it, the harder it was to deny her feelings. There had been that kiss in Philadelphia. A kiss that might have led to more if TJ hadn't pulled away. In Pompeii, neither of them had hooked up with anyone else, even though Marie and Paulo had both made overtures. Then, TJ had turned down a trip to Greece to support her on the tour. Hell, he'd even offered to give her his share of the pay, just so she wouldn't have to deal with Luca on her own. Once he'd committed to the tour, he'd been all in.

Though TJ might have been too intense this morning, it was only because he'd been worried about her. Not once had she thanked him for looking out for her. Instead, she'd totally shut him down.

"Hang on." She pulled out her phone and texted TJ before she lost her nerve.

Sorry I was so grouchy this morning. Thanks for
having my back.

He responded immediately.

I got you, Em. You only need to ask.

The fact that he'd replied without a second of hesitation filled her with an unexpected burst of emotion. Even if the two of them had come to Pompeii as rivals, the dynamic between them had changed. This was a guy who *cared* about her.

She rubbed her hands over her face. "Shit. I'm so doomed."

Cesca leaned in closer. "Hardly. You just need to figure out your next move."

CHAPTER FOURTEEN

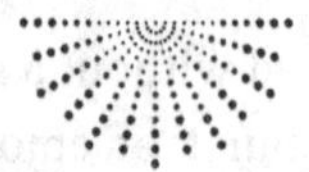

TJ took a screenshot of Emilia's text, in case his messages somehow disappeared into the cloud. He didn't want to lose this one. *Ever.* He couldn't believe she'd sent him an apology. During all their confrontations—at Troy and Pompeii—she'd never backed down from an argument. He wished he could talk to her now instead of having to wait until they were done with the day's outing.

Seated on a bench in a small strip of green space near the Forum, he'd been studying the binder for the last two hours but was growing weary of it. After setting it down, he indulged in a little people-watching. Even if the summer was almost over, Rome appeared more crowded than when he'd first arrived in June. Endless groups lined up to enter the Colosseum, led by guides like the one Buon Viaggio was using.

How many of the tourists took the time to enjoy the sites they were visiting? Were they absorbing the history or counting the minutes until they could go back to their hotels and rest?

Until he started working at Pompeii, TJ had never taken a guided tour of anything. He liked visiting sites on his own or with a group of archaeologists. He also hated being rushed.

Growing up, he'd been the nerdy kid who insisted on reading every placard in a museum exhibit. Give him four hours and a huge building stuffed with antiquities, and he was in heaven. Of all the places he'd visited, his favorite was the Field Museum in Chicago. His dad had taken him there so often that he'd memorized the permanent exhibits.

When his phone buzzed, he peeked at it, hoping Emilia had replied to his last text. Instead, he'd received a message from an unknown number.

SOS. Come immediately! Temple of Vesta.

It had to be from Sandra, the grouchy tour guide in charge of the group. Something must have happened. Despite his trepidation, the adrenaline rush made him feel like Batman receiving the signal from Commissioner Gordon. All he needed was a cape. He sent out a quick response, telling her he'd be there as soon as he could.

He stood up, fully prepared to sprint over to the Forum, but stopped short. Just where was the Temple of Vesta, anyway? He recalled what he'd read about it—an ancient Roman building that had once housed the holy fire of Vesta, tended by six Vestal Virgins. It was located somewhere in the Forum, but the area was so large, so packed with swarms of people, that he wanted to narrow down his search.

His phone vibrated with an incoming call from Emilia. He answered it on the first ring. "Hey, Em. You okay?"

"Yeah. Did you get that SOS from our guide?"

"I did, and I'm on it. Or I will be, once I figure out where the Temple of Vesta is." With one hand, he propped open the binder, trying to find the right section.

"There's a map of the Forum in section three of the binder, right after the stuff about the Colosseum. Cesca and I can meet you there. She knows where it is."

While he could probably handle the emergency on his own, he didn't want to reject Emilia's offer. What if the situation was so dire he needed backup? "Thanks. I'll see you there."

He leafed through the binder until he found the right map. After taking a picture of it, he tucked the giant tome under his arm. Dodging past the Arch of Titus, he ran down the Via Sacra —the main street leading through the Forum. Back in ancient times, the Forum had served as the city's foremost public meeting space, where Roman senators would gather to discuss politics. In addition to a public square, the area had held courthouses, temples, and monuments. Now, it was so filled with tourists that TJ could barely move.

He wiped the sweat from his forehead, hoping to stop it from dripping into his eyes. By now, the midday sun was at its peak. As he got closer to the temple, he paused, overwhelmed by the sheer mass of humanity. How was he supposed to find his group?

Look for red. That's the Buon Viaggio color.

In the distance, Davis stood atop a stone plinth, waving a bright red flag. TJ ran over to him. Panting heavily, he caught his breath before speaking. "I...I'm here. Is everything okay?"

Sylvie Galloway strode over to him, her face blotched with rage. "Everything is not okay. My friend Alice nearly passed out from the heat."

The tour group clustered in a circle on the grassy space next to the main pathway. At the center was Alice, who sat with her head between her knees.

TJ knelt beside her. "Alice? Are you all right?" Given that she was in her mid-seventies and slightly frail in appearance, he hoped her fatigue was weather-related and not due to a serious medical condition.

She raised her head to face him. Unlike Sylvie, she appeared more embarrassed than angry. "I just got so dizzy. I don't think I drank enough water when we were at the Colosseum. I'm sorry for making a fuss, but I was afraid if I kept walking, I might pass out."

The blond tour guide—Sandra—approached TJ with a frown. "We need to get going or we won't be able to visit all the stops on our itinerary. Can you handle this situation or not?"

"Sure, I'll take care of it." TJ turned to Alice. "Do you want to continue with the group? If not, I could lead you at a slower pace or find you a taxi to the hotel."

She reached over and patted his cheek. "Aren't you a dear? I'm not ready to give up the ghost yet. Why don't you lead me around? Even if you aren't an expert, feel free to make things up. I won't know the difference."

He laughed. "I know enough to give you a basic overview." He looked up at Sandra. "You can carry on. I'll make sure we meet up with you at one, as planned."

"Very well," she snapped. "Let's hope there are no more interruptions. We have a tight schedule."

What did it matter if she finished the tour behind schedule? Then again, maybe she had another group lined up after this one and she needed some downtime in between. Having done back-to-back tours at Pompeii, he could sympathize. But she could still show a little more compassion.

Davis handed the tour flag back to Sandra. "Here you go. If you don't mind, I'll tag along on TJ's tour. I'd rather go at a slower pace."

"I'll join you, as well," Sylvie said. "Quite frankly, that Colosseum tour was exhausting."

By now, Sandra was shooting daggers at TJ. He gave her a sheepish grin. "Sorry. We should be good now."

With a huff, she raised her flag high into the air. "Andiamo! We are marching."

After the others had left, TJ viewed the motley trio with a touch of anxiety. It was one thing to take Alice on an impromptu tour but quite another to lead Davis and Sylvie, both of whom seemed very opinionated. "Um…I hope you realize I'm not exactly an expert on this area. I know a lot about Roman history, but—"

"But I'm here, so you don't need to worry. Lucky for you, I memorized this part of the binder." Emilia walked over to join them. Beside her was Cesca, the pink-haired guide he'd met earlier.

The sight of Emilia filled TJ with a burst of happiness. In an attempt to restore their usual dynamic, he smirked at her. "You think you can do a better job than I can, Dr. Flores?"

"Absolutely, Dr. Mayer. You didn't even know where the Temple of Vesta was."

Sylvie narrowed her eyes at him. "Is that true?"

"No," he said. "I just needed a minute to get my bearings. But Em, feel free to lead the way. Aren't you an expert on Vestal *Virgins*?"

Cesca grinned. "I'm totally sticking around for this."

"Joke all you want, but being a Vestal Virgin was a great gig." Emilia pointed to a headless female statue. "These women had it made. In fact, if I'd been born during Roman times, I would have considered myself lucky to snag a spot in this temple."

"Are you serious?" TJ asked. "Wouldn't you miss…um…"

"Sexual relations?" Emilia arched an eyebrow at him. "You can say it, TJ. We're all grown-ups here. Perhaps, but consider this. The Vestal Virgins lived in a luxurious house with a full range of servants. Unlike most women in Rome, they weren't subjected to the patriarchy. They were legally independent and received sizable donations and gifts during their thirty years of service. They even got some of the best seats at the gladiatorial games. I'd say that's a fair trade-off."

"I would concur," Sylvie said. "Sex is overrated, but independence and wealth? Definitely worth striving for."

While TJ didn't agree with her take, he wasn't about to argue. He offered his hand to Alice. "Are you all right to stand up?"

She took it, her grip surprisingly strong. "Yes, please. Lead the way."

After he helped her up, he addressed the group. "Before we continue, I'd like all of you to take a quick water break while I confer with my partner." He led Emilia a few paces away from the others. "You sure you know enough to take on this tour? Neither of us prepared for it ahead of time."

She placed a hand on his arm. Just the slightest touch, but the contact made his heart soar. "I've got this. If not, we can wing it together. We're a team, right?"

Yes. For the first time since they'd embarked upon this tour, he truly believed it.

SOMETHING HAD CLICKED FOR EMILIA. EVEN WITH THE CROWDS, the heat, and the constant questions from Sylvie, she was having fun. This wasn't like leading a group through Pompeii with a prepared script. She was improvising, calling upon her stellar memory to recall everything she'd read about this part of Rome. Knowing she wouldn't have time to cover all the highlights, she skipped a few of the monuments in the Forum and led the group up to Palatine Hill. Back in the day, it had housed the elegant homes and palaces of the Roman elite. Now, it offered a spectacular view of the surrounding area.

She waited patiently as TJ helped Alice up the stairs to the Farnese Gardens. "Sorry for the climb, but you don't want to miss the view," she said. "It's one of the best in Rome."

"As long as you don't mind waiting, I can make it," Alice said. "I need some decent shots for my Instagram account."

"I thought you didn't like apps," TJ teased.

"My grandchildren made me get it," she said. "I agreed to it, but only if they promised to like all my posts."

"We'll make sure you get some great pictures," Emilia said.

Located at the top of Palatine Hill, the Farnese Gardens provided a peaceful oasis filled with shady walking paths, fountains, and statues. Emilia took a deep breath, catching the faint scent of roses. What she wouldn't give to spend a quiet afternoon here reading. Even if she hadn't intended to lead a tour today, she was grateful for a chance to visit this part of Rome.

"These gardens were originally built in the sixteenth century by Cardinal Alessandro Farnese, who was a wealthy nephew of the Pope," she said. "They once included aviaries with all kinds of birds. Take your time walking around, but make sure to observe the view. From here, we can see the Forum, the Colosseum, and the Capitoline Hills."

They stopped at a cast iron fountain with a distinctive curved spout. "Anyone thirsty?" TJ asked. "Now's a good time to refill your water bottles."

Sylvie frowned. "Are you sure the water's safe? When we went to Morocco last year, we wouldn't have dreamed of drinking from a public fountain."

"Our guide told us to stick with bottled water," Alice added. "But even then, a few of us had tummy trouble."

"You won't have to worry about that here," Cesca said. "There are over two thousand of these public fountains all over the city. We call them nasoni—noses—because the spout is like a big nose. The water's not only drinkable; it's also deliciously cold."

As the others filled their bottles, TJ sidled over to Emilia. "You still doing okay? Anytime you want me to pitch in, just say the word."

She poked him in the shoulder. "You wish. You can't stand that I'm showing you up."

"May I remind you that *I* was supposed to be the one saving the day here." He placed his hand over his heart. "I wanted to be the knight in shining armor."

"You already did a lot by letting Alice tour the area at her own pace." She lowered her voice. "Speaking of which, when I talked to Davis yesterday, he told me one of the reasons he panned that Portugal tour was because their guide rushed them through everything. The pace was too intense. It's something we might want to consider. We need to make sure our guests aren't overtired or ask them if they want a less taxing alternative. We might not be able to accommodate every demand, but having two of us means we have more flexibility."

A slow grin spread across his face. "Does this mean you actually *care* about these people? That inside your prickly exterior, there's a sweet center?"

Typical TJ, always pushing her buttons. "Oh, shut up. There's no sweet center, but I never half-ass anything. If we're going to do this, then we're going to give our group the best damn tour we can."

He was still looking infuriatingly smug, like he was the one responsible for her change of heart. She didn't want to give him that much credit, but she had to admit she felt lighter now that she'd told Cesca how she felt about him. While she still intended to banter with him as much as ever, now she didn't have to lie to herself anymore.

At times, he might be too overconfident. Even boastful. And his theories about the Bronze Age sucked. But she *liked* him.

And she suspected he felt the same way about her.

CHAPTER FIFTEEN

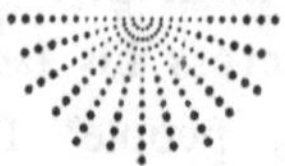

Emilia sat in the hotel's shaded courtyard, enjoying the solitude. Beside her was the binder, but she hadn't cracked it open. Instead, she was using the time to let her mind wander. After her conversation yesterday with Cesca, her thoughts kept drifting to TJ. When had she started liking him? Had it been three nights ago, when they'd spent the evening in her room watching *Gladiator*? Or back in Pompeii when they'd paired up to give tours? Or even last summer while sparring at Troy?

One thing was certain—ever since they'd embarked upon this adventure, he'd been on her mind a lot. Not that she had any idea what to do about it. Obviously, she couldn't pursue him now. The rules didn't allow it. Even after the tour ended, they only had two months left at Pompeii.

Or did they?

What if Dr. Roberti got the funding to extend the project until next June? And what if she and TJ were selected to join the team after proving their worth as tour guides? Then they'd have eight months together in Pompeii. More than enough time for a real relationship to grow.

But was it worth it to invest so much of herself in another person when they didn't have any chance of a future? Once they returned home, they'd go back to being competitors. They'd take jobs wherever they could find them, which meant they couldn't be tied down to anyone or any place.

Why worry about the future? Why not have fun now?

For years, flings had been her default setting, especially as an undergrad. One-night stands, conference quickies, dig hookups —no problem. No ties, no promises, no tearful goodbyes. Just enough physical enjoyment to satisfy her needs without the risk of letting down her walls. The one time she'd opened her heart to someone, when she'd actually envisioned a future with him, he'd fucked her over, in more ways than one. It had ended so badly that she hadn't gotten involved with anyone in two years.

If she could keep TJ in the "fling" category, then she'd be safe. But she suspected it wouldn't be that easy. The more she opened up to him, the more she cared about him. If she truly let him in, there would be no turning back. And once it ended—because with her luck, it *would* end—she wouldn't be able to pretend he didn't exist. Not when she'd undoubtedly run into him on dig sites or at academic conferences. She didn't need that kind of heartbreak.

But she didn't want to shut him out, either. She'd had so much fun with him yesterday, giving their impromptu tour of the Forum and Palatine Hill. After dinner that night, they'd sat at the hotel bar until eleven, talking and sharing stories like old friends. Even today, he'd been texting her off and on for most of the afternoon. Tonight, they were free to have dinner on their own, so he'd suggested they try out a local pizzeria Cesca had recommended.

At the moment, he was out with the group on a day-long excursion to the Vatican and the Castel Sant'Angelo. Rather than join him, Emilia had accompanied the Golden Girls on a low-key tour of the Villa Borghese, a public park filled with gardens, statues, and fountains. The alternative outing had been Sylvie's idea because she and her friends had wanted to sightsee at a relaxed pace. Since TJ had offered to take the rest of the group on the Buon Viaggio-sanctioned tour, Emilia had enjoyed a splendid morning with the four women.

Her phone buzzed with a new message.

> TJ: Bought you two Pope-approved crucifixes at Vat City for your pops and your abuela, as requested. Need any other religious merch? Relics? A hair shirt?

> Emilia: Maybe some holy water to douse my wicked thoughts?

> TJ: Care to elaborate on these thoughts?

> Emilia: Wouldn't you like to know?

She was tempted to send him an image of the Trojan horse, just to tease him, but a familiar voice sent an Arctic chill rushing through her.

"Emilia. How lovely to catch you alone." Luca made his way toward her table and sat down beside her.

As the cloying scent of his sandalwood aftershave filled her nostrils, she resisted the urge to shudder. She silenced her phone and set it in her pocket. "All done with your business dealings?"

"I am indeed. I thought you might be with the group, but I ran into Sylvie in the lobby. She said you took her friends on a private tour. How very thoughtful of you."

"Alice had a hard time keeping up yesterday, so she and her friends asked if I could take them someplace less packed than the Vatican. I offered to escort them to the Villa Borghese." Emilia twisted her hands together, worried she'd broken the rules. "I hope that was okay."

"It's fine. I don't think Angelo would want you making a habit of it, but if a few guests wish to chart their own course, it's wonderful if we can accommodate them." He placed his hand over hers. "You did the right thing, bella."

His closeness made her feel caged in. Trapped. She tried to pull away. "Thanks. I should get back to my room."

"Why the rush? It's lovely out here."

It was, but not with him crowding her. Even if he'd given no sign he intended to pursue her, she didn't want to be alone with him. She scrambled to come up with an excuse. "I…promised my friend Dusty I'd call her. It's eight in Boston, but she's an early riser. Probably built in from years of working on digs, where we had to get up at five in the morning. So…um…I'd better go."

His hand tightened around her wrist. "Before you leave, I'd like to talk to you about something."

"Is this about Davis?" Last night, he'd sat next to her at dinner. Since Luca had been seated at the opposite end of the table, he hadn't been a part of their conversation. Even so, she'd caught him glowering at Davis a few times. "All we did last night was swap travel stories. I stayed on my guard, just like you asked."

"It's fine. That's not what I wished to discuss."

"What's up?"

He stroked his thumb along the inside of her palm. "I'm tired of playing games, bellissima. By now, you must be aware of my feelings. I'm very attracted to you, and if my instincts are right—which they usually are—I suspect you feel the same way. Since we won't have many chances to be alone, why not seize the moment? What say we indulge our secret desires in the privacy of my room?"

Ice water shot through her veins. She'd made herself too vulnerable, sitting alone in the courtyard like this. For the last half hour, she hadn't seen anyone, not even a lone housekeeper.

Don't be an idiot. He's not going to attack you.

She should be relieved he'd made his intentions clear. Now, she could make it equally clear she wasn't available. "I'm flattered, but I can't take you up on your offer."

He raised his eyebrows. "No? With all that spicy Latin blood coursing through your veins, you hardly seem the prudish type."

Spicy Latin blood? What kind of bullshit was that? Heart pounding, she forced herself to ignore his blatantly racist remark. "Getting involved with the guests is against the rules."

"What rules?"

"The Buon Viaggio rules. They're in the binder." She pulled her hand away and flipped through the hefty tome. When she reached the page that listed the tour guide regulations, she pointed to the final line, typed out in all caps. "You see? I could get fired."

He shook his head in amusement. "Perhaps if you slept with one of the guests, but I'm not just any guest. I'm a Roberti, and I'm here as an observer." His smile was like that of a shark, all gleaming white teeth and ravenous hunger. "Trust me, my uncles won't care. They just want my father to invest in Buon Viaggio. The more I enjoy myself on this tour, the more likely I am to give the company a glowing recommendation."

Was that a threat? Even if it was, Emilia wouldn't let it sway her. "I still can't risk it. Call me a prude, but I'm a rule follower."

He brushed his hand across her cheek. When she flinched, he leaned in closer, his dark eyes seeking out hers. "Don't you ever wonder what it would be like to break the rules? I'd make it worth your while."

A flash of memory hijacked her brain as she recalled the way her ex had attempted to coerce her into bed. Like Luca, he'd tried using flattery and seductive language to win her over. At first, she'd kept him at arm's length, joking and flirting with him but never going any further. He'd gradually broken down her defenses until she'd given in willingly, only to regret it once she learned how badly he'd lied to her. After it had ended, she swore she'd never let herself fall victim to any man's compliments or false promises.

Steeling herself against Luca's gaze, she spoke firmly.

"Regardless of how I feel, I agreed to these rules when I signed on as a tour guide. Please don't pressure me into compromising my integrity."

All at once, his smile vanished. His lips thinned into a grim line. "I would never pressure you to do anything, but I think you're being shortsighted."

It's not just about the rules. I don't want you.

He stared her down, but she maintained her cool facade, refusing to let him intimidate her. Despite her outward appearance, her entire body was coiled like a taut spring in anticipation of his reaction. She couldn't imagine he was used to rejection.

Rather than continue his pursuit, he stood abruptly. "I will respect your decision, but I hope you'll remember to follow the rules with *all* our guests."

Was he referring to Davis? While she'd enjoyed talking with him, she hadn't felt a single flicker of attraction. Not to mention, he was a travel reviewer. Hooking up with him would be a serious breach of ethics.

"Of course," she said. "The rules apply to everyone."

Without another word, Luca stalked off. She watched him go, her heart pounding as if she'd downed three shots of espresso. Taking a deep, calming breath, she turned her attention to the binder but couldn't focus. After such a close call, she no longer wanted to be alone in the courtyard. She retreated to her room, making sure to lock the door.

With trembling hands, she texted TJ.

> Can you come by when you get back? I need to talk to you.

CHAPTER SIXTEEN

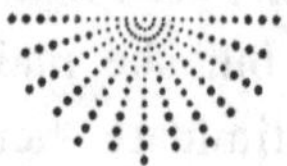

Upon receiving Emilia's text, TJ tried not to overreact. Her request hadn't suggested anything was wrong. Maybe she wanted to review tomorrow's itinerary, which involved checking the guests out of the hotel and accompanying them on the bus to Naples. He sent back a quick reply.

Sure. Everything go okay at the Villa Borghese?

When she didn't respond, he told himself not to imagine worst-case scenarios. She could be napping or out for a run.

But what if something bad *had* happened? Something so dire she couldn't convey it in a mere text?

He wanted to rush back to the hotel and check on her, but he had to stay with the group for their entire excursion—a full-day tour of the Vatican, St. Peter's Basilica, the Castel Sant'Angelo, the Pantheon, and the Museo Nazionale Romano. A lot of sites and a *lot* of people. Given their packed itinerary, he was glad the quartet of older women, which he and Emilia had started calling "the Golden Girls," had embarked upon their own outing.

By the time their bus returned to the hotel, it was almost six. After swapping out his tour guide uniform for a faded Harvard t-shirt and a pair of shorts, he hurried over to Emilia's room and knocked on her door.

When she opened it, her puffy eyes and blotchy complexion suggested a recent bout of tears. Her hair had come loose from her braid, and it fell past her shoulders in a messy tangle. He'd seen her upset before, but never like this. His first impulse was to offer her a hug, but he restrained himself, unsure of whether she wanted to be touched. Instead, he came into her room and shut the door behind him. She led him over to her bed and gestured for him to sit down.

"Em?" he asked. "Are you okay?"

After grabbing her water bottle from the nightstand, she sat beside him and spoke in a shaky voice. "Not really. You were right about Luca."

Fuck. His hands clenched into fists, his adrenaline kicking into high gear. "What did that sleazy prick do? I don't care if he's a Roberti, I'm taking him down."

Her mouth quirked up in a smile. "Don't even think about it. First of all, he'd probably kick your ass. Second, you'd be booted off the tour, and I'm not doing this without you."

"It doesn't matter. If he hurt you, he's gonna pay." Big words, considering TJ had never beaten up anyone before. In middle school, he'd been the one hiding from the bullies.

"Stop it. A knight in shining armor is the last thing I need right now."

"Sorry, but I don't like people hurting my friends."

"He didn't hurt me. In fact, he barely touched me. Well, no more than usual." She rubbed her hands along her bare arms. "But he did proposition me. He asked me to come up to his room so we could fulfill our secret desires."

"That slimeball." Not that TJ was surprised. For the past two days, he'd suspected the bastard was waiting for the right moment to pounce. "What did you do?"

"I said no, of course." She pointed to the binder, which she'd set to one side of the bed. "Lucky for me, you forgot to take this tome to the Vatican. I was studying it in the courtyard when he hit on me. All I had to do was show him the page with the rules."

TJ released a long breath, allowing the tension to ease from his body. "Thank fuck I left it behind. It's the perfect excuse."

"Even so, Luca insisted the rules didn't apply to him since he's the Robertis' nephew. He also hinted he was more likely to recommend Buon Viaggio to his father if he enjoyed himself on this tour."

"Was that a threat? Like, was he implying he'd bad-mouth the company if you didn't go up to his room? That's sexual harassment." TJ was fully aware his voice had risen, but he couldn't help himself. Luca wasn't just an entitled prick; his behavior was completely unethical.

"It's all good. I held him off by convincing him I'm an uptight American prude."

Now it was TJ's turn to smile. "Which is nothing like the Emilia Flores I know."

She gave a short laugh. "Right? Good thing he doesn't know me as well as you do. He bought into it, but only after he warned me not to break the rules with anyone else here."

What a dick. "Like who? Most of the single guys on the tour are over sixty. They wouldn't be anyone's choice for a steamy hookup."

"I think he meant Davis. He really hates him." She looked down, twisting her fingers in the tasseled fringe at the edge of the bedcover. "I should be grateful I got off so easily. It's not like he threatened to fire me or anything, but he just…"

"Made you uneasy?" With a tentative hand, TJ reached over and touched her shoulder. Lightly. "I'm sorry. That's awful."

In all honesty, the outcome was better than he would have

expected. Luca hadn't hurt her, and she'd been able to escape his attentions unscathed. But beneath his touch, she was trembling. While he didn't want to downplay Luca's behavior, her reaction hinted at a deeper issue. "Em? Did something else happen? Before this? If you want to talk about it, I'm here for you. If not, that's okay, too. No pressure."

When she turned to face him, her eyes had misted over with tears. "I know you think I'm a badass, but…"

"You're a total badass. You've traveled all over the world, you spent three summers digging in the jungles of Mexico, and you don't hesitate to put assholes in their place. Anything you tell me isn't going to change that."

She grabbed a pillow and set it on her lap, curling her arms around it. After a ragged breath, she spoke softly. "Two years ago, I was on a project in Sardinia, and I got involved with the dig director—an American archaeologist named Vincent Barnes. Not a professor, but still my boss. Right from the start, he was very clear about what he wanted. He didn't just flirt with me; he also filled my head with compliments. He told me he'd never met a grad student so focused and driven. He said my theories were worthy of publication. He even called me brilliant." She gave a dismissive snort. "Like an idiot, I ate it up with a fucking spoon."

"Cut yourself some slack. Being a grad student means getting your ego pummeled on a daily basis. A little praise goes a long way."

"Maybe, but I always thought I had a good bullshit detector. By the third week of the project, he'd won me over, but I refused to go to bed with him. I told him it wasn't my thing."

"But you've hooked up on other digs, right?" When she frowned, he held up his hands, worried he'd overstepped. "Sorry, not judging or anything. But when we were at Troy, there was that night at the bar when you and Dusty swapped stories about your…um…shenanigans."

"I forgot about that. We were *so* drunk."

"If anything, I was kind of jealous. I've never had much luck on any of my digs." He rubbed the back of his neck, remembering the times he'd been shot down. "It probably didn't help that I bragged constantly about what a hard-core archaeologist I was."

A tiny smile crossed her lips. "Yeah, that might not have been the best approach. But to your point, I fooled around a lot when I was an undergrad. The usual stuff that happens in the field. But *never* with a professor or a supervisor. Once I started grad school, I was more careful. I didn't want to make a mistake I'd regret later." She uncapped her water bottle and took a drink. "With Vince, we flirted a lot, but I had no intention of taking things any further. I liked that we were playing by my rules. Until one night…"

When she paused, TJ's stomach clenched up. If this creep had assaulted her, he might have to track down the bastard and make him pay.

She continued. "Everyone else was out drinking, but he'd asked me to stay behind to help him in the lab. Even though we were supposed to be working, he brought in a bottle of wine for us to share. Just when I'd relaxed enough to let down my guard, he hit me up with a heartfelt confession—how he was falling for me, how he'd never felt this way about anyone before, and how it was killing him that I wouldn't give him a chance. None of the guys I'd ever been with had made me feel like that. Like I was something special."

Her admission just about broke TJ's heart. Damn those other guys for not treating her like the amazing woman she was. "Em… you are special. Take it from me. I mean, yes, you can be a little prickly sometimes, but I've never met anyone like you."

"Thanks. But anyway…I broke my own code. Went to bed with him. Fell for all his lies. I started sneaking around to be with him, letting him take control, and losing all my self-respect in the process."

Based on what he knew of Emilia, TJ couldn't imagine her

being that submissive. Then again, love—or lust—could seriously mess with anyone's head. He'd been there himself, with a woman he'd dated in grad school. A woman who'd gotten him so tied up in knots that he would have done anything to please her. Until she dumped him for someone else.

"The worst part was that he claimed he was in love with me, and I bought into it." Emilia rubbed her hands over her face. "I sound like a clueless freshman, but he totally played me."

TJ's heart ached for her. "It's okay. We all do stupid things when we're in love."

"I don't even think it *was* love. Because love shouldn't be that unbalanced. He kept insisting he wanted us to be together, but after the dig ended, he totally ghosted me. I thought it was my fault, that I was acting too needy. When I got the courage to track him down, do you know what he told me? I wasn't anything special, just another one of his fuckbuddies. Not only that, but he was engaged to be married. Our fling was just a diversion to get him through the summer. It meant *nothing* to him."

Tears trailed down her cheeks. TJ wanted to console her, but the best he could do was pass her the box of tissues on the nightstand.

She grabbed one and dabbed her eyes. "I know I'm better off without him, but at the time, I was crushed. I hated that I'd been used. That he'd fucked with my head by convincing me I was special and then turned around and treated me like garbage."

"I'm so sorry." Hardly adequate for what she was sharing, but he didn't know what else to say.

"It's okay. This thing with Luca? It's not like I was attracted to him, but he gave off a similar energy. Vince was used to getting what he wanted, and Luca's the same way." She blew her nose, then crumpled the tissue and tossed it onto the floor. "Like I said, you were right about him all along."

For once in TJ's life, he would have preferred to be wrong.

"Would a hug help? Or would you rather not have anyone touching you right now?"

"I'd like a hug." She leaned over and allowed him to take her in his arms.

He held her tightly, hoping his embrace would ease her anguish. Outside her window, birds trilled softly, and voices drifted in from the courtyard, but he stayed silent, giving her time to recover. When she pulled away, he passed her another tissue, and she wiped off the last trace of tears.

"Thanks for listening," she said. "Sorry to dump all that on you."

"That's what friends are for." As he said it, he worried he'd assumed too much. In the past, they'd always referred to themselves as enemies. Competitors. *Rivals*. But now, those terms seemed like a way to mask their true feelings. "Just to clarify—we *are* friends, right?"

This time, she gave him a real smile—the kind that illuminated her whole face. "I still think your Bronze Age theories are shit. You're too braggy. And you talk too much. But yeah, we're friends."

As relieved as he was that she'd admitted it, a part of him wished for more. Not that he'd dare bring it up now. After what she'd been through, she needed a real friend, not another jerk trying to get her into bed. "Do you want to make a game plan for dealing with Luca? You shouldn't be alone with him."

"I think I'll be all right. He might turn off the charm now that I've rejected him."

TJ's stomach growled, reminding him he'd eaten a light lunch to save room for pizza. "Any chance I can tempt you into checking out that pizzeria Cesca suggested? I've been dreaming about it all afternoon."

She picked up the pillow and pressed it against her chest. "I don't know if I want to go out tonight. I feel kinda crappy."

"You sure?" He pulled out his phone. On the bus ride back to their hotel, he'd drooled over the mouthwatering photos displayed on the pizzeria's website. "Take a look. You can order by the slice, which means you can try more than one kind. Here's one with crispy potatoes, herbs, and parsley. Or one with sun-dried tomatoes, pancetta, and arugula. This one has zucchini flowers, black olives, and—your favorite—salted anchovies. You're the only person I know who likes anchovies."

"Don't knock my anchovies." She scraped a hand through her hair. "I need to pull myself together. If you're really hungry, you don't have to wait."

Like he'd leave without her? "I don't mind. The hungrier I am, the more pizza I get to try. Don't forget we can charge it to the Buon Viaggio credit card, which means there's no limit to the amount of pizza we can order." He eased off the bed. "Text me when you're ready, and I'll meet you in the lobby."

"Okay. And TJ?"

"What?"

"Thanks." She regarded him tenderly. "For everything."

"Anytime, Em."

He meant it. For the rest of this tour, he'd be there for her, no matter what.

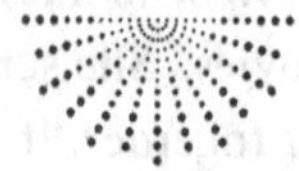

CHAPTER SEVENTEEN

As the Buon Viaggio bus pulled up to the entrance of the Pompeii Archaeological Park, Emilia stood and joined Nico at the front. She found it hard to believe they were already on the fifth day of the tour, which meant it was almost half over. Since today was a weekday, she'd hoped Pompeii would be less crowded, but lines of people had already formed, waiting for the site to open.

She turned to Nico, who was trying to wedge the bus into an open spot. "Don't worry about parking. You can idle here until everyone gets off."

Nico nodded. "This place is always packed—spring, summer, fall. One of these days, I've got to check it out."

"You've never visited? Nico! It's an archaeological gem."

"So I've heard." He offered her a warm smile. "Someday, I promise, but only if you and TJ show me around."

"It's a deal, but you'll have to squeeze it in before we leave in December."

A car horn blared behind them, but Nico paid it no attention. "What time do you want me to pick up the group? You're walking to lunch, right?"

Emilia peeked at the itinerary on her phone. "Yep. We're eating at Stuzzico, which is close by. You want to join us? Lunch is at one, and after that, we'll head over to the ruins at Herculaneum for the second half of today's excursion."

"I'd like that," he said. "I'll meet you there."

TJ was seated a few rows back, talking to Davis. When the bus stopped, he stood and caught Emilia's eye. "Em, do you want me to divide the group into two? Might be easier to do the tour that way."

"Sounds good. Can you get them organized? I'm gonna go on ahead."

When he gave her a thumbs-up, she got off the bus and almost bumped into Giada. The older woman stood at the curb, arms crossed.

"About time," she snapped. "You were supposed to arrive at a quarter to nine."

Emilia stared at her in confusion. "Sorry, but I didn't expect to see you here."

"You think because you're leading a fancy ten-day tour that you can survive without Giada?"

Quite honestly, yes.

But she wouldn't say it. Even if Giada wasn't a part of this tour, Emilia couldn't risk pissing her off. "I think we've got things under control, but thanks for checking on us." Behind her, the guests were slowly disembarking. They gathered in an unwieldy clump, waiting for TJ to give them directions.

Giada peered at them. "Where's Luca?"

"He's not taking part in today's tour. I already showed him around Pompeii when he was here in August. Remember?" His absence meant Emilia could breathe a little easier. Ever since that uncomfortable scene in the courtyard two days ago, he'd changed his tone around her. Instead of doling out compliments, he was quick to chastise her if she made the slightest mistake.

"You're keeping Luca happy, I hope?" Giada said. "Being extra, extra nice to him?"

Emilia repressed a shudder. "I'm treating him like any other guest, which should be more than enough."

Giada blew out a peeved breath. "He's not just 'any other guest.' His father is very important."

I don't care if his dad's the fucking president of Italy, I'm not sleeping with Luca Roberti. End of story. Rather than spend another second talking about him, she pivoted. "Any word from Angelo? TJ and I have been sending him daily updates, but he hasn't responded."

"You think he has time to read all his emails?" Giada said. "I'm sure it's fine. You haven't encountered any difficulties, have you?"

Other than Luca? No. "It's all good. I think the guests are enjoying themselves."

"Don't think—make sure of it! We want five-star reviews from every single one of them." She turned to TJ, who was attempting to herd the group into formation. "What are you waiting for? Your guests need to be right at the gates when Pompeii opens. You only have four minutes to get there."

With that, she turned and stalked off, no doubt in search of another poor guide to harass.

TJ addressed their group in a loud voice. "Okay, everyone. Like I told you earlier, Emilia and I will be leading your tour of Pompeii as a team. We decided to separate you into two groups because some of the areas we'll be visiting are a tight fit. As you got off the bus, I gave each of you a card. If you got a blue one, you're with me. A red card means you're with Emilia. But don't worry—we'll never stray too far from each other. When we reach the end of the tour, we have a special surprise for you."

A surprise? Was TJ intending to take them somewhere that wasn't on the itinerary? If so, they might have to speed through a few of their regular stops. They needed to be done just before one if they wanted to keep their lunch reservation.

Emilia took a bright red flag out of her backpack. "All right, folks, let's get going. It's very crowded here, so if you lose sight of us, TJ and I each have a flag to guide the way."

She led everyone past the line at the entrance and through the priority gate used by tour groups. Though only a week had passed since she'd left Pompeii, she was returning to the site with an entirely different perspective. Today, she wouldn't be a guide-for-hire, leading a random bunch of strangers around the ancient city. This was *her* group, and she wanted them to have the best experience possible.

Part of the fun of guiding tourists through Pompeii was watching their reactions. The site was exceptionally well-preserved, having been suspended in time since 79 AD, when the eruption of Mt. Vesuvius had buried it in volcanic ash and pumice stone. As with the tours she'd given all summer, she paused to describe various points of interest, like the Temple of Apollo, the Forum, and some of the best-known Roman homes and villas, like the House of the Faun and the Villa of the Mysteries. Along the way, she showed them the remains of bakeries, public baths, and thermopolia, or snack bars, where Pompeii's citizens would have stopped after work to grab a bite to eat. Naturally, the tour included a visit to the brothel with its racy wall paintings.

This time, when Emilia glanced at the sensuous images, her thoughts didn't drift to Paulo as they had in August. Instead, a different set of fantasies took hold—ones involving a nerdy, slightly boastful, overly enthusiastic archaeologist who'd gone from being a rival to a friend.

Though she might have teased TJ about it, she *did* consider him a friend. Two days ago, when she'd told him about her toxic relationship with Vince, she'd worried that he'd judge her. That her admission of weakness would forever tarnish her image. But he hadn't treated her like a victim. Instead of letting her wallow, he'd taken her out for pizza, followed by a trip to a nearby gelateria. All thoughts of the past vanished as she devoured a double scoop of dark chocolate and pistachio gelato that made her groan with pleasure.

Now, as she and TJ made their way through Pompeii, he led his group at a brisker pace than usual. A few times, she had to remind him to stop at the public fountains so they could refill their water bottles. Even if the temperature was milder than it had been earlier in the week, a lot of their tour involved standing in the sun.

By the time they reached the outdoor theater where they usually ended the tour, they were twenty minutes ahead of schedule—an unheard-of occurrence. Emilia was about to ask TJ whether he planned to squeeze in any more stops when he called the group to attention. All of them were sitting on the stone steps of the theater, looking down at the stage below.

"Before we leave Pompeii, we have a treat for you," he said. "It's not on your itinerary, nor is it on any of the public maps of the archaeological park. You'll be getting a behind-the-scenes sneak peek exclusive to Buon Viaggio. We're going to visit the House of Venus—the excavation site where Emilia and I have been working since June. We'll also pop into two of the lab buildings to show you where we study our finds."

What? When had TJ come up with this gem?

"Did you get permission?" Emilia asked.

"Not exactly." He grinned. "But since the project's on hiatus for three more days, no one will be working there. Dr. Roberti is still in Switzerland, the excavation site is empty, and the labs are locked up tight. But as luck would have it, I absconded with one of the keys." He pulled it out of his pocket and brandished it with an air of superiority.

"Isn't sneaking into the site against the rules?"

"You always follow the rules, Em?"

Leave it to TJ to keep goading her, even after they'd both admitted they were friends. But she wouldn't have it any other way. She didn't want him to coddle her just because she'd shown him her vulnerable side.

"No, but I don't have a death wish, either," she said. "If we get busted, it's on you."

He turned to the group. "Show of hands—who wants a sneak peek? I can't let you take any photos, but you'll get to visit a place that's only open to professional archaeologists."

When everyone raised their hands, Emilia gave TJ a reluctant nod. Now that he'd gotten their expectations up, she didn't want to let them down. At least Luca wasn't around to rat them out to his uncle.

"All right, but no photos or videos," she said. "TJ and I would like to keep our jobs."

"If you'll all follow me, then we'll get going." He gestured for them to stand up.

As he led them away from the theater, he kept up a steady stream of chatter. They headed back onto the Via Stabiana—one of the main roads running north-south through Pompeii—until they'd almost reached the city walls.

The excavation area was clearly marked, with metal barriers and signs forbidding public access. To Emilia's relief, no security guards were patrolling the area. After she moved the barriers, TJ directed the group inside the remains of the ancient dwelling known as the House of Venus. The house's outer walls were still intact; inside, it was divided into eight rooms surrounding a central atrium. The areas under excavation included the kitchen, the garden, one of the bedrooms, and the triclinium, or formal dining room.

Once they reached the triclinium, TJ stopped and motioned for the group to come closer. "This house was built around 20 BC in what we call the Third Pompeian Style. For the past three months, it's been the primary focus of the Via Stabiana Project. Based on the size and the style of the architecture, we suspect the owners belonged to the upper middle class. Dr. Roberti named it the House of Venus because the wall paintings we uncovered in the triclinium depict scenes featuring the Roman goddess Venus."

"Are we free to walk through all of it?" Sylvie asked.

Feeling like the parent of the group, Emilia spoke up quickly. "Yes, but please be careful. Don't get too close to the edge of the trenches or trip over any of the ropes." Not wanting to dampen their enthusiasm, she gave them a bright smile. "If you have any questions, please ask. TJ and I love talking about this stuff."

Even if she hadn't been on board with his idea at first, she liked sharing this part of herself with the guests. This project was proof that she and TJ weren't just playing at being archaeologists; they were both actively involved in their profession.

"Did you two come to Pompeii as a team?" Davis asked.

He still seemed convinced they were a couple, even after she'd denied it twice. "Nope. We already knew each other because we dug at Troy last summer, but we applied to work here separately."

Alice perked up. "You worked at Troy? I love *The Iliad*. What a masterful epic."

"It was a great experience," TJ said. "If you ever get to Turkey, you should visit the site. There's a giant model of the Trojan horse at the visitors' center that you can climb inside, in case you want to pretend you're a Greek warrior planning to attack Troy."

Damn you, TJ. Emilia couldn't even look at him. Every time he brought up that fucking horse, her mind flooded with racy images. A dark night. A furtive tryst. The two of them lying naked inside the belly of the wooden horse, trying to keep quiet while in the throes of passion.

Whew. Definitely not what she should be focusing on right now.

TJ smirked at her, as if he knew exactly what she was thinking. She'd have to return the favor. Maybe she'd send him some images of the horse when he was least expecting it.

"Have the two of you worked together at any other sites?" Alice asked.

Emilia responded quickly, grateful for the change in subject. "No, but we've dug in a lot of the same countries. We have different specialties, though. I'm an archaeobotanist, which means I study ancient seeds, pollens, and carbonized plant remains to learn what people ate and the type of crops they grew."

"As for me, I'm a lithics specialist," TJ said. "I study stone tools, as well as artifacts made of bronze, copper, and iron. I know a ton about metallurgy, and I even learned how to make my own arrowheads out of obsidian using a technique known as flint-knapping."

"Humblebrag," Emilia muttered under her breath.

He shot her a mock glare. "It's a lot more interesting than studying seeds. Right now, my group has been analyzing the household items we've found to learn more about daily life and determine which items might have been imported from other regions."

When Sylvie and her friends went to check out the wall paintings, Emilia joined them. "Aren't these gorgeous? They still need a lot of restoration, but they're going to be beautiful."

"I used to be an art conservator, back in the day," Sylvie said. "I would have given anything to work at a place like this."

Emilia's curiosity was piqued. "Really? I spent a semester in Florence studying conservation. I'd love to hear more about your experiences."

"I'd be glad to share them. I haven't worked in the field for years, but I own a gallery in Santa Fe. Supporting local artists is a passion of mine. My husband and I started the gallery together, but he passed away five years ago."

"I'm so sorry," Emilia said. "Maybe sometime I could come visit it."

"If you're ever in Santa Fe, I'd be happy to put you up. We could show you all around the area. Right, ladies?"

The other women agreed, sparking a warm glow inside Emilia. "Thanks. Do all four of you always travel together?"

"Yes, indeed," Alice said. "We're widows. We met in a grief support group five years ago and realized how much we hated eating stale donuts and drinking bad coffee."

Another member of their group spoke up. Patsy, age seventy-five. "We started talking about our bucket lists—all the places we wanted to visit but never had the chance. That summer, we took our first tour and had a glorious time. We went to Paris and the south of France."

"That sounds wonderful." As much as Emilia took pride in her solo adventures, traveling with a pack of like-minded girlfriends would be fun. "Where else have you been?"

"After France, we went to Spain, then last year, we did a tour of Morocco," Sylvie said. "Well worth the visit, even if the food didn't always agree with us. There was one rather unpleasant incident when we had to ask the bus driver to make an emergency stop at the nearest restroom."

Patsy shuddered, as though recalling the memory. "It wasn't our finest hour."

"I can relate," Emilia said. "During my first year digging in the Yucatán Peninsula, I had an episode like that. Except the only facilities we had were pit toilets." At the time, she'd been mortified, but now it just made her laugh.

"I admire you, pursuing a career in archaeology," Alice said. "It was something I always dreamed of but didn't have the courage to make happen. Until I met these ladies, I'd never even left the US."

"You should be proud of how far you've come," Emilia said. "For your next trip, consider Greece or Turkey. I've worked in both places, and they have a lot to offer, especially if you like archaeological sites."

Alice beamed at her. "I'd sign up tomorrow if you could be our guide."

When the others nodded, Emilia's heart soared. She'd never imagined how freeing it would feel to let people in. Even if she had no intention of pursuing a career in tourism, the idea that she could handle this much socializing, and truly shine at it, filled her with happiness.

CHAPTER EIGHTEEN

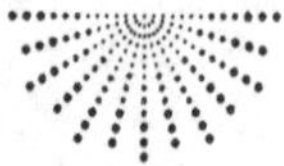

I n all his travels, TJ had never stayed anywhere quite like the Grand Hotel La Sonrisa. Located near the Amalfi Coast, it had originally been built as an eighteenth-century villa but now served as a luxurious resort. From the outside, it resembled a fairy-tale castle, complete with turrets, arches, and Rococo-style architecture. As their bus pulled up to the gated front entrance, he expected liveried footmen to greet them, like in *Bridgerton*—a steamy, Regency-era show that Romily had forced him to watch the last time he was home for the holidays.

The inside of the hotel was even more elaborate, outfitted with frescoed ceilings, inlaid marble floors, giant chandeliers, and wall-to-wall gilded decor. Over the bar was a huge mural filled with plump, winged cherubs. According to the information in the binder, the grounds of the hotel included lavish gardens, fountains, and a large swimming pool with a gazebo.

To think, a week ago, he'd been staying at a funky student hostel, bunking down with three other guys. Life didn't get much better than this.

Once he dropped off his luggage, he ran over to Emilia's room to get her take on the hotel. Since she'd left her door open, he didn't bother to knock. She sat on the bed with her suitcase beside her.

Upon seeing him, she grinned and brandished a handful of rose petals. "Can you believe this? Rose petals—scattered all over my bed. Kind of a waste, seeing as how I'm not here to indulge in a romantic rendezvous."

"Yeah, this hotel could totally serve as Casanova's palace or the setting for *Dangerous Liaisons*. Too bad we don't have anyone to lure into bed."

Though he meant it as a joke, he regretted the words the moment he said them. Because Emilia was sitting right there, on a frilly canopy bed that was easily big enough for two. He swallowed as he imagined what he could do with her on that bed. He'd lay her down on those rose petals, strip off her tour guide uniform, and kiss every inch of her delectable body. She'd moan with passion and beg him for more and...

Whoa. Get a grip. Not gonna happen.

"TJ? You okay?" she asked.

"Yeah. Just...um...overcome by all this luxury. It's like..."

"The castle in *Beauty and the Beast*. Right?" She pointed to a tall wardrobe in the corner embellished with gilt-edged curlicues. "I wouldn't be surprised if this piece of furniture started talking to me."

"Wouldn't that be wild? I'm not sure how our guests would rate a hotel filled with inanimate objects come to life. Speaking of which, everyone seemed impressed at check-in. Davis was in his element filming all of it."

Emilia snorted. "He's not the only one who was in his element. Luca was showing off for the Golden Girls—giving them a full rundown of the hotel's history and all its artwork."

"Well, if he wants to play tour guide, so be it." As far as TJ was concerned, the more time Luca spent with the guests, the less time he had to bother Emilia. He pulled out his phone to check the afternoon's itinerary, but the battery was only at ten percent.

"My phone's just about dead. What's on the schedule for this afternoon?"

"Nico's driving us into Positano for lunch, which might be a stomach-churning ride on those twisty roads. We'll take the group on a short walk through town, then give them a few hours to explore on their own. Dinner's at seven, and it's being held in that huge-ass ballroom on the main floor because we're sharing the banquet space with a group from Roman Pathways Tours. Once we're done tonight, I'm heading for the pool. Wanna join me?"

Did he want to indulge in a late-night dip with Emilia? *Yes, please.* Last summer, when they'd gone to the beach in Turkey, she'd worn a very revealing bikini. Even if they'd been enemies at the time, that hadn't stopped him from fantasizing about her.

"TJ? Hello? What's wrong with you?"

Fuck. He had to stop zoning out like this, especially since ninety percent of his daydreams were Emilia-related. "Sorry. Pool time sounds great."

"Ciao, what's up!" Cesca poked her head into Emilia's room. "Some place, eh? The Grand Hotel La Sonrisa never disappoints."

"You've been here before?" TJ asked.

"Three times. It's a favorite with our groups because it's so over-the-top. Did you see that pool outside?" She did a chef's kiss. "Perfetto."

"Want to come swimming with us?" Emilia asked. "We're going in after dinner."

A twinge of regret tugged at TJ as he realized he wouldn't get Emilia to himself. Then again, maybe it would be better if Cesca served as a buffer. That way, he wouldn't be tempted to break the rules.

"I'd love to," Cesca said. When her phone buzzed, she glanced at it. "We're leaving in fifteen. Do either of you have any candied ginger? Those roads are super twisty, and it helps guests with nausea. I hate it when people hurl on the bus."

"I've got some." Emilia grabbed her backpack off the floor, opened it, and tossed Cesca a bag. "Take this. TJ and I loaded up with supplies when we were in Rome. If you need sunscreen, wet wipes, or hand sanitizer, we've also got those covered."

Cesca grinned. "Aren't you two the cutest team ever? I've gotta go. Ciao."

After she left, Emilia grumbled, "We're not cute. I don't want to be cute." She glared at TJ. "What have you done to me? You're softening all my rough edges."

"Nah, you're still a grouchy pain in the ass most of the time. You just cover it up well."

She threw a pillow at him, but her grin implied she wasn't mad. Not in the slightest.

Probably for the best that they wouldn't be alone in the pool tonight.

❲

AT NOON, NICO TOOK THEM INTO POSITANO—A HAIR-RAISING trip, given that he was driving a giant bus along narrow roads atop five-hundred-foot-high cliffs. A few times, TJ had to close his eyes so that he wouldn't freak out over the hairpin turns— something Emilia couldn't resist teasing him about. Unlike him, she appeared completely at ease, even getting up a few times to check on the rest of the group.

While TJ couldn't deny the Amalfi Coast was visually spectacular, with its sky-high cliffs, picturesque seaside towns, and sparkling turquoise waters, he wasn't a huge fan of the area. Popular spots like Positano and Amalfi were always packed with tourists. But after spending the last five days visiting ruins, monuments, and museums, he was grateful for a leisurely afternoon where everyone could relax and take in the scenery.

At three, the guests were given leave to explore on their own and check out the local shops. Freed from their duties as guides, he and Emilia spent the next two hours at an outdoor bar, where they shared drinks and gossip with Cesca and Davis.

Dinner that night was sumptuous, held in the hotel's ballroom, with musical entertainment by an Italian lounge singer who styled himself as "the next Frank Sinatra." After three hours of conversing with the tour group and listening to all the B-sides from Frank's albums, TJ grew restless. Ever since Emilia had suggested the pool outing, he'd been counting down the minutes.

Once he was off the clock, he slipped away, changed into a t-shirt and swim trunks, and headed outside. Even this late in September, the evening was warm enough for swimming. He approached the pool, inhaling the faint scent of the colorful freesia planted nearby, but stopped short at the sight of Emilia.

She stood at the edge, her figure illuminated in the moonlight. With one fluid motion, she tossed off her sheer black cover-up, revealing a skimpy bikini underneath. She looked sexy as hell, her toned figure on full display, her long black hair falling past her shoulders. Her shapely calves flexed as she poised to jump in.

A hand clapped him on the back. "Caught you looking!"

TJ startled, his heart pounding. Behind him stood Davis, bearing a smug grin.

Heat crawled up TJ's cheeks. "I wasn't looking...um...I was just..."

"Ogling? No need to hide it. Em looks fantastic in that swimsuit."

TJ's shoulders tightened. Was Davis into her? Earlier this afternoon, he'd spent a long time talking to her about their shared passion for the *John Wick* movies. She'd also invited him to join them in the pool.

He must have been shit at hiding his jealousy because Davis laughed. "*Dude.* Relax. It's not like I'd go after her. Total conflict of interest. Besides, she's clearly into you."

"You think?" He was fully aware he'd crossed the line from needy to pathetic, but his ego could use the boost.

"I'm good at observing people. From where I stand, it's pretty obvious."

"Hey!" Emilia yelled at them. "Are you two goofballs going to stand around and stare at me, or are you coming in?"

"Sorry, Em." TJ's face was now a flaming inferno. To hide his discomfort, he shucked off his shirt, ran over to the pool, and plunged in. Seconds later, he popped out, shivering. The water was *not* heated at all. "Holy fuck! That was not what I expected."

Emilia stood at the side, laughing. "You could have tested it first, but you had to be a big showoff." She eased herself in using the pool stairs, gasping as the water hit her bare stomach.

At the sight of her nipples tightening under her bikini top, TJ looked away. Maybe the cold water was a blessing in disguise. Less chance of a hard-on.

Davis jumped in next to him, and Cesca joined them ten minutes later. Like Emilia, she was wearing a bikini that showed off her curves. This time, Davis was the one doing the ogling, which made TJ feel marginally less pathetic.

Once he got used to the chill, the cool water was deliciously refreshing. He swam a few laps, then floated on his back, looking up at the full moon. He couldn't believe he was getting paid to do this. When Emilia swam toward him, he flipped over and dog-paddled next to her.

"Is this the best gig or what?" he said.

"It's awesome. Dinner was unbelievable. Five courses? Three kinds of dessert? That's the way to do Italy. And this pool is a sweet slice of heaven." She gestured to Davis and Cesca, who were talking at the other end. "Think something's brewing there?"

"Maybe. Seeing as how he's not a part of her tour, there wouldn't be a conflict of interest if he hooked up with her. Not like with you."

She frowned. "With me? What makes you think there's anything between me and Davis?"

Unnerved by the force of her glare, he stumbled over his words. "I...um...I didn't say that. But he caught me staring at you. Then he agreed you look fantastic in a bikini and..." His face had heated to such a degree that he wanted to duck underwater to cool down. "Sorry if we were objectifying you, but we're guys, and guys can be idiots. Anyway...I guess my jealousy came across, so he told me he wasn't into you. Not because he finds you unattractive." *Fuck*, he was messing this up so badly. "But because of the conflict-of-interest thing. And, um...I'm sorry. I'll stop now."

He dove underwater, which only worsened the situation because he got an eyeful of Emilia's figure—her full breasts, her flat expanse of bare stomach, and her tanned thighs. When he emerged, gasping for breath, she hadn't moved.

She stared him down, arms crossed. "Back up. Somewhere in that bout of verbal diarrhea, you admitted you were jealous of me and Davis. Did I get that right?"

"Um...yes. Sorry. I won't do it again."

A slow smile crept across her face. "Just wanted to check. Even if it wasn't a conflict of interest, I'm not into Davis. He's not my type."

"What is your type?" The neediness in his voice was cringe-worthy. Maybe he should stay underwater for the next hour to save himself from any future humiliation.

She laughed. "Well...lately, I've been into nerdy, know-it-all archaeologists who can't stop staring at me."

He swallowed but didn't look away. She'd all but admitted she was into him. That he wasn't just projecting his own desire. When her smile widened, he longed to reach out and touch her. If Davis and Cesca hadn't been at the other end of the pool, he would have kissed her, regardless of the rules.

He wasn't just jealous. He was a fucking goner.

CHAPTER NINETEEN

Emilia sat up in bed and flung off the covers. Over the past hour, she'd been trying to fall asleep and failing miserably. Bad enough that she'd spent the entire day battling exhaustion due to the previous night's antics in the pool. She couldn't make that mistake again, not when she had to wake up early tomorrow. In anticipation of their three-hour bus ride to Bari, she needed to have everyone checked out of the hotel and ready to go by eight. She'd gone up to bed at ten, hoping to get a decent night's sleep, only to lie awake in torment.

When she'd agreed to do this tour, she'd thought the biggest issue would be the constant socialization. The need to be "on" for ten days straight. The possibility that she might have to let people in instead of holding them at arm's length. But the tour wasn't the issue keeping her up tonight. The issue was TJ.

When they'd gone swimming, she'd caught him looking. The old Emilia would have berated him for objectifying her. Instead, she'd enjoyed every minute of it. He'd looked at her with such transparent desire that she'd wanted to do more than just banter with him. If they'd been alone in the pool, she might have acted on her feelings. Pulled him closer, kissed him passionately, and delighted in the sensation of his bare skin pressed against hers. She was certain he'd felt the same way.

But even if they weren't bound by the company's rules, hooking up with him was a terrible idea.

Wasn't it?

Or was it just what she needed to revive the old Emilia? The woman who'd had no qualms about expressing her sexuality. Who'd hooked up on digs for the sheer adrenaline rush of sneaky sex with someone she barely knew. Who'd never been consumed with regret or "what-ifs." But after her painful experience with Vince, she wasn't sure she could trust her own judgment.

Rather than spend another minute stewing in her room, she put on her flip-flops, grabbed her key card and phone, and headed outside. Tonight, they were staying near Paestum, at a luxury resort on the waterfront. She ambled down the boardwalk leading to the beach, inhaling the briny scent of the ocean. Above her, the night sky was clear, speckled with stars and a near-full moon. She took off her flip-flops and walked through the water, letting the waves lap at her ankles.

She needed to sort out her feelings for TJ, but she couldn't do it on her own. She texted her friend Dusty, hoping she'd be available to talk. Over the course of the tour, they'd messaged each other off and on but had yet to make time for a phone call. And this was the kind of issue that couldn't be resolved with a few texts.

To her relief, Dusty replied to her request with a thumbs-up. Seconds later, Emilia's phone buzzed with a call.

"Hey, Dusty," she said.

"Em! How goes the tour? Are you still on the Amalfi Coast?"

"Nope. We're in Paestum. About an hour and a half south of Sorrento, right on the Tyrrhenian Sea."

"Did you go to the ruins there? I've never been, but Stuart said they're worth visiting."

"Yeah, the site was fabulous. Some of the best-preserved

Greek temples in the world, plus a great archaeological museum. But honestly? My favorite part of the day was our lunch at Campania Bufa, where they make buffalo mozzarella. We had a tasting with five different kinds of cheese."

"Fresh mozzarella?" Dusty whined. "I'm so jealous. The only cheese in our fridge is a block of stale cheddar. Stuart left for a three-day seminar, and I'm fending for myself."

"You *could* learn to cook, you know."

"Why bother when Stuart is so good at it? His pasta is to die for. Well, obviously not as incredible as the stuff in Italy, but he's a masterful chef."

Emilia plopped down on the sand and brushed off her feet. After putting her flip-flops on, she started walking back to the hotel. While she could happily spend hours chatting with Dusty about random shit, she needed to address the TJ situation.

Fortunately, Dusty brought it up first. "How's it going with TJ? Have you been arguing nonstop?"

"Actually, he's been great. Super helpful, and patient with the guests, and..."

Dusty laughed. Not just any laugh, but a maniacal cackle worthy of an evil villain plotting to take over the world. "I *knew* it. Stuart owes me fifty bucks."

"What?"

"You and TJ. I bet Stuart this tour could go one of two ways—you'd hate each other forever, or you'd end up fucking. Guess who picked door number two?"

Emilia rubbed her forehead. "We're not fucking. Even if we wanted to, it's—"

"Against the rules. I *know*. You already told me about them. They're in that huge-ass binder you carry around everywhere. But you want him, right?"

She did. For the first time since Vince had shredded her heart to ribbons, she was so consumed with longing she could barely focus. "Yeah, but..."

"But what? Once the tour ends, you've still got two months left at Pompeii. What's to stop you from spending every weekend at a cheap hotel screwing your brains out?"

"You're such a romantic," Emilia muttered.

"Well, yeah, because this is just about sex. Clearly, you're ready to get back on the horse, but it's not anything more than that." Dusty's voice trailed off. "Is it?"

Emilia stared at the phone, unable to answer. For the past two years, her sex life had been as dry as a California desert. After the way Vince had hurt her, she'd closed herself off to all sexual and romantic relationships. Instead, she'd focused on writing her dissertation, applying for jobs, and working every side hustle available. From the sound of it, TJ had been operating the same way. Now, they were stuck together on a ten-day tour, both ready to let off a little steam. Of course it was just about sex.

Right?

"Em? Did I lose you?" Dusty asked. "It's okay if you want more than sex. That's what happened with me and Stuart at Troy. We fell in love, and look how well it turned out."

But Dusty hadn't been through the same emotional turmoil. She'd always known Stuart was the one she wanted. Hell, she'd been in love with him for most of her adult life. Emilia hadn't been so lucky. She'd trusted someone and allowed herself to imagine a future with him, only to get her heart broken. Did she really want to take that risk again? Her life was uncertain enough as it was.

"I don't think love is in the cards for me," she said.

"Really? I'm not going to push you, but I think you owe yourself more than that. In the meantime, why not have a little fun? Smoking-hot, no-strings sex with TJ until you leave Italy. Like I said before, what's stopping you?"

What *was* stopping her? Why was she assuming every guy would treat her the way Vince had?

Even if she and TJ couldn't have sex yet, she could let him

know she was interested. And once the tour ended, she could act on it.

~

AFTER ANOTHER HALF HOUR OF CHATTING WITH DUSTY, EMILIA'S fatigue kicked in. She went back into the hotel, fully intending to go up to bed, but stopped when she reached the lobby. To the right of the check-in desk was a sleek lounge with a mid-century modern vibe, containing stylish armchairs in muted reds and yellows, retro light fixtures, and a baby grand piano. Clustered around it was a group of people singing along to Billy Joel's "Piano Man." Among them were the Mangolds and a few others from the Buon Viaggio group.

Earlier that day, she'd noticed a sign beside the piano advertising a lounge singer who made appearances on Fridays and Saturdays. This couldn't be him, not on a Monday at midnight. One of the hotel guests must have gotten the urge to play. She crept closer, not wanting to interrupt, only to come to an abrupt stop. Seated at the piano was TJ.

What the hell? He'd never mentioned he played piano. Not only that, but he wasn't using sheet music or reading from an app on his phone.

She stood there listening as the hotel guests sang along. Given that most of them were over sixty, she wasn't surprised they knew the words to a song from the 1970s. But why was TJ so familiar with it? For that matter, why had he made her a playlist of his favorite Pink Floyd albums? For a twenty-eight-year-old, he had the musical tastes of someone twice his age.

After he was done, he launched into Elton John's "Rocket Man." Another '70s classic. Everyone knew it, even her. She inched a little closer. Even if this music wasn't her jam, TJ's enthusiasm was hard to resist.

The moment he saw her, his expression changed, like a kid

who'd been busted by a teacher. But he kept going until he finished the song. With a flourish, he stood and gave a sweeping bow, beaming when the hotel guests rewarded him with a hearty round of applause.

"That's it for tonight, folks," he said. "I've got an early wake-up call tomorrow, so I should get to bed. Buona notte!"

After a few good-natured grumbles, the group filtered out, leaving Emilia alone with TJ. He sat back down on the piano bench but turned so he was facing her.

She crossed her arms, irked that he'd hidden this talent from her. "You never told me you played piano."

"You never asked." He smirked. "I contain multitudes, Em."

Normally, she would have teased him about his smug attitude, but she was too curious to revert to their usual banter. "When did you learn to play?"

"I started taking lessons when I was six. My dad was a huge music buff. Way back in college, he played keyboard in a band."

"He was in a band? I thought he was an ancient history nerd, like you."

TJ gave her a crooked smile. "He was, but he also loved music. The band wasn't anything big—just a group of guys who played classic rock covers at parties and festivals. Because of him, I took piano for five years." He patted the bench. "Come sit for a sec."

If she was being smart, she'd go back upstairs. Even if she'd finally admitted to herself that she wanted him, she couldn't give in to temptation until their tour ended. But now that she'd seen this side of TJ, she wanted to know more.

She sat beside him on the bench. "How'd you end up serenading the guests?"

He shrugged. "Couldn't sleep. Had a lot on my mind, I guess."

Like me? Not that she'd say it, but she wondered if he was plagued by the same feelings she was. A heavy dose of pining mixed with doubt, frustration, and straight-up lust.

"I remembered seeing the piano earlier, so I came down and

asked the front desk clerk if I could play," he said. "He told me to go for it. Some of our group were at the hotel bar and when they heard me, they came over, and it turned into a sing-along."

TJ was just the type to draw in a crowd while playing hits from the 1970s. She tilted her head to the side. "You said you stopped when you were eleven?" She didn't need to ask why. He was eleven when his dad died. "How is it you're still so good?"

"When I was in college, I used to stress out over grades and assignments and…everything. Music helped me relax. I bought a used keyboard and played whenever I needed a study break."

"Do you only know stuff from the '70s? You're like the world's youngest boomer."

His eyes gleamed with amusement. "Don't knock it. That music was my dad's go-to, so it's like my comfort food." He gave her a gentle nudge. "Come on, I know you liked that Pink Floyd playlist."

"Yeah, it's not so bad." She often listened to it late at night before drifting off to sleep. Whenever "Wish You Were Here" came up in the queue, she thought of TJ.

"After my dad died, I didn't feel like taking piano anymore," TJ said. "Then, when my mom remarried two years later, Al—that's my stepdad—didn't encourage it. Bad enough that he'd ended up with a stepson who'd never played a sport in his life."

"No sports? Not even one?" Though she wouldn't call herself sporty, she'd played soccer since the fifth grade. Her dad had always praised her as if she were the world's best midfielder. Even with the demands of running his own landscaping business, he'd rarely missed a game.

"Nope. My real dad wasn't into sports," TJ said. "He was the type who'd rather visit a museum than go to a ball game. Then Al came along. He's in sports management. My two stepbrothers— Randy and Jake—are super athletic. They both played football and baseball all through high school."

Emilia's heart ached for nerdy thirteen-year-old TJ, feeling out of place in a brand-new family whose passions were nothing like his. "That sounds rough. Did your stepbrothers live with you or with their mom?"

"Their mom died when they were little. Al met *my* mom at a support group for single parents. A year later, we turned into this big, blended, Brady Bunch–style family."

She shuddered, trying to imagine how she would have reacted if she'd had to adjust to a stepmom and a couple of stepsisters. It could have been a full-on Cinderella story. "Were your stepbrothers mean to you?"

"They weren't that bad. Mostly, they just ignored me. Which kind of sucked since you know how much I love being the center of attention."

Maybe he could joke about it now, but it must have been hard for him. Not just missing his dad but having to adapt to a completely different family dynamic.

"Half the time, I still don't feel like I fit in," TJ said. "My stepbrothers don't understand why I spent six years in grad school studying archaeology instead of taking something practical like business or computer science. But growing up with them had one advantage. You know how I always brag about being hard-core?"

For that, she gave him an eye roll. "You might have mentioned it once or twice."

"That's because of my stepbrothers. Randy and Jake belonged to an extreme wilderness group. They used to do these five-day expeditions into the woods with minimal gear just so they could boast about it. Al suggested I go with them, which scared the hell out of me."

"You? The guy who thrives on harsh conditions? You once bragged about battling scorpions in the desert heat." At the time, they'd been going toe-to-toe over who'd dug in the most rugged conditions, with her pitting her experiences in the Yucatán jungle against his in the Jordanian desert.

"That's me now. Not sixteen-year-old me. Before I went on the trip, I researched the shit out of it. No lie, I thought I was going to die out there, but when I was done, I was so proud of myself. Al was shocked as hell."

"Is this how the hard-core version of TJ was born?"

"Something like that. For years, I've felt like I had a lot to prove. Not just intellectually, but in the field, too." He traced his fingers along the edge of the piano bench. "But there are times when I've been a total asshole about it."

Lots of archaeologists were like that, but his behavior seemed less obnoxious now that she'd learned the story behind it. "Maybe you go a little too hard sometimes, but..." She couldn't believe she was saying this. "I'm the same way."

"It's just you and your dad, right?" TJ asked. "I remember you mentioning it at Troy."

She nodded. "My mom died in a car accident when I was twelve. As you can imagine, it was pretty rough. Combine puberty with devastating grief, and you get one messed-up kid. I'm from a big Mexican American family, so I never felt alone or unloved, but it still sucked. The thing is—my dad's always been really encouraging, and he totally supported my decision to go to grad school, but..."

TJ placed his hand over hers. "But you're afraid to let him down?"

She looked away, too self-conscious to meet his eyes. "Exactly. He has such high hopes for me. My mom was a teacher, so he was thrilled when I told him I wanted to get my PhD and become a professor. No matter how many times I've explained that a teaching job isn't a sure thing, he believes I can make it happen out of sheer will."

"Do you want to be a professor?"

Did she? While she'd enjoyed being a TA in grad school, she hadn't embraced it the way her friends Stuart and Olivia had. Her personality wasn't anything like her mom's, either. As a teacher,

her mom had been sunny and outgoing—the kind who greeted her third-grade classroom with exuberance each morning. Even if this tour had forced Emilia to be more sociable, she still wasn't much of a "people person."

"I don't know," she said. "Last year was brutal. Applying for all those jobs in academia, going through the interviews, and getting my hopes up, only to be told, 'Thanks, but no thanks.' The worst part is having to start all over again in a couple of months."

"You can do it. You're one of the smartest, most competitive people I know."

While she appreciated the compliment, the reality still sucked. "Thanks, but I get so tired of hustling. I've been busting my ass since high school. Sometimes I want a job where I could just wake up, go to work, and not worry about being the best in my field."

"I get it. If I think too hard about it, I can't sleep. Looking for jobs last winter was the worst."

"Another thing?" She swallowed, suddenly worried she was saying too much. "I know this is going to sound weak, but...I don't want to compete with you anymore."

"No?" He tightened his grip on her hand.

"Not if we end up hating each other again."

"It's not weak. I feel the same way."

She forced herself to meet his eyes. And then she was lost because the vulnerability she saw matched her own. She wanted to kiss him. Not an impetuous, drunken kiss like in Philly, but a totally sober, passionate kiss that showed him exactly how she felt.

Even if the tour only had three days left, she was done waiting. Taking a deep breath, she flashed him a sultry smile. "Want to come up to my room?"

CHAPTER TWENTY

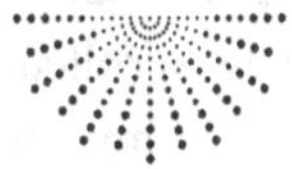

TJ stared at Emilia, too stunned to move.

Had she just propositioned him? Or had he been transported into one of his Emilia-centric dreams?

Either way, he wasn't going to waste this opportunity. After last night's swim, he'd spent hours thinking about her. Today, while leading the group around the ancient site of Paestum, he'd completely lost his train of thought. Even at this afternoon's cheese tasting, he'd barely been able to focus on the delicious samples of mozzarella.

But going up to her room meant breaking the rules. If anyone caught them, they could lose their jobs as tour guides.

Screw it. He craved her so much it was like a physical ache. One night couldn't hurt, could it? Besides, who was going to squeal on them? By now, all the guests had gone up to bed.

"Well?" Emilia asked. "Don't leave me hanging."

While her tone carried a teasing lilt, the hitch in her breath revealed her insecurity. She'd put herself out there, hoping he'd reciprocate. No way was he turning her down.

He squeezed her hand. "Yes. I'd love to. I was just trying to figure out our game plan. Should we go up separately? Maybe ten minutes apart? Before I stop by your room, I can check the hallway to make sure no one's around. I could even bring the binder to make my visit look legit."

She laughed. "The binder's in my room, remember? I think we'll be fine, but I'll go on ahead." She eased off the piano bench and headed toward the elevator.

He wanted to rush after her but forced himself to wait. Ten minutes. Maybe twelve. He scrolled through his phone and checked his emails. After *fifteen* minutes, he took the elevator up to his room on the seventh floor. He let himself in and changed into a t-shirt and sweats, but as he went into the bathroom to brush his teeth, he was beset by a fresh wave of anxiety.

What about condoms? Though he hadn't been with anyone for over a year, he always carried some with him. Would bringing them make him look too presumptuous? Emilia hadn't said they'd be having sex. All she'd done was invite him to her room.

Just bring them, damn it.

Once he was ready, he grabbed his key card and headed into the hallway. Heart pounding, he cast his gaze down the empty corridor. Not a soul in sight. He crept to Emilia's room but hesitated before knocking on her door.

It was one thing to go from being rivals to friends. But if they crossed the line and went from friends to lovers, they'd be taking a bigger step. A step that might not *mean* anything to Emilia except an impulsive quickie. It might be like that night in Philly when all she'd wanted was a physical connection.

But…she wasn't drunk this time, and they weren't enemies. For as much as they teased each other, they'd actually become friends.

Was it too much to hope that she'd be up for more than just a one-night stand?

Stop overthinking it, you idiot.

At this point, he was going to take whatever she offered.

When he knocked on her door, she opened it immediately,

like she'd been standing on the other side, waiting for him to show up. Other than the faint glow of the lamp on her nightstand, the room was dark. He came in and closed the door behind him.

For a minute, he could only stare, too overwhelmed to take another step. She'd freed her hair from its confining braid, and it fell past her shoulders in loose waves. Though she wasn't naked, her boy shorts and skimpy pink tank top left little to the imagination. Under the thin fabric, her nipples were clearly visible.

She inched closer. "TJ? Everything okay?"

"Just to be clear—you're not pranking me, are you?"

"Nope." She grinned. "This is real."

"What about the rules?" He was fully prepared to pretend they didn't exist, but only if she was on board.

She sashayed over to the binder, which lay on the floor beside the nightstand, and kicked it underneath the bed. "Out of sight, out of mind. Right? But we have to be discreet. No boasting about your amazing night to *anyone*."

"That's...ah...one area where I'm not boastful." Not because he lacked experience but out of respect for his partners.

"Good." Her mouth curved up in a sly smile. She crooked her finger, gesturing for him to join her beside the bed.

He thought he'd start slowly. A few gentle kisses to warm her up. But she tugged on his shirt, pulled him toward her, and kissed him hard. Not a shy, tentative peck, but a demanding kiss that left him breathless. When she tangled her tongue against his, he went from zero to sixty, the desire shooting straight to his groin. He cupped her ass, bringing her flush against him until there wasn't an inch of space between them. She placed her arms around his neck and ground into him, kissing him all the while. He stumbled backward and gripped the bedpost to stop from falling over.

She pulled away, breathing heavily, her eyes dilated with

hunger. "Last night in the pool, I wanted you so badly."

"I've been dreaming about you nonstop. I couldn't even focus on today's cheese tasting."

She bit her lip in a gesture that was both sexy *and* adorable. "Are you implying I'm more enticing than cheese? You know I'm from Wisconsin. That's a huge compliment."

"That wasn't what I was thinking of tasting this afternoon."

Her eyes lit up. "You're going to have to make good on that, Dr. Mayer."

"Oh, I intend to, Dr. Flores."

She glanced down at the bulge in his sweats, then flashed him a saucy grin. Turning toward the bed, she yanked off the comforter and blankets and tossed them on the floor, leaving only a top sheet and a pile of pillows. She climbed onto the bed and lay on her back, stretching out in a seductive pose. "Come and get me."

He set his glasses on the nightstand and positioned himself above her. She gazed up at him, her desire so evident that his last shred of doubt vanished. This wasn't anything like Philly. This wasn't a drunken mistake. She *wanted* him.

Lowering the straps of her tank top, he feasted on the sight of her full breasts. He brushed his fingers over her light brown nipples, touching them softly at first, then tweaking them until she gasped. With exquisite tenderness, he ran his tongue over one of the taut buds. He caught the faint scent of orange blossoms on her skin, mixed with a trace of coconut sunscreen.

She tugged on his hair. "Harder, TJ. Please."

When had she ever begged him to do *anything*? He sucked on one nipple, then the other, until she was writhing beneath him. Her gasps fueled his lust, making him desperate to bury himself deep inside her, but he didn't want to rush this. He lifted the tank top over her head and flung it to the side. Even in the dim light of the lamp, her smile was luminous. In all the time he'd known her, he'd never seen her look this happy.

When she tugged on his shirt, he took it off and threw it across the room. She ran her hands along his bare chest and pulled him closer until they were pressed together, skin to skin, igniting the heat between them. But when she reached beneath the waistband of his sweats, he grabbed her wrist.

"No?" she said.

"Not yet. If you do that, I'm going to come."

"What are you—fifteen?" she teased.

"I'm serious. Pent-up lust will do that to a guy." He was so wound up that it wouldn't take much to push him over the edge.

She withdrew her hand, but her eyes gleamed with mischief. "What if I want you to come? What if I want to make you groan until your voice goes hoarse?"

Was it possible to come just from listening to someone? Because, fuck, he was halfway there. "I'd be okay with that, but it wouldn't be fair to you."

"I'll get my turn. Right?"

"Of course." How many times in the last week had he fantasized about spreading her legs and tasting her until she cried out in ecstasy?

"Then let me go first. Got it?" She pushed on his shoulders. "I want you on your back."

She didn't have to ask twice. He lay on the bed, nestling his head in the mound of pillows. She propped herself up until she was looking down at him and gave him a cheeky smile. "Try not to be *too* loud, Dr. Mayer. No matter how good it feels, we can't have the neighbors banging on the walls."

He chuckled. "I'll try to control myself."

She trailed her lips along his bare chest, pausing to suck on his nipples. As the pleasure built up inside of him, he fisted the sheet, trying his hardest to keep quiet. But when she lowered the waistband of his sweats and ran her tongue along the tip of his dick, he let out a harsh groan. "Yes, Em. Please. Like that."

She took her time teasing him with her tongue, so much that

when she finally took him into her mouth, he was dangerously close to exploding. He ran his hand along her silken hair and gripped it tightly. The sensations were a million times better than any of his dreams.

Though, if this *was* a dream? Then he wanted to sleep for eternity. As she took him deeper, he let out another groan.

A sharp knock came at the door, jolting him out of his blissful state.

Emilia pulled away from him and fell back onto the bed. "What the fuck?"

He froze, his body as stiff as an ice sculpture. Had his guttural moans roused the occupants of the room next door? Fate couldn't possibly be this cruel.

When the knocking started again, Emilia called out. "Yes? Who's there?"

"Irene Mangold. It's an emergency. Can I come in?"

An emergency. TJ's hard-on vanished as his mind raced through worst-case scenarios. Yesterday, Giles Mangold had complained of stomach pains. What if his appendix had burst? Or he'd contracted dysentery? What the hell were they supposed to do?

Emilia sprang off the bed, grabbed her tank top, and put it back on. She paused for a moment, as if catching her breath, then called out. "I'll be right there, Mrs. Mangold. Let me grab my robe."

TJ pulled his sweats back over his hips, rolled off the bed, and scooped up his shirt from the floor. He lowered his voice, not wanting Mrs. Mangold to hear him. "I can hide in the bathroom. That way, she won't see me when you open the door."

"Good plan. Wait." She grabbed his arm. "Once I go out there to deal with this emergency or...whatever, you should probably leave. I don't want you to, but..."

He didn't want to, either, and not just because he'd come so close to fulfilling one of his top five fantasies. He'd wanted to make love to Emilia. To kiss her and touch her and taste her until she whimpered with pleasure. To make her cry out his name and cling to him in the darkness. But this wasn't just a close call. It was a sign from the universe, warning them they'd come perilously close to screwing up *everything*.

He locked eyes with her. "I get it. We can't risk getting caught. I'll wait a few minutes, then sneak back to my room. Sorry it ended like this."

"Me, too." She gave him a rueful smile. "I'll make it up to you, I promise."

"I know. Call me if you need help with the Mangolds. If it's a serious emergency, you shouldn't have to deal with it on your own."

"Thanks. We'll get another chance, right?"

"Absolutely. The tour ends in three days."

In the grand scheme of things, three days wasn't that long. And if anyone was worth the wait, it was Emilia.

Once TJ was safely hidden in the bathroom, Emilia put on her robe. Tucking her phone into the pocket, she opened the door and forced herself to smile. Her face still burned like a thousand-watt bulb, and her hair was a tangled mess, but at least the robe covered up her near-nakedness and her perky nipples.

"Sorry to keep you waiting," she said to Mrs. Mangold. "I was asleep when you knocked. It took me a minute to get my bearings."

"You look warm. Feverish. Are you all right?"

"I'm fine. Shouldn't we hurry? Do you need me to call an ambulance? If I ask the front desk to do it, they might get a faster response."

"Oh, dear, I frightened you, didn't I?" Mrs. Mangold chuckled.

"No wonder you look so frazzled. It's a plumbing emergency, not a medical one."

Emilia released a tight breath. *Thank the goddess.* Now she wouldn't have to spend the night in the ER with the Mangolds. "Did you call housekeeping to check on the plumbing? I'm not sure if they have a maintenance person available at this hour, but they could probably take care of it."

"No. I'd rather not go down to the lobby. It would be too humiliating. All we need is a plunger."

"A plunger?" Emilia grimaced. She almost didn't want to know.

"Yes, poor Giles has been stopped up since Naples. Too much rich food and not enough fiber. That's why he had a stomachache yesterday. This morning, I convinced him to take a laxative."

No need for further explanation. "So…he clogged the toilet?"

"Exactly. Can you see why I don't wish to share this issue with the hotel staff? I'd like you to go down to the lobby and request a plunger, then you can take care of it yourself."

Fate, you sneaky bitch. One minute, Emilia was in bed with TJ, preparing to blow his mind. The next, she was about to plunge a stopped-up toilet.

"I hope you're able to deal with it," Mrs. Mangold said. "I tried TJ's room first, but he didn't answer."

"He can be a sound sleeper. That's probably why he didn't hear you." Even as Emilia offered the excuse, she cursed him inwardly for escaping this crappy job.

You owe me, buddy. Next time she got him alone, he'd have to service *her* needs first.

Because there would definitely be a next time. Not on the tour, that was for certain. After such a near miss, they couldn't risk another late-night rendezvous. But after the tour ended, they'd get one more night in Rome. That was when she'd make her move.

CHAPTER TWENTY-ONE

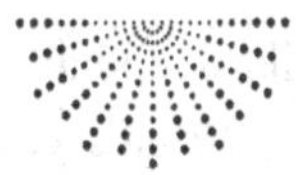

Emilia sat hunched over her coffee cup, trying to keep her eyes open. When her phone alarm had gone off this morning, she'd been tempted to hurl it against the wall. Thanks to the Mangolds' plumbing emergency, she hadn't returned to her room until almost one. Then she'd been up another hour, tormented with regret that she'd sent TJ away. He'd been equally regretful, sending her a series of apologetic texts after he'd learned the true nature of the Mangolds' emergency.

Unfortunately, sleeping in wasn't an option. With a big travel day ahead of them, she needed to have everyone on the bus by eight. First, they were driving from Paestum to Matera, a UNESCO World Heritage site known as one of the oldest cities in Italy. After walking through Matera, they'd have lunch there, then drive to the Castel del Monte for a tour and a wine tasting. Their last stop was Bari, where they'd be spending the night.

Davis sat across from Emilia at the breakfast buffet. Like her, he was rocking a messy bed head and sporting serious bags under his eyes. "I am totally regretting my life choices this morning," he muttered.

She poked at her piece of plum cake. "I thought you went to bed early last night."

"I did, but *someone*—not naming any names—tried to convince me the second *John Wick* movie was the best one in the franchise. I may have started watching the series from the beginning."

She gave him a sympathetic groan. "Please tell me you didn't watch all of them."

"Only the first two. I fell asleep halfway through the third." He raised his eyebrows at her. "What's your excuse? Not gonna lie, you look like crap."

The thought of what she'd done—or almost done—with TJ coaxed a smile out of her. As her cheeks heated, she lowered her eyes. "I'll never tell."

"Did something happen with you and TJ? You have to fill me in." He flipped his phone over. "Off the record, I promise."

"Not without more coffee. Wanna grab me a refill?"

"Miss Flores. Mr. McGowan. Buongiorno." Luca stood over them, having seemingly materialized out of nowhere.

Startled, Emilia knocked over her coffee cup, spilling the dregs onto the table. Grabbing a napkin, she mopped up the mess. Why was it that Luca's appearance always sent her into panic mode?

"Um…hi," she said. "I mean, buongiorno. How are you?"

Luca sat down beside her. "Better than you, apparently. It looks as though the two of you didn't get enough sleep."

Fuck. She couldn't deal with him now, not when she was barely conscious enough to function. Before she could defend herself, Davis chuckled. "I definitely didn't get my full eight hours. I blame Emilia."

Dude. Don't even joke about it.

"What were you two up to?" Luca asked.

"Nothing," Emilia snapped. "Davis insisted on binge-watching the *John Wick* movies last night. *Alone.*" She slid her cup toward Davis. "Can you grab me more coffee?"

"You sure?" His gaze moved between her and Luca, as though he wasn't comfortable leaving her alone with him.

"Yes, please." Once he left, she forced herself to meet Luca's eyes. The scent of his sandalwood aftershave was so strong it almost turned her stomach. "I was up late dealing with a middle-of-the-night emergency. The Mangolds had a plumbing crisis."

"And they called on *you*? I didn't realize being a tour guide meant you'd be serving as a handyman."

A handyperson, you sexist asshole. "Being a tour guide means keeping the clients happy."

"Within reason. Do I need to remind you of the rules?" He pointed to Davis, who was refilling her cup at the coffee station. "Despite my warning, you and Mr. McGowan seem to have grown closer. At Grand Hotel La Sonrisa, the two of you indulged in a late-night swim at the hotel pool, did you not?"

What the hell? Had he been spying on her? "Yes, but—"

"There are no 'buts' where the rules are concerned. A private tryst in the pool is highly inappropriate."

"If you'd let me finish? Davis and I weren't alone. TJ was with us, along with Cesca from Roman Pathways Tours."

"Nonetheless, it's not an ideal situation, putting yourself in temptation's path. I'll be watching you for the rest of the tour. Any impropriety and I'll notify my uncle Angelo."

I'll bet you will, you prick. The phrase "go fuck yourself" was on the tip of her tongue, but she forced herself to exercise restraint. "I understand, but as I said before, I wouldn't dream of breaking the rules. Not with anyone."

Except TJ, until fate had given her a swift kick in the ass.

Luca stood up. "Good to hear. I'd hate to see you lose your job over a foolish indiscretion."

By the time she boarded the bus, she couldn't wait to get the hell out of Paestum. She plopped down next to TJ in the front row and spoke to him in a whisper. "This morning is starting out rough. I'm functioning on four hours of sleep, and Luca was being a dick at breakfast. Can you do the spiel?"

"Sure. What was Luca's problem?"

She scrubbed her hands over her face, wanting to erase the memory of his nasty insinuations. "Nothing serious. Just some bullshit about me and Davis. He implied our swim the other night was a secret tryst, but I was like, 'Hello, there were *four* of us in the pool.' Now he probably thinks we had an orgy."

"What a jerk. If you want, I can also do the tour when we get to Matera."

She wished she could thank him with a kiss, but the best she could offer was a faint smile. "Thanks. You're the best."

"No problem. And…ah…Em?" He spoke so softly she could barely hear him. "Even if you're tired…you don't regret last night, do you?"

He sounded so vulnerable that her heart ached. She didn't want him to think—not even for a minute—that she was upset about anything they'd done. "Not at all. My only regret is not finishing what we started."

"I was hoping we could make up for it in Rome, after the guests leave. Would that be okay?"

"It would be perfect. In fact, I'm going to dream about it right now."

As the bus pulled away from the hotel, she leaned back in her seat and closed her eyes. Despite the untimely interruption from the Mangolds, she and TJ had gotten off to a promising start. For two years, she'd kept her body locked up tight, afraid that if she let someone in, he'd manipulate her the way Vince had. But with TJ, there was no power imbalance, no sense that he'd try to bend her to his will.

The thought of spending an entire night with him, making passionate love—or, as Dusty would put it, "fucking like bunnies"— filled her with a surge of desire. Waiting three more days was going to be a challenge.

"Em? Before you drift off—do you have the binder?" TJ said.

The binder.

She jolted up in her seat. Heart thumping, she grabbed her backpack from the floor. It was far too light. "*Shit.* I left it in my hotel room."

"Are you sure? Maybe you stuck it in your suitcase?"

"No. Last night, I kicked it under the bed. Remember? Then I had to deal with the Mangolds. This morning, I was so tired I totally forgot about it." She recalled stuffing clothes in her suitcase, sweeping through the bathroom to gather up her toiletries, and rushing out the door. She hadn't thought to check under the bed. "What are we going to do?"

"We'll be okay without it. We have the app, plus I photographed a lot of the pages when we were in Rome."

"True, but..." She cringed, imagining Angelo's reaction when she told him what she'd done. "It also had a bunch of maps and restaurant brochures."

"Then we'll go back. Nico's only been driving for ten minutes." TJ leaned over to address him. "Can you drive us to the hotel? We forgot the binder."

"I'm the one who forgot it," Emilia said. "I'm so sorry."

Nico gave a low chuckle. "Happens at least once on every tour. No worries. I'll take you back."

Emilia shot TJ a grateful smile. "Thanks. I feel like such an idiot."

"Don't. It won't put us that far behind. No big deal."

For Emilia, it *was* a big deal. She'd been so careful on the tour, always sticking to the schedule, keeping the guests happy, and trying to ensure they didn't leave anything behind. Clearly, this was the universe's way of reminding her that she couldn't afford any distractions until the tour ended.

When they reached the hotel, she stood and addressed the group. "Hey, everyone. I need to apologize because I left the tour binder in my hotel room. That's why we came back. I'm gonna grab it now, and we can take off in a few minutes."

She didn't wait to hear their responses. If anyone had a complaint, TJ could deal with it. She bolted off the bus and sprinted for the entrance of the hotel. At the check-in desk, she gave the clerk her sweetest smile and explained her situation in flawless Italian. He called the head of housekeeping, who went to look for the binder. When the woman came down with it, Emilia was so relieved she almost hugged her. She thanked her profusely and ran back outside.

Nico leaned against the side of the bus, smoking. Beside him, Luca stood with his arms crossed. He glared at Emilia.

Ignoring him, she faced Nico with an appreciative smile. "Thanks for waiting. I hope no one was too annoyed."

"Eh, they're fine. You didn't take that long."

"It was still a serious misstep on your part," Luca said. "It's hard to believe you could forget something as important as the Buon Viaggio binder. You don't seem to be operating at full capacity this morning."

Heat prickled the back of her neck, making her feel uncomfortably warm. All she wanted to do was crash out on the bus, but instead, she was stuck defending a minor screwup. "Sorry, but I'm still tired after dealing with the Mangolds' emergency last night."

"Not because you were up late, watching movies with Davis?"

"No. If you don't believe me, then ask Irene Mangold yourself." Even as she said it, she worried that the older woman might not be the best witness. Odds were good she didn't want anyone else to know about the humiliating incident.

Rather than go talk to Mrs. Mangold, Luca stood there, his dark eyes drilling into Emilia's like he was hoping she'd crack under his scrutiny.

Nico stubbed out his cigarette. "Cut her a break. Mateo did the same thing on the last tour, except we'd been driving for a good half hour when he remembered. So far, Emilia's been doing a great job."

"She's been performing adequately," Luca said. "It's a shame my uncles couldn't find someone with more experience."

Nico stared him down. "Get back on the bus. We're leaving."

Maybe because Nico was bigger, burlier, and more intimidating than anyone else on the tour, Luca did as he said. When Emilia tried to follow him, her legs wouldn't move. She was trembling all over, her stomach twisting in knots. Not only due to sheer exhaustion, but also because of the sickening nature of Luca's comments.

Nico placed his hand on her shoulder. "Don't let Luca get to you. He's got a giant stick up his ass. I meant what I said earlier. For someone who's never led an extended tour through Italy, you're doing an excellent job. You and TJ have been a pleasure to work with."

"Thanks." Clutching the binder under one arm, she followed him onto the bus. Once he started it up, she addressed the group again. This was her mistake, and she wanted to own up to it right away. "Sorry for the delay, but this binder is like the trip bible." She held it up. "Without it, TJ and I would have a lot harder time leading this tour."

TJ stood up beside her and chimed in. "I don't know, Em. I'm a whiz at memorization. I have most of that stuff down cold."

She was grateful he'd resorted to his usual shtick—bantering with her as though they were a comedic team. Pushing aside her jitters, she grinned at him. "Normally, I'd accuse you of bragging, but you *do* have a great memory. Almost as good as mine." She directed her attention to the group. "How many of you caught TJ's one-man show on the piano last night?" When a dozen hands went up, she added, "He played all those songs from memory."

"Wait," Sylvie called out. "There was a piano concert? Why weren't we notified?"

TJ gave her a sheepish grin. "It wasn't like I planned it ahead of time. I couldn't sleep, so I came downstairs and asked if I could use the piano in the lobby. Most of my repertoire consists of classic rock tunes—stuff by Elton John, Billy Joel, the Eagles, and James Taylor."

"Any Harry Chapin?" Alice asked. "I love 'Cat's in the Cradle.' It always makes me cry."

TJ placed his hand over his heart. "It's one of my favorites. If our hotel in Bari doesn't have a piano, I could find a place to play in town. Then we could do a sing-along, just for fun. If you have any requests, write them down, and I'll collect them later."

"In the meantime, please relax and enjoy the drive," Emilia said. "Before we get to Matera, TJ will give you the full rundown on today's itinerary."

After she and TJ sat back down, she gave a sigh of relief. "Thanks for saving my ass. I think the group is so excited to attend an exclusive TJ Mayer performance that they don't care if I set us behind schedule." She handed him the binder. "Maybe you should hold on to it for now. Luca chewed me out for leaving it in my room."

He set it on his lap and lowered his voice. "Then he's an asshole. It was an honest mistake."

"Thanks." Though she was still shaky from her encounter with Luca, a few deep breaths eased the tightness in her shoulders. Beside her, TJ flipped to the section on Matera. She wished she had a better way to show her gratitude than a simple "thanks." A hug would be nice. A kiss would be even better. If luck was with her, she'd get to express her gratitude in just three days.

CHAPTER TWENTY-TWO

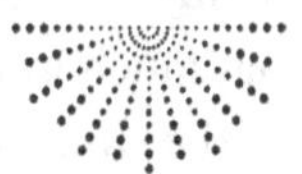

At noon, the Buon Viaggio bus climbed toward the city of Matera, located on a limestone plateau in a region of Italy known for its deep ravines and extended network of caves. Though TJ had seen photos of the town before, the view was more stunning in real life. Above him, the tangle of stone houses, in muted shades of beige and gray, appeared as though they'd been built one on top of the other.

Mixed in with the modern homes were ancient caves carved into the rock, some of which were thousands of years old. Most of the caves were no longer occupied, but a few still functioned as homes, while others had been converted into shops, hotels, and restaurants. The whole area had a biblical feel, reminding TJ of his visit to Israel seven years ago, when he'd worked at the site of Tel Dor.

He shook Emilia's shoulder gently. "Em? Wake up. We're almost there."

"Huh?" She rubbed her eyes. "How long have I been asleep?"

"About an hour, but you didn't miss anything. I gave the group a quick overview ten minutes ago."

She wiped her mouth with the back of her hand. "I wasn't drooling, was I?"

He grinned. "Yep. Like a bulldog. It might be a medical condition."

"Shut up. At most, it would have been a delicate trickle." She turned to peer out the window. "Check out that view."

"It's incredible." Since neither of them had been to Matera before, it made their visit that much more interesting.

Once the bus reached the top of the hill and everyone disembarked, TJ steered them toward a spot that offered a view of the ravine below. He gave them time to spread out and take a few photos before speaking.

"Matera is one of the oldest continuously occupied cities in the world and a contender for the oldest city in Italy," he said. "Over the centuries, hundreds of caves were carved into the limestone, and they served as the primary dwellings for people living in the area. Today, we're going to visit the Casa Grotta, a local history museum set inside a traditional cave house from the nineteenth century, complete with the original furnishings and household goods.

"We'll also visit the Park of the Rupestrian Churches. It contains over 150 cave churches, carved into the cliffs lining the Gravina River. Inside them, you'll see religious frescoes spanning nearly a thousand years of occupation. Fun fact—though the frescoes depict typical Christian iconography, some of the cave churches were used as places of pagan worship before the Christian monks took over."

TJ was glad he'd reviewed the section on Matera during the drive from Paestum. Emilia, on the other hand, had slept for most of the ride.

The nap must have improved her spirits because she raised her hand and waved it around like a kid clamoring for attention. "Dr. Mayer? May I interject with another fun fact?"

"Absolutely, Dr. Flores."

She addressed the group with a wide smile. "I don't know about the rest of you, but I'm a huge James Bond fan. Anyone else here share my love for 007?"

While using pop culture references was part of TJ's routine, he was glad she'd decided to chime in. The tour was always more fun when they worked as a team.

Davis spoke up. "I've seen all the movies, and I do mean *all*. Even the ones with Pierce Brosnan."

"Quite honestly, the franchise went downhill after Sean Connery left," Alice said. She clasped her hands together. "I had the biggest crush on him."

"I was always a Roger Moore fan," Sylvie said. "So suave and debonair."

Emilia chuckled. "Too true, though I find Daniel Craig hard to resist. If you caught him in *No Time to Die*, which came out in 2021, you would have seen Matera. Part of the movie was filmed here." She grinned at TJ. "Sorry for the interruption. You can carry on with the history lesson, professor."

"Thanks. Speaking of movies, *The Passion of the Christ*—Mel Gibson's epic recreation of the last days of Jesus' life—was also filmed here because Matera was so well suited to stand in for biblical-era Jerusalem."

With that, he led the group down a steep stairway, pausing at the bottom until everyone had caught up. Alice struggled with stairs, so he always made sure she had enough time to deal with them. The Casa Grotta was so confining that he split the group in half to avoid anyone feeling cramped. As he walked through it, he could hardly believe how well equipped it was, filled with tools, kitchen implements, a loom, and actual beds. There was even a penned-in area for the family donkey. Though the cave's cool air was a welcome relief from the hot sun, he found the space too claustrophobic for his liking. Give him a wide-open desert any day.

After the Casa Grotta, he led the group through the

Convicinio di Sant'Antonio, which consisted of four interlinked cave churches, and Santa Maria de Idris, an ancient church perched on a rocky outcrop and decorated with centuries-old frescoes. While most of the group barely gave the wall paintings a passing glance, Sylvie and Emilia lingered by them, even after everyone else had gone back outside.

Since people seemed more intent on taking photos than listening to him talk, TJ gave them a fifteen-minute break. The view was so stunning he wanted to make sure they took advantage. When Emilia came out and wandered over to one of the viewpoints, he joined her.

"You feeling any better?" he asked.

"Yeah. Thanks for letting me sleep on the bus. It helped a lot."

"No problem. What were you and Sylvie so interested in? Those frescoes were really faded."

"True, but they made me wish I could restore something with that much historical significance. Like the wall paintings we uncovered in Pompeii at the House of Venus. I hope Dr. Roberti considers me when he puts together the conservation team. I mentioned it when I first got hired on, but he's probably forgotten by now."

TJ remembered her talking about it earlier. "Then you need to remind him once we get back. No need to devote your entire career to studying seeds."

She gave him a cheeky smile. "Mock my seeds all you want, but I've learned a lot from them."

"I know, but you'll never convince me they're more exciting than Bronze Age weaponry."

In the past, his comment might have riled her up. Now, she just laughed and shook her head. "I don't need to convince you, not when I know the truth. Without plant life, humans would be doomed." She gave a little shrug. "Even so, I wouldn't mind getting to use my conservation training for a change."

To anyone else, her casual tone might suggest a mild level of interest, but TJ knew better. This was something she really wanted. Unlike him, she wasn't the type to boast about her abilities or her chances, which meant he'd have to encourage her as much as he could.

"The House of Venus could be the perfect opportunity," he said. "Now that those wall paintings have been exposed, they'll need to be properly cared for. If you get chosen to stay on at Pompeii until June, tell Dr. Roberti you'd like to use that time to help with the conservation process."

"That's a great idea. Would *you* stay longer? If you were asked to be part of next year's team?"

The thought of extending his stay—and getting to do it with Emilia—lit a fire inside of him. Now, he wanted it more than ever. "Hell, yes. Another six months would be perfect. I'd still need to look for academic jobs, but I could do that online. A full year at Pompeii would add even more cachet to my resume." He placed his hand on her arm—just the briefest of touches. "I'll stay if you will."

The smile she gave him could have lit up the entire ravine. "Then I'm holding you to it. Pompeii wouldn't be the same without you."

Though she kept her voice light, there was no mistaking what she was implying. That her feelings for him were more than just a physical reaction to their closeness on the tour. That she wanted more than one night of passion. If they could both stay in Pompeii until next spring, they could have all that. They might even have a shot at a real relationship.

All of a sudden, the future seemed wide-open.

AFTER LUNCH AT A CAVE RESTAURANT IN MATERA, THEY GOT BACK on the bus and headed for the Castel del Monte. While the octagonal castle was considered a medieval masterpiece, TJ sensed a drop in the group's attention level. He kept the tour short, allowing them an extra half hour at the wine tasting, which was held in a nearby vineyard. By the time everyone boarded the bus again, they were drowsy and content, making for a quiet ride.

TJ was half-asleep when his phone buzzed with a text from his sister.

> Romily: You doing okay? I know this week is always rough for you.

For a moment, he was so disoriented that he didn't know what she meant until he checked the date on his phone. The anniversary of his dad's death was in two days. He'd been so focused on the tour—and on Emilia—that he'd pushed it out of his mind.

Maybe this year, the grief wouldn't hit him as hard, but he didn't want to make assumptions. He couldn't risk losing his shit the way he had when he was eighteen, away at college for the first time. He'd been hit by a painful wave of misery that had completely caught him off guard. As a result, he'd spent hours on the phone with Romily until she'd talked him down from his agony.

The only upside of that incident was that it had led to a new tradition. Every year, on the date of their dad's death, they picked one of his favorite movies and did a watch-along.

> TJ: I'm ok right now but the actual day might be hard. Are we still on for our annual movie night? Any preferences?

Last year, he'd chosen the old-school classic *Spartacus*, but she wasn't as wild about gladiator movies as he was.

A text bubble appeared, then disappeared. He stared at the screen, wondering if she was torn over which movie to pick, until her reply appeared.

Romily: I can't do it because I'll be stuck at a
symposium for work. Sorry.

TJ: No worries. I can handle it.

Could he handle it? He wasn't sure, but he didn't want lay a guilt trip on her. He'd just have to deal with it on his own.

He closed his eyes, hoping to fall back to sleep, but it was no use. Next to him, Emilia was dozing again, so he eased the binder off her lap. For the next hour, he brushed up on his facts about Bari, a large port city located on the Adriatic Sea.

Once their bus arrived in Bari, he and Emilia dealt with check-in, got everyone's luggage sorted, and dropped off their own bags. They returned to the lobby to ask the clerk about the possibility of a sing-along. To TJ's relief, the woman told them the hotel bar contained a baby grand piano. Not only that, but it was going unused since the lounge singer who usually entertained the guests was on vacation. After the clerk gave them the go-ahead to host a piano night, she directed the two of them to the hotel's office center, where they could make copies.

Upon opening the door, Emilia burst out laughing. "Not exactly what I'd call a high-tech business hub."

On one side of the room, an ancient-looking desktop computer and an inkjet printer rested on a card table. Beside it was a folding chair and a rolling cart filled with office supplies; a battered copy machine took up most of another wall.

"It's not great, but it's better than looking for a place in town to make copies," he said. "We need to pick twenty songs. I got a lot of requests but eliminated the ones I didn't know, so I narrowed it down to thirty."

She plopped onto the folding chair and booted up the computer. "This is giving me flashbacks to freshman year when I went through this annoying phase where I wanted to be a DJ. Once we pick the songs, I'll look up the lyrics and print them out.

We can make booklets for everyone on the tour, plus a few extras, in case some randos decide to join us."

He grinned at her. "You're really getting into this, aren't you?"

She rolled her eyes as if to remind him she was still Em, despite her uncharacteristic display of enthusiasm. "The sing-along is a nice gesture, and it allows you to show off your piano skills. It doesn't mean I'm going soft."

The thing was—she *was* softening up. Compared to her attitude back in August, when they'd been stuck doing weekend tours of Pompeii together, she'd opened up a lot. Not just to him but to the guests in their tour group. This Emilia seemed intent on making people happy.

He passed her the notebook where he'd written the requests. "Here's the short list. Any suggestions on what I should cut?"

She scanned it, grabbed a pen from the rolling cart, and crossed out one of the songs. "No 'American Pie.' It's fifteen minutes long."

"It's only eight and a half, and everyone loves it."

"No, everyone thinks they love it until they get to the fifth verse, and then they just want it to be over."

"Fair enough. Anything else that needs to go?"

"I'd limit the Elton John numbers to two. Same with the Beatles. Let's mix the ballads with the up-tempo songs to keep things lively."

He nodded, pleased she was taking this so seriously. "I'll let you arrange the order of the songs, DJ Flores. Any other suggestions?"

She regarded the list with intense concentration, her brow furrowed. "Why isn't 'Piano Man' here? You killed it the other night."

"Since I already played it, I figured people wouldn't want to hear it again."

"But not all our guests were there. You should include it, especially since I didn't get to hear it all the way through." Her lips quirked up in an affectionate smile. "You *are* the piano man, TJ."

"Okay." He loved that she'd given him that nickname. It made him feel special. Not just hard-core archaeologist TJ or Harvard-grad TJ, but a guy who could entertain people in a way that had nothing to do with his degree or his background. In a way that had clearly made a strong impression on Emilia.

Once they narrowed down the list, she looked up all the lyrics, printed out the pages, and made forty song booklets. She even created a cover featuring a photo of a piano superimposed over a silhouette of Italy. She was so excited about it that it took all of TJ's willpower not to use their precious time alone to take her in his arms and kiss her until she was breathless.

After dinner, the guests assembled in the hotel bar. Everyone showed up except Luca, who'd informed them earlier that he had no interest in attending "amateur hour." Just as well. The less TJ saw of him, the better.

Emilia handed out the booklets, and TJ took his place at the piano. The white baby grand was fancier than he was used to, but the sound was marvelous. He couldn't remember the last time he'd had this much fun playing. All through college and grad school, music had helped him cope, but he'd rarely performed for anyone but himself. As he launched into "Ob-La-Di" by the Beatles, he could understand why his dad had formed a band with his friends.

The choices he and Emilia had made seemed to resonate with the group, who sang along with gusto. When he played "She's Always a Woman"—another Billy Joel classic—he couldn't help thinking of Emilia. He peeked over at her, only to catch her with a dreamy expression on her face. Did she realize he was serenading *her*? Maybe it was better that she had no idea.

Before his last song, he paused to take a water break. Beside him, Alice was talking softly to Emilia. "I used to play the piano," she said. "Six years of lessons, but it was a lifetime ago. It's one of those things that fell by the wayside as I got older."

"You could always take it up again," Emilia said. "Just for fun. I only had two years of piano when I was a kid, but hearing TJ makes me wish I'd kept at it."

Wait. Why hadn't she disclosed this earlier? "Em?" he said. "You didn't tell me you played."

She shook her head. "I don't. Not like you. I can't even read music anymore."

"I think our next number should be a duet." He peered around the group. "Don't you?"

When everyone nodded, Emilia groaned and put her head in her hands. "It'll never work. I don't remember anything except 'Jingle Bells' and the theme from *Star Wars*."

"I'll bet you know 'Heart and Soul.' Everyone knows that one." TJ patted the piano bench. "Come on—you can do the left hand. It's the easy part."

"How generous of you," she muttered. But she didn't back down. Instead, she sat beside him, so close that her thigh brushed against his. He was suddenly aware of her physical presence, the scent of her shampoo, and the tantalizing heat of her body. The last time they'd sat together on a piano bench, they'd gone up to her room, and she'd almost...

As if she knew what he was thinking, she gave him a hard nudge. "Don't get distracted. Our guests are counting on us."

Right. He started off with the melody, keeping it simple before adding a few flourishes. She joined in without missing a beat. It was a deceptively easy song, but it sounded so good when both parts came together. For once, he and Emilia were in complete harmony. Partners in the truest sense of the word.

When they were done, the group applauded. Emilia flushed with pleasure, then got off the bench.

"Why don't you finish up?" she said to him. "After that, we'll call it a night. Tomorrow, we have another big travel day: Metaponto, the archaeological museum at Taranto, and Lecce."

For the last song, he'd chosen "Sweet Caroline," which everyone knew, even the group of Australians who'd been drinking at the bar for the past hour. When he was done, the applause made his heart soar. Best of all was the way Emilia beamed at him. Like she was so proud of him. Not because of his Harvard PhD or his dig experiences but because he'd given their group a night to remember.

In the past, he'd always believed the best way to make people like him was to impress them. To show them what he'd accomplished and how much he knew. But he was starting to realize that bringing people joy could be more rewarding than trying to be the smartest person in the room. All because he'd joined this tour to help Emilia.

When in reality, she'd been the one helping *him*.

CHAPTER TWENTY-THREE

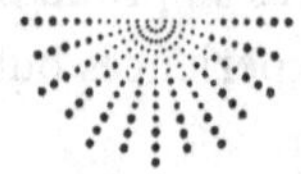

As Emilia boarded the bus, she was gripped with a rush of exhilaration. She and TJ had almost made it through the entire tour.

Two nights ago, they'd enjoyed a memorable evening in Bari, thanks to his prowess on the piano. Then, last night, they'd had dinner at an agrotourism restaurant in Lecce, where they'd experienced a wonderful farm-to-table meal. Everyone had enjoyed it, even Luca, who'd turned on the charm with the group sitting at his table. Though his presence still made Emilia uneasy, he hadn't bothered her again.

For their final day of the tour, they were driving from Lecce to Rome. Since the trip took almost seven hours, they hadn't planned any stops. The only big event left on the schedule was their farewell dinner at seven. Tomorrow morning, everyone would disperse, most of them heading for the airport to fly home. By noon, the Buon Viaggio "Archaeological Treasures of Southern Italy" tour would be officially over.

Emilia was glad she and TJ didn't have to rush back to Pompeii. Instead, Angelo was comping them another night in Rome, with the assumption they'd spend the entire time writing their full report on the tour. Given that Mateo had often submitted reports twenty pages long, Angelo had high expectations. Rather than wait until the end of the trip to begin writing, TJ had suggested starting it when they were in Naples. Since then, they'd kept up with it so diligently that they'd almost finished the whole thing. If they could polish it off after the guests left tomorrow afternoon, they'd have all night to indulge in a few rounds of sneaky hotel sex.

Hotel sex. Had there ever been a more enticing phrase?

Emilia had expected TJ to be at his most exuberant, thrilled that they'd pulled off the tour so successfully. Instead, he'd been painfully subdued at breakfast. A few times, she'd caught him staring off into space, his expression troubled.

Was he depressed their tour was almost over? That they'd no longer get to work together as a team? While she was sad their partnership was coming to an end, she was eager to take the next step with him. To give in to their desires and see where they led.

For the first few hours of the bus ride, most of the guests napped or chatted among themselves. To make up for TJ's listlessness, Emilia took charge, pointing out sights along the way. At three, Nico stopped the bus in Teano at an Autogrill—an Italian highway rest stop chain that functioned as a combination gas station, coffee bar, deli, buffet, and liquor store. What Emilia liked most about the chain was the bizarre array of products for sale—giant stuffed animals, three-foot-long sleeves of cookies, huge chocolate bars, weird off-brand toys, and enormous bottles of booze.

She was about to address the group, but TJ beat her to it. As at breakfast, his voice lacked its usual positive energy. "We'll be taking a twenty-minute break. Now's the time to use the restroom, grab a drink, and pick up a few snacks, but please don't lose track of time. We still have a way to go before we reach Rome."

He waited until everyone had exited the bus before turning to Emilia. "Are you coming? I'm going to grab a soda."

"That's all you're getting?" she said. "You won't be tempted to buy a giant bar of Toblerone or a cheap bottle of limoncello? Or a stuffed turtle that looks suspiciously like a non-licensed Pokémon character?"

On any other day, he would have teased her back, but he merely gave a sad little smile. "Not today."

"You okay?" she asked.

He shrugged. "I'm good. Just tired. Do you want anything?"

"I'll be there in a sec. You can go on ahead."

This morning at breakfast, she'd told him she was eager to be done with their tour. Maybe he thought she was eager to be done with *him*. Far from it. Even if they got the chance to fulfill their fantasies tomorrow, one night wouldn't be nearly enough.

As she picked up the binder on TJ's seat, she noticed his phone resting underneath. She retrieved it, intending to bring it to him. When it buzzed twice, she startled and dropped it. On the screen, she could make out a bunch of texts. If she looked closer, she'd be able to read them.

Though she had no right to invade his privacy, her curiosity got the best of her. With a sense of trepidation, she picked up the phone and saw a series of messages between TJ and his younger sister, Romily.

Romily: Sorry today's so hard.

TJ: I'll get through it. It shouldn't hurt this much. It's been 17 years.

Romily: I wish I could be there for you. How about this weekend? Will you be back in Pompeii then?

Romily: TJ? You there?

Emilia stared at the screen, waiting to see if Romily would

follow up with another message. When none appeared, she placed the phone back on TJ's seat. Clearly, she hadn't been imagining things. He *was* depressed, so much so that he'd reached out to his sister, who was seven time zones away. But what had set him off? Up until now, he'd always faced each day with unflagging optimism.

Rather than wait until later to seek him out alone, she wanted to take action now. To figure out what was wrong. But how?

The inspiration came to her in a flash. She needed to call Romily.

She flipped through the binder until she found the itinerary. At the top, she and TJ had listed their contact information, along with two emergency numbers, in case they were seriously injured or hospitalized during the trip. Under TJ's name, he'd listed two people—his mom and his sister, Romily Mayer.

Emilia added Romily to her contacts and stepped off the bus. Around her, the lot was filled with cars, motorcycles, and other tour buses. A few people stood in the shade next to the entrance of the rest stop, taking a smoke break. In the distance, the steady roar of the highway functioned like white noise.

She walked over to a stretch of grass past the fuel pumps. As she punched in Romily's number on her phone, she was fully aware her actions bordered on intrusive. But she was too worried about TJ to care. If the tables had been turned, he'd do the same for her.

Romily picked up on the first ring. "Hello? Who's calling?"

"Hi. Is this Romily? This is Emilia Flores. I'm co-leading the Buon Viaggio tour with your brother, TJ."

"Is he okay?" Romily's voice sounded breathy and anxious. "He wasn't answering his phone just now."

"He's fine. We're at a rest stop in Teano, and he went to get a soda. I actually wanted to talk to you alone. Um...this is kind of awkward, but..." Emilia hesitated. While she didn't want Romily to hate her, she didn't want to lie, either. "He left his phone on the seat next to me. I saw a few texts from you, and I…might have read them. I'm sorry, but I was worried about him because he hasn't been acting like himself today."

The pause that followed was so long Emilia cursed herself for being honest. What had she been thinking? She braced herself for Romily's anger, but instead, TJ's sister burst out laughing.

"You like him, don't you?" Romily said.

"What?"

"You like TJ. Right? He didn't believe me, but I totally called it. I *love* being right."

Emilia released a drawn-out sigh. "Yeah. I like him. More than I should."

"This is the *best*. When he called me the night before the tour started, I told him to give you time. I said you'd come around eventually."

Wait. That would have been the night she and TJ had watched *Gladiator* in her room. Did that mean he'd wanted her then?

Of course he did, you idiot. He'd sought her out alone just to spend time with her.

While Emilia was dying to know exactly what TJ had told his sister, she needed to stay on track. "I don't want to pry, but is everything okay with TJ? He's been in a weird funk since breakfast."

"Today's the anniversary of our dad's death. TJ always takes it really hard."

It's been seventeen years. Now his message made sense.

Over at the parking lot, a couple got out of their car and led a toddler into the rest stop. Another family emerged from the building with two little girls in tow. Both were clutching giant stuffed unicorns in a vibrant shade of pink. Families were everywhere, and TJ had lost a part of his, just like she had. It would *always* be hard.

"When my dad was alive, we used to celebrate our birthdays with this special tradition," Romily said. "You could pick any movie you wanted, and we'd all watch it together, no judgment. I usually went for Disney movies, like *The Parent Trap* or *The Princess Diaries*. My mom liked musicals, and TJ was into sci-fi, but my dad loved cheesy movies set in ancient Greece and Rome."

"Like *Gladiator*?" No wonder TJ had been so keen to watch it.

"Nah, though he liked that one a lot. He preferred older flicks like *Spartacus* or *Ben-Hur* or this trashy Greek mythology epic called *Clash of the Titans*. The one from the '80s, with the janky stop-motion animation. So TJ and I started our own tradition where we'd pick one of those movies and do a watch-along on the anniversary of our dad's death. But this year, it's not going to work out."

"Because of the difference in time zones?"

"It's not just that. I'm spending all day—and most of the evening—at a symposium. It's ironic because I usually work from home, but the one time he needs me, I'm stuck at a conference center in St. Louis."

"I could do it," Emilia said. After tonight's farewell dinner, everyone would probably turn in early. She and TJ could easily squeeze in a movie.

"He'd like that," Romily said. "Then I wouldn't feel guilty about abandoning him."

"Okay. Thanks." Emilia checked her watch. In five minutes, their break would be over. If she wanted to grab a snack before Nico fired up the bus, she needed to hurry.

"No problem," Romily said. "But Emilia? TJ can be a lot, but if you decide to take things further, please don't hurt him. He really likes you."

I know. I feel the same way.

BY THE TIME DINNER STARTED AT SEVEN, TJ HAD SHOVED ALL HIS emotional angst into a deep well. Now wasn't the time to brood. He had one last night with the Buon Viaggio group, and he wanted to leave them with the best impression possible. Not just because he was hoping for stellar reviews but also because he'd genuinely enjoyed leading them around Italy. Even Sylvie, who seemed demanding at first, had revealed a softer side once he'd gotten to know her.

At his table, he encouraged his group to share their favorite memories, and he shone with pride when a few people told him how much they'd loved his piano performance in Bari. After finishing up dessert, he couldn't maintain his cheery facade any longer. He bid them good night, with the promise to see them off at breakfast tomorrow. By the time he got back to his room, he was wiped. He changed out of his polo shirt and jeans, got ready for bed, and turned on the TV. If nothing else, he could block out the pain with a little mindless entertainment.

At least today was almost over. Once the sun rose tomorrow, he'd move on, like he always did. Maybe next year, his schedule would line up better with Romily's, and they could resume their movie night.

When a commercial came on with a father and son—some awful ad for razors—the grief hit him hard. He let it in, wallowing in agony until his eyes welled with tears.

If his dad could see him now, would he be proud of him? Or would he be embarrassed? TJ might have a PhD from Harvard, but he was working as a *tour guide*. Even if he'd used his archaeological skills to secure a place on the Via Stabiana project, it wasn't a permanent gig. After December, he had nothing lined up.

But what if he and Emilia could stay at Pompeii for another six months? A full year of work at the site would look great on his record. If that didn't pan out, hopefully Dr. Roberti would write him an outstanding letter of recommendation. All the weekends TJ had spent giving tours had to count for something. He hadn't just done them for the money but also to show his boss he was a team player. That he was willing to put in the work, even during his days off.

Was it too much to hope that fate would smile on him once he left Italy? All he wanted was a job at a decent university or a well-respected museum. A post with a comfortable salary, health insurance, and a title that would impress his stepdad.

A sharp rap at his door shook him from his trance. He hoped it wasn't one of the guests with another emergency. When he got up to answer it, Emilia stood outside his door, clad in a baggy Yale t-shirt and a pair of sweats, her hair in a messy braid. Under her arm was a cloth shopping bag from a local supermarket.

"Hey, Em," he said. "Everything okay?"

"Can I come in?"

He gnawed on his lip, torn between wanting her company and wanting to avoid temptation. "I'm not sure that's a good idea."

"This is a platonic visit, I promise." She gestured to her shirt, which was at least two sizes too big. "I'm not exactly dressed for seduction."

It didn't matter. Being around her stirred feelings he couldn't control. If they were alone in his room, he'd want to continue where they'd left off the other night. "You're still awfully hard to resist."

"I'm not here to make a move on you. If you're up for it, we could celebrate the end of the tour with a movie. You know, since we watched *Gladiator* on our first night here."

He stepped back and allowed her to come in. She closed the door and pulled a plastic container of Italian butter cookies out of the shopping bag. "I even brought your favorite treats."

"Um...thanks." He still didn't understand why she was taking such a big risk. Why not wait until tomorrow, when they'd be off the clock?

"I thought we could watch *Clash of the Titans*. The 1981

version with Harry Hamlin as Perseus and Laurence Olivier as Zeus. It's streaming on Peacock, so I had to sign up for a free trial. Remind me to cancel it by the end of the week."

As TJ put the pieces together, his throat closed up. A rush of emotion coursed through him, so powerful he could barely speak. "How…how did you know?"

"You weren't being your usual obnoxious self today. Like, I've never seen you this quiet. I called Romily to ask her what was up."

"You called Romily?" He could hardly believe what he was hearing. Emilia hadn't just been worried about him. She'd *acted* on it.

"Yeah." Emilia kicked off her flip-flops and sat on his bed with the container of cookies on her lap. "Sorry today's been so rough."

He sat down beside her. "Thanks. I keep telling myself it shouldn't hurt this much. It's been seventeen years."

"Grief isn't linear. At least, that's what the middle school counselor told me after my mom died. The pain can crop up at any time. Birthdays and anniversaries are the worst. I didn't want you to deal with it alone. Unless—would you rather be alone? I don't want to intrude."

"No. Please stay." He placed his hand over hers. "I didn't expect this, but it's really nice."

Giving him a warm smile, she laced her fingers through his. "Just don't tell anyone. I don't want people to think I've gone all soft and mushy."

"It'll be our secret. I promise."

She scooted onto his bed until she was leaning against the headboard. When he moved to sit beside her, she placed two pillows between them. "This is the boundary line. Got it? No touching, no kissing, no cuddling. For tonight, we're just going to be two friends watching a movie together."

He let out a ragged breath, unable to properly express the depth of his gratitude. "I'll behave myself."

"I know." She grabbed the remote. "Also, fair warning—I watched the trailer for this movie earlier, and *woof*. I don't care how much you love it—I'm making snarky comments through the whole thing."

He couldn't help but smile. "Honestly, Em? I'd be disappointed if you didn't."

CHAPTER TWENTY-FOUR

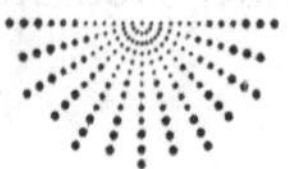

The buzz of her phone woke Emilia from a sound sleep. She blinked and tried to orient herself. Where was she?

As her eyes adjusted to the darkness, she got her bearings. She was in TJ's room, sitting on his bed. Beside her, he was slumped over, eyes closed, his hands still clutching the container of butter cookies. On the opposite wall, the TV had gone dark; the movie must have ended ages ago. The last thing she remembered was a battle between Perseus and two giant scorpions.

On the nightstand, the digital clock read 5:10 a.m. *Shit.* Even if her visit had been purely platonic, she'd spent the entire night in TJ's room. Heart pounding, she searched for her phone and found it wedged under a pillow. She was almost afraid to look at it. What if she'd slept through a huge emergency?

To her enormous relief, only two texts appeared on the screen. Both were from Davis, sent two minutes ago.

Getting ready to head out. Catching an early
train to Milan.

If you're awake, come say goodbye. Room 673.

Why not? Going back to bed was futile since she was supposed to be up by six.

She glanced at TJ and brushed a lock of hair from his face. A sharp pang of affection tugged at her heart. Even if the movie had been complete trash, watching it had brightened his mood—so much that he'd joined her in making snide remarks.

She found a piece of hotel stationery in the nightstand drawer and dashed off a quick note.

I didn't want to wake you, but I left the butter cookies to tide you over until breakfast. XOXO Em

XOXO? Since when did she sign her notes this way? What had happened to her rough edges?

Like she had to ask? TJ had happened. Not just TJ but this tour and all its demands. Over the last eleven days, she'd had to shed her personal armor and let people in. She'd experienced the rush of making people happy, and in return, she'd reveled in joyful moments of her own. Above all, she'd had the courage to open her heart to someone, confident he'd never treat her the way Vince had.

Would she come to regret all this openness? Would it eventually bite her in the ass? Maybe so, but right now, it felt good to let down her walls.

She eased off the bed, popped into the bathroom, and did a quick self-assessment. Not great. Messy hair spilling loose from her braid, wrinkled t-shirt dusted with cookie crumbs, bags under her eyes. Fortunately, Davis wouldn't care. She'd stop by his room and say goodbye, then go clean up for breakfast.

She let herself out of TJ's room and slunk down the hall. When she knocked on Davis' door, he opened it and motioned for her to come in. "Hey, Em. Hope my text didn't wake you."

"Nah, I was up already." She scanned his room, startled at the amount of stuff still piled on his bed, including two large bottles of limoncello. He'd be lucky to fit all of it into his suitcase. "Why are you leaving so early?"

He gave her a rueful smile. "I'm an idiot, that's why. A friend of mine is vacationing at Lake Como, and he invited me to join him. So I thought, why not take the early train to Milan and get a jump-start on my visit? Except I forgot how much I hate getting up at the butt-crack of dawn."

"It's—what—a three-hour trip?"

"A little longer, plus I need to take the bus from Milan to Lake Como. I'm going to work on my video during the train ride, so that'll give me something to fill my time."

"Already? That's so quick." He hadn't posted the Portugal video until a month after the tour ended.

"This is just an overview—a teaser—with my general thoughts. I'll do four or five more shorter videos after that, going into greater detail. That way, I can stretch out my content."

"Makes sense." She gnawed on her lip, curious about his "overview" but hesitant to put him on the spot.

As if he could read her mind, he offered her a playful grin. "For the record, I'm giving this tour the full five stars. You and TJ were awesome."

She let out her breath in a whoosh. "Thanks. We tried our best. I appreciate how supportive you were, especially when we gave that impromptu tour of the Forum and Palatine Hill."

"That was one of the best parts of the trip. You guys did a great job, plus you made it enjoyable. And the two of you had fun, didn't you?" The gleam in his eye suggested he knew exactly what was going on between them.

She flushed. "Yeah. More than I expected."

"Glad to hear it. Anyway, I should finish packing. My taxi's gonna be here in twenty minutes, and I have no clue how I'm going to fit all this shit into my bag. Thanks again for a great time."

"You bet." She opened the door, but as she was leaving, he motioned for her to stop.

"Hang on." He grabbed some euro notes out of his wallet and pressed them into her hand. "Your tip. Half of it is for TJ, but I'm guessing he's still asleep."

"Thanks. I'll give it to him at breakfast." She stuffed the bills in the pocket of her sweatpants.

"Any chance I could get a hug before I go?" he asked.

"Absolutely." She leaned in and hugged him, inhaling the faint scent of his marine-scented bodywash. "After Lake Como, are you coming back this way or heading north to Switzerland?"

"I'm coming back. I still want to visit Sicily and Sardinia, and, ah…Cesca said she'd show me around Naples." Now it was his turn to flush.

Interesting. Maybe Emilia had been right when she'd sensed something brewing between them during that night in the pool. "Nice. Well, if you get to Naples before December 18, let me know. TJ and I would be happy to meet you there for drinks."

"You got it. Safe travels, Em."

"Safe travels, Davis."

After he closed his door, she turned to walk down the hall, only to come face-to-face with Luca. She froze in place, her pulse rate spiking. What was it about this guy? He was always creeping up on her, like a stalker. "Um…hey, Luca. You're up kind of early."

He was clad in a snug blue compression shirt and a tight pair of running shorts that left little to the imagination. If she hadn't found him so repellent, she might have been impressed by his muscular hotness. Instead, all she wanted to do was flee in the opposite direction.

"I'm going out for a run," he said. "What's your excuse for wandering the halls at this hour? Coming from a late night with Davis?"

"Excuse me?" She brushed a few crumbs off her shirt. Even if she was messy and disheveled, that hardly implied she'd spent the night engaging in a passionate tryst.

"I saw you sneaking out of Davis' room just now. Don't deny it."

"I wasn't about to. Since he's leaving before everyone else, I stopped by to see him off."

Luca's lip curled in a sneer. "That's quite the effort on your part, seeing as how it's barely five in the morning."

Seriously? "We're just friends. Even if we weren't, I'd want to leave him with a good final impression since he's a travel influencer who'll be leaving a review. Not that it's any of your business. Now, if you'll excuse me, I'm going to get ready for breakfast."

She turned and left, not caring if she'd pissed him off. At least she only had to endure his loathsome presence until the tour ended. After that, she could put him out of her mind for good.

At breakfast, she made a beeline for TJ's table. Beside his plate was a mug of cappuccino, and he'd loaded up with sweets—two pieces of apple cake, a cornetto, and a jam tart—as if he hoped the sugar would give him a boost of energy.

When she slid into the seat across from him, he flashed her sad puppy-dog eyes. "I'm so sorry."

Had she missed something? "About what?"

He lowered his voice. "You were so thoughtful last night, and then I went and fell asleep on you. Not *on* you, but before the movie ended. That was a dick move on my part."

She could have strung him along with some gentle teasing, but he looked genuinely contrite. "Don't worry about it. I fell asleep, too." She spoke softly, not wanting anyone else to hear them. "I didn't wake up until five."

"*Fuck.* I'm sorry."

"It's all good. I got a text from Davis when I was sneaking out. He asked me to come by his room and say goodbye." She fished some euro notes out of her pocket and handed them to him. "Here's your half of the tip."

"Thanks. I'm bummed I missed him."

"He'll be back in a month to visit Sicily and Sardinia. I told him to hit us up if he gets to Naples, then we could meet him and Cesca for a drink."

"Good plan. Other than that, are we okay? Did you make it back to your room without getting busted?"

She was tempted to tell him about her encounter with Luca but decided against it. TJ would only feel worse if he learned how Luca had treated her. "No one suspected a thing." She snitched a piece of apple cake from his plate and took a bite. "You still up for tonight?"

He gave her a wide grin. "I wouldn't miss it for anything."

~

EMILIA PACED IN HER ROOM. HAD SHE AND TJ GOTTEN THEIR signals crossed? After dinner, she'd told him to stop by at eight. But it was twenty past, and he hadn't shown up. A quick peek at her phone—for the fifth time in less than two minutes—revealed no new texts.

Maybe he just needs more time to pack. The two of them had been busier today than she'd expected. She'd assumed all the guests would be gone by noon, but the Mangolds' flight had been delayed two hours. With time to kill, the elderly couple had treated her and TJ to lunch. A delightful treat, even if it had put them behind schedule. They'd spent the next four hours finishing their report for Buon Viaggio but decided to send it the following morning. That way, Angelo would think they'd spent all evening working on it. TJ had returned to his room to pack but promised he'd be back by eight.

Was he having second thoughts? Or was he worried he wouldn't live up to her expectations? This was different from that night in Paestum when she'd invited him to her room on a whim. They'd acted so impulsively that they hadn't had time to overthink their actions. But now, after three days of anticipation, the pressure to create the perfect night might be too much for him to handle. If he wasn't ready to take this step, so be it, but he needed to tell her face-to-face. No wimping out via a text or a phone call.

With a grunt of frustration, she went out into the hall, intending to track him down. As she rounded the corner, she almost careened into him. For whatever reason, he was still wearing the ugly red Buon Viaggio polo. She skidded to a halt. "Where have you been?"

"Sorry. I…ah…"

"You changed your mind?" She kept her tone light, not wanting to reveal the extent of her disappointment. No matter how badly she wanted him, she wouldn't force him to do something he wasn't ready for. "No problem. We could do another movie night."

"No. It's not that. It's just…" He rubbed the back of his neck. "I feel like a total cad."

Despite her uncertainty, she couldn't help but smile. "A cad? What are you—a character in a Regency novel?"

"Not quite. But this doesn't seem right. I've never taken you on a date. I didn't have time to buy you flowers or chocolate or *anything*. And here I am, planning to barge into your room in the hopes you'll have sex with me."

She bubbled over with laughter. "What makes you think I want any of those things? You came on this tour to support me. You covered for me when I was too tired or frazzled to socialize. You listened to me whine about my ex. Honestly, you've done more for me than any of the guys I've been with."

"But I want to go the extra mile. I want you to feel cherished. That's how I operate."

She moved in closer and smoothed the collar of his polo shirt.

"You know how you can go the extra mile? By being a thoughtful lover, attending to my needs, and giving me a couple of really good orgasms. I'll take those over roses any day."

He swallowed, his Adam's apple bobbing. "I…I'll do my best."

"I know you will. Come on. We've both waited long enough."

CHAPTER TWENTY-FIVE

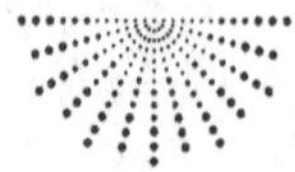

Emilia unlocked her door and led TJ inside her room. In anticipation of their night together, she'd turned off all the lights except the tiny lamp on her nightstand. While she'd never had any qualms about exposing her body in broad daylight, the faint glow of the lamp set a more romantic tone. She went over to the double bed and pushed aside the comforter and pillow shams. "There. Now we have a little more room. How's that?"

He didn't answer. Though he'd followed her to the side of the bed, he had yet to make a move.

Was he nervous? From their past conversations, she knew he'd been with a few women before, most notably the grad student he'd dated while he was at Harvard. Maybe he was too wrapped up in this ridiculous notion of being a gentleman to take the next step.

Then I'll do it.

With a saucy smile, she stripped off her t-shirt and shorts, revealing a lacy black bra and matching panties. Normally, she wasn't the sexy lingerie type, but she'd purchased them a month ago, hoping to use them with Paulo. She was infinitely happier that TJ would reap the benefits, especially since he was staring at her in slack-jawed admiration.

She cocked her hip. "Your move, Dr. Mayer."

"Sorry. I was momentarily overcome by…ah…the sight of you." He pulled a handful of condoms out of his pocket and set them on the nightstand. "But I brought supplies, so we're covered there."

"Thanks. Just so you know—I'm clean. After I learned about Vince's 'double life,' I got tested, and there hasn't been anyone since." While admitting the extent of her sexual drought was embarrassing, she wanted to be as open with TJ as possible.

"Same with me. I mean, I got tested after my last girlfriend cheated on me, and, yeah, it's been a minute." He gave a self-deprecating laugh. "If you want to be precise, it's been a year and a half, so we're kinda on the same page."

"Good to know. We don't have to worry about birth control since I have an IUD."

A slow smile spread across his face. "So I won't need to use a condom?"

"Not unless you want to. I trust you."

"Okay, then. Now that we've gotten *that* out of the way." He gestured to his polo shirt. "I kept this on for a reason. Once I remove it, I'm officially off the clock as a tour guide and will no longer be subject to the rules set forth in the Buon Viaggio binder."

She laughed. "Ooh, yes. Take it off. But *slowly*."

With a little hip roll, he pulled it over his head, twirled it in the air, and flung it across the room. She gazed at his bare chest, taking her time to appreciate the view. His shoulders and arms were nicely muscled, his chest dusted with light brown hair. She continued staring as he stripped down to a pair of red boxer briefs that barely hid his erection. Taking his hand, she tugged him onto the bed with her. Even if they had all night, with no chance of interruption, she didn't want to wait any longer.

After placing his glasses on the nightstand, he settled himself beside her so they were lying face-to-face. With gentle fingers, he traced the curve of her cheek. "I can't believe I'm here with you. I feel so privileged."

Her heart soared at the tenderness in his voice. Clearly, this meant more to him than a quick romp in bed. She kissed him, softly at first, her lips barely grazing his. A delicate dance, teasing and promising more while building up the anticipation between them. When he tangled his fingers in her hair and pulled her closer, she responded with passion. Kissing him harder, sweeping her tongue against his, nipping at his lower lip. A bolt of desire shot through her, filling her with an ache that demanded more than kisses.

She pulled away and quickly unclasped her bra. After tossing it aside, she pressed her bare skin against his, inhaling his scent and delighting in the warmth of his body. With the same gentleness he'd shown earlier, he pushed her onto her back and positioned himself over her. For once, she was more than willing to cede control. His warm brown eyes captured hers, showing not just lust but affection. Like he truly *wanted* her to feel cherished. She was thrumming with need, ready for him to take things further.

Until he whispered, "You're so beautiful. So gorgeous and—"

"Stop." She stiffened, an icy fear taking hold where the warmth had been. "No compliments. Please. I don't need them."

After Vince and Luca, she didn't want anyone else filling her head with meaningless praise. She wanted honesty.

He looked down at her with a pained expression. "I can't seduce you and say nothing. That's not right."

"I…just. *Please.*"

"Fine. How about this?" He nuzzled his lips against her collarbone, feather-soft kisses that made her tingle all over. "You might be stunningly beautiful, but you're also stubborn as hell. You're one of the most stubborn women I've ever met."

"Mmm. Yes. That's good. More of that, please." She wound her fingers through his hair.

More kisses followed, trailing from the hollow of her throat to the valley between her breasts. He chuckled softly. "You're a brilliant scholar, but you constantly one-up me at every turn. It's annoying as fuck."

She gave a grateful moan. "I *love* annoying you."

He swirled his tongue around her nipples, teasing them with the lightest of touches before sucking on them until she gasped. "I don't know which dreams I've enjoyed more," he murmured. "The ones where I'm making love to you or the ones where I'm forcing you to admit I'm right at an academic conference."

The sensations were so delightful she could barely think straight, but she loved what he was doing. She was on fire, her body as primed as Mt. Vesuvius, ready to explode. After two years in the desert, she'd finally found her oasis. When he tugged on her panties, she shimmied them down past her hips and flung them to the side. But he only let her sit up for a second before pushing her back onto the bed and taking control again.

Yes. Take control. Have your way with me.

With a nudge, he parted her legs and slid his fingers between them. The pressure was exquisite. When he found the right spot —like a pirate knowing exactly where to dig for treasure—she gave a little cry. "*Yes.* Like that."

"You're so wet, Em. So wet and sexy and…shit, I can't think of any other insults." His lips traced a path around her navel while his fingers continued stoking the fire within her, igniting her further.

She rocked her hips, urging him on. She was so tantalizingly close that she couldn't bear the thought of him stopping. "My… my Bronze Age theories," she gasped. "What about those?"

He placed soft pecks along the inside of her thighs, his breath warm and seductive. "Your theories are so messed up. No basis in reality. You'll never convince me climate change caused the collapse of the Bronze Age. Not in a million years."

"Ohhhhh. I'm right, and you know it. You just…" She gasped again as he dove in, burying his face between her legs, licking her sweet center until she shuddered with pleasure. "You…just can't admit it."

"I'll *never* admit you're right."

She raked her hands through his hair, digging her nails into his scalp. "TJ?"

"What? More?"

"Yes, but can you stop talking? Please?"

Because right now, she couldn't focus on anything except what he was doing with his tongue, bringing her closer and closer to her peak. It felt so good, like bathing in an icy-cold waterfall after spending hours trekking in a steamy jungle. As the tension built up inside of her, she moaned and clutched the sheet, poised to jump off that cliff into a shimmering pool of pleasure. The orgasm hit her hard, the sensations rolling over her like a tidal wave, churning her up until she was wrung out on the shore.

And then he did it again.

By now, she was panting, her heart thudding, her entire body trembling. With a breathy plea, she begged him to stop. Her nerve endings were so sensitive she couldn't handle a third time. When he faced her with a cocky grin, his lips wet with the taste of her, she burst out laughing. "How is it you brag about everything except *that?*"

"You liked it, huh?"

"Did you not hear me?" Hopefully, the walls were sturdy enough that their neighbors hadn't gotten an earful.

"You sounded so sexy. Are you okay to keep going, or do you need a moment to recover?"

"Keep going. Please." She waited until he'd taken off his boxer briefs and flung them aside. Reaching down, she guided him inside of her. But when he didn't move, she caught his eye. "Are *you* okay?"

"I'm great. Just trying to figure out how to make this last longer than thirty seconds. Listening to you moan was the most intense turn-on ever."

She loved how honest he was. Honest and funny and completely TJ. She ran her nails along the ridge of his spine. "Do you want me to talk about seeds for a while? Or remind you my GRE scores were four points higher than yours?"

He laughed. "My cumulative GPA was higher. By half a percentage point."

She grabbed his butt and gave it a squeeze. "What if I called you a *treasure hunter?*"

His eyes gleamed with amusement. "Now you're getting nasty. And you're going to get it, Dr. Flores."

"Am I, Dr. Mayer? Then you'd better give it to me. *Hard.*"

He moved inside her, slowly at first and then in a steady rhythm, his eyes never leaving hers. She wrapped her legs around him, wanting to bring him closer. She was still so keyed up, her entire body sizzling from his touch, that the pleasure built up quickly. And when he hit the right spot, she urged him to go deeper. Harder. Faster. She sucked in a breath as the sensations coursed through her again, closing her eyes as her world spiraled out of control and exploded into a million stars. Seconds later, he released himself with a shudder and groaned loudly, burying his face in her shoulder.

When they were done, she held him for a long time, stroking his hair as they slowly fell back to Earth. No matter what happened tomorrow—or next month, or even next year—they'd always have this night.

~

TJ ENJOYED FEW THINGS MORE THAN WAKING UP TO A BEAUTIFUL woman in his bed. While he loved sex as much as the next guy, he often worried he wouldn't be able to live up to his partner's expectations. But that feeling of drifting off with a lover and spending the night in her arms? Sheer bliss.

Waking up with Emilia was all that, times ten. When he first opened his eyes, the digital clock on the nightstand read 6:30 a.m., so he tried to go back to sleep. No chance of it, not when he couldn't stop thinking about last night. How much he'd enjoyed teasing her during foreplay. How amazing the sex had been—not just the first time but the second as well, when she'd been on top and had ridden him to a world-shattering climax. And how deliriously happy he'd felt lying beside her afterward, talking softly until they fell asleep. As tired as he'd been, he hadn't wanted their night to end.

He buried his face in her hair, inhaling the faint scent of orange blossoms that lingered from her shampoo, until her sharp voice startled him. "Are you gonna talk to me or sniff my hair like a weirdo?"

He laughed. "I'm gonna be a weirdo. I can't help it."

She rolled over and grinned at him. "Did you sleep okay?"

He couldn't get over how adorable she looked—her dark hair sleep-mussed, faint tan lines marking her light brown skin, her breasts barely hidden by the sheet. He placed a gentle kiss on her forehead. "Incredibly well. How about you?"

"Like a fucking dream. I'm not sure if it's because I'm officially done with the tour or because my studly boyfriend wore me out. Either way, I'll take it."

Studly boyfriend? Now, there was a compliment he appreciated. "I could be of service this morning, if you want."

She wagged her finger at him. "First things first. You need to send the report to Angelo. Do it now before we forget."

Yesterday evening, after compiling the sixteen-page report on her laptop, she'd sent it to him, and he'd attached it to an email he'd drafted to Angelo. All he had to do was hit Send. After putting on his glasses, he grabbed his phone and took care of it. "There. Done. Sent to Angelo, cc'd to Dr. Roberti and Luca, and out of our hands. Now can we have sex?" He'd already grown hard in anticipation of their next few hours together.

"Sure, but…"

"But what?"

Her mouth turned down in a cute little pout. "I wish we didn't have to leave today."

"Well, actually…" Though he hadn't mentioned it last night, he'd already planned for this very scenario. "Since it's Saturday, we don't need to rush back yet."

"Wait. It's Saturday?" She ran her hand through her hair, messing it up even further. "I'm so disoriented after being on the tour that I don't even know what day it is."

"It's definitely Saturday. So, what's to stop us from spending another night in Rome? It's not like we ever go into work on a Sunday unless we're giving tours, and I can't imagine you'd want to do that."

She gave an audible shudder. "Hell, no. I don't want to put on that polo for at least another week."

"Right, so we could spend tonight in Rome, then head back tomorrow afternoon. That'll give us time to unwind before we have to be back at work on Monday."

Her eyes lit up. "Great idea, but Angelo would never comp us another night here. He'd suspect something's up."

TJ wasn't deterred that easily. "Then we don't tell him. We check out of this place at noon, like we planned, then check into another hotel for tonight. I found a guesthouse a block over that's a lot more affordable. A small room with a queen bed is less than eighty euros a night." A total steal, given the high cost of hotels in Rome.

She eyed him suspiciously. "Less than eighty euros? Are you sure it's not a dump? What's it rated?"

He pulled it up on his phone and passed it to her. "It has 4.2 out of 5 stars on Tripadvisor. Check it out."

As she looked it over, he was struck by an unpleasant sense of déjà vu. The last time he'd picked out a cheap hotel for them had been the previous summer in Istanbul, when he'd made a terrible mistake. A mistake he'd *never* apologized for.

"If you're worried this is going to be Istanbul all over again, I promise it won't be." He softened his tone. "I'm so sorry for how I treated you. If I pay for this place in Rome, will you forgive me?"

She placed her hand on his shoulder and gave it a gentle squeeze. "You giant dork. That was last year when we barely knew each other. I've already forgiven you, and I'm fine with paying for my half tonight."

"Please let me pay. In lieu of flowers or chocolates or gifts you don't need?"

"Okay." Laughing, she passed him the phone. "Go ahead and book it. But in return, I get to take you out to dinner tonight. A nice place where we can sit outside, drink wine, eat pasta, and flirt with each other shamelessly. Deal?"

"Deal." Now he could relax, knowing they had a full twenty-four hours left together. "Are you okay if we take it easy today? No museums or ruins?"

She grinned at him. "As long as there's sex and gelato, then I'm good."

He glanced at the clock. "It's a little early for gelato, so…"

"Sex it is, then." She pulled him closer, wrapped her arms around him, and kissed him deeply.

Once again, he was lost in the blissful embrace of the woman who'd captured his heart.

CHAPTER TWENTY-SIX

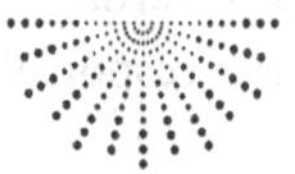

Emilia didn't want to get out of bed. Getting up would burst this sweet little bubble she and TJ had created. A bubble where they'd spent hours teasing each other, having sex, snuggling, sleeping, and having more sex, interrupted only by the occasional break for food. But checkout was at noon, and their train left Rome at two, which meant they couldn't linger.

She should be grateful she was returning to a job she enjoyed. For as much fun as she'd had leading the tour with TJ, she was better suited to the role of archaeologist, using the skills she'd spent years honing. How many people got to work on a site as extraordinary as Pompeii? Landing this gig had been one of the best things that had ever happened to her. If fate smiled on her, maybe Dr. Roberti would choose her and TJ to stay on until next spring.

But right now, this bed was so cozy and inviting that it was hard to make herself move. Unlike the crappy hotel in Istanbul where she and TJ had stayed last year, their tiny room in this guesthouse was perfect. A comfy queen bed, a standing shower big enough for two, and a stunning view of St. Peter's Basilica in the distance.

She lay beside TJ, tracing patterns on his bare chest with her fingernails. "I don't want to get up. You can't make me."

"Oh, really? Yesterday, you said to me—and I quote —'Whatever we do, we can't miss that train.' Do you remember?"

She groaned. "That was yesterday. Now we have to put on our clothes and go back to being responsible adults and start hating each other again."

He froze beside her. "Wait. Hating each other? I thought…we were going to stay together."

Wanting to console him, she placed a soft kiss on his shoulder. "Sorry, I should have phrased that better. *Acting* like we hate each other again."

Because honestly, even when she'd first started working with him at Pompeii, she'd never truly hated him. At times, he'd been exasperating beyond belief, but sparring with him had always been a challenge she relished.

"Can't we admit we're together?" he asked. "If we don't, you'll have to spend the rest of your time at Pompeii secretly pining for me. Letting out dreamy sighs every time you see me, craving my touch but being unable to act on it."

She smacked him in the chest. "Your ego is the worst. I've never given a dreamy sigh in my life."

He smirked. "You did last night. Several of them, in fact."

"That was in the heat of the moment." Even as she said it, she knew he was right. What good did it serve them to keep acting like rivals? "But you make a fair point. Working at Pompeii would be a lot more fun if we're a couple."

"Really?" His voice rose with enthusiasm. "You're okay with making this public?"

"Hang on a minute." She sat up quickly, wanting to take control before his excitement got the best of him. "Before we do anything, we need to make a plan. First, we wait two weeks before telling everyone so it doesn't look like we hooked up while we were on the tour. We don't want Angelo thinking we broke the rules. He'd use it as an excuse to dock our pay."

"Smart move. Especially since we *actually* waited until the tour was over."

"Second, we'll stage a big fight scene where we go from enemies to lovers and end up kissing, much to everyone's shock and amazement."

"I love it." He grinned. "A sort of Han Solo-Princess Leia vibe."

"Whatever, nerd. Third, before we make things public, you should let Marie down gently, and I'll do the same for Paulo." Even if she didn't like Marie, the girl didn't deserve to be blindsided.

"Don't worry about that one. Haven't you been checking Instagram?" TJ reached for his glasses, then grabbed his phone and scrolled through it.

"Not really. Other than posting a few photos for Buon Viaggio, I've barely looked at it." As TJ passed her the phone, she gaped at the picture on the screen. Paulo and Marie on a beach in Mykonos with their arms around each other. "Whoa. Didn't see that one coming."

"Apparently, they were an item two years ago. Being on a sun-drenched Greek island must have brought those feelings back."

"Perfect. We'll get back to Pompeii, bicker like always, then stage a passionate fight scene in about two weeks. The weekend after that, we'll book a getaway in Naples so we can have sex. Sound good?" She was getting turned on just imagining it.

"It's perfect, but that's a long time to wait for sex."

"I know, but think how good it'll be." She rubbed her hands together. "All that waiting will make it even more spectacular."

Her last two months in Pompeii suddenly looked very promising. And if they were both picked to stay until next June?

Even better.

As TJ followed Emilia off the train at Ercolano, he almost took her hand but stopped himself in time. If he wanted their ruse to work, he needed to play by her rules. For the next two weeks, he couldn't touch her, kiss her in public, or give any hint he was into her. Though the term "into her" barely scraped the surface of what he was feeling. He wasn't just "into her"; he'd fallen head over heels in love. Not that he'd told her yet. If he hit her with a heartfelt confession so soon after having sex, he might scare her away. Instead, he'd work up to it over the next month and profess his love during one of their weekend getaways.

She stopped walking and peeked behind her. "You coming? Or are you staring at my butt?"

He gave a half-hearted groan. "One last stare. Remembering how it felt to—"

"I'm gonna stop you right there. No more of that. We have to behave like rivals. I'm going to be grumpy Emilia again, and you can revert to being overly enthusiastic, thoroughly obnoxious TJ."

"I'm not *that* obnoxious."

"In the mornings? When you try to talk to me before I've had my coffee? All sunny and cheery? I'd call that obnoxious." She hitched her thumb forward. "Let's go."

He followed her in silence, his mind drifting as he imagined their next rendezvous. He'd already found a small hotel in Naples that would suit them perfectly. It was affordable, well reviewed, and had an available room with a queen bed and a balcony overlooking the city. They'd have a few drinks, go out to dinner, and spend the rest of the night making good use of that bed. He gave a little chuckle as he imagined how he'd tease her during foreplay.

"Stop that," she muttered. "I know what you're thinking."

"I was thinking about Bronze Age metallurgy."

"Bullshit. You were already daydreaming about our next getaway. Cut it out."

How had she read him so well? She wasn't even *looking* at him. He scurried to catch up with her. "Haven't you been imagining it?"

"Of course I have. But I'm keeping it to myself."

As gruff as she sounded, she was smiling. Even if she was reverting to her old self, there was a light in her he'd never seen before. An inner glow. He'd like to think it was because of him, but it wasn't just that. During the tour, she'd let down her walls enough to allow people in, and she'd enjoyed it. They both had. The ten-day tour had brought out their strengths and allowed them to lean on each other in moments of weakness.

TJ had always taken pride in charting his own course and relying only on himself, but he'd come to realize how incredible it was to work with a partner. With someone who could help him, prop him up, and make him an even better person.

When they reached the hostel, it was practically empty—no surprise for a warm Sunday afternoon. They split up to unpack and get organized. Back in his dorm-style room, TJ surveyed the scene with revulsion. As always, it was a mess since the other archaeologists who shared the room were total slobs. Next to one bed was a pile of dirty laundry and a couple of empty liquor bottles. The overstuffed garbage can was topped with a crushed pizza box stained with grease. The whole room smelled like feet and beer.

Ugh. After two weeks of staying in nice hotel rooms, dorm-style living was a harsh return to reality. If he and Emilia were invited to stay at Pompeii until June, they could try to snag one of the two-person rooms in the hostel. Though it might be a little pricier, he'd gladly pay more to have some privacy.

After dinner, he and Emilia ended up on the rooftop, drinking beer to commemorate the end of their journey. She was sitting on a bench across from him, giving no sign they'd ever been lovers, when the rest of the cohort returned. She held up her beer bottle in a salute as Paulo and his friends came to join them, followed by Marie, Chloe, and the rest of the Swiss contingent.

Paulo pulled up a bench and sat beside them. "Welcome back. How was the tour?"

"Not bad," Emilia said. "A lot of work, but we got to stay in some classy hotels. Much nicer than this dump."

Marie settled on the bench next to Paulo. "It was so hard coming back after our trip to Greece. That hotel in Mykonos was so romantic, wasn't it Paulo?" She ruffled her fingers through his hair and gave TJ a pointed look, as if to say, "See what you missed?"

TJ held back his laughter and sensed Emilia was doing the same thing. "So…you two are together now?"

"We are," Marie said. "It's been absolute bliss."

Paulo turned to Emilia with a sorrowful expression. "Sorry, but Greece is a very romantic location, and I needed someone to share my bed. I hope you aren't too upset."

Emilia shrugged. "I'll get over it. I'm glad you two had fun."

"Same here," TJ added. This whole scenario meant neither he nor Emilia had to feel guilty about ditching their prospective partners.

"What about the two of you?" Paulo asked. "Any 'Trojan horse' moments where you snuck off to have sex? I seem to recall there are a lot of hidden tunnels beneath the gladiator's floor at the Colosseum. A perfect place for a rendezvous."

"Don't be silly, Paulo," Marie said. "They had to follow the rules. Remember the list Emilia showed us?"

"Ah, but rules are meant to be broken, are they not?" He raised his eyebrows as though challenging them to deny it.

Emilia wrinkled her nose. "Not this time. There were *no* steamy moments. We're lucky we didn't kill each other."

TJ forced himself to glare at her. "Yeah, and I had to be extra cheerful to compensate for Em's grumpiness. It was a giant pain."

"Hey, I wasn't that grumpy," she snapped. "At least I didn't dominate every stop on the tour with scads of useless information. You never shut up."

"People *loved* my information. I was a total rock star." He almost laughed at how easy it was to fall back into their old patterns, except this time, their words weren't intended to hurt. If anything, they could use these barbs to fuel their foreplay when they got together in Naples.

"Enough fighting," Paulo said. "I hope you two weren't this bad around the guests."

"We were very well-behaved," Emilia said. "Right, TJ?"

"Right. We kept our true feelings under wraps, but I don't think we'll *ever* volunteer for anything like this again. Not as a team." He caught Emilia's eye but had to look away for fear of revealing the truth.

Keeping a secret this big wouldn't be easy, but it would make for a passionate reunion.

CHAPTER TWENTY-SEVEN

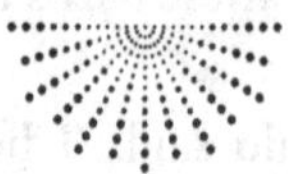

During her morning commute on the train from Ercolano to Pompeii, Emilia could barely keep her usual scowl in place. It was hard reverting to her grouchy persona when she was positively bubbling over with good vibes and steamy memories. She couldn't even look TJ in the eye for fear she'd start grinning like a lovesick idiot.

Why had she suggested they wait two weeks before revealing their feelings? She needed to reassess. Sitting this close to TJ and not touching him or even sharing a smile was maddening.

After their ride into Pompeii, she was free from temptation since she spent all day in the lab, working with the archaeobotanical team. They'd set up a flotation tank to separate out the carbonized plant remains and animal bones they'd excavated from the west corner of the kitchen. Emilia kept herself busy, jotting down notes, sharing observations with Paulo, and comparing their finds to the botanical material they'd found in the garden area of the house. An hour and a half before the end of the workday, she received a text from Giada, asking her to report to the Roberti brothers for a tour debriefing session.

Finally. She cleaned up her station, told Paulo where she was going, and headed out. Unlike the first time she'd been summoned to Dr. Roberti's office, she wasn't burdened with trepidation. Even if the reviews for the tour had yet to come in, she and TJ had done an outstanding job. During their final breakfast with the guests in Rome, they'd received lavish compliments and generous tips. The Golden Girls had even invited her to visit them in New Mexico once she was back home in the States.

Outside the office, TJ stood waiting with the binder tucked under his arm. He flashed her a quick smile. "Hey, you. Ready to bask in the stunning success of our kick-ass tour?"

"More than ready. Can we go in yet?"

"Giada told me to wait. You know how much she loves bossing us around."

Emilia snickered. "I'm sure it killed her that we led a tour for ten days without her telling us what to do." She raked her gaze over him. "You're looking good, by the way. I had a hard time controlling myself on the train this morning."

"Same. Any chance we could cut our wait time to one week instead of two? I can't handle not touching you."

Before Emilia could reply, Giada opened the door and poked her head out. "Emilia. You first."

"Can't we go in together?" she asked. "We were both leading the same tour."

Giada frowned. "Nope. The Robertis want to talk to each of you separately."

All of a sudden, the meeting felt more like a police interrogation than a friendly debriefing, but Emilia wasn't about to argue. Once it was over, she'd be receiving a hefty paycheck. Even if TJ had agreed to give her his half of the pay, she wasn't holding him to his promise. Instead, she was going to suggest they use the money for their weekend getaways. Would it be more prudent to pay off some of their debt? Possibly. But she'd rather spend it on hotels in Naples and Sorrento without worrying about the cost.

When she entered the room, she almost tripped over a pile of books. The office was even more cluttered than she remembered, the shelves crammed with artifacts, buckets, and folios. Despite the onset of cooler weather, the space was uncomfortably stifling. Dr. Roberti sat at his desk with his brother Angelo beside him. Giada went to stand next to them and gestured for Emilia to sit in the folding chair facing the desk.

Emilia eased into the chair and offered the two men a gracious smile. "Good afternoon. I want to thank you for the privilege of leading a tour through Italy. It was a real delight. Did you have a chance to review the report TJ and I sent?"

Angelo nodded. "I glanced at it. Very thorough, which I appreciate."

But he wasn't smiling, and neither was his brother. Her heart rate accelerated as they continued staring at her. Not in gratitude but with judgmental expressions that suggested she was on trial.

Was she on trial? She'd done nothing wrong. Unless Angelo had found out what she and TJ had done in Rome. But even then, they hadn't broken the rules. They'd only had sex *after* the tour had ended.

With a hesitant voice, she forced herself to speak up. "Is there anything you wanted to ask me? About the tour? Or how it went?"

Angelo blew out a ragged breath. "As you know, our ratings are of the utmost importance. We're a small company, so we can't rely on our website or our social media presence to reel in tourists. We need word of mouth. Strong reviews. This way, when our tour comes up in a search on Viator or Tripadvisor or any other aggregator, travelers will choose it over Roman Pathways or one of the bigger companies offering the same services."

Had someone left a bad review? Emilia tried to recall if any of the guests had acted disgruntled when they'd left, but she came up blank. "I'm sorry, but did one of our guests complain?"

Giada let out a snort. "On the contrary. You got a rave review." She turned to Angelo. "May I show her?"

"Please do," he said.

The older woman passed Emilia her phone. "This video was posted this morning. It's a short overview of the tour—with more to come later—but the reviewer was quite exuberant in his praise."

Emilia smiled at the sight of Davis' face, front and center in the video. The subject line was "Best Italy Tour—Ever," which boded well. She glanced up at Angelo, who *still* wasn't smiling, and tried to comprehend why he looked so peeved. "I don't understand the issue. This looks great. Before he left, Davis told me he was going to work on it, but I'm amazed he posted it already. Did you watch the whole thing? Was it okay?"

Did they want her to watch it *now*? If so, then she'd oblige, just to hear what Davis had to say. But Angelo gestured for her to return the phone, so she passed it back to Giada.

"We both watched it," Dr. Roberti said. "Davis McGowan gave a glowing review of the tour overall and praised you in particular."

"That's good, right?"

Why did they look so angry? Why was Giada regarding her like she was a piece of dog shit on the sidewalk? Heat prickled the back of her neck. She had a sudden urge to turn on the box fan in the corner but forced herself to stay seated.

"I know it's a short video," she added, "but Davis said he'd post more later about our excursions to Matera and Paestum and a few other stops. That stuff takes a while to put together. In the meantime, this is ideal. Even if he doesn't have many followers, his base has been growing steadily."

"Normally, we'd be thrilled," Angelo said. "An honest review from a travel influencer can go a long way, but not if it's earned through illicit means."

Illicit means? Emilia's spine stiffened. "Are you suggesting I bribed Davis? I don't have that kind of money. If I did, then I'd be the one going on these tours instead of serving as a guide."

"I never said you bribed him with money," Angelo retorted.

What the fuck?

As the realization hit her, the shock froze Emilia in place. A rush of heat enveloped her, making her cheeks flame with discomfort. When she regained the ability to speak, her mouth was so dry she could barely form the words. "Are...are you suggesting I slept with Davis?"

Giada crossed her arms. "He's not suggesting. He knows it happened, you little tramp."

"I'd just prefer if you admitted it outright," Angelo said.

Emilia sprang to her feet, her distress turning to outrage. "There's nothing to admit. What makes you think *anything* happened?"

"Sit down, Miss Flores," Angelo barked.

She did as he said but glared at him. "That's Dr. Flores to you." *Asshole.*

"This morning, Luca asked to meet with us," Dr. Roberti said. "He's the one who showed us the video. At first, we were extremely pleased, until he told us what you'd done. Perhaps you didn't realize it, but he was keeping a careful eye on you. He said your behavior with Davis was wildly inappropriate. Flirting with him. Sneaking off for a late-night tryst at the hotel pool. And spending the last night of the tour seducing him."

"But I didn't—"

"Luca caught you doing the walk of shame back from Davis' room at five in the morning," Giada said. "Do you deny it?"

I don't answer to you, bitch. She kept her focus on the Roberti brothers. "On the last morning of the tour, Davis texted to tell me he was leaving, and I went to say goodbye. My messy appearance was because I'd fallen asleep in my clothes while watching a movie. But that was it. You want me to call Davis? I can do it right now, and he'll verify nothing happened."

"Like we'd believe him?" Angelo asked. "The fact is you not only broke the rules, but you also did it in a way that could compromise us as a tour company. Can you imagine what people would think if they learned our guides were exchanging sexual favors for ratings? It would tarnish our name in the tourism industry."

Emilia was tempted to mention she'd heard rumors to that effect about Mateo, but she didn't say anything. For all she knew, they were just rumors, and she wasn't about to drag down a guide she'd never met.

She took a deep breath, trying to respond calmly. Yelling at the Robertis would only aggravate them even more. "I understand your concern. You put the rules in place for a reason. That's why I followed them during the tour. Davis and I were friends but nothing more. If he gave us a high rating, it's because we did a great job and made the tour fun."

When they didn't respond, she held her breath, hoping they'd believe her.

Angelo shook his head. "It's your word against Luca's. If I have any hope of gaining his father's investment in our company, I need to appease him. Therefore, I have no choice but to relieve you of your Buon Viaggio duties."

So he wanted to play it that way? Then the fucking gloves were off. She stood again, more incensed than ever. "You want the truth? Luca filled your head with this bullshit because I bruised his ego. He hit on me when we were in Rome, and I turned him down. If I'd gone to bed with him, then we wouldn't be having this conversation. This is his way of getting back at me."

"You're such a liar," Giada spat out. "Luca would never behave like that."

"Oh, please," Emilia said. "You're the one who told me to wear lipstick and show off my cleavage when he was on my tour in Pompeii. You're the one who asked if I was keeping him happy. Obviously, if I had, I wouldn't be getting fired."

"That's enough." Angelo pointed to the doorway. "Get out."

"Fine. I'd rather work as an archaeologist anyway. That's what I was hired for." Fuck Angelo and his stupid tour company. If he and his sniveling lackey Giada were going to slut-shame her for something she hadn't done, she never wanted to work for them again.

Dr. Roberti stood abruptly and marched over to her. He got up in her face, so close she could smell the onions on his breath. "Did you not hear my brother? You're fired. Not just from Buon Viaggio but from the entire project. You have an hour to pack up your things and leave Pompeii."

Tears welled up in her eyes. Hot, furious tears, sharp and stinging. Her throat closed up in rage, the painful knot making it hard to swallow.

Being wrongfully accused sucked. Being made to suffer for it sucked even more. She blinked, trying to hold the tears at bay. She'd rather cut off her arm than let these men see her cry. "That's not right. You hired me because of my skills and training as an archaeobotanist. My position here has nothing to do with Buon Viaggio."

"I don't care," Dr. Roberti said. "You cross anyone in my family, and you cross me. You're out. I'll see to it that you never work in Pompeii again."

No.

This couldn't be happening. Not after all the efforts she'd made. The weekends spent leading tourists through Pompeii. Smiling through her exhaustion and never missing a shift. Giving thirty-three people a truly memorable tour of southern Italy. Busting her ass at the site, never taking a day off, even when the heat spiked to ninety-five degrees. And for what? To end up fired because some prick couldn't handle a blow to his ego?

"What about my pay for the tour?" she asked. "I put in a lot of work."

"You won't get another dime out of us," Angelo said. "I suggest you leave before we throw you out."

She'd leave all right, but not without a parting shot. "Go fuck yourself, Angelo. You, too, Maurizio. And tell Luca he can burn in hell. Tell him…I'd rather be fired than let him fuck me. Got all that?" She strode out, slamming the door behind her.

WHEN TJ HEARD YELLING FROM DR. ROBERTI'S OFFICE, HE GREW worried. Had he and Emilia been found out? Were they chastising her for breaking the rules?

But we didn't break them. We waited, damn it.

Even so, he was worried they'd screwed up and Em was taking the heat for it.

Or had something else happened? Had one of the guests left a bad review? A rant so spiteful that they were both in terrible trouble?

The door burst open, and Emilia stormed out. Her face was red, her eyes glistening with tears. Before he could ask her why she was so upset, Giada poked her head out again. "You." She pointed to TJ. "You're up next."

"I…just give me a minute, okay?" he said.

The older woman scowled at Emilia. "You need to leave. If you're not gone in twenty minutes, I'm sending security after you."

Emilia flipped her the finger. "Fuck you, Giada."

TJ stood there, too stunned to move, until he realized Giada was still waiting. "I need a minute."

"One minute, then I'm dragging your skinny ass in here." She closed the door.

Once she was gone, TJ approached Emilia. He wanted to take her in his arms and comfort her, but she held up her hand. "Don't. If you touch me, I'm going to bawl like a baby, and I can't do that here. I have to go before they kick me out, but I need you to do two things for me. Can you agree to that?"

His stomach knotted into a tight ball. "Wait. I don't understand. What just happened?"

"They fired me." Her voice wobbled like she was on the verge of tears, but she didn't cry. "Davis posted his first review, and it was great. Five stars. But they think he did it because I fucked him. As a bribe."

"What?" TJ's heart pounded frantically. While the words registered in his brain, they made no sense. "Why would they think that?"

"Because that's what Luca told them. Clearly, he couldn't handle it when I rejected him, so he cooked up a story to discredit me. He claimed I spent the night with Davis, and his uncles bought into it. They said I 'compromised' Buon Viaggio by trading sexual favors for a five-star review."

"That's total bullshit. I can vouch for you." TJ needed to do something—*anything*—to fix this situation.

She gave a rueful smile. "You can try, but I doubt they'll believe you. Plus, I just told them to go fuck themselves, so I think they're done with me."

Shit. There was no coming back from that. "What about your job at Pompeii?"

"It's over. Dr. Roberti fired me because I messed with his family." She wiped her eyes. "Anyway—about those favors?"

TJ still couldn't believe this was happening. One minute, he and Emilia had been on top of the world, and now, the Robertis were tossing her out like she was yesterday's garbage. "What do you need?"

"I can't face the others. Not like this. But I don't want to lose my equipment. Once you're done, can you go by my lab and grab my stuff? Paulo will know which tools are mine."

He wanted her to slow down, to stop, to rewind *everything*, but he could only nod. "Um…sure. I can do that."

"The second thing. Don't be a hero. Defend me if you want, but don't quit on my behalf. Got it?"

"But…" How could he continue working for the Robertis when they'd behaved so badly?

She frowned. "I don't want you quitting in solidarity or telling them off. I know how much you need this job."

He was about to protest but stopped short. Deep in his heart, he knew she was right. No matter how much he cared about her, he couldn't risk blowing up his future. "Are you sure?"

"I'm sure. No grand gestures. *Please*." She squeezed his arm. "I have to go."

With that, she turned and left. He wanted to run after her, but Giada opened the door to the office again. She gave a jerk of her head. "Get in here. Now."

He followed her inside, hoping he'd find a way to make things right.

CHAPTER TWENTY-EIGHT

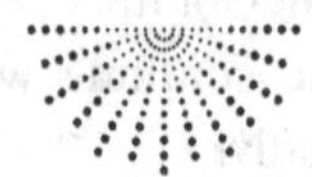

As TJ entered Dr. Roberti's cramped, stuffy office, the thick dust tickled his nose, forcing him to hold back a sneeze. Giada gestured for him to sit in a folding chair, but he waved her off. Instead, he approached the two Roberti brothers, who sat behind a desk piled high with books, papers, and artifacts. He wanted to tackle the issue of Emilia before they sidetracked him with questions about the tour.

He set the Buon Viaggio binder on the desk, grateful to be done carrying it around. "Sorry to make you wait. I was just talking to Emilia. She told me you fired her?"

"We had no choice," Angelo replied. "She broke the most important rule in the binder and compromised our company's integrity."

TJ brushed his hands against his jeans. "With all due respect, sir, she didn't do anything wrong. I don't know what Luca told you, but—"

"He told us enough to take action. She behaved deplorably, offering herself up to that trashy influencer, Davis McGowan, in exchange for a five-star review. Perhaps her intentions were good, but that's not how we operate. It's highly unethical."

Fucking Luca. Now TJ wished he hadn't given the asshole so much leeway. Ever since Emilia had rejected that prick's advances in Rome, he'd treated her poorly, but TJ hadn't done a damn thing about it for fear of pissing him off. He should have shut down Luca right from the start.

"I'm not sure what Luca thinks he saw," he said. "But I can vouch for Emilia. She didn't sleep with Davis. Trust me, I was with her for the entire tour. I would have known if she'd done something like that."

Giada barked out a harsh laugh. "Oh, really? Unless you were with Emilia every night—which I doubt—she could have easily deceived you. You're not the sharpest tool in the shed."

Ouch. Rather than let Giada bait him, he turned to Angelo and addressed him in a humble voice. "If you want, I could contact Davis. Would that help? Once you talk to him, I'm sure he'll clear this up. Then there would be no issue of impropriety."

"I have no need to contact him," Angelo said. "The matter is closed. I trust my nephew's judgment, and I stand by my decision. I don't wish to discuss it any further."

TJ swallowed, tasting grit and dust in the back of his throat. How could he stay silent when he was the only one who could speak up for Emilia? But his resolve weakened under the force of Angelo's piercing stare.

"If you persist in defending your colleague, the door is that way," Dr. Roberti said. "However, I'd caution you against making such a rash move. You clearly have a bright future ahead of you. If I can secure the funding for another six months at Pompeii, I promise you'll be at the top of the list."

This was the prize TJ had been hoping for. The reward at the end of his trials. But as he recalled Emilia's face when she'd left this office, his stomach churned. After the despicable way the two men had treated her, how could he continue working for them?

But how could he not? If he left Pompeii in a huff, what would he do? Where would he go? Hadn't Emilia begged him not to be a hero?

Maybe he could compromise. For now, he'd play along just to get through this meeting. Once he was done, he'd head back to Ercolano and talk to Emilia. Then, he could help her figure out her next move.

"TJ!" Giada snapped. "Angelo asked you a question."

"Sorry." He pushed Emilia from his thoughts. "What did you want to know?"

"If you'll take a seat, I'd appreciate it if we could discuss the tour in more detail," Angelo said. "In particular, I'd like to hear about the musical entertainment you provided for the guests. Though it wasn't on the original itinerary, your report suggested they enjoyed it a great deal."

The sing-along he'd done with Emilia in Bari. *As a team.* He felt like a traitor, but he sat down and gave Angelo his falsest smile. "Sure. I can tell you all about it."

After leaving TJ outside Dr. Roberti's office, Emilia forced herself to keep moving. Without making eye contact, she walked past the labs, past the barriers surrounding the excavation project, and through the crowded site until she reached the exit. She followed the familiar path to the station and got on when a train appeared. All through the ride, she could barely stop shaking. It wasn't until she was off the train that the shock hit her, but she kept going until she reached the sanctity of the hostel.

As she entered the building, she was grateful to see it so empty. With the other archaeologists still at the site, few people were around to witness her shame. Clutching her stomach, she ran to the bathroom and threw up. Not since she'd been ill with the flu, five years ago, had her body reacted so violently. Upon getting to her feet, she leaned against the bathroom sink and released the tears she'd held back for the past hour. She shook with sobs as she relived the agonizing scene with the Robertis.

When she was done—her body purged of all toxins—she stared at her reflection in the mirror, furious at what she saw. A woman who'd let herself be bullied and shamed. Who'd barely defended herself. Who'd cried more in the past month than she had in a year.

I thought you were supposed to be a badass. What happened?

In the past, she'd had no qualms about challenging anyone: misogynistic supervisors, arrogant dig bros, and racist assholes. But now she'd gone soft. She'd lowered her defenses and let people in. And in doing so, she'd made herself vulnerable.

The last time she'd been this weak had been two years ago, during her final confrontation with Vince, when he'd told her how little she meant to him. Back then, her heart had suffered. This time, it was her professional career. Irrevocably tarnished, all because Luca Roberti couldn't handle rejection.

For a second, she imagined what would have happened if she'd followed a different path—one in which she'd responded favorably to Luca's overtures. In this alternate scenario, she would have followed him to his room and submitted to him in bed. And pretended to enjoy it, just to make him happy.

No.

Never.

Even though she'd been kicked out of Pompeii, forced to leave in disgrace, she'd *never* regret turning him down.

She took the stairs to the rooftop patio and sat on a bench in the sun, her teeth chattering, feeling like she'd never be warm again. She needed a plan. Staying in Ercolano was out of the question, but she didn't know where to go.

With shaky hands, she texted Dusty with an SOS, hoping her friend would respond immediately. Since it was early morning in

Boston, Dusty would probably be in her apartment, working on her illustrations.

When Emilia's phone rang with a FaceTime call, she swiped her finger across the screen. Even if she looked a mess, she wanted to connect with Dusty face-to-face.

"Em?" Dusty said. "What happened? Are you okay?"

"Not really. Are you free to talk? Alone?" As much as Emilia respected Stuart, this wasn't something she could share with him right now.

"Sure. Stuart left for the university an hour ago. He's teaching an early morning Latin class. But…Olivia's here. She's in Boston for a symposium at Harvard. Is it okay if she listens in?"

Emilia nodded. Though she'd never been on a dig with Olivia, the two of them had bonded four years ago at a big conference, when they'd been the only Latinas in a panel filled with white male archaeologists. After the panel, they'd gone out for drinks and spent hours sharing stories. They'd stayed in touch ever since.

Olivia's face appeared on the screen next to Dusty's. "Hey, Em. Dusty and I were having coffee, but I'm totally cool with hiding out in the bedroom if you'd rather talk to her alone."

"It's okay. The more female solidarity, the better. I was totally fucked over, and…" Emilia's voice caught. "It hurts so bad."

"Do you need me to fly over there and punch someone out?" Dusty demanded. "Say the word, and I'll do it. I've gotten way too domesticated living with Stuart. I could use a good brawl."

Emilia laughed and wiped her eyes. "No punching. Not until after you hear my story. Do you have time to listen?" She was sure they had places to be, especially Olivia, but they both agreed.

She tried to condense her recap into a quick and dirty series of events, but even the short version was fairly long and involved a large cast of characters. As she recounted her experiences, her earlier shame vanished, replaced by a steadily growing rage.

She'd pulled off that tour like a rock star. She deserved kudos and extra pay, not a kick in the ass.

Apparently, Dusty agreed because she was swearing a blue streak by the end of the story. "Those absolute dickheads. They've got no right to treat you like this. I'm going to burn them to the fucking ground."

While the thought of Dusty barreling into Pompeii and taking on the Robertis made Emilia smile, the reality of her situation still stung like hell. "I feel like such a loser. When Dr. Roberti kicked me out of his office, I barely fought back."

"Sounds to me like you did as much as you could," Dusty said. "First of all, they totally blindsided you. Second, they held all the power. I'm just glad you told them to fuck off instead of slinking out in silence."

"It probably didn't help my cause," Emilia muttered.

"Even if you'd accepted their decision gracefully, it wouldn't have mattered," Olivia said. "When you're a woman in the field, sometimes the odds are stacked against you."

Emilia nodded, appreciating the solidarity. "You're right. And I shouldn't waste any more emotional energy on those pricks. I need to make a plan. Since I don't have a job—as an archaeologist *or* a tour guide—I can't afford to stay here. And…I can't go home a failure."

Shame washed over her as she imagined flying home to her father and explaining how she'd been wrongfully accused. He'd be furious on her behalf, but more than anything, he'd be sad and frustrated that he couldn't help her.

"Then don't go home," Dusty said, pivoting from anger to excitement. "Since you're halfway across Europe, why not go on to Egypt? You could stay with my mom at our family's apartment in Cairo. When the dig season starts in January, I'll bet she could find you a spot on an excavation. Wouldn't you love to work in Egypt?"

The thought was tempting, especially since Dusty's mom was

a world-famous Egyptologist with a ton of connections in the field.

"I could also tap into my Turkish network," Dusty added. "Even if the Troy dig is on hiatus until next summer, there's usually lab work available at the Institute of Nautical Archaeology in Bodrum."

"That's a great idea," Olivia said. "Rick and I worked there two years ago. I loved Bodrum. It's right on the Aegean Sea, and it's not that far from the ruins at Ephesus."

While their suggestions sounded good—not just good but incredible—Emilia couldn't summon her normal level of enthusiasm. Usually, she was always up for an adventure. A new dig site, a new crew, a new place to explore. But not anymore. Her confrontation with the Robertis had stripped away her armor, leaving her vulnerable. For the first time ever, she was afraid to take a chance on anything unknown.

"Thanks," she said. "This is going to sound weak, but I don't think either option's going to work for me. Right now, I'm so tired of hustling. Of starting over somewhere new, trying to make it work, and hoping no one screws me over. I..." She paused, feeling even more like a failure. What was wrong with her? Why wasn't she jumping at the chance to work in Egypt?

"Emilia?" Olivia's voice was soft. "You're not weak. Maybe you just need time to regroup in a place where you don't have to hustle or deal with unwanted male attention. Would you be up for doing contract archaeology in Southern California? There's so much construction going on in Ventura County that Rick's boss is always scrambling for new crew members. You've done salvage archaeology before, so you'd be a huge asset to the team."

Emilia allowed herself a small measure of hope. Even if contract work wasn't the dream, she was good at it. Working with someone as trustworthy as Rick would also mean zero chance of harassment. She wiped her eyes with the back of her hand. "I'd love to take you up on it, but rent in California is so pricey. I couldn't even afford to stay in a trailer." It didn't help that she hadn't been paid for all her work on the tour.

"You could stay with us," Olivia said.

"Hardly. You and Rick live in a one-bedroom apartment. I'd totally cramp your style."

Olivia grinned. "I didn't tell you, did I? The chair of the Classics Department at UC Santa Barbara is on sabbatical this year. She's spending ten months in the Mediterranean, researching a book that traces the path of Homer's *Odyssey*. When she found out I was a cat person, she asked if I'd be available to house-sit. So, in exchange for looking after three cats, Rick and I are living in this sweet two-bedroom bungalow in Ojai, rent-free. We're also supposed to take care of the garden, but I'm not much of a plant whisperer. If you came, you could have the extra bedroom in exchange for your green thumb."

Emilia drew in a shaky breath. After everything she'd been through, Olivia's offer seemed too good to be true. "Don't you and Rick want your privacy?"

Olivia dismissed the question with a wave of her hand. "We're archaeologists. If we have a room with a bed and a door that closes, then we're good."

"Let me know if you need to book a new flight," Dusty said. "I love playing fast and loose with my mom's frequent-flier miles. She has millions of them."

Emilia's heart overflowed with gratitude. At most, she'd expected advice or sympathy, but her friends were offering her a job, a free flight to the States, and a place to live, all because they cared about her. "I don't know what to say."

"Say you'll do it," Olivia said. "I'll call Rick tonight and tell him."

Emilia paused and drew in a shaky breath. "I want to, but I hate feeling so needy."

Dusty glared at her. "Get over it. There's nothing wrong with needing help *or* with accepting it. If the tables were turned, you'd do the same for either of us."

It was hard to argue with Dusty's logic. "Okay," Emilia said. "Thanks so much."

"What about TJ?" Dusty asked. "It's pretty obvious you both wanted more than just two nights of steamy hotel sex."

The question made Emilia cringe with guilt. She'd been so distraught, so focused on figuring out her next move, that she'd left TJ out of the equation. She dug her fingers into a groove on the wooden bench. "I...I'm not sure."

"Can we back up a minute?" Olivia asked. "I was so worried about finding you a job that I almost forgot you and TJ had sex." She gave Emilia a cheeky grin. "I have to know—is he as boastful about his prowess in bed as he is about everything else?"

A smile tugged at Emilia's lips. "Nope. He was sweet and wonderful and really thoughtful. And...um...surprisingly good at oral sex."

"Yes!" Dusty said. "Don't you love it when guys have that skill set down? Please tell me it's not over. You could do the long-distance thing until he comes back in December. Right?"

With all the stress and humiliation of being fired, Emilia hadn't thought ahead to everything she'd be missing. Not just her job and her colleagues but the opportunity to spend the next two months with TJ, indulging in stolen weekends together.

But now? If she was in California and he was in Italy, how could they sustain a relationship? "I don't think it would work. Dr. Roberti might extend TJ's contract through next June, which means we'd be apart for eight months. And once TJ's done in Pompeii, who knows where he'll end up? He's so determined to land a prestigious job that he'll take one wherever he can get it. I'm not going to tie him down."

Nor would she suggest he join her in doing contract archaeology. From what he'd told her, it wouldn't be impressive enough to satisfy his judgmental stepdad.

"Maybe he wants to be tied down," Olivia said. "He might do it for you."

Emilia didn't want to counter with negativity, but she needed to be realistic. Her unjust treatment by the Robertis only served to remind her that life was unfair more often than not. If she expected a happy ending, she'd end up bitterly disappointed.

"He might, but not if it meant turning down a tenure-track position," she said. "If he gets an offer on the East Coast or in the Midwest, then who am I to stand in his way?"

When neither of her friends responded right away, Emilia suspected they didn't agree with her. Then Dusty gave a world-weary sigh. "I hate to say it, but I get what you mean. Those jobs are competitive as hell. When Stuart went through the application process last year, he got so stressed-out. He was fully prepared to move anywhere he had to."

"Same here," Olivia added. "I guess I'm just a sappy romantic at heart. After everything you've been through, I want you and TJ to end up together."

Emilia blinked quickly, trying to stave off a fresh round of tears. Why did life have to be so hard? "I'd like that, too. But right now, I need to put myself first."

Even if it hurt like hell, it was better to make a clean break now than spend the next few months growing apart from TJ, knowing they didn't have any chance of a future together.

CHAPTER TWENTY-NINE

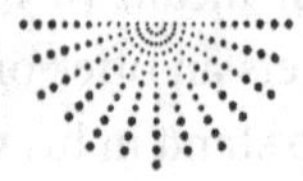

For the last half hour, TJ had been forced to give the Robertis a full rundown of his experiences on the tour. Never mind that he'd already emailed them a sixteen-page document describing each day in painstaking detail. Angelo wanted more. To be precise, he wanted TJ to assure him the tour had gone so successfully that all the guests would leave five-star reviews.

Every time he stroked Angelo's ego, TJ felt more like a hypocrite. To make matters worse, he had to act as though he'd pulled off the tour single-handedly because the Robertis scowled at him whenever he mentioned Emilia. So, he'd played along. In return, Dr. Roberti had suggested—once again—that TJ would be at the top of the list if the Via Stabiana Project was extended into next spring.

Once he was dismissed, TJ bolted out of the office and checked his phone for messages. Nothing from Emilia. Since she hadn't wanted to face the other archaeologists, she'd probably returned to the hostel. He went into the archaeobotanical lab, where Paulo and two of his colleagues were working.

"Hey, Paulo. Can you help me gather up Emilia's tools?

She's…um…" He paused, unsure how much to reveal. "She's leaving Pompeii and asked me to grab her stuff."

Paulo put down his notebook. "Why? Was she fired? Did something go wrong on your tour?"

TJ didn't want to get into it. "It's not really for me to say, but the Robertis made some shitty accusations. She denied them, and then…she told them to fuck off. So, she's out."

Paulo gave a rueful shake of his head. "That sounds like something she'd do. What did they accuse her of?" His colleagues moved in closer, their ears attuned to juicy gossip.

"Can we not discuss this now?" TJ begged. "I just need to get her things. I can tell you more later."

With a huff of annoyance, Paulo set Emilia's tools and her notebooks in a cardboard box. "Here. But I'd like to know what's going on. Not so I can spread gossip but because I care about her."

TJ nodded. He wished Emilia had taken the time to talk to Paulo, but he could also understand why she'd fled so quickly. If she'd stayed, she would have made herself vulnerable, and she hated anyone to see her that way. "I'll tell her. I promise."

"Do you want to wait a few minutes?" Paulo asked. "We're almost done for the day. Then we can go back together."

"Sorry, but I need to talk to her right away. I'll catch you later."

While TJ didn't believe Emilia would leave Ercolano without saying goodbye, she was in such a volatile state that he couldn't predict her behavior. Tucking the cardboard box under his arm, he left the lab and hurried through Pompeii, weaving around tourists until he came to the exit. Once outside the site, he didn't bother to walk to the train station. He needed to get back to the hostel before the others returned so he could have a few minutes alone with Emilia. Upon sighting a taxi, he flagged it down and gave the driver the address. So what if the fare was exorbitant? Now wasn't the time to quibble over money.

At the hostel, he ran up the stairs until he came to Emilia's floor. The door to her room was open, so he walked in. She was sitting on her bed with her backpack and suitcase set to the side. Her red-rimmed eyes and blotchy complexion hinted at an earlier bout of tears.

"Em, I'm so sorry." He set the box on the floor. "Okay if I sit down and give you a hug?"

When she nodded, he sat next to her and took her in his arms. She wasn't crying—not even trembling—which meant she was probably done grieving. She wasn't the type to wallow in misery for any longer than necessary.

She broke free of his grasp and gave him a weak smile. "Thanks. How did your meeting go with the Robertis? Did you get in trouble?"

After all this, she was worried about *him*? "No, it was fine. I tried defending you, and I offered to contact Davis, but they shut me down."

"I figured that might happen." Her brow creased. "You didn't quit, did you?"

He winced with discomfort, wishing he could tell her he'd stormed out in anger. Instead, he had to own up to his cowardice. "I didn't, but I still can. What they did to you isn't right. I'm not sure if I should work for them anymore."

"Don't quit. You've got too much at stake. Did Dr. Roberti offer to keep you on if the project is extended?"

He swallowed the guilt in a giant lump. Bragging about his offer would only make Emilia feel worse, but he couldn't lie to her, either. "Maybe? It depends on whether he gets the funding for next year. But he said I'd be one of the first people he'd consider."

"Good." Emilia leaned down to pick up the box from the floor. "Thanks for this. I should have told you to leave my notebooks there since they're meant to stay with the project, but I'm glad you took them." She gave a snort. "That asshole Maurizio probably would have thrown them in the garbage."

TJ wished he could do more to help her. After all her hard work—at Pompeii *and* on the tour—he couldn't stand that she'd been treated so poorly. "I haven't gotten paid for the tour yet, but when I do, I can send you the money once you get settled." He pointed to her suitcase. "Do you know where you're going?"

He didn't want her to leave, but he knew it would be too hard for her to stay in Ercolano with the other archaeologists.

She twisted the luggage tag between her fingers. "Don't worry about the money. Euros won't do me any good in California."

California? What the fuck?

At most, he'd thought she'd go somewhere else in Italy, like Rome or Florence. When had she decided to go to California? "You're flying back to the States? When are you leaving?"

"In two days. Since my original flight was nonrefundable, Dusty booked me a new one with her mom's frequent-flier miles. Comfort Plus, if you can imagine."

She might be able to smile about it, but TJ could hardly believe his ears. Rather than demand answers, he kept quiet, listening as she explained her new plan: leaving Italy, flying to Los Angeles, moving in with Olivia and Rick, and taking a temporary job in contract archaeology with Rick's crew in Ventura County. Somehow, in the space of an hour, she'd gone from being fired to turning her life in a new direction.

When she was done, she took TJ's hand and gave it a squeeze. "I'm sorry. I didn't want to end things like this. I was really looking forward to spending the next two months with you, but it's not going to work."

His frustration bubbled to the surface, making his words come out harsher than he intended. "It sounds like you didn't even consider staying in Italy. Why not? There are loads of other sites besides Pompeii. What about Sardinia? You've worked there before. Or Florence, where you studied conservation? There has to be something."

She frowned. "Even if there was a job available and I applied, I doubt I'd get hired since I can't use Dr. Roberti as a reference. Sure, I can claim I worked at Pompeii, but then I'd have to explain why I was let go. It would mean a ton of hustling, and I don't have it in me."

"So you're taking the easy way out?" His response was far too judgmental, but he couldn't help himself. This wasn't the Emilia he knew.

Her eyes blazed with a sudden fury. "Why shouldn't I? I've spent the past ten years busting my ass, and for what? To get fired because I wouldn't fuck my boss's nephew? Do you have any idea how much that sucks? Of course not, because you're a man, and you'll never have to deal with this shit. So, please forgive me if I just want a fucking job."

Guilt swamped over him. He didn't want to make this about him, but he didn't want to lose her, either. "Sorry. I was out of line. But what about us?"

She gave a sad little shrug. "There's no 'us.' Not anymore. You're staying here, and I'm going to California, and that's too many miles."

No. He couldn't let her go that easily. "But I'll be home in December. That's only two months away. We could do the long-distance thing until then."

"What if you stay until June? Because if Dr. Roberti asks, you're gonna stay, aren't you?"

Of course he was. He'd be a fool to turn down an opportunity like that. Another six months of work and a stellar recommendation could make the difference between landing a job next year or coming up short. "Would you blame me if I did?"

"No." She let go of his hand and stood up, as though too agitated to sit still. "I'd understand it. Your career comes first. It always has. I totally respect that about you."

Did she? Because right now, she sounded pissed. But he couldn't promise he'd leave Italy in December. Not even for her.

"The thing is," she added, "we were fooling ourselves if we thought we had any chance of a future. Once you're done here, you're going to look for a job wherever you can, right?"

"Right." Was that a bad thing? He'd always thought his perseverance was an asset. Suddenly, he wasn't so sure.

"If that's the case, who knows where you'll end up?" she asked. "It probably won't be Southern California, which means we won't be together. It's better to end things now."

He looked down, overcome with gut-wrenching misery. He should be grateful she was giving him an easy out. She wasn't begging him to come back to the States or find a job in California. She was urging him to follow his dreams, regardless of where they took him. So why did he feel so awful?

Time to put everything on the line. "I get what you're saying, but I don't want to lose you. I'm in love with you."

She closed her eyes and took a deep breath. "Don't say that. *Please*. It'll make this too hard."

"It's the truth. I fell in love with you on that tour, and I—"

"Stop. I don't have any room in my heart right now. I just lost everything—my job, my gig as a tour guide, my reputation, and my chance to be with you until December. I'm gutted and exhausted, and I can't make you feel better right now. I just can't. What we had on the tour was wonderful, but it's over." When her phone pinged, she pulled it out of her pocket and glanced at it. "That's Cesca. She just finished giving a tour of Herculaneum, and she's coming to pick me up in fifteen minutes. I have to finish packing."

"Please don't leave like this. Or at least wait until you've had a few days to recover. You might feel differently then."

He didn't want to come across as patronizing, but she was in a heightened emotional state. Making huge, life-altering decisions before she'd had time to calm down and think them through. In a week's time, she might realize how much she wanted him in her life, even if the most he could offer her was a long-distance relationship.

She gave a sad shake of her head. All her anger had vanished, leaving her with a regretful expression that broke his heart. "I don't think so, TJ, but I'll let you know if something changes. In the meantime, could I get one last hug?"

He didn't want to say goodbye. Not after everything they'd shared on the tour—their camaraderie, their teasing friendship, and their nights of passion in Rome. But he couldn't walk away in anger, either. He stood and took her in his arms, fully aware this might be the last time he ever hugged her.

CHAPTER THIRTY

One Month Later

Emilia was leaning her head against the passenger-side window of Rick's truck, halfway to dozing off, when the song "Piano Man" came on the radio. She reached over and turned down the volume.

"Not a Billy Joel fan, I take it?" Rick asked with a grin. Even after a long day of hot, grubby work on the excavation site, he always maintained his good humor. "You can switch the channel if you like."

"Sorry. It's not Billy Joel—it's this song." A pang of despair washed over her as she recalled TJ playing it on the piano in Bari while she and the rest of the tour group sang along.

"You doing okay?" Rick asked. "You seemed kind of down today. No one in the crew is giving you trouble, are they?"

"Nope. It's all good. But..." She didn't want to admit how much she was missing TJ, so she focused on the other issue that had been nagging at her. "I feel kind of guilty. It's been a month since I moved in with you and Olivia. Aren't you craving more alone time?"

Rick exited the 101 freeway and turned into the In-N-Out

drive-thru in Ventura. "The only thing I'm craving right now is french fries. Don't tell Olivia, or she'll get annoyed. She always thinks I'm going to spoil my dinner." He chuckled. "Like I'd ever turn down anything she cooks? This is just an appetizer."

"Can you get me a Diet Coke? I could use the caffeine."

"You got it." He inched his truck forward into the drive-thru line. "To answer your question—we like having you with us, and the cats adore you. Ever since they started sleeping on your bed, I get Olivia all to myself at night. You don't mind them, do you?"

Emilia couldn't help but laugh. Every night, she went to bed with three cats snuggled beside her. "I like the cats. They're so sweet and cuddly. But that's not the issue."

"There's no issue. We enjoy your company, and you've done wonders with the garden." He moved his truck further down the line. "Unless you'd rather have your own place?"

"Not really. Even if it wasn't beyond my budget, I think I'd get too lonely." If it hadn't been for Rick and Olivia, she would have found it too easy to dwell on the heartache of leaving TJ behind. "I guess a part of me still regrets leaving Pompeii without fighting back. Instead of demanding justice, I fled to the States with my tail between my legs."

"Don't beat yourself up. There are times when the odds are stacked against you, and it's better to cut and run. That happened to me on a project in Crete two years ago. Like you, I was accused of shit I hadn't done, all because the dig director wanted me gone."

"I didn't know that."

"Yeah. I didn't fight him on it, either. Just took off and hoped the next project would be better." He grinned. "And it was. I got a gig on a field school in Cyprus, and that's where Olivia and I met up again. So maybe this is where you're meant to be."

Was it? She was pondering the thought when the staticky voice of the drive-thru operator came through the window. "Welcome to In-N-Out. What can I get for you?"

"One order of french fries and a large Diet Coke, please," Rick said. He drove up to the window and paid the cashier before turning his attention back to Emilia. "Just to be clear—you're welcome to stay as long as you want. Or at least until Olivia's boss comes back. At that point, we'll have to find a new place, too, but that's not until June."

Emilia let out a relieved sigh. "Thanks. I appreciate it. The job, too. It's been great."

"Good to hear. I know it can't compare to working at Pompeii. Not gonna lie, digging in California will never hold a candle to Italy."

"But you're okay with it? You worked on projects all over the Mediterranean. Don't you miss that life?" For as many dig stories as Rick had shared with her, he'd never shown any remorse over what he'd given up by coming back to California.

He shrugged. "Not that much. There's nowhere else I'd rather be than with Olivia, and I'm still doing what I love. Ultimately, that's what matters."

A twinge of sadness tugged at Emilia's heart. What would it be like to have a partner like Rick? Someone who cared enough about her that he'd be willing to compromise if need be.

She shook off the thought. Rather than dwell on what she was lacking, she should be thankful she'd landed on her feet. She'd left Italy in tears and disgrace but ended up with a decent job and a place to live. Even if doing contract archaeology in California wasn't as glamorous as excavating in Pompeii, at least she was working in her field.

With each day that passed, she felt stronger as her anguish over leaving Italy gradually faded. Only two things still troubled her: she had yet to tell her father the truth, and she'd cut TJ out of her life. She hadn't wanted to hurt him, but after she'd arrived in California, his texts had gotten so needy that she'd asked him to stop. But she still missed him terribly.

At night, when she was in bed, her thoughts drifted to him

and the memories of their time together on the tour. Not just the steamy moments but the fun they'd had quizzing each other on the binder, bantering during their presentations, and talking late into the night as they planned out each day's itinerary. No matter how tired or grumpy she got, he always managed to coax a smile out of her. She'd give anything to wake up and find that he'd miraculously appeared at the breakfast table with the coffee already brewed. Extra bold, just the way she liked it.

Once they'd gotten their order, Rick merged back onto the freeway. Twenty minutes later, he pulled into the driveway of the bungalow. At the front entrance, a plastic skeleton sat in a lawn chair, wearing a pirate hat. Three elaborately carved pumpkins were piled at his feet. With Halloween a few days away, Emilia had insisted they set up a display to lure in trick-or-treaters. As she followed Rick into the house, she was hit with the mingled scents of cumin, chilies, and garlic, which made her mouth water.

Olivia stood in the kitchen, stirring a pot on the stove. At the sight of them, she laughed. "You two are positively filthy. We've got about twenty minutes before dinner's ready, so you both have time to grab a shower if you make it quick."

One of the few downsides of the bungalow was that it only contained one bathroom. Emilia turned to Rick. "You want to go first?"

"Nah. You go on ahead." He sauntered over to Olivia and put his arms around her waist. "I'm going to harass the cook."

"Hands off, mister," Olivia said. "You're way too dirty."

He nuzzled her neck. "You like it when I'm dirty. Don't you, princess?"

Emilia took that as her cue to leave. After shucking off her filthy clothes in the bathroom, she jumped into the shower. Under the warm spray, she let her mind wander as she imagined a different scenario. One in which she wasn't crashing in anyone's spare room but living in a place of her own, coming home from work each day to a loving, affectionate partner.

Someone who respected and cherished her the way Rick did Olivia.

Someone like TJ.

~

OVER A DELICIOUS DINNER OF CHICKEN ENCHILADAS WITH MOLE sauce, black beans, and lime-cilantro rice, Emilia was lulled into a sense of complacency. As always, the food was amazing—Olivia had learned to cook from her parents, who owned a Mexican restaurant in San Diego—and the conversation was lively. Olivia was teaching a junior-level seminar on the Roman Empire at UC Santa Barbara, and some of her female students had *very* strong opinions about the patriarchy. But just as Emilia was taking a mouthful of rice, Olivia hit her with a question that chilled her blood.

"Em? I hate to put you on the spot, but there's something I need to talk to you about. Are you up for it?"

Emilia swallowed quickly, washing down the rice with a swig of beer. Maybe Rick had been wrong when he'd said she was welcome to stay. "You want me to move out? Is that it?"

"No. Of course not. I like having you here. Besides, the cats would never allow it. They're madly in love with you. It's about TJ."

"Did something happen to him? Is he okay?" Emilia's gut twisted as her mind raced with worst-case scenarios.

Olivia gave her a knowing look. "That response right there? Total proof you still care about him. He texted me yesterday because he's worried about you. He wanted to make sure you're doing all right."

Emilia looked down at her plate, too ashamed to face her friend. "I…cut him off because it was too hard, but he hasn't messaged me for weeks. I assumed he'd moved on."

"TJ? Move on?" Rick said. "The guy is nothing if not persistent. He even texted *me*."

"Could you throw him a bone?" Olivia asked. "Send him a message to let him know everything's good? Even if you're upset with him, it's not right to leave him hanging."

Emilia frowned. "What makes you think I'm upset with him? I never said that."

"But you're pissed he stayed at Pompeii. Right?" Rick asked.

She shook her head emphatically. "I told him to stay. I would have felt guilty if Dr. Roberti had fired him." One of the cats brushed past her ankles and meowed. She reached down to pet him, grateful for the distraction.

"Are you sure?" Olivia grabbed the bowl of black beans and scooped more on her plate. "It's okay if you were mad. Rationally, it makes sense that you didn't want him to quit. But emotionally? Maybe you *wanted* him to stand up for you."

"I've never needed anyone to stand up for me. I'm not some damsel that needs rescuing." Ever since she was eighteen, Emilia had fought her own battles. And yet—deep down, a small part of her couldn't help but resent TJ for the way he'd caved so readily. How he'd done whatever the Robertis wanted, just to stay on at Pompeii and secure a glowing recommendation.

"This isn't about being rescued," Olivia said. "It's about wanting your partner to do the right thing, regardless of the risks involved."

"Maybe TJ just needs a nudge," Rick said. "A sign from you that you want more from him. Do you really want it to end like this?"

Emilia pushed the food around on her plate. "Even if I wanted him back, it's not like we had any chance of a future, not when our lives are going in different directions."

"Where have I heard that before?" Rick said with a smile. "Oh, that's what Olivia told me when she broke my heart in Cyprus."

Olivia placed her hand on his arm. "I was *so* wrong, but I was convinced we couldn't make a go of it because we didn't know where we'd end up. Even when we were together last year, my job search threw us for a loop. I knew if I wanted to teach college, I'd have to apply everywhere I could. Getting hired to work at UC Santa Barbara was such a relief since Rick could keep his job here, and we could both be close to our families."

Emilia looked between the two of them. "What if you'd gotten hired somewhere else? Didn't you make the short list for two other schools?"

"I did," Olivia said. "Rick and I talked about it. I would have taken whatever I could get, especially if it was a tenure-track position."

Rick nodded. "I said I'd go with her, no matter what. One way or the other, I'd find work."

Emilia let their words sink in. She'd known the job hunt had weighed heavily on Olivia, but she'd never realized how big of a sacrifice Rick was willing to make just to be with her.

"So—this thing with TJ?" Olivia said. "If it's more than just a fling, then maybe it's worth the effort."

"How can it be? I only spent two nights with him in Rome, and the tour wasn't even two weeks long. But..." Emilia set down her beer, groaning as the realization hit her. "I'm still stuck on him. I always have been. Even at Troy, when he provoked me constantly, I loved challenging him. Same with our tours at Pompeii. Whenever I was around him, he lit a fire inside of me."

She didn't miss the knowing look Rick and Olivia gave each other. Like they understood *exactly* what she meant.

"After the tour ended, I was so glad we'd get more time together. We'd already planned our first weekend getaway. But...I need to move on." She took a deep, shuddering breath. "If I think too much about everything I've lost, it's too hard to keep going."

"Sorry. I didn't mean to harp on it," Olivia said. "We can talk about something else. Sofia called me today with some interesting news."

Rick smirked. "Did she call while you were teaching class? She has the worst timing of anyone I know."

Even if Olivia's younger sister, Sofia, was a globe-trotting influencer, she didn't seem to grasp the concept of time zones or people's schedules.

"She's just too impatient to wait," Olivia said. "She was like that even as a kid. Whenever she had news, she insisted on sharing it immediately. Fortunately, she didn't disrupt my class today. She called when I was getting dinner ready. Talked my ear off about a new discovery in the Yucatán Peninsula. Some kind of lost city? Javier told her about it."

Emilia had met Sofia's fiancé, Javier, before when she'd dug in the Yucatán as an undergrad. "The Maya temples there are amazing, but I was never lucky enough to uncover a lost city. That's Indiana Jones-type stuff."

"Sofia's dying to go there and check it out. Like, she somehow presumes she could machete her way through the jungle and visit the site." Olivia snorted. "But we both agreed we should plan a group trip to the Yucatán Peninsula next year. Wouldn't that be a blast? I've been to Mexico to visit my dad's relatives but never to that part of the country."

They spent the rest of dinner talking about the Maya temples they wanted to visit, and Emilia recounted her experiences digging at Calakmul, a site buried deep in the jungle.

But that night, while in bed with the three cats snuggled beside her, she picked up her phone and looked at her last text from TJ. By now, she'd read it dozens of times.

> Em, I miss you so much it hurts. Out of respect for your wishes, I won't text you anymore. I hope things work out for you in California.

Her fingers hovered over the screen as she considered responding. She wanted to tell him how much she missed him. That she wished she could have stayed in Italy and that they could have spent their weekends sneaking off to Naples and Sorrento.

But her life wasn't like Rick and Olivia's. Fate might have smiled on them, but she'd always been a fickle bitch to Emilia.

With a sigh, she set her phone on the nightstand and turned out the light.

For now, it was best to relegate TJ to her dreams. The reality was just too painful.

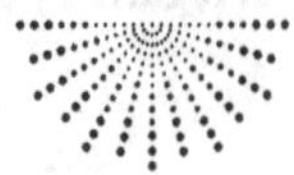

CHAPTER THIRTY-ONE

Upon leaving Pompeii at the end of a long workday, TJ made it to the station as the train pulled up. He hopped in quickly, but when a familiar voice ordered him to hold the door, he braced himself against it.

Marie dashed inside and claimed the first available seat. "Thanks. I hate waiting, especially on a Friday."

"Same here." He snagged the seat across from her and raised his voice so she could hear him. "Any big plans for the weekend?"

She blew out a frustrated breath. "I wish, but all those getaways to the Amalfi Coast have started adding up. I need some extra cash, so I agreed to give tours this weekend. Maybe we'll get paired up together. That could be fun."

He was surprised to hear her say it, given that she'd been ignoring him ever since she'd taken up with Paulo. "Sorry, but I worked the last four weekends in a row, so I'm taking a break this Saturday. I'm headed to Naples to meet with my friends Cesca and Davis."

"Are they archaeologists, too?"

"No. She works for Roman Pathways Tours, and he's a travel influencer."

He'd been pleased when Davis had contacted him about getting together. They'd chosen to meet in Naples since Cesca would be home visiting her family, and she'd promised to take them to her favorite bars in the city.

Marie made a face. "Davis? Is he the YouTube guy who was on your tour? I heard *all* about him and Emilia."

A burst of anger flared up inside of TJ. After Emilia left Italy, he hadn't revealed the truth to anyone. When pressed, he'd told the others she'd had a disagreement with the Robertis, but he'd never breathed a word about Luca, Davis, or the accusations Angelo had made. "What are you talking about?"

"Last weekend, Chloe gave a couple of tours, and she asked Giada why Emilia left Pompeii so suddenly. Apparently, Em was fired after she slept with Davis to boost the company's ratings. She hardly seems the type to seduce anyone, but that's a sleazy thing to do."

TJ clenched his fists. He willed himself not to go on an expletive-laden rant against Giada or Angelo. Marie didn't deserve to be subject to that, not when she was only parroting what she'd heard. But she needed to know the truth. He'd kept quiet to protect Emilia, but he didn't want anyone judging her for a crime she hadn't committed.

"That's total bullshit," he said. "Angelo's nephew Luca made that stuff up. Emilia didn't sleep with Davis."

"How do you know?"

What did it matter if he fessed up now? "Because Emilia and I were together. We didn't want to get in trouble for breaking the rules, so we kept it quiet."

"Wait. What?" Marie's voice was so loud that the businessman sitting next to her glared at them. "You and Emilia? But she couldn't stand you."

"Not at first, but..." A ghost of a smile crossed his face. "We grew closer on the tour."

"Did you tell the Robertis that?" she asked.

"No, but I stood up for Emilia. I told them there's no way she would have slept with Davis. It would have been a total conflict of interest."

The train came to a sudden halt, rocking TJ so much he almost fell off his seat. He grabbed the metal bar next to him and clutched on tightly. Of all the times to be stuck on the train, why did it have to be now when Marie was staring him down with murder in her eyes?

"You mean to tell me those assholes fired Emilia on false pretenses?" she said. "And you were okay with it? What the hell, TJ?"

He wiped his brow, suddenly aware the AC had shut off. "I didn't say I was okay with it."

"But you stayed and kept giving tours for Buon Viaggio? You're a coward."

He took a sip from his water bottle, hoping the liquid would quench the dryness in his throat. Over the past month, he'd harbored the exact same thoughts. That he was a coward who should have done more for Emilia. "Em told me to stay at Pompeii. She didn't want me to ruin my future by quitting."

Marie threw up her hands, further annoying the businessman next to her. "She might have said it, but she didn't mean it."

"She did. She made me promise not to quit. You know how Em is—she's stubborn as hell. I was just following her wishes."

Be honest. You were following your own ambition.

On the one hand, Emilia wouldn't have appreciated him trailing her to California, unrooted and jobless. But on the other? He hadn't considered any alternatives besides staying at Pompeii and working for the jerks who'd fired her.

Marie narrowed her eyes at him. "So...how'd that decision work out for you? Are you still together? Or did she ghost you after she left Italy?"

Ouch. He could have lied and claimed he and Emilia texted on a daily basis. But after sending her a few desperate messages, he'd gotten a terse reply from her, asking him to stop. She hadn't even wanted to stay friends. "She cut me off."

Marie smacked her hand against the metal bar. "You see? You blew it. Some boyfriend you are."

TJ's throat closed up as he remembered how distraught Emilia had been when she left Dr. Roberti's office. "The thing is… even if I'd wanted to help Emilia, there was nothing I could have done. They weren't going to take my word over Luca's. When I tried to speak up on her behalf, they threatened to fire me."

He almost wished they had. Or wished he'd been bold enough to defend the woman he loved. Instead, he'd backed down, all for a chance to keep working at Pompeii. But with every week that passed, he grew more and more resentful. He hated the way Dr. Roberti had him on the hook. How he constantly suggested—no, *insisted*—that TJ spend his days off giving tours of the site. Each time, he reminded TJ that the more effort he put in, the more likely he'd get to stay until June. TJ was starting to suspect his boss was lying, especially since none of the other archaeologists had heard about the project being extended.

"Why don't you do something now?" Marie said. "When I worked with Dr. Roberti two years ago, he had a reputation for being vindictive. I heard a bunch of rumors, but I wasn't sure what to believe. If he and his brother are really that bad, you should make them pay."

TJ wanted to argue that he had no power, that he was an American working in Italy on a visa, that he was no one in the grand scheme of things. But Marie was glaring at him with such ferocity that he nodded quickly. "I can try, but I don't know what I could do."

As the train jolted forward, Marie gripped onto the bar beside her. "You're a smart guy. I'm sure you'll think of something."

For the rest of the ride, she ignored him, choosing to scroll through her phone rather than make eye contact. TJ sat in silence, letting the guilt wash over him, as the train made its painfully slow journey to Ercolano.

That night, rather than join his cohort when they went out for dinner, he retreated to the hostel's rooftop patio to be alone with his thoughts. Marie's accusations buzzed in his head like a swarm of furious bees. Was he wrong for not leaving Pompeii after the Robertis had fired Emilia? Even though she'd asked him not to quit, he could have left in protest, as a show of solidarity. But even if he had, Dr. Roberti wouldn't have cared. Not when he could easily find another archaeologist to take TJ's place.

What TJ really wanted, more than anything, was to get justice for Emilia. To show the Robertis they couldn't treat a woman so unfairly and get away with it.

But how?

As furious as he was at the Roberti brothers, he was too much of a professional to compromise the Via Stabiana Project. That meant tampering with the site or the labs was out of the question. If he wanted to make an impact, he'd have to take on Buon Viaggio Tours.

He tried to think of what would hurt Angelo the most. The answer was almost *too* easy.

Bad reviews.

For the first time since he'd lost Emilia, TJ felt a small glimmer of hope.

~

The following night, TJ met up with Cesca and Davis in Naples. They were seated outside at a table on the Via dei Tribunali—a popular street that cut through the oldest part of the city—and the area around them was packed with tourists and locals enjoying a balmy Saturday evening. Cesca had ordered drinks for all of them and a huge charcuterie plate piled high with mozzarella, prosciutto, salami, tomatoes, and olives.

Though TJ was desperate to hit them up with his plan for taking down Buon Viaggio, he didn't want to come across as too self-centered. Instead, he asked Davis about his trip to Lake Como. Then, Cesca regaled them with anecdotes from her last excursion—a weeklong jaunt through Tuscany, complete with three wine tastings. When she was done, TJ was ready to present his idea. Before getting them on board, he filled them in on everything that had happened to him and Emilia after the end of their tour—their two nights in Rome, their blissful return to Pompeii, and her brutal confrontation in Dr. Roberti's office.

"Well, fuck," Cesca said after he'd finished setting the scene. "When I picked up Em in Ercolano, she was a wreck. She said she was leaving Italy because the Robertis fired her, but she didn't give me the details. I figured it was bad, but not this bad."

Davis swiped a hand through his floppy blond hair. "I'm so sorry. I liked hanging out with her, but I never intended to get her in trouble."

"You didn't do anything wrong," TJ said. "It was that shithead Luca. He couldn't get over the fact that she turned him down."

"I never liked him," Davis muttered. "He gave off stalker vibes."

"So, now Em's working in California?" Cesca asked. "Is that where she's from?"

"She's from Wisconsin," TJ said. "But we have a good friend who works in salvage archaeology in Southern California, and he offered her a job. She seems to be doing okay—not that she's told me herself. My friends have been sending me updates. I think I fucked up by not taking a bigger stand when she was fired."

Cesca popped an olive into her mouth. "There wasn't much you could do. It was your word against Luca's, and he's family. Em told me Luca's dad is a bigwig who's thinking of investing in Buon Viaggio. I'm guessing Angelo and Maurizio needed to keep Luca happy, and firing Emilia was an easy way to do it. But it totally sucks."

Davis signaled the waiter over and ordered another Aperol spritz. "What a bunch of assholes. Now I wish I'd never left those glowing reviews. Even if you and Em gave a great tour, the company didn't deserve my videos."

TJ took a deep breath, then launched into his pitch. "About that? Last night, I came up with a plan to torpedo the company, but I'll need your help. It's a huge favor, so you can say no if you're not okay with it."

"I never mind stirring up shit," Davis said. "You've watched that review I left for Global Adventures. More people liked that video than any of my other ones."

"This would be even more scathing," TJ said. "I was hoping you'd be willing to create a new video about the tour. One where you spilled *all* the tea. You'd tell everyone how the Robertis falsely accused Emilia and then fired her, all because of Luca."

Cesca pounded the table. "Fuck, yes! Davis, you've gotta do it."

To TJ's relief, Davis grinned. "I'd be up for it. The title could be...'Why I'm Never Touring with Buon Viaggio Again' or something like that. Total clickbait. TJ, you need to write down everything you just told me and email it to me." He paused as though thinking it through. "In my video, I won't mention Em's name or reveal you two were together, but I'll focus on the injustice she suffered. And I'll explain to my subscribers how my own name was smeared by this company. How those lowlifes accused me of demanding sex in exchange for a five-star review. This is gonna be epic."

TJ eased out a grateful breath. Davis wasn't just on board; he was excited about it. "Thanks. As a follow-up, I was thinking I'd contact everyone else who was on the tour."

Cesca rubbed her hands together. "Ooh, this sounds diabolical. Do you have a way to get in touch with them?"

"Yeah. Two days ago, Angelo asked me if I'd email all of them to offer them a twenty-percent discount if they booked another tour within the next twelve months. Instead, I could tell them what happened to Emilia. Most of them left great reviews, but they could always submit new ones. Right?"

"Right." Davis grabbed the last piece of salami from the platter. "A lot of them liked Em. If they knew what the Robertis did to her, they might speak up."

"It's a great idea," Cesca said. "A bunch of shitty one-star reviews could have a big impact, especially if they left them on an aggregator like Tripadvisor or Viator."

TJ nodded. He'd send out the emails tomorrow before he lost his nerve. He had no idea if any of the guests would respond or if they'd be annoyed at him for making such a huge request, but it was worth a try.

"Um...TJ?" Cesca said. "Just a warning—if you go through with this and the Robertis trace it to you, then you'll probably get fired."

Davis let out a snort. "No, you'll *definitely* get fired."

TJ downed the rest of his Campari and set his cocktail glass on the table. Was he making an enormous mistake by letting revenge fuel his actions?

No. Not when he'd been mired in regret for weeks. Working for a pair of assholes. Wallowing in shame, fully aware he'd been too weak to take a stand. Even the prospect of staying another six months didn't energize him. These weren't the people he wanted to work for.

"It's okay," he said. "If I'm going to be fired, I'll go out in a blaze of glory." If Emilia were here, she'd tease him about sounding boastful, but she'd say it with a smile. Like she admired him for making the effort.

"This isn't just about getting revenge, is it?" Cesca said. "You're in love with Em."

While TJ was embarrassed his feelings were so transparent, he didn't want to lie. "Yeah. I'm all in, but I don't think she feels the same way. Before she left Ercolano, I told her how I felt, and she said she couldn't deal with it."

"Because she'd just gotten fired," Cesca replied. "That wasn't about you."

"You need to try again," Davis added. "Hitting her with a big romantic confession when she was at her lowest wasn't the smartest move."

TJ knew that now. But what stung was the way she'd cut him off after she arrived in California, which meant he hadn't gotten another chance. Even so, he was going to fight for her. "I'm not sure if she'll take me back, but I still want justice for her. Whatever it costs me."

"Dude, you're doing the right thing," Davis said. "But you might want to figure out your next move, especially after you go back to the States. No chance in hell you'll be getting a recommendation from Dr. Roberti."

True. After the way Emilia had begged him not to quit, he didn't want her to get upset that he'd blown up his future. But was he really blowing it up? Pompeii wasn't the only gig on his resume. He'd worked on projects all over the Mediterranean and the Middle East and had held research assistantships for three Harvard professors.

"I think I'll be okay," he said. "I'll just have to dig deep and reach out to all my contacts. Everyone I've ever dug with, every professor who's ever recommended me, anyone who could give me a boost. And hell, I might even mention Pompeii. If they want to know more, I'll tell them I left because my employer was a sexist asshole."

Just thinking about it eased a little of the heartache that had plagued him over the past five weeks. A sure sign he was making the right call.

"Okay, then," Davis said. "Once you send me the details, I'll get started on the video. I just wish…"

"What?" TJ gnawed on his lip, suddenly worried Davis was having second thoughts. Without the video, their plan wouldn't have the same impact.

Davis twisted the stem of his cocktail glass between his fingers. "I wish I had a bigger platform. My views have been increasing steadily, but not as fast as I'd like. I want everyone to hear this. If I had more connections, then—"

"Hang on," TJ said. "My friend Olivia has a younger sister who's a big travel influencer. I met her in Cyprus a couple of years ago. Her name's Sofia Sanchez, but she goes by SoFood SoFia, and she's got a ton of subscribers."

Davis' eyes widened. "Whoa. You know her personally? I'm a major fan of her work."

"You think she'd be willing to help?" Cesca said. "This is a big ask."

"I can try." For once, TJ couldn't resist using one of his stepdad's motivational quotes. "You know what they say—you miss one hundred percent of the shots you don't take."

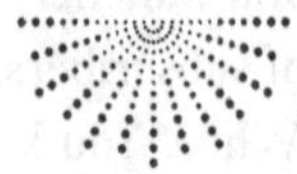

CHAPTER THIRTY-TWO

With a yawn, Emilia grabbed the coffeepot from the warmer and topped up her cup. She passed the pot to Olivia, who sat beside her at the breakfast bar. Relaxing on a weekend morning was a rare occurrence for Emilia. Usually, she tried to stay busy by going on long runs or spending hours in the garden. Since today's forecast called for heavy rains, she hadn't bothered to change out of her pajamas.

Rick sat on the couch with his head bent over his laptop. Though he claimed he was drafting a report for work, Emilia knew the truth. He was scouring travel sites for a weekend getaway with Olivia. He'd wanted to take her somewhere romantic for her birthday in October, but they'd both been too busy. Emilia had encouraged him to go for it because she suspected he was planning to propose. Even if she lacked any semblance of a love life, she wanted her friends to be happy.

When Olivia's phone rang, she picked it up with a huff of annoyance. "Sofia. Does she not realize it's barely seven?"

Emilia laughed. Even if Olivia's younger sister was crap at paying attention to time zones, she was always so bubbly and upbeat it was hard to stay mad at her. "Aren't you going to answer it?"

"Nah. It's too early. If it's important, she'll call back."

"Do you want me to make more coffee?" Emilia asked. "My head's still fuzzy from last night."

"Yes, please," Olivia said. "I totally regret opening that second bottle of wine with dinner. It didn't help that Calcite woke us up so early this morning."

Rick patted the tabby cat sleeping next to him. "Hey, the little guy caught a mouse. I don't blame him for being excited about it."

"I guess, but I would have preferred a few more hours of sleep." When Olivia's phone started up again, she groaned. "Now she's calling me on FaceTime. I hate it when she does that first thing in the morning. She knows what my hair looks like." She pushed her messy curls away from her face, swiped the screen, and put the call on speaker. "Hey, Sof. What's so urgent you had to call me at seven in the morning?"

"Good morning, Liv!" Sofia's perky voice came through clearly. "It's seven there? Wow. So early. It's already nine in Chicago."

"Yes, that's how time zones work," Olivia muttered. "What's up?"

"Is Emilia around? I have big news for her."

Emilia went to stand next to Olivia and waved at the screen. "I'm here. How's it going?"

"It's going great! Like, *fantastic*. Did either of you catch my latest video? Well, it wasn't *my* video, but the one I shared on my YouTube channel on Tuesday?"

"Sorry," Olivia said. "I've been busy with a ton of grading. I'll watch it later today."

"You need to watch it now!" Sofia demanded. "It's about *you*, Emilia."

"What?" Emilia downed the rest of her coffee, hoping the jolt of caffeine would jump-start her foggy morning brain. "You made a video about me?"

"I told you, *I* didn't make it. Your friend did. Davis. The guy you met in Italy? He made a video about your tour and how those fuckers at Buon Viaggio screwed you over. Then he asked me to share it—well, *he* didn't ask me, but TJ did. And I still remember good old Teej from Cyprus, so I said yes. And it got *so* many views. Like, even more than my last video, when I taste-tested five kinds of Chicago-style deep-dish pizza—which was a total masterpiece if I do say so myself."

Emilia's head swam with confusion. Why would Davis post a video about her? And why *now*?

"Hang on, Sof," Olivia said. "Are you saying Davis created a new video about the Buon Viaggio tour, and then TJ asked you to share it?"

"Did you not hear me?" Sofia sputtered. "You're a little slow on the uptake this morning. I shared it four days ago, but you haven't commented on it, so I had to make sure you saw it."

"Thanks," Emilia said. "I'll check it out. I'm sure Davis appreciated the boost. You probably have a lot more subscribers than he does."

Sofia laughed. "That's putting it mildly, but it was no problem. I'm always happy to take down the patriarchy, one asshole at a time. Or three assholes, in the case of the Robertis. I've gotta go because Javier's taking me out for waffles, but you need to watch it ASAP. Catch you later."

Already, Emilia was pulling out her phone, going to YouTube, and bringing up Sofia's channel. The first video she saw was the one Sofia had shared from Davis. It was labeled, "Why I'll Never Tour Italy With Buon Viaggio Again—And Why You Shouldn't Either!" The title alone made it the perfect clickbait.

When Emilia hit Play, Olivia watched over her shoulder. At first, Davis praised Emilia's performance on the tour, reiterating the things he'd said in his original video—the one that had gotten her in trouble. But then he let loose, telling everyone what the Robertis had done to her. While he didn't mention her by name, he made it clear she was an innocent victim who'd been let go because she'd refused to sleep with the boss's nephew. Not only was Davis pissed at the Robertis for firing her, but he also hated that they'd accused him of trading reviews for sex. After the video ended, Emilia stared at the screen, astonished that he'd taken the time to do this for her.

Rick spoke up. "Holy shit. I just checked Buon Viaggio on Tripadvisor, and their ranking for that ten-day tour of southern Italy is way down. There's a one-star review from a Sylvie Galloway and another from an Irene Mangold."

Emilia rushed over to him. "Can I see?"

As she scanned the recent reviews of Buon Viaggio, an ache tore at her throat. Nine of the guests who'd left five-star reviews in September had posted new ones, downgrading the tour to one star after learning how the company had treated Emilia. She'd been vindicated.

"I...I can't believe it," she said.

"Believe it," Olivia said. "TJ must have engineered this. He really came through for you."

Tears welled up in Emilia's eyes. "I should go talk to him. Right?"

When Rick and Olivia nodded, she ran outside. She plopped down on a bench facing the garden, not caring that it was damp with dew, and punched in TJ's number. When he didn't answer, she hung up without leaving a message. Her head was so muddled that she wasn't sure what time it was in Italy. For all she knew, he could be sound asleep.

Or maybe he's not answering. You haven't texted him in over a month.

She stared at the phone, wondering if she should try again, when it buzzed in her hand. At the sight of TJ's name, she answered immediately, her voice shaky with nerves. "TJ?"

"Em. Sorry I missed your call, but I didn't want to talk with my roommates around. I had to go up on the roof."

With all her heart, she wished she could be there with him. "I saw the video. I can't believe you did that."

"Most of the credit goes to Davis. He put it all together. And to Sofia for sharing it on her channel. She has so many subscribers."

"But you lit the match. You…you…" She paused. "*Shit*. You got fired, didn't you?"

He laughed, his glee evident. Like he was glad he'd gotten in trouble. "I was *so* fired. Giada saw the video the day it came out, and she told the Robertis. When they summoned me into their office, they thought you were the one behind it, but I made it clear you had nothing to do with it."

"You didn't have to do that." He'd put his future at risk, all because of her.

"I totally did. After the way they smeared your reputation and treated you like garbage, they needed to be called on their behavior. That's worth more than any job. They took turns yelling at me, then they fired me, and *then* Dr. Roberti told me I'd never work at Pompeii again."

She cringed, imagining the scene. But despite the consequences, she was grateful TJ had fought for her. "So, what are you doing now? Did you find work somewhere else?"

"Here's the funny thing—I *am* working at Pompeii. Cesca got me a job with Roman Pathways, giving half-day tours of Pompeii and Herculaneum. Turns out her boss hates Buon Viaggio so much that he was thrilled to employ someone who'd tried to take down the company. Did you see all the negative reviews of our tour? There's a vicious one on Tripadvisor from Alice. I never knew she had it in her."

Hearing TJ's voice was like a balm to Emilia's soul. It also hammered home just how deeply she'd missed him. "I'm glad you found something to tide you over. Are you just doing half-day tours? Or are they going to send you on any longer excursions?"

"Just the short tours. The only way I'd do one of those long-ass trips would be if we did it together. I miss you so much."

She wiped her eyes with the sleeve of her pajama top. "I miss you, too. I'm sorry I cut you off after I got here. It was just too hard and..."

"I get it. I should have quit right from the start. Even though you asked me not to, I didn't feel right working for the Robertis. I'm sorry I waited so long to stand up for you."

His apology was so heartfelt that she wanted to jet across the miles and hug him. "It's all right. I don't blame you. No one's ever done anything like that for me."

"You deserve it, and so much more. I know you aren't some damsel that needs rescuing, but I wanted to get justice for you."

She couldn't help but smile at the way his words mirrored her earlier thoughts. "Thanks. I'm starting to realize it's okay to accept help from people who care about me."

"I *do* care. Maybe it's too soon to ask, but do you think we could be friends again?" He paused. "Or...maybe something more?"

She gave a deep, shuddering sigh. After everything he'd done for her, she couldn't keep her walls up any longer. She needed to let him back in, even if it meant risking more heartache. "I'd rather have more. I never told you this before, but I...I'm in love with you. Sorry it took me so long to admit it."

"Em." His voice broke. "You already know how I feel, but I'll say it again. I fell in love with you on that tour, and my feelings haven't changed. I don't want to lose you."

If he could make himself vulnerable, then so could she. "I don't want to lose you, either. You're coming back to the States in December, right?" *Please say yes.*

"You bet. I'm flying home in six weeks. Even though I'm a masterful tour guide, I need a real job. I've already started looking, but as of today, I've decided to narrow my search. West Coast only, preferably Southern California."

She drew in a breath, stunned at what he was implying. "I didn't ask you to do that."

"I know, but what's the point of landing an amazing job if it takes me thousands of miles from the woman I love? I've applied everywhere I can think of, and I'd even be okay doing salvage archaeology if Rick's boss would be willing to hire me. I think we could make it work as long as you're on board with it."

She was about to argue that he shouldn't sacrifice his career goals for her, but she stopped herself. Why *shouldn't* he make this sacrifice? Wasn't she worth it? Maybe fate would smile on them for once.

"I'm definitely on board," she said. "If you could find a job in California, that would be ideal. I really like it here."

"And you like what you're doing?"

"I do. It's a good fit. I'm not sure if I'll stick with contract archaeology long-term, but for now, it's perfect." The rain began falling, the drops spattering her hair and shoulders, but she didn't move from her spot on the bench. After days of hot, dry weather, the cool drizzle had a cathartic effect. "It's going to be so hard to wait until December to see you."

"It'll go by quicker than you think. In the meantime, I'll send you sexy texts. Racy images from the lupanar at Pompeii. Photos of the Trojan horse. I'll make you videos where I'm serenading you on the piano. Whatever it takes to keep us connected until we can meet in person again. Does that sound okay?"

Even across the miles, his eagerness was irresistible. How had she ever thought she could cut him out of her life? "It sounds perfect."

Maybe it didn't matter what fate had in store for them. This time, they'd take the reins and take control of their future. Together.

CHAPTER THIRTY-THREE

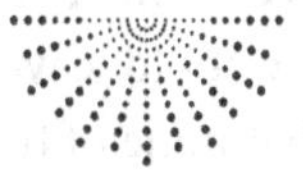

ix Weeks Later

Emilia sat in traffic, cursing the owner of the big rig who'd jackknifed into the side of the road. While snow in Wisconsin might be the norm in December, the first big storm of the season always left the freeways a sloppy mess. She'd already passed three other accidents, including a car that had spun off into a ditch.

She was tempted to send TJ a message telling him she'd be late, but she didn't want to get busted for texting and driving. As it was, she was already on edge, excited and nervous at the prospect of seeing him again. Like her, he was visiting his family for the holidays, so they'd agreed to meet at a restaurant halfway between her home in Milwaukee and his in the north Chicago suburbs.

Ever since she'd called him about Davis' video six weeks ago, they'd stayed in contact. In their phone calls, they'd opened up to each other. She'd shared stories of her mom, admitting things to him that she'd never told anyone. The acute pain of losing someone she loved and the void that still lingered in her heart. TJ understood her in a way few other people could since he'd lost his father at the same age.

When she'd confessed that she hadn't told her dad the truth about Italy, TJ encouraged her to reach out to him. Over the Thanksgiving break, she'd flown home to Wisconsin and had a long, heartfelt conversation with her dad about Pompeii. He wasn't mad at her—not even a little. Instead, he asked if he and the rest of the Flores family could leave scathing reviews of Buon Viaggio, despite the fact that none of them had ever visited Italy.

As a bonus, he was so grateful to TJ for exposing the Robertis that he'd encouraged Emilia to invite him over to dinner this week. While she appreciated the offer, she didn't want her reunion with TJ held under the prying eyes of her extended family. Her cousins were so nosy that they'd "accidentally" drop by during mealtime just to check him out. Instead, she and TJ had made plans to meet up for dinner in Lake Geneva at a bistro serving Italian fare.

But now she was ten minutes late, with no sign the traffic would start moving.

After ensuring no cops were nearby, she sent TJ a message.

Stuck in traffic. I'll be there as soon as I can!

WHEN TJ'S PHONE BUZZED WITH A TEXT FROM EMILIA, HE WAS relieved she was on her way. A week ago, when he'd made their dinner reservation, he hadn't counted on the weather wreaking havoc on their plans. Fortunately, the winter storm meant the restaurant was less full than usual, so no one had hounded him for nursing his glass of Cabernet for twenty minutes.

Inside the bistro, the space was cozy and intimate, with rustic wooden tables, framed black-and-white photos of Italy, and big picture windows. But outside? The snow was coming down harder—thick, wet flakes that coated the sidewalk. Maybe he'd been an idiot, asking Emilia to drive all this way. But after waiting two and a half months to see her, he'd wanted their reunion to be memorable. The location he'd chosen—Lake Geneva—held a special place in his heart. Back when his dad was still alive, his family had often taken weekend getaways at the popular resort town.

As he stared out the window, watching the snow fall, he let his mind wander. While he was glad to be back home, he definitely wasn't ready for the full onslaught of a Midwestern winter. He was tempted to text Emilia and suggest she turn back but couldn't come up with the right words. The last thing he wanted to do was imply that she couldn't handle the snow. Then again, he didn't want to put her safety at risk, either.

The door to the restaurant opened, letting in a blast of chilly air. He looked up, hoping Emilia had made it through the storm. To his immense relief, she strode in, her long, dark hair dusted with snowflakes. As she took off her parka, his breath caught at the sight of her. Clad in a figure-hugging green velvet dress and a pair of death-defying heels, she looked so sexy he instantly wished they were meeting somewhere a little less public.

She took off her coat, slung it over her arm, and glanced around the restaurant. When their eyes met, she ran over to his table but stumbled as she reached him. He bolted out of his seat and caught her in time.

She gazed at him with a wry smile. "Obviously, I still haven't mastered the art of running in heels."

"It's okay. I'm here to catch you whenever you need it."

Having her this close was far too tempting. He was gripped with the urge to run his hands along her curves and kiss her passionately, but he didn't think the other restaurant patrons would appreciate the display. He settled for pressing his forehead against hers in an act that felt almost as intimate as kissing.

"Hey, there," he murmured.

"Hey, yourself. It's *so* good to see you."

"I was worried you wouldn't make it." He released her slowly, not wanting to break contact even for a minute.

She brushed a damp strand of hair from her face. "Sorry I'm late, but there were four accidents on the road, not to mention all the people who acted like they'd never driven in snow before. Idiots, all of them."

That sounded like the Emilia he knew and loved. "I'm just glad you're here, and…" He took a minute to admire her alluring ensemble. "I have to say it—you look stunning in that dress."

That earned him one of her familiar eye rolls. "It's a bit much. I feel like a sexy Christmas tree. And the heels? Definitely not what I should have worn during the first big snowfall of the season. But my cousins were visiting, and one of them insisted I borrow the dress and the shoes. They told me I couldn't show up for a romantic reunion wearing jeans and boots."

To be honest, he would have been happy no matter what she was wearing. "I appreciate it. You know how much I love seeing you in heels."

She sat down and tossed her coat onto the chair beside her. "Tell me *all* about it, Dr. Mayer. All your dirty little fantasies."

Laughing, he took his seat across from her. "Before we get carried away, let's get you some wine."

"And bread. And an appetizer. I'm starving."

EMILIA COULDN'T BELIEVE SHE AND TJ WERE FINALLY TOGETHER, flirting, sharing a bottle of Cabernet, and munching on fried goat cheese and bruschetta. After weeks of phone calls and videos, he looked so much hotter in person, wearing an olive-green button-down that made his brown eyes pop. His tawny brown hair was neatly trimmed but still curled, ever so slightly, at the back of his neck. She wanted to kiss that sensitive area and make him groan in response.

Down, girl. Don't get all worked up when you can't do anything about it.

Since they were both staying with their families for the holidays, sex was out of the question. Her father was such a light sleeper that she'd never be able to sneak TJ into her childhood bedroom. Even though her dad wouldn't judge her for it, she'd still feel awkward as hell. She didn't want to end up in TJ's bedroom, either, not if it meant running the gauntlet of his entire family. They'd just have to plan a getaway in January.

Not that Emilia had any clue what TJ intended to do after the holidays. Over the last two weeks, he'd been surprisingly tight-lipped about his job search, so much so that she was afraid to ask how it was going. For now, she was just glad he was on the same continent.

After their server cleared the appetizers away, TJ took her hand. "I have some news. I've been dying to tell you, but I wanted to do it in person. I got a job in Southern California." He gave her a smug grin. "You're looking at the newest assistant curator of antiquities at the Getty Villa in Malibu."

Relief flooded over her, so palpable she could barely speak. She'd been to the Getty Villa a few times with Olivia, who liked visiting it on the weekends. It was a gorgeous museum, built to resemble an ancient Roman villa, and it housed the Getty's collection of Greek, Etruscan, and Roman antiquities.

"You absolute stud," she said. "That's awesome."

"Yeah, I'm so pumped. I reached out to everyone—and I do mean *everyone*—that I could think of with ties to colleges and museums on the West Coast. Then Dusty and Stuart told me about an opening at the Getty Villa. Since Stuart's dad is the director of the antiquities department there, he knew about the posting before it was made public. I didn't mention it earlier because I thought it was too much of a long shot."

Thank you, Stuart. Emilia's friends had done such a terrific job of supporting her that she was grateful they'd been able to help TJ, too. "I'm so glad you applied."

He squeezed her hand. "I was amazed when I got it, but then I was afraid that maybe you'd applied, too. I hope I didn't deprive you of the opportunity. I want you to be happy."

Her heart soared. This wasn't the same TJ she'd known in January, back when he'd been her fiercest competitor. This was a guy who'd put his career at risk just to avenge her.

"I *am* happy," she said. "Not just because you're finally here, but because I like what I'm doing. I'm also taking advantage of Stuart's connections to the Getty but in a totally different way. I applied for a post-doc at the Getty Conservation Institute, starting next September. Full funding for two years and a chance to work on some incredible projects."

He beamed at her. "That's fantastic. I hope you get it."

"Me, too." For once in her life, she was surprisingly optimistic about her chances.

"Before I forget, I have one more bit of news," he said. "It's from Cesca, but I convinced her I should be the one to tell you."

"What is it?" From the gleeful expression on his face, it had to be good.

"Just before I left Italy, she told me the tour company she works for—Roman Pathways—is planning to acquire all of Buon Viaggio's assets. Their buses, their equipment, their mailing list —everything."

"Really? I thought Angelo wanted to expand the company, not sell it off."

"He did, until things went to shit." TJ chuckled. "First, there was Davis' viral video, then all those bad reviews poured in. Then, in November, two American women left a couple of scathing reviews after taking the company's weeklong tour through Tuscany."

"Please tell me these reviews mentioned Luca." The thought of that sleazy bastard receiving any kind of comeuppance filled Emilia with exuberance.

"Right on the first guess."

She pumped her fist. "*Yes*. Couldn't happen to a more deserving guy."

"Apparently, he was accompanying the tour and thought he'd make a play for them. He got so pushy that they retaliated by taking their complaints public. It just so happens that one of the women is a micro-influencer with over four hundred thousand followers on TikTok."

No wonder TJ had wanted to share this delightful news in person. "That's awesome. What happened after that?"

"Luca went back to Milan in disgrace, his father decided not to invest in Buon Viaggio, and Angelo lost all his tour bookings for December, including his overpriced 'Christmas in Rome' package tours."

With a laugh, Emilia held up her wineglass. "Here's to the power of honest reviews."

TJ clinked his glass against hers. "I'll drink to that."

Once their pasta arrived, they took turns sharing stories about their visits home. She told him how much she'd enjoyed spending time with her dad and her cousins. He shone with pride when he described how impressed his family had been with his new job. They'd even offered to fly out to California next spring to visit him.

Emilia was so focused on TJ that only during dessert did she turn her attention to the view outside the window. "It's coming down even harder. Driving back is gonna be a bitch."

"If you want, we could find a place to stay for the night." He waggled his eyebrows. "I think our families would understand, given that this is an actual snow emergency."

She flashed him a playful grin. "It's the perfect excuse."

The thought of being with him tonight instead of waiting until January, made her quiver with excitement. All during dinner, she'd been fighting back her desire, knowing she couldn't do a damn thing about it. But now? They could indulge in a passionate night of steamy hotel sex. She fanned herself with the dessert menu as a flush of heat warmed her entire body. She couldn't wait to take off this dress. *No.* She couldn't wait for *TJ* to take it off.

"I'll see if I can find us a place." He pulled out his phone. "Any preferences?"

"All we need is a room with a bed. Preferably a queen or larger."

After a few minutes, he gave a cry of excitement. "This is perfect. The Geneva Inn. Our family used to stay there when I was a kid. It's kind of pricey, but I can afford it, seeing as how I'm going to be a big shot at the Getty."

She poked him in the chest. "You don't have to sound so smug about it."

"Come on, Em. I have to boast a little. That's how I roll." He glanced at his phone again. "In case you were worried it might be a dump, the hotel is rated 4.5 out of 5 on Expedia."

"Perfect." It could be rated two stars and she'd still be up for it. For once in her life, she wasn't worried about reviews. All she cared about was spending the night in TJ's arms.

CHAPTER THIRTY-FOUR

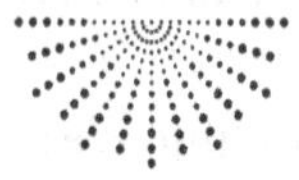

By the time TJ left the restaurant with Emilia, the visibility was almost zero. The hotel was only a few blocks away, but he drove slowly, checking in his rearview mirror to make sure she was following him in her car. They parked outside, made their way through the snow, and went into the lobby, which was fully decorated for Christmas, with an eight-foot tree in one corner. Emilia dashed over to the brick fireplace and warmed herself by the blazing fire. Around it were four overstuffed plaid armchairs, providing the perfect spot for a late-night drink. If TJ hadn't been in such a hurry to whisk Emilia off to bed, he would have suggested they sit by the fire with a glass of wine.

"I'll go check us in," he said. "Any requests?"

"Nope." She settled herself in one of the armchairs. "I'm going to call my dad and let him know I won't be home until tomorrow."

"Good plan." At check-in, he paid for the room and purchased some sundries—two toothbrushes and mini tubes of toothpaste, a packet of makeup wipes for Emilia, and a couple of t-shirts they could wear while lounging in the room. Once he received their key cards, he sent Romily a text, asking her to tell his family he'd decided to spend the night in Lake Geneva. She replied immediately, her message punctuated with hearts and smiley faces.

Emilia came up to him. "I just talked with my dad. He was relieved I didn't try to drive home. He always worries when the weather's bad."

"I'm glad you got hold of him. We're all set. I even got us some supplies." He handed her the bag.

She peeked inside and pulled out a shirt. "Ooh. 'Life is better by the lake.' That's *so* not my vibe, but it's perfect for tonight. Thanks."

He took her arm. "Let's go up and make good use of that room."

Was he rushing her? Maybe, but based on the enticing smile she gave him, he suspected she was just as eager as he was.

They took the elevator up to the third floor, grinning like a couple of giddy teens. By the time they entered the room, his pulse was racing. He flicked on one of the lamps, softly illuminating the space around them. He couldn't have asked for a more romantic setup —a big four-poster bed, a balcony overlooking the lake, and an oversized soaking tub in one corner.

After they'd draped their coats on a chair, Emilia walked over to the bed and set the bag of supplies on the floor. When he joined her, she grabbed him and pressed him up against the wall. With nimble fingers, she unbuttoned his shirt, slid it off his shoulders, and tossed it aside. She stripped off his undershirt, then ran her hands along his bare chest and brushed her lips against his collarbone, lighting a fire inside of him. He wanted to tell her to slow down, but it had been far too long since he'd felt this good.

When she pulled away, her dark eyes flashed with desire. "Am

I going too fast? Sorry, but I've been dreaming about this for weeks."

What had he ever done to deserve a woman this incredible? "Me, too. But maybe we should take our time. Don't you want to make this last?"

A burst of laughter tumbled out of her. "Nope. I'm too greedy. We can take it slow later. I wasn't planning on getting a lot of sleep tonight."

He loved that she was just as passionate as he was. "Turn around. I want to unzip you out of that dress."

Tossing her hair over her shoulder, she turned and faced the bed. He took a moment to appreciate the delightful view of her backside, so lusciously presented in that tight velvet dress, before drawing the zipper down to her hips. It was like opening a package on Christmas morning. She slipped out of it, revealing a silky black bra and matching panties.

He traced his finger along the curve of her spine, then let it rest on her butt, barely covered by the scrap of black fabric. "Is this the same lingerie you wore in Rome?"

"No, my cousins took me shopping yesterday, and I bought a few more items. I wore this tonight on the remote chance we might get lucky."

"Excellent call." He pressed his body against hers and cupped her breasts. Tweaking her nipples gently, he nuzzled the back of her neck and inhaled the familiar scent of her orange blossom shampoo. When she rubbed up against him, his dick twitched, demanding release. He quickly took off his shoes and socks, then undid his belt and removed his khakis and boxers, giving a groan as his bare skin came in contact with hers.

"Hold on to one of the bedposts," he murmured.

Her laughter rang out, even more gleeful than before. "Why? Are you going to make me so weak that I won't be able to stand up?"

"Challenge accepted, Dr. Flores."

She did as he said, gripping the bedpost tightly. With one hand, he continued playing with her nipples while his other dove beneath her panties, seeking out her slick, wet folds until she gasped with pleasure. "Yes. Right there. Please, TJ. Don't stop."

"You're so wet already," he whispered. "You were thinking about this in the restaurant, weren't you?"

"Yes. I…" She arched her back. "More. *Please.*"

He kissed her neck and shoulders as he continued stroking her, growing more aroused every time she moaned. When her body trembled under his touch, he kept going until she shuddered, let out a breathy cry, and sagged against the bedpost.

When she turned to face him, her cheeks were flushed, her smile radiant. "I'm still standing. But just barely."

"I'm not done yet. Sit down on the bed. But leave your heels on."

"Oh, yes, Dr. Mayer." After pulling aside the comforter, she sat on the edge of the bed and gave him a coy smile.

He set his glasses on the nightstand, knelt in front of her, and removed her panties, making sure she kept her heels on. Starting with her ankles, he stroked his hands along her calves. He'd never gotten this turned on by a woman in heels before, but then again, he'd never been with anyone like Emilia. After parting her legs, he ran his lips along the inside of her thighs, inhaling the scent of her. "You're so fucking sexy. I can't wait to taste you."

"Yes, please. I love it when you do this. I even bragged to Dusty and Olivia about it."

What? Raising his head, he met her eyes, unsure if he'd heard her correctly. "You bragged about *me?*"

"Mmm-hmm. I'm hoping you've still got it."

For all the times he'd boasted about his accomplishments, he'd never considered his bedroom skills to be brag-worthy. But if Emilia felt this way, he wasn't about to let her down. "I'll do my best."

Gripping her bare butt, he buried his head between her thighs, licking and tasting her, so wet and sweet and ready for him. With each gasp, he wanted her more, and when she dug her fingers into his scalp, he thought he might explode.

"Like that," she demanded. "Right there. *Yes.* Please don't stop."

She let out a loud moan, her body bucking in response as she reached her climax. But he kept going. He wanted to make her come again and again, to hear her call out his name each time she hit her peak. But when she gasped for him to stop, he pulled away. Looking up at her, he was overcome with longing for this wild, sexy woman who'd stolen his heart.

With a saucy grin, she slid her feet out of the heels. "As much as you love these, I need to take them off." She removed her bra and lay down on the bed. "Anytime you're ready, Dr. Mayer."

His breath caught at the sight of her, so glorious in all her naked beauty. He felt like the luckiest bastard on the planet.

After climbing onto the bed, he placed his body over hers. She angled her hips, allowing him to thrust deep inside of her. As she pulled him closer, they moved together in harmony. Once again, he battled the desire for release. She was so soft and warm, her body so pliant against his, her breathy cries so compelling, that he was close to the point of no return.

He clenched up, trying to distract himself, trying to think of *anything*—ancient pottery types, Roman emperors, the Greek alphabet—that would delay the inevitable, but she felt so good underneath him. He kept going, telling himself it was a test of his will, that the longer he held out, the better it would be. But when she cried out and pressed her face into his shoulder, he let himself go, succumbing to an intense wave of pleasure that racked his whole body.

As they came down from their high together, he held her tightly, still overwhelmed by the feelings she'd elicited in him. For the longest time, all he wanted to do was hold her. To reassure himself that she was really with him and not thousands of miles away.

Releasing her gently, he lay on his back and let out a satisfied sigh.

She nestled her head against his chest. "Mmm. That was totally worth the wait."

"It was. I love you, Em."

"I love you, too. Even if you did make me risk my life in a giant blizzard."

He couldn't remember a time he'd felt so content. For all his boasting and competitiveness, for all the times he'd tried to get ahead, the best things had happened when he hadn't put himself first. When he'd cared about other people, loved someone with his whole heart, and put himself on the line for her. Back in November, when he took on the Robertis, he hadn't known what would come of it. He'd had no idea if he'd find a job or win Emilia back. All he'd wanted to do was get justice for her.

But now, he was gainfully employed, reunited with the woman he loved, and ready to take on life's challenges.

It was a far better future than he ever could have predicted.

After their second round of delicious, toe-curling sex, Emilia dozed off in TJ's arms. When she woke, the room was still dark, but she was too curious about the storm to go back to sleep. Easing out of bed, she found the bag with the shirts and slipped one over her head. It fit her more like a dress, the hem falling halfway down her thighs, but she loved the way the soft fabric caressed her bare skin. She crept over to the window and pulled back the drapes. Outside, the sun was just rising, the whole world covered in a blanket of white.

As a kid, she'd loved days like these. Snow days when school was canceled, when she'd spend hours playing outside and then warm up with her mom's spicy hot chocolate. It was one of the memories that still filled her with a twinge of sadness when she recalled how much she'd lost.

Though she'd always have a small void where her mom had been, she was slowly filling the well by letting people into her life. Not just colleagues or dig buddies but people she cared about. Friends like Rick, Olivia, Dusty, Stuart, and Cesca. The people on the tour group who'd reached out to check on her after posting their one-star reviews of Buon Viaggio in November. And TJ, who'd helped her break down her walls. Thanks to him, she'd opened herself up to love, realizing it didn't have to end in hurt and humiliation. After the way he'd come through for her, she knew she could trust him with her whole heart.

At the sound of his voice, she turned to face him. He sat up in bed and grabbed his glasses from the nightstand. "Everything okay, Em?"

"I woke up and had to check out the snow. Looks like we got at least a foot. Come see."

He got out of bed, found the other t-shirt, and put it on with a chuckle. "I didn't realize these were extra-extra-large."

"They're adorable, but if you tell anyone we were wearing matching lake shirts, I'll have to kill you."

He came over to join her. "So, no taking a selfie of us and posting it online?"

"Don't even. I can't have anyone thinking I'm a 'lake person.'" She gestured to the view outside their window. "How much do you think we got? Maybe a foot?"

"Or more. I'm glad we didn't have to drive in it last night." He grinned. "I know this might sound selfish, but I'd call this a perfect storm."

She felt the same way. Thanks to the blizzard, they'd been able to truly reconnect. And now, they had so much to look forward to. In the space of one year, her life had changed completely, and not in ways she ever could have imagined. She'd led a ten-day tour through southern Italy, gotten fired, rebooted her life in California, and fallen in love with her fiercest rival.

Whether it was fate, luck, or sheer persistence, she'd ended up exactly where she was meant to be.

EPILOGUE

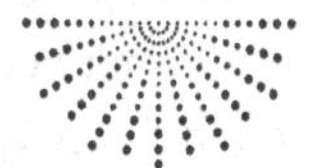

One Year Later

"Any further questions?" Emilia scanned the audience one last time. When no one raised their hand, she spoke up again. "On behalf of the Getty Conservation Institute, I'd like to thank you for attending my presentation on technological advances in the conservation of wall paintings at Pompeii and Herculaneum. If you think of any follow-up questions, I'll be at the conference all weekend, and my email address is on the handout."

She waited until everyone had filed out, then went to grab her laptop. As she was tucking it into her briefcase, a familiar voice addressed her. "Excellent job, Dr. Flores."

A smile tugged at her lips. She turned to face TJ, who was looking sharp in a navy blazer, a light blue button-down, and a striped navy-and-gray tie. Whenever he dressed in full professional mode, her hormones went into overdrive. Even now, she wanted to drag him by the tie, press him up against the wall, and have her way with him.

But since they were at an academic conference, she kept her

urges under control. "Thank you, Dr. Mayer. I hope you were paying attention and not ogling my legs."

He smirked. "Well, you know how I feel about you in heels. But no, I was listening. Your presentation was fantastic."

"Thanks." She took his arm. "We should get going. My talk ran a little late, and I don't want to lose our table." In a conference hotel filled with hungry archaeologists, securing a reservation in one of the on-site restaurants hadn't been easy.

"No worries. Dusty took off ten minutes ago so she could grab the table. If anyone challenges her, she'll take them down."

"Perfect. Let's go."

As they walked down the hall, she passed a few anxious-looking men and women clutching briefcases. In all likelihood, they were grad students, coming from their interviews. She gave an involuntary shudder, grateful neither she nor TJ had to worry about finding a job.

After moving out to California last January, he'd started working at the Getty Villa, a position that suited him perfectly since it involved research, exhibit preparation, and a fair amount of schmoozing. She'd stayed on with Rick's crew in Ventura County until she learned she'd received a Postdoctoral Fellowship from the Getty Conservation Institute. Not only was it an incredible opportunity, but the benefits included a generous stipend, a study trip allowance, and an apartment in the Getty Scholars housing complex. No one had been more excited for her than TJ, who'd immediately booked them a romantic getaway at a seaside hotel in Laguna Beach.

She'd started her fellowship in September, and TJ had moved in with her shortly after that. Together, they were learning to cook, and they'd even adopted a kitten.

It was hard to believe that just two years ago, they'd clashed at this very same conference. Now they were attending it as a couple, both representing the Getty with all their expenses comped. Life didn't get much better than that.

When they reached the restaurant, she scoured the crowd, hoping to find her friends. Dusty waved them over. She and Stuart were sitting at a six-top laden with beverages.

Emilia grabbed a seat across from Dusty. "Whoa. Got enough to drink?"

"I ordered a round for all of us since our server was getting antsy," Dusty said. "A mojito for you, an IPA for TJ, white wine for me and Stuart, and two brandy sours for Rick and Olivia."

"Thanks," TJ said, sitting beside Emilia. "I'll get the next round."

"Hell, yes," Dusty said. "You can write it off to the Getty's tab, Mr. Big Shot."

A few minutes later, Rick and Olivia joined them, grabbing the last two chairs. When Dusty passed Olivia a cocktail, she squealed with delight. "Is this a brandy sour? Thanks! That drink brings back *so* many memories of Cyprus." She flashed Rick a quick grin.

He raised his cocktail glass in a salute. "It sure does. Sorry for being late, but Olivia's session was on the other side of the hotel. I'm so annoyed they scheduled her talk and Emilia's at the same time. Sorry we missed your presentation, Em."

"It's fine. All the sessions are being recorded." Emilia held up her glass. "Time for a toast. Here's to all of us and to a summer filled with more adventures."

After everyone clinked glasses, Dusty spoke up. "What's going on this summer?"

Emilia couldn't help but grin. "The Getty Conservation Institute is sending me to Pompeii for two weeks in July. I'll be working with a couple of Italian conservation experts to study the wall paintings at the House of Venus."

"No way!" Dusty smacked the table. "Here you thought you'd 'never work in Pompeii again.' Isn't that what Dr. Roberti told you?"

"He did, but the joke's on him. Apparently, he's not at Pompeii any longer. He was replaced, though I'm not sure what happened. Something about a misappropriation of funds? I asked Paulo to sniff around for gossip."

Last winter, Emilia had reached out to Paulo and apologized for leaving Italy so abruptly. Over the past year, she'd stayed in touch with him and a few others from the Via Stabiana Project, including Marie, who'd warmed up to her considerably.

"Are you going to Pompeii, too?" Olivia asked TJ.

"Definitely. Gonna do a little recon for an exhibit the villa is planning for next year. A joint venture with the Conservation folks. This time, Em and I aren't staying in a cheap hostel. Five-star hotels all the way."

Emilia shivered with excitement. Even if she and TJ spent every night together at their apartment, nothing beat the allure of hotel sex. "After Pompeii, we're going to take some vacation time and travel a little. I have to admit, I've missed the Mediterranean a lot."

"I've got news, too," Olivia said. "I was asked to serve as the assistant director of the University of California field school in Cyprus. The same one where Rick and I met. Luckily, it starts in July, so it won't interfere with our wedding in June."

Emilia had been thrilled when Olivia and Rick had announced their engagement, and she'd had fun helping Olivia and Sofia plan the wedding.

"Are you going to join her?" she asked Rick. "You can't miss a chance to go back to Cyprus."

"Yep. I'll be helping with the survey component of the field school since *someone*—not naming any names—still has no sense of direction." He tossed Olivia a teasing grin.

"Hey, I'm not that bad," she said. "As long as I have a GPS, I don't get lost. Well, not much, anyway."

Stuart gestured toward Olivia with his wineglass. "If you and Rick are going to be in Cyprus for the summer, you should jet over to Turkey afterward. Dusty and I will be going back there in July. I got full funding for two more dig seasons at Troy."

Dusty nodded. "I can't wait. I just got a commission to illustrate a new translation of *The Iliad*, so I'll be splitting my time between that and my archaeological illustrations." She gestured to Emilia. "If you and TJ want to visit after you're done in Italy, you could come join us, too."

"We'd love to have you there," Stuart added.

"Quick question for you about Troy," TJ said. "You know that giant Trojan horse near the visitors' center? Is it accessible after hours? Or do they lock it up tight?"

Emilia reached under the table and squeezed his thigh. He never missed a chance to tease her about that damn horse.

Stuart frowned. "I'm not sure. Why? Were you planning on sneaking in and…" His voice trailed off. "Never mind. I don't want to know."

Dusty laughed. "Ooh, now you're giving *me* ideas."

As Emilia looked around the table, she couldn't believe how far they'd come. A few years ago, they'd all been single, trying to find their way, struggling to balance love and relationships with the demands of archaeology and academia. Now, they were paired up and employed, with so much to look forward to.

"We all sound so grown-up," Dusty said, giving a sad little pout. "Do you think this is the end of our shenanigans?"

Stuart placed his hand on her shoulder. "Hardly. There are tons of adventures to come, but now we don't have to face them alone. Right?"

When everyone nodded, Emilia couldn't have agreed more. She caught TJ's eye and smiled at him. For all the times he'd challenged and teased her, he'd also offered her love, passion, and unflagging support. As long as they were together, she was ready to face whatever life had in store.

Thank you for reading *Tour Wars.*
If you enjoyed this book, please consider leaving a review.
Thanks! Your support is much appreciated!

Want to find out what happens when TJ and Emilia return to
Troy (and get their chance to sneak inside the Trojan horse)?
Click here to download your free bonus epilogue or grab it with
the QR code below.

Website and Newsletter Signup
www.carlalunabooks.com

ACKNOWLEDGMENTS

If you're still reading, thank you!! I wouldn't have gotten to where I am today without all the people who've taken the time to read my books. Now that you've finished *Tour Wars*, treat yourself to a delicious bowl of pasta and a glass of wine. You've earned it!

I'd also like to thank:

My awesome team of professionals—Bailey McGinn, for capturing my characters perfectly and giving me a gorgeous pink cover; Serena Clarke at Free Bird Editing for her meticulous copy edits and thoughtful suggestions; and Sandra Dee at One Love Editing for the final proofreading polish.

My beta-readers—the writers who helped me take my writing to the next level: Jennifer Rupp, Gail Werner, Michelle McCraw, Liz Czukas, and Susan Keillor; thanks also to Brandy Shaw, Serena Bell, and Elise Kennedy for helping me smooth out the opening chapters.

My writer friends—Lolly Rzezotarski, Jennifer Motl, Lisa Minneti, Virginia Small, Michelle McCraw, Ofelia Martinez, Kristin Lee, Brandy Shaw, Jazz Matthews, Amy Reichert, M.K. Wiseman, Carrie Lofty, Natalie Caña, and Melonie Johnson. A special shout-out to Liz Lincoln and Liz Czukas for providing me with equal doses of support and snark.

My critique partner—fellow romance writer Tricia Quinnies, for brainstorming help and much-needed feedback, and for supporting my decision to give TJ his own story!

The Penzeys crew—especially my boss, Byron, who was

totally cool with me taking ten days off to go on an impromptu trip to Italy.

The Italy contingent—when I traveled to Italy as research for this book, my friend Jackie Dhein and her daughter Holly gave me a list of places to eat in Rome. Not only that, but Jackie also took me to the bus depot at 5:30 a.m. so I could make it to the airport on time! A tip of the hat to the guides who made my trip so enjoyable, whether it was a guided tour of Pompeii ("by a real archaeologist") or a delicious food tour in Rome. My experiences on these tours played a big part in creating this book.

The Getty—years ago, upon receiving my master's degree in archaeology, I was fortunate to land a job at the Getty Research Institute in Los Angeles. Working there was such a formative experience that I couldn't resist featuring the Getty in the last few chapters of this book. For all the people I worked with, *especially* the women (Erin, Maria, Daisy, Kim, Jenny, Donna, Lillian, Ann, Amy, Wendy, Sabine, and Kathy), thanks for the memories, the solidarity, and the laughter.

My late parents—Dulcie and Mario Luna, who raised me with a passion for art, history, and archaeology that has lasted my whole life. And my brother, John Luna, who understands the value of cheesy movies.

My family—my two (adult) children, Tasmine and James, who are endlessly supportive. Thanks to James, for inspiring the "Piano Man" scenes, and to Tasmine, for insight about graduate school in the 2020s. Finally, I'm forever grateful to my husband Mike, for the love and encouragement he's given me over the years.

Grazie mille!

ABOUT THE AUTHOR

Carla Luna writes contemporary romance with a dollop of humor and a pinch of spice. A former archaeologist, she still dreams of traveling to far-off places and channels that wanderlust into the settings of her stories. Her books have been called "escape reads," perfect for perusing during a beachside vacation, a long flight, or a relaxing weekend at the lake. In addition to being a voracious reader, she loves baking, Broadway musicals, whimsical office supplies, and pop culture podcasts. Though she has roots in Los Angeles and Vancouver Island, she currently resides in Wisconsin with her family and her spoiled Siberian cat.

For sneak peeks, giveaways, and book recommendations, sign up for Carla Luna's newsletter:
www.carlalunabooks.com

THE ROMANCING THE RUINS SERIES

Field Rules

Digging up the past takes on a whole new meaning when graduate student Olivia Sanchez is forced to team up with her ex, Rick Langston, while working at an archaeological dig in Cyprus. Given that their last fling almost led to their academic ruin, they can't afford to repeat their past mistakes. But as they work together under the scorching Mediterranean sun, the heat between them proves impossible to ignore.

Troy Story

For years, Dusty Danforth has harbored a secret crush on her best friend Stuart Carlson. Hoping to take things further, she jumps at the chance to join him on an archaeological dig at the legendary site of Troy in Turkey. But keeping the excavation on track is harder them either of them expected. Just as their long-simmering passion ignites, their boss's treacherous behavior puts the entire project in jeopardy.